The al-Andalus trilogy

Book One

THE

SHINING CITY

The Scottish novelist Joan Fallon, currently lives and works in the south of Spain. She writes both contemporary and historical fiction, and almost all her books have a strong female protagonist. She is the author of:

Daughters of Spain
Spanish Lavender
The House on the Beach
Loving Harry
Santiago Tales
The Only Blue Door
Palette of Secrets
The Eye of the Falcon (al-Andalus series Book 2)

(all are available in paperback and as ebooks)

www.joanfallon.co.uk

JOAN FALLON

THE SHINING CITY

Scott Publishing

ISBN 978 0 9576891 6 9
First published in 2014
Scott Publishing
Windsor, England

ACKNOWLEDGMENTS

My sincere thanks to my editor Sara Starbuck, author of the 'Dread Pirate Fleur' series of children's books, whose advice and support has been invaluable. My thanks also to Angela Hagenow, who took time out of her busy life to proof read the manuscript for me and to JG Harlond, author of 'The Chosen Man', for her clear and concise appraisal.

AUTHOR'S NOTE

An explanation is perhaps needed regarding the different levels of society in al-Andalus in the 10th century. By the time Abd al-Rahman III became caliph in the year 929, his empire encompassed many different people. At the top, holding all the most important administrative positions, were the Arabs. Next came the Berbers who were originally from North Africa and, although they were also Muslims, were never treated as true equals. Then there were the Mullawadun converts, who were either educated new Muslims or the descendants of converted Christians. Last were the dhimmi, the name given to all Christians and Jews who lived in al-Andalus; they were allowed to worship their own faith and live normal, productive lives. Outside of society and at the bottom of the pile were the slaves - all non-believers. If a slave converted to Islam then he or she would receive her freedom as it was forbidden to have Muslim slaves.

Although I explain how al-Mari was sent to work in the galleys as a galley-slave, I have to point out that in actual fact, slaves were not usually used in the galleys. The navies of the time preferred to employ free men rather than slaves. My apologies for the poetic licence.

One further point is regarding Isolde and her village in a remote part of Saxony. Although by 10th century most of the Germanic people had converted to Christianity, some isolated villages, particularly in the north of Europe, held on to their pagan beliefs.

MADINAT AL-ZAHRA

In the southern part of Spain, in the province of Andalusia, lies the archeological site of Madinat al-Zahra, the city-palace of Abd al-Rahman III, who was the caliph of al-Andalus in the 10th century. Once, long ago, this was the most beautiful city in the western world and home to one of the most powerful and cultured rulers of the time. Today it is all but forgotten.

Work began on the city in the year 940 and by 946 AD the Khalifa Abd al-Rahman III was in residence. This was to be a monument to his fame, a fitting city for an Omeyyad caliph that had united the warring princes of the Iberian peninsula into one Islamic kingdom. It was designed to tell his enemies and followers alike that he was now their supreme ruler.

One of the tragedies of history is that this magnificent city endured no more than seventy-five years. After the death of Abd al-Rahman III, his son Hakim continued with the construction of the city but when he died in 976 AD, the city was abandoned and the royal court returned to Córdoba. The new caliph, Hisham II, had been a mere child of eleven when he inherited the title from his father and the Grand Vizier, al-Manzor wrested power from him and began to rule the country in his place. It was he who moved everything, the royal Mint, the judiciary, the administration, the army, all back to Córdoba.

11

So with the passing of the years the beautiful palaces of Madinat al-Zahra were stripped and dismantled, their marble pillars and floors removed, buildings broken down and used to construct walls to corral livestock. Bit by bit the city deteriorated, disappearing into nothing more than a pile of rubble that nature gradually covered with a blanket of green.

This is the story of that city as seen through the eyes of those who lived there. For what is a city if it is not its people?

PROLOGUE

Córdoba
987 AD

The old man sat in the shade of the mosque wall. It was still early but already the heat was building with its usual summer ferocity. He loosened his robe slightly and fanned himself with the napkin he had in his hand. Omar was not a rich man but neither was he poor. His djubba was made of the finest white cotton, with long narrow sleeves and over that he wore his djellaba, a hooded cloak of the same material. It was light, cool and comfortable. He was of the generation for whom appearances mattered. Even his cap, crocheted in a green and white design, sat elegantly on his long, white hair. His beard was trimmed and shaped; once it would have been touched with henna but now it was as white as his hair.

'More tea, old man?' the waiter called from the entrance to his tiny shop.

Omar waved him away, irritated that he did not automatically come over and refill his cup. That was so typical. Standards were slipping all the time. He took off his cap and scratched his head.

'There you are, uncle. We've been looking for you everywhere.'

It was his nephew, Musa, the youngest son of his brother Ibrahim. He was with his friend, Ahmad. Omar looked at them and smiled. Lanky youths, with their hair cut short in the latest fashion, they behaved as though life was theirs for the taking. If only they knew what vicissitudes lay ahead of them. Not that they would pay any heed. He certainly hadn't at their age. The boys sat down beside him. The two were never apart; it was as if they were joined by some invisible rope. Where one went, so did the other. They reminded him of his own childhood; he had had a close friend named Yusuf. Just like these boys they had done everything together and were so similar in looks and mannerisms that they were often mistaken for brothers.

'Drinking tea, uncle?' Musa said.

'Would you like some?'

The boys nodded and Omar waved across to the waiter, who still lounged in the doorway.

'Another pot of tea and two more glasses, please,' he said.

He turned to his nephew and asked, 'So child, you have been looking for me. What is it that you want?'

He already knew the answer: nothing, just the opportunity to drink mint tea and listen to Omar's stories.

'We wanted to see if you were all right.'

'And why wouldn't I be?'

The boys looked at each other and giggled.

'Is it true that you are more than a hundred?' Ahmad asked.

'No, it's not true, although I certainly feel like it some days. Now what is it you want to know?'

'Have you ever been inside the Khalifa's harem?' Musa blurted out.

'The Khalifa's harem?'

'Yes, what's it like?' they both chorused.

'Well ...'

The waiter arrived and set the freshly brewed mint tea on the table.

'Maybe something sweet for the boys to eat,' Omar said, looking at the waiter.

'Churros?'

'Excellent.'

Omar turned back to his eager audience.

'So, what were you saying?'

'The harem.'

'Oh yes.'

The old man smiled; for a moment he let his thoughts drift back to when he was young. He sighed and turned back to the boys.

'Yes, well, let me see. The harem you say?'

'Yes uncle,' his nephew said, barely keeping the impatience from his voice.

'You do realise that no man is permitted to enter the Khalifa's harem, other than the Khalifa himself. It is an offence punishable by death.'

The boys nodded.

'We know that, uncle.'

'Very well, as long as you do not tell anyone that I was once there, I will tell you about the most beautiful harem in the world.'

He paused and looked at the boys; their eyes were as round as moons.

'Now, in the year 947, when I was not much older than you, my father took me with him to work in the new city, Madinat al-Zahra.'

The boys looked at each other and smiled. Omar's stories always began in that way.

'Our ruler, Abd al-Rahman III, wanted to build a city-palace worthy of the title of Khalifa so he sent his engineers and architects out to find the perfect location. And they did. They found a spot in the foothills of the Sierra Moreno, green, fertile, sheltered from the north winds, with as much water as you could wish for, yet set high enough above the plain so that you would be able to see anyone approaching. From there you could see across the valley of the Guadalquivir to Córdoba and beyond.'

'He called it after his favourite concubine, didn't he?' Ahmed said with a smirk, urging him to get to the more interesting details.

'His favourite concubine was certainly called al-Zahra and he lavished every possible luxury on her so it is possible that that was why he called the city al-Zahra. But do you know what else the name means?'

He looked at the boys, who shook their heads.

'It means shining, glistening, brilliant. Possibly his concubine glittered and shone with all the jewels and beautiful silks he showered upon her but then so did the city. It was indeed the Shining City. When visitors entered through the Grand Portico, passing beneath its enormous, red and white arches, when they climbed the ramped streets that were paved with blocks of dark mountain stone, passing the lines of uniformed guards in their scarlet jackets and the richly robed civil servants that flanked their way, when they reached the royal residence and saw the golden inlay on the ceilings, the marble pillars, the richly woven rugs scattered across the floors and the brilliant silk tapestries, when they saw the moving tank of mercury in the great reception pavilion that caught the sunlight and dazzled all who beheld it, then they indeed knew that they were in the Shining City.'

It was a shame that his nephew had never been to Madinat al-Zahra and probably would never go. Soon the city would be as if it had never been, its stone buildings returned to the rock from which they came.

'But they say that he loved his concubine more than anyone else,' said Musa.

'Maybe. Who knows what goes on in the hearts of men, even less in the heart of a Khalifa.'

'They say she was the most beautiful woman in his harem.'

'She was certainly very beautiful, but the most beautiful, no. There was another more beautiful than her, more beautiful than all his wives and concubines.'

'Who was she? What was her name?' asked Ahmed.

'Jahwara,' he whispered.

He could still feel the pain as he said her name. The boys waited, eyes wide in anticipation but Omar did not elaborate.

'Did you ever see him? Did you see the Khalifa?'

'Yes, once.'

'What was he like? Was he big and strong?'

'He was a bit on the stout side.'

He could see the disappointment in the boys' eyes.

'But he was a good-looking man, with white skin and blue eyes,' he added.

'White skin? Wasn't he an Arab?'

'Of course he was. Who else but an Arab could be Khalifa? But his mother was from the north. She was captured from one of the ruling families during the war and became his father's slave and concubine. Abd al-Rahman inherited his fair skin and hair from her.'

'I heard that he used to dye his beard,' Ahmed said.

'Yes, I believe he did. He wanted to look more like his subjects.'

The boys nodded wisely. Omar stifled a smile.

'Tell us more about the harem,' Musa insisted.

'What can I tell you? There were hundreds of beautiful women, trained in all the arts of love and music; they knew a thousand and one ways to please their lord and master.'

'The Khalifa?'

'Of course, who else? Every woman who entered the Khalifa's harem belonged to him and no-one else.'

As he said the words, he could hear the bitterness creep into his voice.

'They were slaves?'

'Indeed they were. Even if one of them wanted to leave she could not. The Khalifa would never permit it.'

Before the boys could start another stream of questions, he said, 'Here, eat your churros and then you should be off. Is there no school today?'

He saw Musa blush. His nephew was a good boy and not able to tell a ready lie.

'We're going now, uncle. Come on Ahmed.'

The boys picked up the churros, doused it with honey and crammed it into their mouths.

'Ma'a salama uncle,' Musa said, honey dripping down his chin. 'See you later.'

'Goodbye, Hajj,' Ahmed said, hurriedly eating the last piece of churros and following his friend.

Omar watched the boys skip down the road. If they hurried they would be in time for the first lesson of the day. He wished he had asked them what they were being taught these days. When he had been at school the curriculum was very strict: reading, writing, geometry, arithmetic, the Quran and the sayings of the Hadith. Everything in Arabic of course, although not many spoke it in the streets in those days; people retained the habit of speaking a variety of the local language among friends and family. That was normal. He signalled for the waiter to come over and paid him for the tea and churros. It was time he took some exercise. His doctor had said it was important to walk every day even if his knee was paining him. He would walk across the old Roman bridge and see if there were any fish in the river this morning. It was his favourite walk these days because he would stop half-way across and look back at the city of Córdoba and its beautiful mosque, towering against the skyline. This ancient city was once again the centre of power, his beloved Madinat al-Zahra abandoned and neglected since the young Hisham II had inherited the throne. Today the boy-Khalifa was isolated in Madinat al-Zahra, alone, living the life of a recluse, his city crumbling around him.

As he stood up a sharp pain shot through his knee and up his thigh. He grasped the ebony stick that he always carried with him these days and used it to propel himself forward. A wave of longing for his old home leapt to his breast. It had been years since he had visited Madinat al-Zahra yet there was never a day when he didn't dream of its beautiful palaces and its fragrant gardens; when he closed his eyes he could still hear the sound of the fountains that fed the tranquil lakes and smell the orange blossom that used to grow outside his house. But he knew he could never return; the pain would be too great. The city lay only a couple of Arab miles to the west of Córdoba and yet it might as well have been in distant Arabia. Yes, there were many tales he could tell Musa about his days in Madinat al-Zahra.

FORTY YEARS EARLIER
947 AD

CHAPTER 1
A REMOTE VILLAGE IN NORTHERN EUROPE

The screams woke her. At first Isolde thought it was part of her dream but then she heard loud shouts and an enormous crash as the door to their hut was kicked open. The monstrous figure of a man filled the doorway. The axe in his hand glinted menacingly, its sharp blade glowing red from the flames of their neighbour's burning house. Instinctively Isolde reached for her young brothers, lying curled up by her side. They too had heard the noise and whimpered in their half-waking state. Hans, the older of the two, sat up, rubbing the sleep from his eyes. The man shouted again. He wanted them to leave. Isolde could not move; she was paralysed with fear but her mother jumped up, wide awake and screaming. She rushed towards the man, beating at his breast with her hands. Nobody was going to harm her family. What she thought she could do against such a monster, who knew, but she was prepared to defend her children to the death. And that is exactly what she did. Isolde watched petrified, as the intruder picked up her mother as though she weighed no more than the bag of straw she used as a pillow and threw her against the wall. Her mother's screams died in her throat as she slipped slowly to the ground, with barely a moan. The man strode into the room, knocking over their stove and kicking the animals out of his way. Again he shouted at them to leave. Isolde ran across to where her mother lay motionless, blood trickling down her face and soaking into the earthen floor of their home. Isolde wanted to help her but she didn't know what to do. She tried shaking her gently.

'Mama,' she cried. 'Mama, wake up.'

There was no reply, no movement from her; she stared at her daughter with unseeing eyes.

'Mama.'

Isolde shook her again, this time harder. Nothing. She did not move.

'Mama,' she cried again and again but her mother could not hear her.

By now, both Isolde's brothers were awake and crying; they huddled together in the corner, their terrified eyes on her.

'Isolde, what's happening?' the younger boy asked. 'Who's that man? What's the matter with Mama?'

'It's all right; it's all right. I'm here,' she said, turning to them.

'Out,' the man said again, more loudly than ever and moved towards them.

Now Isolde knew who he was. He was a viking, a foreigner from across the sea. She began to tremble. They had all heard about the vikings; their infamy had spread far and wide. They were cruel, hard men who took what they wanted and killed anyone who got in their way. The man held the axe aloft and roared at them again, 'Out.'

Isolde tried to move but she could not stop shaking. This could only mean one thing; like their mother, they were going to die. At last she managed to take control of her trembling legs and stood up, reaching for her brothers.

'Come on boys. Here take my hand,' she said.

She had to remain calm for their sake. She led them out into the yard and stopped in horror at the scene before her; it was a nightmare. The God of War himself had turned on them. The villagers' wooden houses were in flames, their thatched roofs burning like bonfires and lighting up the night sky. Her friends and neighbours were herded together like animals in the village square. One woman sat on the ground, cradling her dead baby in her arms and wailing. What manner of men were they that they could kill an innocent baby she asked herself. The night air, normally home to the sounds of nothing more than a barn owl or the occasional howl of a wolf, was now filled with cries of pain and despair, the sound of the women's anguish so strong it drowned the squeals and snorts of the terrified pigs that skittered around, desperately seeking an escape. Her neighbour's donkey, the one she gave a tidbit to each morning, kicked against his stable door, braying in terror while chickens ran wildly around the yard, trying to avoid the vikings' axes. People and animals alike were terrified.

Isolde stumbled forward, gasping. By now the air was thick with black smoke. She tried to cling to her brothers but one of the vikings pulled them away from her. They struggled to free themselves, kicking and screaming but he wound a length of rope around their wrists and tied them to the other children.

'Isolde, don't let him take us,' her younger brother cried. 'Don't leave us. Don't leave us.'

'What about this one?' the viking asked, pointing at Isolde.

The leader of the raiding party, a huge brute, with a long red beard, pulled her towards him and held a burning torch up to her face while he studied her. He wore a cloak of animal fur around his shoulders; she could smell the rank odour of the skins and twisted her head away, trying to pull out of his grasp. He was obviously a man of some importance because his cloak was fastened with an enormous double clasp of twisted gold and on his head he wore a helmet embellished with golden figures; he was a rich man, a powerful man but also a cruel one.

Isolde could feel her knees give way. She thought she would collapse with fear. The man continued to study her for a moment, turning her head first one way then the other.

'Mmn. She'll do. Put her with the other women for now. I think we'll get a good price for this one, so don't rough her up. I don't want to see any marks on that pretty face. And keep the other men away from her; that's an order. I don't want her deflowered; a virgin brings a higher price and this one is destined for a king.'

One of the vikings grabbed her arm and shoved her towards the group of crying women. She collapsed on the ground next to them. What did he mean, destined for a king? What was going to happen to her? What was going to happen to them all? She looked around her; escape was impossible. There was no way they could get away from these men; they were no more than a few dozen women and some children. They could not fight them. But who could save them from the vikings? Her father and the other men were away, deep in the forests of Saxony; they were fishing in the lakes and wouldn't be back for two more days at least and the nearest village was at least an hour's walk away. She knew the answer to her question; there was no-one to help them.

She thought of her father and her uncles. Would they understand what had happened to their families? Would they realise where their loved ones had gone? What would they do? Would they come after them? She was sure her father would try to look for them but he might be too late; by the time he returned they might all be dead. At the thought of her mother lying on the floor of their hut, her eyes, wide and staring, Isolde started to cry. Once started, she could do nothing to stop; the tears just coursed down her cheeks, soaking her dress.

'Can't you shut those women up?' one of the men said. 'Get them out of here; take them down to the ships.'

While some of the vikings ransacked the village looking for food and valuables, the others dragged the captives down towards the river. Two long-ships were moored by the bank; their curved oak prows stood tall against a sky reddened by the burning village. She couldn't believe that these enormous ships, both as long as the tallest trees in the forest, had managed to come so far up the river; the raiders had rowed upstream in the middle of the night without anyone realising it. Even the dogs, usually alert to any intruder, had been taken by surprise.

The vikings bundled their captives on board the ships, separating the women onto one ship and putting the children on the other.

'Lie down and keep quiet,' roared the man with the red beard.

He glowered at them. Despite her fear, Isolde knew she had to take one last look at her village. She turned and faced back the way she had come. It was easy to see. Beyond the trees, the flames had turned night into day. Her village was ablaze, sending a cloud of acrid black smoke high into the sky and blotting out the stars. Isolde began to sob, uncontrollably. That was her home; she had lived there all her life. Now it was gone. Worse still, her mother was lying there, her body burning along with everything else. Why had the gods let this happen to them? It was too hard to take in; she wanted to wake and find that it was all just a bad dream. She wanted to cuddle up next to her mother and listen to her tell her that everything would be all right, that when the sun rose she would laugh at her night fears. But this was no dream. She looked at her brothers, huddled together in the bow of the next ship, their faces blackened by the smoke. What was going to happen to them? Would she ever see them again? What was going to happen to her? The unanswered questions rattled around in her brain making her dizzy with fear.

The rest of the vikings came back to the ships; they seemed happy with what they had achieved. They herded the animals they had managed to round up onto the ship with the children. They were laughing and joking amongst themselves. One was gnawing on a ham bone that he had stolen; another was eating a hunk of bread. How relaxed and pleased with themselves they looked. She hated them all. Silently she prayed for the gods to strike them dead. But the gods were not listening to her small voice that night. No flash of lightning hit their long-ships, no giant wave raced up the river and overturned them, no plague of insects chased them back into the woods. Nothing happened to save the women and children. They were doomed to go where fate had decided to send them. With despair in her heart she watched as each man took his position at the rowlocks and the long-ships pulled away, downstream towards the sea.

***

She did not remember much about the journey except that it was long and cold and uncomfortable. There was no shelter on the ships; they were war-ships, built for speed and were nothing more than wooden shells with oars positioned their full length. For the captives there was nowhere to shelter from the elements; she sat huddled in the bow with the other women, people she had known all her life. Now their chatter was stilled; they sat in silence, heads down, hugging their bodies as though they could make themselves smaller and remain unnoticed. No-one had the energy to talk. At first they had asked about her mother but she could not answer them; the tears had welled up again, closing her throat and filling her eyes. Her mother was dead; she was sure of it. She could never have survived that conflagration. And what of her father and the other men? They would be back any day. Had any of the vikings stayed behind ? Would they be waiting for them? Would they walk into a trap? She voiced her fears to one of her neighbours, an older woman who acted as a midwife when any babies were born.

'No. The vikings will be far away by then. They only attacked us because our men were not around. Cowards, that's what they are. Only interested in the women and children.'

'But why? What good are we to them? They have taken our money and our food, even our animals. Why do they want us?'

'Don't you know who they are?' asked the woman whose son always played with Isolde's brothers.

She looked at Isolde in astonishment.

'They're slavers. They raid the villages and take people to sell as slaves. We're better than food or money to them. They will take us to the slave markets of Iberia and sell us to the highest bidder. Our lives are over.'

'We might as well be dead,' said another woman.

So she was to be sold as a slave. They all were. That was what the viking leader had meant. He had looked at her face and decided that she would bring a higher price than some of the others. Good news for him but what did it mean for her? Her heart beat wildly in her chest at the thought of what might lie ahead for her. Whatever it was, it would not be good; of that she was certain. Her life was about to change forever and only time would tell if she would have the strength or the good fortune to survive. All she could do was put her trust in the gods. But first, they had the sea to cross. She looked up at the dragon's head carved into the prow of the ship; it stared ahead into the murky darkness, seeing what dangers she feared to know.

***

She had never been at sea before and to begin with she was so frightened that she could hardly breathe. The forests and mountains of her homeland gradually disappeared into the mist and all that was left was sky and sea. Everywhere

she looked there was water, an icy, oily grey expanse of
endless water. As they pulled away from the shelter of the
coast, the sea became rougher, the waves towered above
them, lashing at the ships in fury; even the screams of the
seagulls whirling overhead died away as the birds headed
back to calmer waters. Now her fear became secondary;
she was too ill to be scared. Every time she tried to move,
her stomach heaved, her head spun and she retched
violently. She huddled in the bow of the ship, frightened to
move, so cold and wet that she wished she were dead.
There was no respite from the fierce wind that blew directly
from the north, cutting through her flimsy night-clothes
and turning her bones to ice. Her nightdress was soaked
and clung to her body like a second skin; her face and hair
were encrusted with salt. None of the women were crying
now; they were all too exhausted to cry. She tried to stand
to see if she could spot the other long-ship, but the wind
blew her back, knocking the breath from her body. There
was no sign of it; the ships had become separated. Now
she feared for her brothers; how would they survive without
her? They were so small; it would be easy for them to be
washed overboard. Suddenly a giant wave lifted the long-
ship out of the water and for a brief moment she caught a
glimpse of the second vessel. Then it was gone, hidden by
the crashing waves. Tears streamed down her wet cheeks.
They were all going to die. It was impossible that these
flimsy ships could withstand this battering for much longer;
there was no way that they could survive. Again a wave
lifted the ship out of the water and this time she was sure
they would capsize. Her stomach heaved and seemed
about to leave her body. Maybe the God of the Sea was

going to grant her wish; maybe he was going to drown them after all. As she silently prayed to him she told herself that even death would be better than a life of captivity. But the ship shuddered, regained its balance and ploughed on through the waves.

Their captors offered them food and water to drink but she had no stomach for either; she tried to drink a little but she could eat nothing. Even the thought of food made her want to vomit. Anyway, she asked herself, what was the point of eating? She no longer wanted to live; she wanted to die. The other women had painted a grim picture of what it was like to be a slave. Women and young boys could expect no mercy from their owners, they said; they treated their animals better than their slaves. If her life was to be a living hell then she would prefer to die now, here in this odious ship.

But she didn't die; she survived. For five days and five nights they sailed. The ship kept heading south and soon the weather became calmer and warmer; gulls flew out to greet them; great fish could be seen swimming alongside them until, at last, they landed on a rocky shore.

CHAPTER 2
MADINAT AL-ZAHRA

Qasim was awake before the cock began to crow; it was habit. His body was used to rising before dawn and today was no exception. He stretched, feeling the stiffness in his joints as he did so. On the bedroll next to him lay, not his wife Fatima, but his youngest son, Omar. Fatima and his daughter slept indoors, in the only room that was properly finished while he and Omar slept on the patio. It was no hardship. He might be old now but he was still strong. He was a big man, broad and solid, like a rock. Born of the land, he was a common man; his feet were large and worn hard like leather. Even his hands were as tough as goat hide. That was the clay. Years of moulding it and shaping it had dried out the skin and cured it as well as any tanning agent.

He rolled onto his back and looked up; already there was a pink tinge on the horizon that grew steadily as he watched. Stars strewn across an indigo sky were dimming and gradually fading away altogether as the sun rose. When he was in the army he had often slept under the stars. He had enjoyed his days as a soldier, the comradeship, the common cause, following the man he had respected almost as much as he did his father. And he had been good at it, rising to the rank of commander within a year, a trusted and loyal follower of Omar ibn Hafsun. It had all seemed so simple; ibn Hafsun had been his hero in those days. But that was then, before he had betrayed Qasim and the rest of his Mullawad followers.

At last the cock crowed, and then again, twice more; more persistently than ever it seemed.

'All right. I'm getting up,' he muttered.

He moved quietly so as not to wake his son. He would have to rouse him soon but for now he could sleep. Qasim preferred to have these first few minutes to himself; this was the part of the day he liked best. He filled a bucket with water from the pump and washed himself thoroughly then dressed in his usual grey djubba; he combed his greying hair and beard and placed the red ghifara that Fatima had made for him, on his head. Then he picked up his prayer mat and moved to the corner of the patio that he had allocated for worship; kneeling down, he began his morning prayers.

He loved this moment, alone with Allah, his family safe and sleeping around him. How different things could have been if Allah had not looked down on him favourably. And yet here he was now, in his own house, albeit a still unfinished house, but his own, nevertheless. And paid for by the Khalifa, Allah bless and keep him. He tried to remove from his mind all thoughts of the silver dirhams he had been given. It was not right to be saying his prayers with thoughts of money and avarice running through his head. But still they returned. He could hardly believe it when he had heard that the Khalifa was giving four hundred silver dirhams to anyone who wanted to move to his new city, Madinat al-Zahra and build themselves a house there. He had hesitated a mere moment or two then set off to the government buildings to apply. He had not been alone; many others had taken advantage of the Khalifa's generosity and still they came pouring in. Soon there would be a continuous line of houses linking the old city with the new. Before long Madinat al-Zahra would rival Córdoba in wealth and grandeur.

Mentally he rebuked himself. No, he must not dwell on his good fortune or Allah might take it away from him. Pride was a sin. He must be humble and empty his mind of material things. With a supreme effort he turned his body towards the quibla and began to recite his prayers.

***

A movement inside the house told him that his wife was now awake. He walked into the room where she lay. So far he and Omar had only completed one room, the one where the women slept. They had constructed the exterior walls with limestone ashlars and laid out the interior patio, paving the floor with bricks; they had built a latrine in the corner of the building and installed a pump and sink for water. Outside, attached to the north wall, they had constructed the <u>alfarería</u> and installed a large brick kiln to fire the pottery. They had drawn up plans for the rest of the house and stacked the materials ready. There were to be four symmetrical rooms on the ground floor and a staircase leading to a large upstairs room for the family to gather and relax. Above would be a wide flat roof where Fatima could dry her washing and they could sit in the cool of the evening, watching the sunset and maybe even sleeping when the heat was too great to sleep inside. It would be splendid when it was finished; he could see it in his mind's eye. The problem was that it was taking a long time. The rest of his family was still in Córdoba; there was only Omar to help him and he was not much use. All Omar liked to do was work on his new designs.

'Good morning wife.'

'Good morning Qasim,' Fatima murmured.

She looked sleepy.

'Where is my little princess?' Qasim asked, reaching down to his ten-year old daughter and tickling her.

The child shrieked with pleasure and wriggled further under her blanket.

'Come on, you sleepy-head, it's time you were up.'

'I'll get you some breakfast,' Fatima said, pulling her robe around her.

'No, it can wait. Say your prayers first,' he told her. 'I'm going to empty the kiln.'

The dawn prayers were the only ones he could really be sure that everyone in his family said. Once he began work and the family set about its business he lost control of them. Of course they all said that they prayed five times a day but he could not be sure. Even at night Omar was not always back in time to pray. It did not matter, his son told him, he did not have to be at home to pray; he could go to the mosque. Qasim did not argue with him. Allah would know if he prayed or not. Qasim had done his duty as a father; that was what mattered.

He walked back to the patio and gave his son a gentle kick with his foot.

'Time to get up. You're late for prayers.'

His son grunted and rolled over. A minute later he was up, his head under the pump washing the sleep from his eyes.

Qasim went into the alfarería and began to unload the kiln, holding each plate up to the light for inspection as he did so. One had a slight chip on the rim so he tossed it into the corner with the other rejects. He could not keep any failures. These plates were to be painted by Omar with Qasim's new glazes and then re-fired. He wanted them all to be perfect.

His thoughts returned to Ardales and his youth. It was strange; he had not thought about those days for a long time. In fact for many years he had deliberately kept them from his mind. But now, for the second time that morning he found his mind straying back to his home town.

He had been a potter before he joined ibn Hafsun's rebellion, working alongside his father in a small town, high above the green and fertile Guadalhorce valley. In those days the country was in a state of turmoil; the Sultan's rule was constantly challenged by a succession of princelings eager to usurp him. Omar ibn Hafsun had been one of them. The renegade had come to the area with his band of followers and built a fortress at Bobastro, only an Arab mile from Qasim's home. He told everyone that he was going to build a better world, an independent kingdom of the Mullawads, here in al-Andalus and he would be their king. He was tall, handsome and charismatic. Everyone believed him. They flocked to join his army and Qasim too had been swept up by the enthusiasm of the man; he immediately left his work as a potter to join him. He felt an ache in his chest as he remembered his youthful passion. Passion or foolhardiness? If only he had had the wisdom then that he now possessed.

'Baba, breakfast is ready,' his daughter said, peering through the curtain that hung across the entrance to his workshop.

'All right, princess, tell your mother I will not be long.'

He placed the last of the plates on the workbench, ready for his son to paint and went to join his family.

CHAPTER 3

Isolde was bewildered and scared; they all were. After days and nights of walking they had finally arrived at a small inland town and were camped on the outskirts. The countryside about them was dry and arid, sparsely populated by grey leafed trees and enormous boulders that loomed out of the sandy soil like sleeping giants. They had passed few animals, only a flock of goats that ran away, bleating frantically as they approached. In the far distance she could see the blue outline of mountains and high above them, in a cloudless sky, eagles soared. This country was nothing like home; she felt a tug at her heart as she thought of the deep forests that surrounded her village, of the morning mists that hung like silver clouds along the river, of the cattle lowing in the fields. Here the trees were poor specimens, small and stunted, twisted into strange shapes by the sea winds, not tall oaks with branches wide and strong enough for her and her brothers to climb. The forests of Saxony were home to squirrels and birds and the forest floor was carpeted with bluebells and tiny white flowers. She remembered how her mother sent her into the forest to collect kindling with her brothers or to gather mushrooms, how it was her job to bring in their cow from the fields for milking. The thought of her mother made her sad. She wondered if her father had returned yet and whether he knew what had happened to them. She had no idea of how many days had passed since she had been captured but she felt sure that he would try to find them. If only she knew where she was. If only she could send word to him to come for them.

A movement from her captors caused her to look up. Some men were approaching on horseback. The soft, sandy soil muffled the sound of the horses' hooves but there was no mistaking the cloud of dust that they sent into the air as they galloped towards them. She felt her stomach tighten with fear. What was going to happen to them now?

The horsemen stopped beside the encampment and one, a tall, swarthy man, dismounted; he had come to bargain for them. He was unlike any man she had seen before, with a black beard and a gold ring in his ear and he wore long robes instead of homespun trousers. But he was no stranger to her viking captors; they seemed to know him and greeted him warmly in a tongue she did not recognise. The viking with the red beard waved towards his captives, who sat roped together like cattle, and smiled, inviting his visitor to inspect them.

The man examined them all; even the old women. He looked at their teeth and pulled up their skirts; he tested the boys' strength by squeezing their forearms; he pinched the women's arms and buttocks. As he leaned over to look at her he smelled of stale fish and onions. She thought she was going to be sick again. At last, he seemed satisfied and pulled out a bag of gold coins which he gave to the vikings. Then he led his new purchases to a tent where they were expected to sleep. Sleep? She felt she would never be able to sleep again.

***

At dawn she awoke. The vikings had left. At first she thought the man with the gold earring was going to keep them and put them to work for him but then she realised that he was a slave merchant. He had no intention of keeping them; he wanted to sell each of them for a handsome profit.

They were still roped together, but the women and children were now all in the same tent. Isolde edged her way across to her brothers. It was her first opportunity to speak to them.

'Hans, Per, are you both all right?'

The boys looked scared but they bravely smiled at their sister.

'I'm all right, Issy,' Per whispered. 'But I'm frightened of those men. I want Mama.'

She swallowed hard. Per was the youngest, no more than four years old. How could she tell him that his mother was dead?

'Mama is not here. She stayed behind.'

'Will she come and get us later?' he continued.

'I don't think so.'

The little boy frowned at her.

'We're a long way from home. How will she find us?' he asked, tears filling his eyes.

'She's dead, stupid. You saw that viking kill her,' Hans said, angrily. 'She's never coming to find us. She's dead.'

Isolde looked at her brother's frightened face. There was no point denying it.

'Yes, Hans is right. Mama's gone to live with the gods,' Isolde said, choking back her own tears.

'What's going to happen to us now?' asked Hans.

'I don't know. I think they mean to sell us as slaves.'

'Where's Papi?' asked Per. 'Why doesn't Papi come for us?'

He was having great difficulty understanding what was happening.

'Papi doesn't know where we are, Per. He can't help us.'

The boy began to cry.

'Don't want to be a slave,' he said angrily. 'I want Mama.'

'I know, sweetheart, but you have to be brave, both of you. Maybe we will be lucky and someone will buy the three of us. Then it won't be so bad if we are all slaves, together,' she said.

The boys looked at her.

'Why don't we run away?' Hans asked.

'Where would we go? We don't even know which country we are in. We've been travelling for weeks. All we know is that it's a long way to go home even if we could escape without being seen.'

She would love to take them by the hand and run away, back to what remained of her village, back to the forests and streams of her homeland, back to Papi but she knew it was impossible. The men would hunt them down and punish them. No, they would have to hope that the gods looked after them and kept them together.

'In the meantime, just keep close and look after each other,' she told them.

Some of the women and a few of the children were sold at the first town they came to; Isolde was sad to see them go. Now she felt even more alone; their little group was diminishing. At the next town Per was sold to a man who wanted him to work in his kitchen. The little boy cried and struggled so much when they separated him from his brother that she thought the man was going to hand him back to the slave merchant. But he didn't; he just put Per across his shoulder like a sack of potatoes and strode away with him. She called out, pleading with him to take them all, not to separate them but the slave merchant pulled her away and tied her up with the horses, where nobody could hear her. Then Hans, along with some bigger boys, was sold to another trader who wanted to trade them in one of the nearby towns.

At their next stop, one of their guards tried to take Isolde out with the others but the man with the gold earring stopped him. So Isolde was made to stay in the tent while the others were paraded up and down like cattle and eventually auctioned off for the best price. Soon only she and a couple of skinny boys remained; the rest, her neighbours and friends had all been sold. She had been spared for now. But spared for what? The slave auctions that she had witnessed had been brutal and she had no great hope of being treated any better, wherever she was going.

***

They arrived at last in a great city. Isolde had never been to a city before. She had heard pedlars talk of them, on the occasions when they stopped in her village to sell their wares or buy supplies, but they had sounded cold, dreary places, crowded with people and animals. This southern city was like nothing she had ever heard about or even imagined in her dreams. The buildings were huge and built of stone but they were not dreary; they glowed a

42

warm amber colour in the evening sun. They towered above her, casting pools of bluish shadows across her path. The slave merchant led them down narrow paved streets lit by oil lamps, under red and white painted arches, through winding passageways, past marble columns and heavy oak doors that were three times as tall as she was. And the people, they were everywhere, hurrying to and fro about their business, all dressed in the same flowing robes as her captors. Their complexions were dark and they chattered in a tongue that was as far removed from her own Saxon language as it was possible to be. Some were obviously working people, tradesmen and labourers but many looked like chieftains or wealthy merchants, their clothing was so fine and rich. Even though night was drawing near, the evening air was warm and filled with the scent of blossom. There were fountains of running water, open spaces where people sat talking and drinking something from tiny cups, balconies filled with flowers, entertainers playing musical instruments. They passed a market, where the stalls were stacked with so many different goods that she had trouble identifying most of them. For a brief moment, so lost in curiosity was she about this vibrant, colourful city, that she forgot she was a captive, powerless to do as she wished.

The slave trader stopped and spoke to someone. Whatever exchange took place between them, it made him angry. He turned to his men and shouted.

'What's happened?' one of them asked.

Isolde could just make out what he said; he spoke in a dialect not unlike her own. It seemed that the Khalifa was not here anymore; they had to move on. She could see that the slave merchant was not happy with the news. As they turned to leave, the men grumbling and moaning about the change of plan, a richly dressed man approached them. He pointed at Isolde and leered then offered the merchant a purse of money; it seemed he wanted to buy her. Isolde felt her stomach lurch with fear. Was this to be her destiny, to be a slave to this repugnant old man? She thought she would be sick. But the slave merchant had other ideas and, shouting at him in the same strange language, pushed him roughly away. This angered the old man; he put his purse back in his pocket, shook his stick at the slave merchant and shouted some abuse at Isolde. From his gestures he seemed to be saying that Isolde wasn't worth it, anyway. Whatever had passed between them, the slave merchant was angry at the old man's words. He grabbed Isolde by her arm and turned her round and round, so that he could have a good look at her. Then he thrust her back to one of his men and disappeared into the depths of the market.

Isolde looked down at her dress; it was torn and stained with her mother's blood. Her hands, and surely her face too, were blackened from the soot of the fires; her feet were dirty, caked with mud and salt, her nails broken and her hair matted from the salt spray of the journey. No wonder the old man had been so rude about her.

A few minutes later the merchant reappeared with a bundle of clothes in his hand.

'Take her away and wash her. Then dress her in these,' he said, shoving the clothes at the man, who spoke Isolde's language. 'And get one of the women to comb her hair. I want her to look like a princess before we get to Madinat al-Zahra, not some street urchin.'

So that was where they were going, Madinat al-Zahra; at last she knew her destination. Madinat al-Zahra, the name had a musical ring to it.

CHAPTER 4

The market of Madinat al-Zahra was busy by the time Fatima arrived; people were setting out their wares on mats in front of them, peasants who had come in from the outlying countryside to sell aubergines, endives, radishes, leeks and artichokes. There were fresh figs, dates and even a few grapes, although it was still a bit early for them. Others were selling spices: sticks of cinnamon, cardamon, cumin seeds, scarlet chilli pods, garlic cloves, pepper, whole nutmegs, fresh coriander, aniseed and mint. The air was pungent with their fragrance. Fatima made straight for the usual stall where she bought her meat and chose a shoulder of lamb. The butcher chopped it into small pieces for her and wrapped it in a vine leaf. She would cook it slowly in a tagine with saffron, cumin and coriander and maybe she would buy an aubergine and some onions to add as well. Next she went to the sweet stall. Her family would expect her to bring something back from here. She chose a few pieces of candied fruit, some almonds and some sticks of sugar cane. She looked at her shopping. To think that she used to collect most of this herself when she lived in the country. Her parents had fruit trees in their garden and there were almond trees and olives at hand; she could gather asparagus in the fields and even find sugar cane by the wayside.

'Anything else?' the stall holder asked her.

'Not today, thank you,' she said as she handed him a small silver coin.

A burst of loud laughter caught her attention. There was a crowd gathering at the far end of the market so she collected up her purchases and made her way towards it. She pushed her way to the front to see what was happening. A group of foreigners were talking in loud, harsh voices and gesticulating wildly at the crowd; they were dark, bearded men who spoke Arabic with a thick accent. She had seen them or their like before. They were Jewish merchants who traded in slaves. They brought them from the other side of the Mediterranean to sell in al-Andalus. The crowd were jeering at them because they had brought a motley collection of slaves to sell today. Nobody wanted to pay the prices being asked and she could understand why. There were six slaves in all: four men and two women. Men, hardly, they were no more than boys and puny lads at that. One of the slavers pulled a boy forward, yanking at his chain and barking orders designed to make him stand up straight and look stronger. The poor child tried as best he could but nothing the slaver said or did would put muscle on those thin arms or straighten out his crooked back. In the end someone bought him for a pittance. For a moment Fatima wished she had done so herself.

They had been talking of getting someone to help with the heavy work in the house but so far Qasim had done nothing about it. He did not like her going to the slave market. He knew how much she hated seeing the slaves being treated badly. It wasn't that she didn't believe in slavery; after all these were heathens. They were not people

47

of the Book. But she didn't like the way the slavers pulled them around, especially the way they treated the women, lifting their dresses up so that everyone could see their legs and poking and pulling them. If they were beautiful then they dressed them in skimpy rags, so that their breasts showed and made lewd remarks about them. It was disgraceful. She would not treat an animal like that. Everyone deserved some dignity, even a slave.

She was about to turn and leave when the crowd went quiet. One of the slavers had moved to the front of the group. He was leading a shrouded figure, tall and slim but obviously female. The crowd waited expectantly and then, as he pulled the shroud from the figure, a gasp went up. It was a woman, a young woman, no more than sixteen, the most beautiful woman that Fatima had ever seen. She was fair and her eyes were as blue as the summer sky. Her blonde hair hung down her back like a river of corn; her hips were full, as were her breasts and her legs were shapely. Dressed in a plain white robe she was like some foreign goddess. She stared at the crowd, showing no fear. Her look defied anyone to speak. However, once the crowd had recovered from the shock of seeing this lovely creature, the bidding started in earnest, each one trying to outdo the other. The slavers looked pleased with themselves; at least they would make some money with this one. Then a voice silenced them all. It was the Chief Black Eunuch, the head of the Khalifa's harem. His name was Yamut al-Attar; everyone knew him. He was a tall man and his skin shone like polished ebony.

'Fifty silver dirhams,' he said.

'What? Is that an insult? Do you think I am going to give away this beautiful young virgin for a measly fifty dirhams? I paid more than that for her and I've had to provide for her too, feed and clothe her for weeks. You must be mad. I could get five hundred for her in Córdoba,' the bearded man said, holding his captive by the arm. 'She is from a royal family, a princess of the north.'

Fatima could see the red wheals on the girl's arm where his fingers gripped her. What was a princess doing being auctioned off by such a man? More likely she was some poor, country girl, snatched from her family in the dead of night.

'One hundred.'

'Three.'

'One hundred and fifty.'

Something in the Chief Eunuch's tone said that this was as high as he would bid, so the slaver nodded and handed over the girl. She would be a new addition to the Khalifa's harem. Everyone knew that there was no point in being too greedy when dealing with the Khalifa's men.

The girl rubbed her arm and stepped towards the eunuch, who took a cloak from his assistant and threw it around her, covering her from head to toe. Then he counted the silver coins into the merchant's hand and led her away. She was the Khalifa's property now.

The crowd began to disperse. There was no more to see. The Khalifa's men were taking the girl back to the alcázar.

Fatima still had more tasks to do before she could return home and the morning was gradually slipping away. She lifted her basket and set off in the direction of the baker's shop.

***

The baker was already loading his oven with bread dough when she arrived. The sweat was running down his neck and his djubbah had a large damp patch down the back.

'As-salama alaykum,' she said by way of greeting. 'Any room for a couple more?'

'Wa alaykum e-salam, Fatima,' the baker replied. 'How are you today?'

'Very well. I wondered if you could bake these for me?'

She took the dough she had prepared the night before from her basket and handed it to him. She had already divided it into three portions: two of equal size and one a bit smaller to give to him as payment.

'Of course. You're just in time; this is the last batch until tonight.'

'And this is for you,' she said handing him the smaller piece of dough.

He nodded and put it to one side. Then he placed her loaves on a long wooden paddle and slipped them into the oven along with his own. She had marked them with a little cross so she would be sure to get her own bread back after it was cooked.

'It'll be ready in half an hour,' he told her.

'I'll come back later,' she said.

Her house was just around the corner. Once she had prepared the meat and put it to cook slowly on the stove, she would return to collect the bread.

Although it was only mid-morning, the sun was already fierce and as she stepped out from under the awning that

50

shaded the shop, she felt the heat hit her like a blast from the baker's oven. It was the same in this city as it had been in Córdoba - an unrelenting dry heat in the summer that made her eyes sting and filled her throat and nose with dust and a fearsome cold in the winter. Never was the weather as temperate as it had been in Ardales, the place of her birth. She still felt homesick when she thought back to that little white town, perched high on a hill, overlooking a wide, green valley that stretched all the way down to the city of Málaga and the sea. Even in summer the cool sea breezes seemed to reach them. As a child she had climbed the hills above the town, taking the goats to pasture and sat and looked across the hills to El Tajo and the deep lakes that spread out below her. That had been her life until she had married Qasim. Then one day he came home and told her that it was no longer safe to stay in Ardales; they had to flee. They had to leave the town where she had been born, where her brothers and sisters lived, where her parents lived, leave her friends and neighbours, her in-laws, everyone she knew and loved. They could no longer stay there; it was too dangerous. There was to be no more mention of his hero, Omar ibn Hafsun, no more mention of rebellion. They were going to live in Córdoba and from then on they were to be loyal subjects of the Sultan.

They had left the same night, taking all their possessions and a camel her father gave them. She was just seventeen, newly married and expecting her first child. What else could she do but follow her husband, no matter what the cost.

***

As Fatima walked back towards her home she noticed a crowd gathering by the Bab al-Sura, the gate of the Statue. It looked as though the Khalifa was expecting some important visitors. Who would they be today, members of the Imperial Frankish court, ambassadors from Byzantium or the representatives of the Christian kingdoms in the north of the country? She wandered towards the crowd of people already jostling for the chance to see these exotic travellers.

The Khalifa's visitors did not arrive by the normal Los Nogales Road, which ordinary travellers and merchants walked; they took the ceremonial road, Las Almunias, direct from Córdoba. The paved road was covered in rush matting; it was lined with a double row of soldiers, smartly dressed in their full uniform, some in armour and all holding silken banners. Her oldest son, al-Jundi, was a soldier. He had told her that the entire road, all the way from Córdoba to Madinat al-Zahra, was lined with soldiers in this way, in order to display the full might of the Khalifa's army to the foreign dignitaries. She peered at the nearest of the soldiers, trying to see if al-Jundi was amongst them. He had said how the Khalifa liked to impress his visitors with his wealth and power. They would be met at the Portico by government officials and members of the Khalifa's household, all sumptuously dressed and lined up on either side of the Arms Square and all the way to the Khalifa's political reception hall. Then the visitors would be led through the marble passageways and courtyards, past pavilions hung with rich tapestries, through ornate gardens and past lakes full of fish until they reached the high terrace where the Khalifa was waiting to receive them.

Al-Jundi had never been into the inner reception hall but he said that those who saw it, told how it was a wonder to behold, more beautiful than anything in Córdoba and, some said, even Baghdad had nothing to compare with it.

A stir in the crowd told her something was happening. They were coming. How splendid they looked. First came a procession of the Khalifa's guards, marching in double formation, a hundred of them at least; then behind them were members of the foreign court, some walking, some on horseback. The king, because she was sure he was some sort of king, rode behind on a magnificent black horse; he was followed by groups of dancing girls in flowing robes, with jangling beads on their wrists and ankles and behind them, bare chested eunuchs. She did not know who this dignitary was, although someone in the crowd said he was from the north. He was a slight, dark-haired man with a wispy beard and he wore chain-mail armour that glistened in the sun. Despite his show of wealth he did not look as powerful as the Khalifa.

She waited for the procession to pass and then the crowd began to disperse. The sun was now high in the sky; it was time she returned home. Qasim would be looking for her and, besides which, the meat she had bought would need at least two or three hours to cook. If she didn't start soon the dinner would be late.

'Fatima. As-salam alaykum,' said a shrill voice behind her.

'Elvira, wa alaykum e-salam,' she replied to her friend.

'Have you been watching the procession?' Elvira asked.

'Yes. I hoped to see Makoud but he wasn't there.'

'Al-Jundi?'

'Yes. He's in the Palace Guard now.'

'I missed most of the excitement. Who was it this time?'

'Some king from the north, I think. There were no camels, only horses.'

This was always a good indication that the visitors were northerners and not from Africa. She liked to see the camels, with their saddles stuffed with amber-gris and stitched with gold thread and the tassels swinging from their headdresses. It had been one of her jobs as a girl to feed her father's camels and despite the fact that they could sometimes be bad-tempered animals and would spit at her, she had been fond of them. They had no camel now; it had been sold when they arrived in Córdoba all those years ago.

'Are you heading home?' Elvira asked.

'Yes.'

'I'll walk with you then.'

Elvira hoisted the bags she was carrying up onto her wide hips, one either side and waddled along beside Fatima.

'There're more people building in the medina,' she said. 'We have two lots of new neighbours.'

'I know; I've seen the houses going up. It's soon going to be very crowded. I'm glad we got our plot when we did.'

'Yes, you were lucky to build inside the city walls, not like us.'

Elvira's husband was a merchant; he imported spices from the East and supplied the traders in the bazaar. Their house was an impressive five-roomed building close to the Nogales Road, well positioned for passing traders and craftsmen.

'That's because of the alfarería; we have to be inside with the other craftsmen.'

'Whatever the reason, you are very lucky; it's so much more convenient. I hate living by the main road.'

Fatima smiled. Elvira was always complaining about something. She knew as well as her that Fatima's husband had no choice in the matter; their alfarería had to be with all the other workshops, in the artisan quarter.

'We are buying a slave,' Elvira said with a satisfied smile. 'You know I've been on at Hassam for years to get me some help; well at last he has agreed. He says he will go to the slave market and choose one for me.'

'Be careful he doesn't choose a beautiful young slave girl. You might find that he decides to take her as another wife,' Fatima said, thinking of the lovely slave girl she had just seen.

'Why would I care? If it means he leaves me in peace and I have someone to help with the work around the house, that would be fine. If he wants more children that's up to him. He can have as many new wives as he wants. I just want some peace and quiet in my old age.'

Elvira was not that old, maybe a few years older than Fatima but she understood what she meant. Fatima knew many women who shared their husbands with other wives; her own father had had two wives. Qasim had never talked about it. He seemed happy to just have her. She felt privileged that he thought so much of her that he had never needed anyone else. She often thought that it was because of those early years, running from the soldiers in fear of their lives; a bond had grown between them that still held true. Whenever Qasim had anything on his mind, instead of going to the hamman and discussing it with his friends, he talked to Fatima. Like all husbands, he made the important decisions in their lives but he still wanted her opinion and she felt she exerted a real influence on him.

Elvira stopped and put her bags on the ground; she was wheezing from the exertion and her breath came in harsh gasps.

'Are you all right, Elvira?'

'Just give me a moment to rest and I'll be fine,' she said, squatting down beside her shopping. 'Tell me, how is your little Layla? Have you chosen a husband for her yet?'

'A husband? No. She's far too young to be thinking about marriage.'

'I don't know about that. How old is she? Ten? I was promised to my husband when I was eight.'

'But that was then. Things are different now. No, Layla is going to have a good education; she is going to become a doctor.'

'A doctor? Well, you do have fancy ideas for her. Personally I don't see the point. What's the use in giving her all that education if she is going to end up as someone's wife. Any husband will expect his wife to stay at home and look after him and the children, not go out doctoring. Men are only interested in their home comforts.'

Fatima bit her lip; she had heard this argument before. But Layla was not like her other children. She was lively and intelligent like Omar but she was far more difficult to control. She had an independent streak that the others lacked. Her inquisitive mind and her persistent questions often caused her to cross the line between curiosity and propriety and Fatima sometimes felt that she failed to show the respect for her elders that they were due.

When they had come to Córdoba all those years ago Fatima had been amazed to see the freedom that women held in the city. She could not believe it when she saw women doing the same jobs as men, women who trained as doctors and lawyers, women scribes who copied out the Quran. She saw wealthy women who supported public works, who paid for the upkeep of gardens and parks, who financed hospitals and libraries, women who were mystics, women who were icons of fashion. Even though it was too late for her, she had wanted that freedom for her daughters. Her eldest daughter, Sara had married but now there was Layla; she would have the chance that they had both missed.

'Well I'd better be getting home,' Elvira said, hauling herself to her feet.

'Are you feeling all right now?'

'Yes, but I'll be glad when we get that slave; he can go to the market for me and I'll stay at home with my feet up.'

She laughed. They both knew that was not likely to happen.

'Ma'a salama, Fatima.'

'Alla ysalmak. Take care of yourself.'

CHAPTER 5

When Omar was young he wanted to be a soldier like his oldest brother but his parents would not allow it.

'There have been enough soldiers in this family,' his father had said. 'You will do something else with your life.'

It was unfair of him to say that. Makoud, his oldest brother, nicknamed al-Jundi—the soldier—was in the army. He was part of the Palace Guard; his job was to protect the Khalifa and the Khalifa was a good man, even their father agreed on that. According to the old men who sat gossiping in the tea shop each evening, there had never been such a period of prosperity and peace.

Although his father's decision had annoyed Omar at first and, in his youthful rage he had thought of rebelling and running away to enlist, in the end he had to admit that his father was right. He knew he was not as strong as his brother and would probably have made a pretty poor soldier. Al-Jundi was built like his father, tall and broad and as strong as an ox while Omar had to admit that he was a puny specimen beside him; he was thin and wiry, favouring his mother's side of the family. So when his father put him to work as his apprentice, he had at first acquiesced and then decided that he actually enjoyed the work. He liked working with his hands and the designs that he created filled him with a pleasure that he could not put into words; they danced around in his head day after day until he saw them made whole, displayed in all their splendour for everyone to see and admire. He had served his apprenticeship well and then, when his father had got his hare-brained scheme of moving to Madinat al-Zahra, he had followed him here. That had been a mistake, although if the truth were told he had not had much say in the matter. His father needed him, not only to help build the house that they were to live in but also to assist him in the alfarería. He had protested that his friends were in Córdoba, that his father could employ someone else to help him, that Ibrahim could go in his place but it was all in vain. He was to go to Madinat al-Zahra and his brother Ibrahim would stay in Córdoba and look after the alfarería there.

He pulled out his designs and spread them on the floor in front of him. They were coming on well. His father would be pleased. This, his latest idea, would make an excellent pattern for a plate, or maybe even a deep dish. His father, as usual, had been right; there was a good demand for pottery here. This city, although unfinished, was the centre of the caliphate; the Khalifa lived here now and because of that people with money and power had left Córdoba and set up home here as well. They needed new houses and they needed furnishings for them. Not everything could be bought from the merchants who flocked in from the East with their camel trains laden with rich and exotic goods; there was plenty of room for locally produced merchandise too. Even working people were making more money these days and they too wanted to buy well-made pots for their homes. Only the other day the local baker had come in looking for something special for his wife who had just presented him with his first son; he had bought her a bowl, decorated with two birds and carrying the word 'blessing' interleaved with their feathers. Omar had been particularly pleased with that piece and charged the man a substantial price for it. That's how it was; he and his father were working day and night to meet the demand. That was the reason it was taking so long to finish building their house and why they were still sleeping under the stars.

'Mama says do you want any breakfast?' his sister asked, arriving in the doorway to the workshop. 'Or should she give it to the dog?'

His sister, Layla, was a cheeky little thing but he was fond of her. She had a wicker basket in her hand; it was covered with a cloth.

'It's churros,' she added.

He already knew that. He had smelt the hot sweet scent of the churros while his mother was frying them and it had made his stomach rumble.

'Put it down there. It would only make the dog fat.'

'She said it would have been nice if you could have stayed and eaten breakfast with us,' the little girl continued, putting the basket on the ground next to him.

'No she didn't. You're making that up.'

His sister wagged her finger at him in an exact parody of her mother.

'Go on, off to school with you. I've got work to do,' he said, stifling a smile.

'There's plenty of time,' she said, sitting down beside him.

'I told you I'm busy.'

'Mama says that it's time you got married and had another woman running after you instead of her.'

'Where do you get these tales? Off with you before I tell Baba that you are still here.'

The girl jumped up at that and pretended to be scared. He knew it was all an act. Even if he told his father, Baba would just laugh and pat them both on the head before returning to whatever he had been doing. Layla could do no wrong in his father's eyes.

'If you're going to be mean to me, then I'll go.'

'Good.'

But she remained where she was. He pulled out some more drawings and ignored her.

'That's pretty,' she said.

It was. Like most of his work it was based on a hexagon; the underlying design was one of six inter-linked outer circles and a central one.

'Show me how you do it,' she said, sitting down again beside him.

'All right, but then will you go and leave me to get on with my work?'

'Yes, I promise.'

He picked up his compass and drew a circle then moved the compass to the circumference of the circle and drew an arc. He then moved the compass to where the arc crossed the circumference and repeated the process until he had inscribed six arcs. Next he took his rule and joined these six points with straight lines to make his hexagon.

'That's pretty. You've made a daisy inside a square,' Layla said. 'Can I have a go?'

'No. And it's not a square; it's a hexagon. Now get off to school before I get cross with you.'

'Layla? Is that you Layla?'

It was her mother.

'Yes, Mama.'

'Why are you still here child? Hurry along with you. You'll be late.'

'Yes Mama.'

She skipped to the door then turned to her brother.

'Ma'a salama,' she said, with a little bow.

'Goodbye.'

As soon as she had gone he opened the basket and helped himself to a piece of the churros. It was good. He loved his mother's cooking. When he did marry he hoped his wife would be able to cook as well as his mother.

'Have you finished that new pattern yet?' his father asked, coming into the workshop with a sack of clay blocks in his arms.

'Almost. What do you think of it?'

His father nodded. He stacked the clay blocks against the wall with the others.

'Good.'

Good? Did this mean he thought it was good or that it was good that he had almost finished it? He could never tell with his father. He was a man of few words and they often passed the day working in silence, each locked in their own thoughts. They shared the work in the alfarería but each had specific tasks. His father had promised that they would buy a slave to do the menial tasks but for now they fell to Omar. He prepared the clay, moulding it with his feet first to make it malleable and then with his hands to form a cone to put on the wheel. His father created the pots and plates which Omar then stacked into the kiln, once they were dry. His father also made the glazes and did all the firing while Omar designed and painted the patterns that they used as decoration. His father was very secretive about the components he used to make the glazes, especially since he had developed a new lustre glaze that was becoming very popular with the Khalifa's court. He had promised to teach Omar how to mix it but so far had not done so. Even Ibrahim, who had worked with father longer than he had, did not know what special ingredients he put into it to make those wonderful iridescent metallic colours.

His father seemed hot. Omar watched as he took the jarrah from the stand and lifted it up in front of his face, tilting the jug so that the cold, clear water came out in a stream, straight into his open mouth. He wiped the water from his chin.

'Omar, I want you to get some supplies. Go to the apothecary and buy me some sulphur and some manganese. Then run round to the baker and ask for a small sackful of ashes. I shall need them for my next batch of glazes,' he said.

'All right, Baba.'

Omar put his designs away carefully. He didn't want them to get spoiled; they were almost complete and tomorrow he would be able to paint them onto a new batch of earthenware plates. He loved this part of his work. When his father told him he was to work with him and his brother in the alfarería in Córdoba, he had expected that he would only get the worst jobs to do: preparing the clay, loading the kiln, washing the old clay off the wheel at the end of the day, delivering the pots to the bazaar. Instead his father had set him to work learning how to create the designs that were now making their pottery famous. He had showed him some plates that he had bought from a merchant from Baghdad; they were spectacular: intertwined leaves and swirling patterns painted in blues and greens, lattice work and flowers, tiny stylized birds that filled the gaps between interlocking circles and all of it carefully executed, in exact proportions and the pattern repeated not once but many times. They were perfect works of art, too beautiful to eat from.

He had protested that he could not produce anything as intricate as these designs but his father had explained that it was all a question of practice. Everything was possible if you knew how to go about it.

'You did geometry in school, didn't you?' he had asked.

'Of course.'

'Well there you are. These designs are all based on geometric principles. Work out what they are and make something similar. All I can tell you is that everything you see before you is based on a very simple idea. Look for the simplicity behind the ornate. Master it and repeat it.'

He had been working on those instructions ever since. He had found the simplicity that he was looking for and from it he had created designs both intricate and beautiful. Between his designs and the new lustre glazes that his father was working on they would soon be able to create ceramics the equal of the East. Maybe the Khalifa himself would want to have some for his new palaces.

'Don't take all day about it, lad,' his father said as he pulled out the big bowl he used to mix his glazes.

He always did this, sent Omar out on some errand or other when he wanted to be alone to mix the ingredients. One day he would pass on the formula to Omar, he said, when he was too old to do it himself. Omar could not understand this. Why in the name of Allah didn't he let him learn how to do it now? Why make him wait? It was Ibrahim's fault, he was sure. Ibrahim had been furious when their father had said that he must remain in Córdoba and continue with the business of making boring earthenware pots and plates. He felt that Omar should have been the one to stay and that he should be learning the finer techniques of the craft. But Omar knew and so did his father that Ibrahim had no artistic talent. He was a good craftsman and his pots were true and solid but there was no intrinsic beauty to the shapes he created, no spark of anything that made them out of the ordinary. Ibrahim would have been better as a soldier but his father needed him to continue working in Córdoba; his domestic pottery sold well and provided them all with a good living. It was what allowed his father to risk something new, here in Madinat al-Zahra. Omar knew it was difficult to compete with the beautiful ceramics that came from Damascus and Baghdad but so far it seemed to be working. Already people came to the door of the workshop asking for the alfarero, the potter; they had seen his work and they wanted some for themselves. His father had even instructed Omar to sign it with the name ibn Qasim, son of Qasim. In that way both their names were on it. But Qasim had three sons and Omar did not want his brothers to take the credit for his work, so he slipped in an additional letter, his initial O. If his father noticed, he said nothing; Omar had woven both their names into the fabric of the design.

***

Omar could hardly believe his eyes.   He was walking through the market, on the way back from the apothecary with his friend Yusuf, when he saw her.   It was a mere glimpse but a glimpse of such beauty that it took his breath away.   He thought it must be the sunshine playing tricks with his eyes.

'Allah be praised, did you see that girl?' he asked Yusuf.

'The slave girl?'

'Yes. What a beauty.'

'Do not even consider it.   You know who that is that's just bought her?   The keeper of the Khalifa's harem.   So forget it.   You'll never see her again.   Which is just as well because the Khalifa doesn't like men to lust after his women.'

Omar could not reply; he was struck dumb by her beauty.   He couldn't get the vision of her loveliness out of his head.'

'I have to meet her.'

'Aren't you listening to me?   That's the craziest thing I have ever heard you say and you've said some crazy things in your time.'

Omar was taking no notice; all he could think about was how was he going to arrange to meet her.

'Anyway I thought you were betrothed to some girl in Córdoba?' Yusuf asked.

'Muna?'

'So?'

'So what?'

'Well you can't go round looking at slave girls if you're about to get married,' his friend said, rather pompously.

Omar looked at his friend. Yusuf had become unbearable since the date had been set for his own wedding. He seemed to have turned into an old man overnight.

'I don't see why not; I'm not married to her.'

'But you will be soon.'

'In the name of Allah, she's only twelve. That's just two years older than my sister. I can't possibly think of marrying a child when there is a beautiful woman like that here, just waiting for me to sweep her into my arms.'

'More likely you'll be swept into the dungeon; that's if you survive,' Yusuf added. 'Anyway you couldn't afford a slave like that. Didn't you hear what he paid for her? That's more than a year's wages.'

Omar did not reply. He was thinking about Muna and her family's expectations of him. She would probably make him an excellent wife when she was older but it was hard to think of her in that way at the moment. He knew he should be grateful that his father had found him the daughter of a good family; her father was a teacher in a school in Córdoba. She was a Muwallad like himself but whereas Omar's family had been Muslim for centuries, Muna's grandfather had been a Christian who had converted to Islam. That was acceptable; Mullawads were treated equally whatever their ancestry and the main thing was that they were true Muslims now.

'I haven't seen her since we moved from Córdoba,' Omar said. 'And anyway I'm too young to marry'.

'You're not much younger than me,' Yusuf protested.

'Yes, but you love your wife-to-be. I'm fond of Muna but I don't love her.'

Yusuf blushed. It was true. He had told Omar many times how much he loved Zilma and how he couldn't wait to marry her.

'I have known her all my life,' he said, unable to keep from smiling. 'You'll feel the same about Muna when she's older.'

'Maybe. There's nothing wrong with Muna but I am not ready to get married. Maybe when I'm forty I'll think about it then.'

Yusuf let out a snort of derision.

'Forty. You'll be past it by then. No, if you want lots of healthy sons you need to marry earlier than that.'

'Look I have to go. My father is waiting for these things. I'll see you tonight.'

'Very well. Usual place?'

'Yes. Ma'a salama.'

'Alla ysalmak.'

Omar headed back to the workshop. His heart was still racing from the vision of the slave girl in the bazaar. All he could think about was when and how he going to see her again.

CHAPTER 6

Abd al-Rahman ibn Muhammad ibn Abd Allah al-Nasir li-Din Allah, Defender of God's Faith and supreme ruler of al-Andalus, woke from a deep sleep. He had once again been on the battle fields, fighting the Christian armies that threatened his kingdom. He sighed; for now this battle was consigned solely to his memory. The country was at peace at last, although an uneasy one he had to admit; there were still enemies on his borders: the troublesome Christians in the north and the upstart Fatimids threatening to advance into his territory in Morocco.

He stretched and felt twinges of pain in his leg where he had been wounded during the defeat at Alhandega. He had been lucky that day. Fifty-thousand of his men had been killed and he had barely escaped with his life. It was in the year 939, 'The Year of Alhandega' they called it still. What a rout. It could have been the end of al-Andalus if those quarrelsome Christian princes had banded together. But no, their internecine behaviour had been a blessing for him that day, giving him time to replace his slaughtered army and regroup his troops.

He groaned as the pain shot up his leg again. He was getting old and there was nothing he could do about it.

A slight movement to his right told him that his servant, Gassan, was waiting to attend to him. He would have been watching over him all through the night, ready to do his bidding the moment he awoke. Abd al-Rahman sat up and pushed the silken sheets aside. He was alone in the bed. His concubine had been dismissed earlier when he had finished with her. She would be with the others now, somewhere in the enormous maze of rooms that was his harem.

He lifted his hand slightly and Gassan was instantly there with his robe.

'Your bath is ready, my lord.'

'Send in my masseuse. My bones are aching today.'

'Yes, my lord.'

Gassan was an old man now but he was someone that Abd al-Rahman could rely on. He had been his first personal slave, given to him by his mother when he was a mere boy and he had been with him ever since. After his escape at the Battle of Alhandega, Abd al-Rahman had first thanked Allah for his mercy and then given Gassan his freedom. He was in no doubt that Gassan had saved his life that day; his slave had tended to his wounds and kept him alive until they could reach a doctor. His old friend had happily accepted his freedom but would not leave him; he wanted to remain by his master's side, a free man.

Abd al-Rahman had been glad of it; he needed men he could trust. His first job when he inherited the throne from his grandfather was to remove all the old Arab aristocracy from positions of power and replace them with his own people. He chose young men mainly, talented men who were just starting out in life, men of ambition who would owe him for the great opportunity he was giving them. In return he expected their unswerving loyalty and he had it; he felt sure. The country was governed well, the administration functioned perfectly and the power of the aristocracy had been curbed.

He walked across to the bath chamber, his silk slippers silent on the marble floor. This was a moment he looked forward to, an opportunity to relax before the rigours of the day began. The orange light from the flickering lamps threw shadows in the corners of the rooms and created an intimate, sensual atmosphere. He slipped out of his slippers and stepped into the first of the bath chambers. The green marble, that he had had specially imported from the East, was cool beneath his feet; water flowed from bronze fountains, each skilfully shaped in the form of an animal or a fish, and tumbled into the shallow pool. A Nubian slave took his robe and stood to one side while the Khalifa stepped into the first pool and stood there as a second slave poured cold water over his body.

'Enough,' the Khalifa said, with a slight shiver and moved on, into the second chamber where aromatic candles burned, filling the air with their sweet fragrance.

He went down the steps into the warm water and sat there while a muscular young man massaged his shoulders and back. The warmth eased the pain in his leg. He looked down at the long jagged scar on his thigh; it would always be there to remind him that his power was ephemeral. His body was criss-crossed with battle scars but this was the only one that had nearly cost him his life. He touched it lightly.

Abd al-Rahman had fought long and hard to achieve peace and establish his rule over an united al-Andalus, now his task was to consolidate it and part of that plan was here, in Madinat al-Zahra. A khalifa's role was not just to rule but to rule wisely and, above all, to secure his dynastic line. His Omeyyad ancestors had conquered al-Andalus from the pagan Visigoths and converted it to Islam, but they left him with a kingdom fractured and warring. There were thousands of brigand chiefs, plundering and raping the land; each province had its own petty ruler and none of them paid allegiance to the Sultan. It had taken him many years to unite the country and get rid of the tyrants, the last of them being the most persistent of all, Omar ibn Hafsun. But he and his sons were dead now and all his followers exiled. Abd al-Rahman had created order and prosperity throughout the land. He deserved to be Khalifa, supreme political and religious leader of all the Muslims in al-Andalus. It was the only way to ensure that no young upstart would dare to challenge him; no true muslim would ever challenge the Khalifa. His title could not be disputed and everyone was better for it.

That was why it was so important to finish this beautiful city; it was to be the most magnificent city in the world, even more magnificent than Córdoba whose fame was known to all. More importantly, he was following the tradition laid down by other khalifas before him, whereby each new ruler founded a new city, more splendid than any that had been before. Madinat al-Zahra would be a fitting home for him and his heirs.

His favourite masseuse entered the bath chamber; she bowed low and he watched as her long black hair fell forward, almost touching the ground in front of her. She was a slave from the far east and he never tired of looking at her strange almond eyes and skin that was the colour of apricots. He nodded for her to begin. Slowly and firmly she began to massage his back and legs with fragrant oils until gradually his muscles relaxed and the aches disappeared from his bones.

That felt good. With a wave of his hand he dismissed her and passed into the third chamber of the bath house. This was the hot pool. He lowered his body into the scalding water and waited while a young slave bathed him, rubbing away the excess oil with perfumed soap. The slave was al-Magribi, a young man captured in North Africa, whom Gassan was training to take over some of his personal duties. He eyed the slave, taking in the youth's physical beauty and strong arms; he was competent and meticulous in all he did. He would make a good replacement for the faithful Gassan.

The heat from the pool was making him sweat. His physician had told him that this was good. It removed any toxins from his body and, apparently, having regular baths was an excellent precaution against disease as well as being a way of purifying the soul. Once he would not have bothered listening to his physician - all that mumbo-jumbo was for women and children - but now he was much more aware of his passing years and of how finite his time on earth. It was important to take care of his health.

He looked down at his body. It was in good shape for a man of his age: his stomach was flat and taut, his back was still strong and his chest was as wide as a barrel. He had a few years left in him yet and probably a few more sons too.

'Where is my barber?' he asked al-Magribi.

'Here, my lord,' said a voice.

The barber, a round man with little hair himself, appeared at his side.

'Cut my beard, but not too much, mind. And get rid of that red hair that's starting to show.'

'Of course, my lord.'

He leaned back, allowing the barber to first trim his hair and whiskers, then apply a mixture of black dye to his beard. As the supreme ruler of a land where virtually everyone was of mixed blood it seemed ridiculous that he should bother to hide his own mixed ancestry but, since childhood, he had been conscious of the physical difference between himself and his brothers. They were swarthier than him, with Arab eyes and black hair. His blue northern eyes, designed for cloudier skies, had made him stand out. For that he blamed his mother. She was a beautiful woman, one of his father's concubines and a Christian captive. He had spent much of his youth living in her harem and she had personally seen to it that he had the best education available. She used her influence to make sure that he was groomed for his future role as leader and that he mixed with educated people. Though how she knew that his grandfather would pass over his own sons and choose him as his successor, he had no idea. Sometimes he wondered if, by some magic, she had contrived the whole situation. He twisted the gold ring that he wore on his second finger, remembering how his grandfather had given it to him as he lay dying. He had loved the old man and he, in turn, had loved al-Rahman and trusted him with his kingdom.

'Where is Gassan?' he called.

'I am here, my lord.'

'Gassan, get me my chief minister and my secretary. I want them here by the time I get back from the mosque.

We have a trade delegation arriving today from Aquitaine,' he said.

'Yes, my lord.'

'I'll meet them in the Courtyard of the Pillars,' he added. 'Oh and tell my son, al-Hakim to be there, too.'

CHAPTER 7

The pots were stacked up in the drying area; they would not be ready for their first firing until tomorrow. Qasim looked around the workshop. There was still a lot to be done. When were they ever going to get enough time to finish building their house? It was impossible. All they could fit in was a couple of hours each evening and by then he was dog-tired. He couldn't really ask Omar to do any more than he was already; he worked twelve hours a day in the workshop as it was. It would not be fair to expect much more from him. He had to have a life. After all he was his son not his slave. He looked across at Omar, his head bent over his work. His dark hair hung down hiding his face from his father. He was doing well. Qasim was proud of him. He had been quick to learn the potter's craft and was always coming up with new ideas to make their pottery more marketable. He would have to teach him the last of his secrets before long.

'Omar. I'm going out. Keep an eye on everything will you.'

'Of course, Baba.'

'I won't be long.'

His son did not reply; he was engrossed in his work.

Qasim had made up his mind. It was time to buy a slave. They could afford it now; the alfarería was doing well. He would look for a strong one, young and used to hard physical work. But he wouldn't come cheap; he knew that. There were always more women for sale than men; young males were scarcer and came at a higher price, especially if they were white. He didn't mind what colour the slave was; he wasn't intending to impress anyone. He didn't want a slave as a sign of his wealth; he wanted one who could work hard. He knew some who liked to educate their slaves so that they became more valuable then they would put them to work writing letters or doing accounts but his needs were more basic; he needed one with brawn.

There had been an auction at the slave market that morning but he had been too busy to go. Now he was hoping that he might be able to catch the traders before they left. He headed out through the south gate towards their encampment. Each day there seemed to be more and more people camped outside the city walls. Some were itinerants, men like the slave traders, only here until they had sold their wares, others were newcomers to the city, men in search of work, with their families in tow. The smell of roasting meat drifted across to him, making him feel hungry; women were lighting fires and getting out their cooking stoves. It would soon be time to eat. A couple of snarling dogs were scrapping over some bones that one of the women had thrown to them. He passed a group of newly arrived families; they were busy marking out the plots for their new homes. The men looked young and fit. It wouldn't take them long to get their houses built.

He suddenly felt tired and his back ached. He was getting old; not many more years and he would be seventy. He wished he had had more sons to help him in his old age. They had tried but after Omar was born Fatima had had nothing but a series of miscarriages and stillborns so they had abandoned the idea of more children. He had been considering taking a second wife, although his heart was not in it, when Layla arrived. It had been such a surprise. He said she was a gift from Allah and put aside any thoughts of new wives.

The slave traders were camped by the river. There were six of them, all swarthy men from beyond the Maghreb. He couldn't see any slaves. He felt disappointed. He was too late; they had all been sold.

'As-salam alaykum,' he said to the taller of the men.

'Wa alaykum e-salam,' the man replied, stepping towards him. 'What can I do for you?'

'I am just walking in the cool evening air,' he replied.

'Sit and have some tea with us.'

'Thank you.'

Qasim moved into the shade of the tent and sat down. The man said something to one of his companions who disappeared into the back of the tent then reappeared carrying a tray with glasses and tea. Qasim waited until all the civilities had been performed then asked, 'You have done well today?'

The man nodded.

'Where are you from?' Qasim asked.

The man waved his hand in a general direction and replied, 'Wherever the wind blows. We travel all over, sometimes to North Africa, sometimes as far as Byzantium. It depends on what we are looking for and who can give it to us. Tomorrow we leave for the north of Iberia.'

Qasim sipped his tea and waited.

'I didn't see you at the slave market this morning,' the slaver said at last.

'No. I was busy.'

'So what is it that I can do for you now that the slave market is closed?'

'Maybe I wanted to buy a slave.'

The man stroked his long beard.

'Only maybe?'

'You have none left,' Qasim said, looking around him.

'What is your fancy? I can bring you back a plump white-skinned girl from the north, the next time I am here, someone to wash your back and keep you warm at night.'

Qasim smiled.

'No. I have a wife to do that. No, what I want is someone who can work hard. A man, strong and fit.'

The man threw back his head and laughed.

'Well you should have come earlier. All that I have left now are the runts of the litter. You can have a look if you like.'

He clapped his hands and one of the men went into the tent and brought out two bedraggled slaves: an old man and a thin boy with spindly legs.

'You can have them both for thirty dirhams. I'd be glad to be rid of them.'

'Neither of them looks very strong to me,' Qasim said.

'Their looks belie their strength,' the slave trader said.

Qasim shook his head. They would be of little use to him. He needed someone who would be able to pull his weight. These two would just be extra mouths to feed. The boy was staring at him, beseeching him to buy him. His tow coloured hair hung lankly over his eyes. Poor kid;

he must be frightened out of his wits. He was a pretty child; what would the men do with him if nobody bought him?

'All right then, twenty-five,' the trader said at last.

'Come here boy,' Qasim said. 'How strong are you?'

'As an ox, sir.'

'Ah, he speaks Arabic.'

'A few words only, but he's a quick learner.'

'How old are you boy?'

The boy shrugged and looked at the trader.

'He's about ten but he's strong and there're lots of years in him. Fifty at least. He's a bargain at that price. And he's intelligent. You'll be able to teach him exactly what you want in no time at all.'

Qasim looked at the boy then at the old man. They would probably do if they were cheap enough.

'What about the old man? Where did you find him?'

'He was begging in Almeria but he says he is from the far north. He was a hard man in his day but now he is old. Look at the callouses on his hands. He is no stranger to hard work.'

He gripped the man's hands and turned them over for Qasim to see.

'I won't lie to you, you won't get many years out of him but you'll get a few,' he continued. 'And he brings experience with his years.'

'All right I'll take them off your hands, but for twenty dirhams only, not more.'

'What? Are you trying to beggar me?' the trader said, throwing up his hands in horror at Qasim's offer.

'Twenty dirhams is what I am offering you.'

The man looked as if he would refuse then changed his mind and said, 'Agreed.'

The slave trader gave a nod to his companion who untied the shackles on the slaves' legs and handed them over to Qasim.

'Ma'a salama. Have a good journey,' Qasim said.

'Alla ysalmak.'

The slave trader counted the money carefully into his pouch and sat down once more. Qasim imagined that he was delighted with himself for selling the last of his goods; he was twenty dirhams better off than he expected to be. Qasim looked at his new purchases; they were a sorry sight indeed. He hoped he hadn't made a mistake.

CHAPTER 8

Fatima had covered the low table with a leather cloth and set out the plates for their evening meal; she arranged each person's mat in its designated place, with Qasim at the head and herself at the foot. The meat was almost ready. She lifted the lid on the pot to check it; it looked perfect. Now all that she was waiting for was her family to come and eat.

'Layla, leave that now and go and tell your brother and your father that the meal is ready.'

'All right, Mama.'

She placed a plate of cold tongue and a dish of pickles on the table. They would eat that first then they would eat the braised lamb. She had prepared asparagus and aubergines to accompany the second course and after that she would bring out the candied fruit that she had bought that morning.

She poured herself glass of water and sat down to rest. The patio was shaded perfectly from the evening sun. Suddenly the door opened and her husband stood there, a wide grin on his face.

'Fatima. Look what I have for you,' he said.

'What is it husband?'

'Come outside and see for yourself.'

She followed him out to the alfarería. Two ragged strangers stood there in the middle of the workshop. Her son, Omar was looking at them with an expression of disbelief and Layla was struggling not to laugh. Who were they and what on earth was going on?

'What is it? Who are these people?' she asked, turning to her husband. 'Why are they here?'

Had he invited a couple of beggars to share their evening meal with them? It was just the sort of thing Qasim would do. Could she make the food stretch for two extra, she wondered.

'They are a present for you,' he said, his smile even wider by now. 'I bought them for you from the slave merchants.'

'For me? Slaves you say?'

They were not beggars, but slaves.

'Yes. Well not just for you, my dear wife, for us all. You have complained for some time that the work on the house has been very slow so I decided we needed some help. Omar and I can't continue to sleep on the patio in the winter and I know you want somewhere for Sara and the children to stay when they visit you. We need more rooms and we can only have them if we have more hands to build them.'

'But ...'

'No buts. I know what you are going to say.'

'Do you husband?'

'Yes, you think I have been too extravagant buying two when one would have done, but it was a bargain. I have to admit that I got them for a very fair price.'

Layla could not contain herself any longer and burst out laughing.

'Baba, if you needed someone to help you, why did you buy a grandfather and a child smaller than me?'

'Exactly. What help are they going to be to anyone?' asked Fatima. 'If you wanted to buy a slave why not get one that would be of some use to us?'

The words were out before she could stop them. Her husband's face darkened. He did not like her speaking to him like that, especially in front of his children. He turned to go into the house.

'I'm sorry Qasim. I spoke in haste; I'm sure we can find something for them to do,' she said, backtracking a little. 'Bring them into the house and they can eat with us while we decide where they will sleep.'

She motioned for the slaves to follow her.

'Husband, do you know where they are from? Do they speak Arabic? How will they understand us?' she asked.

'The boy understands a little. So far the old man has not spoken a word. I will try to talk to them later, after supper,' he said.

Fatima took the boy by the hand and led him to the pump, motioning for him to wash himself.

'He's filthy. They both are. Here Layla get them some soap and towels while I set two more places to eat. And see if there is something that they can wear; I'm not having those flea-ridden rags in my house.'

The boy scrubbed himself under the running water and gradually, as the dirt and grime were washed away, she was surprised to see that he had golden hair and pale skin. His eyes were round and blue; he reminded her of the slave girl she had seen in the bazaar.

'What about the old man?' she asked her husband.

'Don't worry. I'll take him down to the public baths. We won't be long.'

'Take these with you then,' she said, indicating the clean clothes that Layla had laid out for him. 'The food will be ready when you return.'

***

The slaves had eaten well and she had found two mats for them to sleep on. They lay curled up, already asleep on the patio that they would have to share with Omar and Qasim for now.

'Well husband, where do we go from here?'

'Tomorrow I will leave Omar in charge of the alfarería and I will show them what I want them to do on the house.'

'Do you think they will be all right? The man is as old as my father.'

'Yes and look at your father, still working in the fields and as fit as a flea.'

'That's true; he is very strong for his age. Perhaps you are right. The old man may be sturdier than he looks.'

The truth was that both of the slaves looked a lot better since they had washed. The old man had cut his beard and hair, so now he too looked more presentable and no longer quite so decrepit; an old djubba belonging to Qasim hung loosely about his frame but at least it was clean.

'We need names for them,' Qasim said.

'Yes. What do you suggest?'

'Let's call the boy al-Sagir, little one.'

'Yes and the old man?'

'The slave trader said he found him in Almeria, so how about al-Mari?'

'It's all right. What else can we call him when we don't know anything about him. Did he say anything to you at the baths?'

'No, nothing apart from asking for the scissors.'

'So he speaks Arabic?'

'Yes, that was a surprise. He seems to speak it well and with a local accent.'

'How is that then? Do you think he was originally from this area?'

'I don't know. As soon as I tried to question him, he shut up like a clam.'

'Well maybe when he has settled in, he will tell us more.'

'Don't expect too much, wife. He is a slave and there must be a reason for that. Maybe he was a prisoner of war or captured as a child, like the little one. There could be lots of reasons why he can speak our language.'

'He seems a quiet old man. I just hope he can do the work you want him to do.'

'Where's Omar gone?' Qasim asked. 'He was in a hurry to leave this evening.'

'He didn't say. Just that he had to go out. He's probably gone to play chess with Yusuf. Has he spoken to you about them?' she asked, pointing to the sleeping slaves. 'What does he think?'

'No, he hasn't said a word. He's angry, I know. He wanted someone to take over some of the work in the alfarería. Maybe he's right, maybe they won't be much use, but at least we can try. The little one will learn quickly; I'm sure about that. He's bright and if he's willing I might even use him in the alfarería later on. That would make Omar happy; he's always grumbling about having to do the messy jobs.'

'Would you like any more food?'

'No, I'm going to prepare for bed.'

The sound of the muezzin calling the faithful to prayer had alerted him to the hour. It was time for the family to pray. She followed him to the quibla and knelt down beside him.

Once her husband had gone to bed, she tidied the kitchen, removing any remnants of food that could attract the rats and went into her room. Layla was already sprawled out on her mat, fast asleep.

It had certainly been a surprise. Now maybe they would get the house finished before winter was upon them. How lovely it would be if there was an extra room ready for Eid. Her elder daughter, Sara was coming for the festivities and bringing her children with her; Ibrahim was coming too. Even al-Jundi said he would be with them for part of the time. It would be good to have all the family together. That's what fiestas were for, to share with your family.

How strange that Qasim had never mentioned buying a slave before. She smiled to herself. He was a very soft-hearted man for all his bluster. She could imagine him looking at those two unwanted slaves and feeling sorry for them; he would have convinced himself that he was getting a bargain when really he was doing them a favour. It was what he believed in, helping those who were more unfortunate than himself. Of all the people she knew, he was the one who tried to follow the teachings of Mohammed most carefully. He was no zealot but he was a true believer in the one God. His life, he said, was based on the five pillars of Islam. Qasim donated ten percent of his earnings to the poor; he never missed his prayers, no matter how busy he was and he fasted to purify his soul. He tried to encourage his family to be more strict in their religious duties and she did attempt to do so. It was just that sometimes she was too busy to stop and pray at midday or if she did she hurried it, which Qasim said was almost as bad as not praying at all. He told them that their prayers would take them half-way to Allah, fasting would bring them to the door of Allah's palace and giving money to the poor would allow them to enter. All this he adhered to rigidly. The only thing that he had never done was go on a pilgrimage to Mecca; she knew it was his dearest wish but it was unlikely that it would ever happen now. He was too old to make such a journey.

She lay down on her mat. It was a warm night and she hoped she would be able to sleep. A fleeting thought made her smile; she could just imagine Elvira's face when she told her that they had bought, not one, but two slaves.

CHAPTER 9

Her reflection gazed back at her and smiled sadly. Isolde never tired of looking at herself in the mirror. Such things were unheard of in her village. She had only ever seen her own face reflected in a bucket of water. Now she could sit and look at it as much as she liked. It fascinated her. She brushed her hair until it shone then plaited it into a long braid which she let hang loose down her back. Gold earrings dangled from her ears and around her neck was a necklace of pearls and coral beads. If only her mother could see her now. She looked like a fine lady. But, she reminded herself as she did constantly each day, she was still a slave and her mother was dead. Once again the pain returned as she remembered her mother lying on the floor of the hut, her eyes unseeing, her blood seeping into the ground. If only she had been able to help her. Isolde put down the mirror and turned towards her new friend and confidante.

'Would you like me to help you shape your eyebrows?' Najm asked her.

She was the one that the Chief Eunuch had told to look after Isolde. Like her, she was from northern Europe and, also like her, she had been captured in a viking raid. So for the moment she was Isolde's translator and friend.

'Do I need to?'

There did not seem to be anything wrong with her eyebrows but Najm was insistent. She took a pair of tweezers and carefully plucked out a few hairs.

'There, that's much better.'

Najm was her harem name; it meant star. She had told Isolde that when she lived in Saxony her name was Gerda. They had changed Isolde's name too; the Chief Eunuch had decided to call her Jawhara, the jewel. Najm said that she was being groomed because he wanted her to be noticed by the Khalifa.

Everything here in the alcázar was different, even the way of eating; she had had to learn the simplest things anew. They did not help themselves from one common plate of food as she was used to at home; there were separate plates for each person and different courses of meats, vegetables, fowl and sweets. There was an etiquette about where you were allowed to sit and you could not eat with your hands; you had to use knives and forks. The water was poured for you from elegant jugs into glass beakers. She was constantly getting things wrong. Then there was the bathing. She had never had so many baths in her life. These people seemed obsessed with cleanliness. At home she and her brothers had bathed in the river in the summer and in the winter they had not bothered. It had done them no harm.

She could hardly believe that all this was happening to her. It was three months since the slave merchant had sold her to the Khalifa. She had expected to be working in the kitchens or scrubbing floors but instead here she was, being groomed and pampered like a lady of the court.

'There are so many women here, hundreds and hundreds. Who are they all? Are they all slaves?' she asked Najm.

'Some are slaves and some are the Khalifa's family. The harem has a strict hierarchy.'

'I know. The Chief Eunuch spoke about it when I was in the school but I didn't really understand him,' Isolde replied.

'Would you like me to explain it to you?'

Isolde nodded. There were things she had already grasped about this cloistered place, like the fact that it was forbidden for men to enter. Only the black eunuchs could enter and only then with permission. Yamut al-Attar, the Chief Black Eunuch, appeared to wield enormous power not only over the women in the harem but also over the eunuchs who worked for him. He had direct access to the Khalifa and to the Royal wife. Everyone was terrified of him and Isolde was no exception.

'Well there are three classes of women in the harem. The lowest class are the slaves who work as servants, then above them are women like us, slaves learning to be concubines. But even then there are divisions. At the moment you are a pupil at the school of the harem. When you finish there you will become a graduate, like me and that is how you might stay for the rest of your life. I have been here three years and I have never seen the Khalifa once.'

'How does one get to see the Khalifa?'

'That is not up to us to decide. Maybe the Chief Black Eunuch will arrange for you to dance for him or maybe he will just notice you one day. If that happens you move to the next category, that of "being noticed". That does not necessarily mean that the Khalifa will call for you but everyone knows he has seen you. In any case until you have learnt all that the school has to teach you, you remain here as a pupil.'

'And then?'

'Then if you are lucky enough to get noticed, you may become one of his concubines. But that does not mean much unless you become pregnant. That is the one and only true way to promote yourself.'

'So, if I were to have a baby the Khalifa would marry me?'

'Not necessarily but it can happen. It depends on how many wives he already has. At the moment he has four, so he is unlikely to take another one.'

'But the Khalifa can have as many wives as he wants, can't he?'

'Islamic law says that a man may have up to four wives. I don't know if the Khalifa is allowed to take a few more but at the moment that's all he has. As I said, there is a strict hierarchy here in the harem and everyone knows their place. You have to. The Royal wife has the power of life and death over the rest of us. It's best not to cross her.' she added.

'So where are we in this hierarchy?' asked Isolde.

'A long way down. In the first group are the Khalifa's wives and female family members. The most important woman here used to be his mother, but now she is dead so his Royal wife, the mother of al-Hakim is the first lady. She has supreme power over us; we cannot enter the harem or leave it without her permission. Then after her are his second wives, those that have given him sons. They are free women now and they live here with their children and their servants. There are also women who are the Khalifa's favourites; they are all very beautiful and they live in splendid apartments, with their own personal maids, slaves and even their own eunuchs.'

'But they are not his wives?'

'No. You have heard of al-Zahra?'

'Yes. They say she is very beautiful.'

'She is the Khalifa's favourite concubine. She lives in a splendid palace, almost the equal of his wives.'

'So it is unlikely that I will ever see the Khalifa?' Isolde asked.

She did not know whether that was a good thing or not. The life here was very comfortable and extremely luxurious but it was strange and she was often homesick. She yearned for her previous life, her parents, her brothers.

'Who knows. Yamut seems to be very impressed with you. He knows the Khalifa's taste in women. It all depends on what happens at the school.'

Isolde sighed.

'There is a lot to learn. I am still struggling with Arabic and now they want me to learn to dance.'

'And there'll be a lot more, I can tell you. Your education is designed to teach you the many ways to make a man happy. You will be expected to play the lute, sing and recite poetry. You will be taught the erotic arts. If they think you are capable they will teach you to read and write. I am told that the Khalifa particularly likes those who are good storytellers. Do you like telling stories?' Najm asked.

'I used to tell stories to my brothers,' Isolde said and for a moment she was transported back to the woodland village where she had grown up.

Her eyes filled with tears as she recalled snuggling up beside her brothers in the dark and telling them the folk tales that her mother had taught her.

'But I don't think the Khalifa would like stories about children getting lost in the woods and big, bad wolves,' she said, sadly.

Najm laughed.

'Probably not.'

She smoothed Isolde's eyebrows into place.

'They're fine now. If you want to get dressed you can come to the bazaar with me. I want to buy some ribbons and some perfume.'

'What if I wanted to leave?'

Najm looked at her in astonishment.

'Leave? Leave the harem? You can't leave. You belong to the Khalifa. The only way you could leave is if he were to sell you to someone else or give you your freedom. I can't see why he would do either when he doesn't even know you exist. No, your best choice is to get yourself noticed. Remember we are both a long way from home now. There is no going back.'

Najm seemed annoyed with her for asking such a thing. Isolde sighed. She was right. Even if she could find her way back to Saxony, there was nothing there for her; her mother was dead, her brothers had been taken, her village destroyed and who knew where her father was. She wondered if he was looking for her and her brothers. She felt that old emptiness return. Despite all this luxury her heart yearned for her old, simple life.

***

The bazaar was crowded when they arrived but people stood back to let them pass as soon as they saw that they were accompanied by one of the Khalifa's black eunuchs. How different it was from the first time she had been in this market, shackled and dragged along by the slave trader. Now she was dressed in pure cotton and the sandals on her feet were of the softest leather, intricately stamped with patterns of leaves and flowers. She wore an embroidered veil over her long hair and it was hard not to notice how the townspeople stared at her in admiration.

'Look at this, Jawhara. What do you think?' Najm asked.

She held some coloured ribbons up for her to see.

'They are very pretty.'

'Yes, I think so. I'll have them.'

She nodded to the eunuch, who paid the woman with a small coin.

'What else do we need?' asked Najm.

'Soap?'

'Yes. I love buying soap and perfume. Follow me; I know the best stall in the bazaar for that.'

Najm led them deeper into the bazaar, past pottery stalls and men selling leatherwork, past women selling fruit flavoured drinks and sweet pastries, past spice stalls and basket weavers until they arrived at the perfume stall.

'What wonderful smells. Here, try this one,' she said pushing a bar of pink soap into Isolde's hand. 'I just love this fragrance.'

Isolde sniffed at it; it smelt of roses.

'Yes, it's lovely. I'll have a bar of that,' she said.

'So will I. Two bars please,' Najm said to the stall holder.

'Excuse me, is this yours?' a voice asked in perfect Arabic.

Isolde turned round to see a young man smiling at her. He was tall and wiry with creamy brown skin and enormous eyes that sparkled at her as though he had been waiting for just this moment all his life. He was holding a veil in his hand, her veil; it looped around his wrist and hung like a silken rainbow. She put her hand to her head; her veil was gone.

'Yes it is. How ...?'

'It was on the ground,' the young man said, pushing his long, black hair back from his face.

He was staring at her and she felt herself blush.

'Thank you so much,' she said, taking it from him. 'I didn't want to lose it.'

As he handed it to her, their fingers touched and it was like lightning running up her arm. He was so handsome, not like the boys in her village with their rough ways and their untidy mops of blond hair, but in a more romantic way, like a prince in a fairy tale. She looked into his deep brown eyes and shivered with excitement. Nervously she stepped back and wound the veil around her head, covering her hair but not her face.

'You're a stranger here, aren't you?' he asked.

She nodded. He continued to smile at her as he said, 'I thought so. May I introduce myself, my name is Omar ibn Qasim. I am a potter.'

'Good day, Omar ibn Qasim,' she said, struggling with the strange vowel sounds.

'And your name, beautiful lady?'

'Jawhara.'

He smiled and whispered, just loud enough for her to hear, 'Ah, the jewel. I should have known.'

Najm pulled at Isolde's arm.

'We must go now. Hurry.'

The eunuch had, by now, realised what was happening and moved to interrupt them.

'Ma'a salama, and thank you,' Isolde said.

'Alla ysalmak, Jawhara,' the young man said and quickly slipped away into the crowd before the eunuch could intercept him.

'We are finished here now,' Najm told their chaperone. 'We are going back to the alcázar.'

She took Isolde's arm and steered her away from the stall.

'You cannot talk to men in the street, Jawhara. It is expressly forbidden. If this got back to Yamut we would all be in trouble.'

'I'm sorry; I didn't realise.'

'I don't think he will say anything,' Najm said, nodding at the eunuch who was walking in front of them. 'He knows Yamut would punish him too. But please don't do it again.'

'He was only returning my veil,' Isolde protested.

But as she said it, she knew it had not been as innocent as she made out. When their hands had touched, something had passed between her and that lanky young man, some chemistry that told her he would be in her thoughts for some time to come. She looked back, hoping to see him standing there watching her but he had vanished into the crowd.

CHAPTER 10

Abd al-Rahman III had bathed, prayed and now was dressed in his finest robes. Today he was receiving an ambassador from Baghdad and he intended to impress him. He wanted to dispel, once and for all, the notion that al-Andalus was still a warring backwater. It was time that the kingdoms of the East realised the importance of the caliphate and acknowledged that Córdoba was now the equal of Baghdad and Damascus in terms of culture and learning.

'You wanted to see me, my lord?'

It was Hasdai ibn Shaprut, his minister of foreign affairs.

'Yes. Have our visitors arrived?' he asked.

'Yes, my lord. They have been waiting in the ante room for almost an hour.'

'Excellent. They can wait a little while longer then I will go to see them. First I need your advice.'

Some remarked that ibn Shaprut had become too close to the Khalifa for a man in his position; he was a practising Jew. Al-Rahman did not agree. His minister was an excellent man, wise and charming. In fact he relied on him for many things. Ibn Shaprut had joined the royal court originally as his physician but his many talents meant that al-Rahman had come to depend on him and, above all, to trust him. Apart from al-Hakim, he was the only man that he could confide in.

'What is my lord? I thought this visit was merely about trade agreements.'

'It is. I don't want to talk about the delegation; I want to speak to you about something personal.'

'I am at your service, my lord. I will do what I can to help.'

'I remember that some years ago you developed an antidote against a number of poisons.'

'That's right, my lord. It is particularly effective against snakebites. I have cured many men who were bitten.'

'I hear that it also helps with other ailments,' he continued.

'Indeed. It is efficacious when someone has jaundice and has even been known to hold back the effects of the plague.'

'Is that all?'

'It has also been known to cure impotence, my lord. But surely a man like you does not need such help?'

'I know I can trust you not to speak of this to anyone but I have, of late, been distinctly uninterested in the women that Yamut brings me. Do you think that this medicine of yours would help me?'

'It may do, my lord. It may revive your flagging desire to what it once was,' ibn Shaprut said. 'Would you like me to prepare some for you?'

'I would, Hasdai. But not a word to anyone.'

'Very well, my lord.'

'Tell my son and the ministers for trade and culture to join you in the throne room and wait there for me. I will be along directly. Advise my guards what is happening.'

'Naturally, my lord.'

Ibn Shaprut bowed and backed out of the room.

Al-Rahman walked out onto his patio and looked down at the alcázar gardens below him; the sun glinted on the ornamental lakes, dazzling him. He breathed deeply, enjoying the scent of the myrtle bushes that bordered the garden paths. Some women from his harem were throwing bread to the fish. He watched them lazily, trying to identify them. One of them in particular caught his eye; he did not think he had seen her before. He prided himself on the fact that he could recognise every one of his concubines, even if he had only slept with them once. This was not one of them.

He turned to Gassan who, as usual, was not far away.

'Bring Yamut al-Attar to me.'

'Yes, my lord.'

He continued to watch the girl. She was sitting by the edge of the lake now, trailing her hand in the water. She was obviously not a servant. Servants were not allowed to sit about like ladies all day. Yet he was sure she was not one of his concubines. The more he watched her, the more intrigued he became. One of the other women was speaking to her and, as she lifted her head to reply, the sunlight caught her hair, making it shine like a river of gold.

'My lord?'

'Ah, Yamut. Who is that girl?'

He pointed to the women by the lake.

'They are women from your harem, my lord.'

'But that one, there on the right, sitting by the pool? Why have you not brought her to me before now?'

'That is Jawhara, my lord. She has only been with us a short time; she is still attending the school. I intended to keep her as a surprise for you.'

'Good. Bring her to me as soon as she is ready.'

'I will my lord.'

The eunuch waited a moment and when al-Rahman walked back into his rooms, asked, 'Will that be all, my lord?'

Al-Rahman nodded. It was time to meet the ambassador; he had kept him waiting long enough.

***

When he arrived, Al-Rahman's son and his ministers were standing by the throne, waiting for him and the walls of his royal reception room were lined by Palace Guards, all resplendent in their usual green and gold livery. The guards were all tall men, mostly Slavs from eastern Europe who were, more often than not, referred to as 'the silent ones' because they spoke so little Arabic. Their lack of culture made no difference to him; they were strong, brave men and they were loyal to the Khalifa.

He walked to his throne and sat down to await the arrival of his visitor. The air was heavy with expectancy. His son smiled at him and bowing low, said, 'As-salam alaykum, father. Here is your sceptre.'

He handed the royal insignia to his father.

'Wa alaykum e-salam, my son.'

Al-Rahman looked around his reception room. No visitor could fail to be impressed. He sat on a raised throne at the end of a long room; above his head was a ceiling of

pure gold, supported by two rows of red and white
horseshoe arches, each one resting on a column of blue
marble. Behind him, was an identical arch and on either
side the stucco-covered walls were carved from floor to
ceiling in exquisite patterns of birds, plants and flowers, all
delicately painted in reds and blues; the floor, made from
the finest marble and polished like glass reflected it all back
to him. Everything about the room was a feast for the
senses. From the twelve gold statues, cast in the shapes of
animals and birds and encrusted with precious jewels, that
poured clear spring water into a huge green marble basin, a
gift from the Emperor of Constantinople, to the suspended
tank of mercury that dazzled the beholder whenever the
sun's rays touched it, it all spoke of wealth and power.

He raised his hand to indicate he was ready to receive
his visitor. The outer doors opened and in came the
ambassador. The ambassador advanced a third of the way
into the room then stopped and bowed. After a moment's
wait he walked the same distance and repeated his action.
Then and only then, following the protocol of the court,
was he permitted to approach the Khalifa's throne and kiss
his hand.

'Welcome to my humble home,' al-Rahman said. 'As-
salam alaykum.'

'Wa alaykum e-salam, Abd al-Rahman, Defender of the
Faith. I bring you greetings from my lord and master, al-
Muti, Khalifa of the Abbasid dynasty and ruler of all
Baghdad.'

Al-Rahman looked carefully at the ambassador. Surely
he realised that news had already reached al-Andalus that
the Khalifa of the Abbasid dynasty was in trouble and that

his kingdom was on the verge of breaking up. Ruler of all Baghdad? He was barely ruler of his own court.

The ambassador clapped his hands once and a stream of servants entered, each carrying a gift for al-Rahman. These they placed on the ground in front of him: exotically carved ivory boxes, exquisite pottery, silver jewellery, gold amulets and much more.

'This is most generous of your master,' al-Rahman said and motioned for his own servants to reciprocate. 'Please convey my most grateful thanks to Khalifa al-Muti.'

This was one way to show that pathetic ruler in Baghdad, who continued to call himself Khalifa even though his power had diminished, that al-Andalus was capable of sending him gifts that were even more magnificent than anything Baghdad could offer. He leaned back and watched as his servants paraded past, showing the ambassador the wonderful gifts he was to take back to his master: embroidered textiles, bales of silk so fine that the light could pass through it, delicately woven cotton, richly patterned rugs, scented candles, ivory from North Africa that was finely carved with the names of al-Rahman III and al-Muti; there were saddles stuffed with precious aromatics, slaves and pure bred Andalusian horses. All these the ambassador would take back to Baghdad as a sign of the Khalifa's power and generosity.

Once all the intricacies of court protocol had been completed, Abd al-Rahman indicated that his ministers should withdraw and leave him and the ambassador alone.

'So, ambassador, you have spent some days in Córdoba already, I believe?'

'Yes, your excellency. It is a marvellous city.'

'I hope you had the opportunity to visit our universities. They are the hub of learning for all the western world. Savants and professors from all over the world come here to study. Our libraries contain over four hundred thousand books.'

'They are very impressive, my lord.'

'I hope, ambassador, that when you return to Baghdad you will encourage your learned men to visit our city. They will not be disappointed, I can assure you. Muslim scholars are always welcome here.'

'The fame of your city for wisdom and learning has already reached us. I think you will find that many of our philosophers and writers are already here.'

'And its beauty, too, I hope.'

'Of course, my lord.'

'Now that you are my guest, here in Madinat al-Zahra, you must stay a while and enjoy my new home. You will find that everything you have seen in Córdoba has been surpassed by the beauty of this city. We have created buildings that are truly unique. My architects have taken ideas from Damascus, from our own Roman and Visigoth predecessors and put their own mark on them; they have created an architecture that is truly unparalleled in its beauty. In centuries to come, people will look at my palaces and say, not that they are Visigoth palaces, nor Roman, not that they are Omayyad, but that they are the work of the Iberian Omayyads, of the khalifas of al-Andalus.'

'Indeed they will, my lord.'

'Now you must leave me. My son, al-Hakim will speak to you about other matters.'

He watched the ambassador rise and bow his way out of his presence. Later he would speak to Hakim and find out how his meeting had gone. He knew he could trust his son to impress the ambassador and ibn Shaprut would be there too; he would work his charm on the meeting and make sure all went well. Yes, those two men could be relied upon to impress the ambassador. Of all his children, Hakim was the most sensitive and cultured. His love of books was greater even than his own; it was his son's dearest wish to expand the libraries both in Córdoba and here in Madinat al-Zahra. Al-Rahman knew he would do his best to persuade the ambassador to send them more men of learning from the universities in Baghdad.

CHAPTER 11

Omar's head was spinning. He had actually spoken to her and she was every bit as lovely as he knew she would be. Her voice was soft and gentle and her accent, as she struggled with the strange Arabic vowels, made his spine tingle. He repeated his name, just as she had said it. It was music to his ears. She was adorable. No wonder they had named her Jawhara; she was a perfect jewel, the most desirable woman he had ever seen. He sighed. When could he see her again? It was all he could think about.

'What's up with you today?' his father asked. 'You've been mooning about all morning. Leave that now and show al-Sagir how to empty the kiln. We've got all these plates to glaze by tomorrow.'

'All right, Baba.'

Al-Sagir was in the house, helping the old man plaster the walls of the new room. It was almost finished and, as soon as it was dry, Omar would be able to sleep inside. Much to everyone's surprise the new slaves were working well; al-Mari, despite his years, was strong and capable and the boy was eager to learn. The two had formed a close friendship and Omar could see that al-Sagir looked on the old man as a father. At first the child had been very withdrawn and his tear-stained cheeks each morning spoke of his unhappiness but now, with al-Mari as his friend, he seemed to have settled in. Omar wondered what had happened to the boy's real father. How had he allowed him to be captured? He had tried asking him where he was from but the boy just shook his tow coloured head; he either didn't know or preferred to keep it to himself. What did it matter; his family was probably dead anyway.

'Sagir, I need you in the workshop,' Omar said, touching the drying plaster lightly with his finger.

He saw the boy look at al-Mari, unsure of what to do. The old man nodded and said to the boy in Arabic, 'Run along. I can finish off here.'

Omar was growing fond of al-Sagir. He found it easy to communicate with him, even though the slave's grasp of their language was still a bit weak. He was an intelligent lad and would soon be speaking like a native. The boy followed him back to the workshop where Qasim was waiting.

'Ah, there you are. I've got to go out. When you've emptied the kiln, start painting the designs on those plates so that I can fire them tonight. I may already have a customer for them so give them your best attention,' his father said, pointing to the plates already stacked on Omar's workbench.

Omar nodded but his mind was far from his work. All that he could think of was Jawhara. What would become of her? Was she going to be locked in the alcázar forever? Would he ever see her again? He felt despair clutch at his heart. There had to be some way to find her. He would talk to Yusuf. His friend was working in the alcázar; he would know of a way to see her. He would help him.

The boy stood silently, waiting for Omar to give him his instructions.

'All right, al-Sagir, let me show you what to do. This is the oven where we bake the pottery,' he explained. 'Never go near it when it's hot. Always check that the fire is out first before you open the door. At the moment it's cold.'

He touched the kiln door with his hand before opening it and continued, 'I want you to unload the pottery very carefully and stack it over by the bench. Make sure you don't chip any of it because then it can't be used. Put the pots over there and place the plates at the end. Later I will coat them in a fine white glaze and we will fire them again. After that I will decorate them and give them their final firing. Do you understand?'

'Yes, master. But why do you have to fire the pots so many times? Why not do it all in one go?'

Omar laughed. The boy had an inquisitive mind; he liked that.

'You will see. Here, look at this plate; it has been fired twice and now I can paint it with a special pattern.'

He held up one of the plates that his father had left out for him; it was glazed a glossy white.

'I have to make sure that the first coating of glaze is not crazed. See, here. This one won't do because it's covered in fine cracks.'

He put the plate to one side and picked up another.

'But this one is perfect so I can proceed with the second coat of glaze.'

He looked to see if the boy understood him. Al-Sagir was staring at the two plates.

'What happens to the bad plate?' he asked.

'Put it over there on that pile. We sell them off cheaply in the bazaar. Now do you understand what you have to do?'

'Yes, master.'

He waited to be sure that the boy was taking sufficient care in removing the pottery from the kiln then returned to his own work. He took down the pots of glaze and stirred them thoroughly. They contained his father's special lustre glazes. He picked up one of the plates and carefully drew a pattern on it then began to paint it with the secondary glaze; the paint flowed freely onto the smooth surface. It was painstaking work and he did not want to make any mistakes. Until it had been fired a third time and removed from the kiln, he would not know the exact colours of his design but he did know that it would be basically green with a lustre of reds, browns and gold. That was what made his craft so exciting; you never knew exactly how the glaze would turn out. It was magical to see the transformation.

'Shall I throw these out?' al-Sagir asked, holding up some broken shards of pot.

'No. Keep them. We use them for packing around the pottery when we fire it. It helps to keep the temperature of the kiln even. Just stack them on the floor for now.'

The boy was learning well. They worked on in silence for a while then al-Sagir asked, 'Do you want me to do anything else or should I go back to al-Mari?'

'No, not yet. Get in some wood and fill the stove ready for tonight.'

The boy stopped and looked at the design Omar was painting.

'Do you like it?' Omar asked.

The boy nodded, unenthusiastically.

'It's a bit dull,' he said. 'But the pattern is pretty.'

'Ah, but when it is fired you will see how it will change. Its colours will be revealed. It will glow like the fire it has come from.'

The boy looked unconvinced. He went outside and began chopping the wood for the evening.

Omar picked up another plate and began again, tracing out the design and stage by stage filling in the spaces with the glaze. Each plate would be slightly different even though the basic geometric design he was using was identical. The variations that he could create were endless. He loved to invent new ones. For a while he was engrossed in his work then his thoughts began to wander back to the beautiful slave girl; he was becoming obsessed with her. How was he going to see her again? The question would not leave him alone; it buzzed around in his head like an agitated bumble bee.

Once he had a number of plates ready for firing he decided to take a rest. He would slip out before his father returned and go to find Yusuf. He picked up his robe and a satchel of tools and said to the boy, 'Al-Sagir, I have to go out. You must stay here until my father returns.'

'Don't you want me to go back and help al-Mari?'

'No. You mustn't leave the alfarería unattended. You can sweep the floor and clean down the wheel. I won't be long.'

As he stepped out into the street he was assailed by a strong stench of camels. A caravan was making its way into the medina, laden with sacks of goods. The man leading the first camel was black, a negro from beyond the

Maghreb. He strode into the medina, his white robes billowing around him and a long striped turban wound around his head and partially covering his face. They were merchants from North Africa, nomads that wandered through al-Andalus buying and selling whatever they could. Their arrival had set the local dogs barking and a few ran out to snap at the camels' heels but the stoical creatures ignored them, picking up their broad padded feet daintily and continuing to march solemnly on. He stood by the door, waiting for them to pass; there were at least twenty camels and half-a-dozen pure-bred horses that walked with their heads held high and tails up. The women and children followed behind, leading mules laden with their possessions. One of the nomads, a Berber by the look of his dress, seemed to be the leader. He had a gleaming, curved sword tucked into his belt and shouted for the others to halt. Normally Omar would have lingered to see what wares they had brought and talk to them about where they had been and what they had seen on their travels but today he had no time for that. He wanted to find Yusuf and get back to the alfarería before his father returned. He manoeuvred his way through the crowd that was beginning to form around the travellers and headed for the north gate.

When he and Yusuf had been talking the previous evening, his friend had mentioned that he was currently working on the wall panels of one of the rooms of the Grand Vizier's new palace. Omar knew he was not allowed to go in there unless he had official business but he was sure he could bluff his way past the guards.

As he entered the alcázar he could see a group of workmen in the far room. He prayed that one of them was Yusuf.

'Who are you? What's your business here?' asked one of the Palace Guards.

Omar had been hoping to see his brother or one of his brother's friends but this impressive mountain of a man was not someone he recognised.

'I'm looking for Yusuf. He's a stone mason. I've brought some tools for him.'

The guard peered at him, curiously.

'Your al-Jundi's brother, aren't you?' he asked.

'Yes.'

'Go on then. He's through there, with the others.'

The guard pointed to the group of workmen.

'Thanks.'

He walked towards the room; the entrance had three horseshoe arches resting on marble pillars. The arches and all the area surrounding them were covered in intricately carved stone; it was a magnificent sight even in its unfinished state. Later it would be painted in shades of blue and red; he knew this from other buildings. Inside, the stone masons were working in complete silence, each carving the white soft stone tablets that covered the inner walls. Omar watched, fascinated, as their designs of carefully entwined leaves and flowers gradually took form. They worked independently, each on his own section but carving identical patterns and all with the same intense concentration. He wondered how long it would take them to finish an entire wall, weeks probably. He must have spoken aloud because Yusuf turned round to see who was standing behind him.

'Omar? What on earth are you doing here?'

'Sorry, I didn't mean to startle you.'

Yusuf's face and clothes were covered in a fine white dust. He looked anxiously around him but the guard was not in sight and the other stone masons were too busy to be worried about Omar.

'I wanted to see where you worked.'

'But how did you get in? This is the Vizier's new residence. How did you get past the guard?'

He brushed some of the dust from his face.

'I told him I had some tools for you,' Omar said.

He pushed the bag forward so that Yusuf could look inside. His friend laughed.

'Those are potter's tools. What am I supposed to do with those useless bits of wood? Not much good for carving stone, are they.'

'The guards wouldn't know the difference. They're mostly foreigners anyway; they don't know what tools you use.'

'Probably not, but it was a bit risky of you, all the same.'

He frowned at Omar.

'I hope this is not about that girl.'

Omar smiled his most persuasive smile.

'I just wanted your help. I mean, here you are in the alcázar, close to where she is living. Surely you could help me to see her again without that bossy eunuch sticking his nose in?'

'Definitely not. You know as well as I do that no-one is allowed to enter the Khalifa's harem. Do you want me to be executed as well as you?'

'Don't exaggerate. Nobody's going to be executed. I just want to get a message to her.'

'Well I can't help you.'

Yusuf turned back to his work. It really was beautiful, freer in form that Omar's designs but still very controlled. The pattern seemed to repeat itself over and over and the winding, undulating stalks of the plant seemed to have no beginning and no end. It was an illusion, a deception of the eye. Omar found it amazing that his friend had created such movement, such fluidity in a medium as inflexible as stone.

'That's very good,' Omar said, tracing his finger along the design. 'I am impressed. I never realised you were so talented.'

'It's a craft, like any other; the more you do, the better you get. I've been doing it since I left school.'

'This plant, it's carved everywhere,' Omar said looking around the unfinished room.

The Quran forbade them from making images of living things in case it encouraged idolatry but plants and trees were acceptable.

'It's the tree of life, a traditional symbol. It's used to define the indivisible and infinite nature of God. Look, you'll have to go. I can't afford to make a mistake; one slip and the whole panel would be ruined. This work is all about concentration. If my boss saw me talking to you I'd probably lose my job.'

'It looks so real. How do you make those tiny holes where the stalks of the plants cross over? Surely you can't get your chisel in there without breaking bits off?'

'No, of course not; I use this.'

He took a trepan out of his pocket and handed it to Omar. Omar tested the point with his thumb.

'It's pretty sharp. I bet you could do some damage with that if you wanted to.'

'The only damage I'm going to do to anyone, is to you if you don't go away.'

'But you're my friend Yusuf; who else can I turn to in my hour of need?' he pleaded.

'Omar, I can't do anything for you. I'm sorry. Really I am.'

'But surely there must be a way? Don't you know anyone who has access to the harem?'

'Yes, Yamut al-Attar.'

'Who's he, a friend of yours?'

'Not exactly. He's the Chief Eunuch. Now go away and leave me in peace.'

His colleagues were beginning to take an interest in their conversation and Omar could see that Yusuf was not happy about it.

'All right. See you later tonight then?'

'Yes. Now go.'

'But you will think about it?'

'Go. Peace be with you,' he added.

'Thank you, my friend,' Omar said.

He would have to hurry. Baba would be looking for him. He nodded at the guard as he passed through the gate and out into the medina. A cold wind had sprung up;

Omar pulled up his hood and thrust his hands into the pockets of his djellaba. Amongst the coins and assorted bits and pieces that he always carried was something new, something sharp. He pulled it out; it was the tool he'd picked up from Yusuf, the trepan. He stopped. He ought to go back and return it but that would mean telling another lie to the guard and then he'd be late getting back to the alfarería. Well, he was sure his friend had another; he'd give it to him tonight.

CHAPTER 12

First Qasim decided to check up on the work that al-Mari was doing. He was not the fastest of workers but he was very thorough and Qasim was pleased that he had bought him. Without the additional help it would have been impossible to finish so quickly. Now the lower part of the house would be ready before Eid al-Adha, the Feast of the Sacrifices, so Fatima could have all the family to stay with them for the holiday.

'How's it going, old man?' he asked the slave.

Al-Mari put down his tools and straightened up to answer his new master. With a wave of his hand, he indicated the bricks he had laid for the floor. He hardly spoke to anyone except the boy and when he did it was difficult to understand him; he had a tendency to mumble and never looked at you when he spoke.

'Good. Good work,' Qasim said.

The bricks were evenly laid, giving the floor a smooth flat surface. He couldn't have done it better himself. Qasim felt a warm satisfaction in his bones. His house was going to be one of the best in the medina. For the first time since he had left Ardales he truly felt at home here, in this house. It was his house, built with his own hands and those of his household. This was a house that would last for years; it would be a home for his grandchildren and their children. He would end his days here, surrounded by his family.

***

He had never wanted to leave Ardales but in the end he had had no choice. His family were marked as traitors. His father had been the cousin and right-hand man of Omar ibn Hafsun, the most troublesome of all the rebels. Ibn Hafsun had been a thorn in the side of Abd al-Rahman and his predecessors for many years. From the tales that were told about him, ibn Hafsun had been born a rebellious child and grew into a violent and headstrong youth. He had been forced to flee the country to evade punishment for the murder of a neighbour and would have stayed in exile except that he heard of a rebellion against the Sultan, so he returned to join forces with the rebels. The Sultan's men labelled him a bandit and a renegade but Qasim's father had not seen him like that, not in those days anyway. Later perhaps. Ibn Hafsun built himself a castle at Bobastro, a mere stone's throw from Ardales. All the young men, Qasim's father and his friends included, had flocked to join his army; ibn Hafsun was a Mullawad like them. He told them he was fighting for their right to equality with the Arab ruling class. His followers idolised him.

But in the end ibn Hafsun was nothing more than an opportunist. After a series of defeats by the Sultan's army he abandoned his men and went to Córdoba to join the Royal Guard. Qasim's father could not believe that he would betray them in that way, but he did. He had joined forces with the enemy. So Qasim's father returned to his old life in Ardales, disappointed and disillusioned with his cousin and former hero.

That would have been the end of it except that ibn Hafsun was not treated with the respect he felt entitled to in Córdoba so, after a few years, he returned to Bobastro in an attempt to create his own independent kingdom. He rallied his old followers and gained new ones, including mercenaries from North Africa. That was when Qasim, young and headstrong, had joined him. His father warned him that he was making a mistake but he would not listen. At first the rebels fought a series of successful battles; the neighbouring towns of Mijas, Archidonna and Comares fell to ibn Hafsun's army and suddenly he began to pose a serious threat to the Sultan. This time it looked as though he was going to win and who knows how things would have gone if ibn Hafsun had continued conquering the towns one by one? He had thousands of loyal men and his strength was growing day by day. Then he did the inexplicable, something for which, even now, Qasim could not forgive him; ibn Hafsun renounced Islam and converted to Christianity. It was in the year 899; Qasim would never forget the date. He felt betrayed. It was the beginning of the end for ibn Hafsun because it cost him not only Qasim's loyalty but also that of thousands of other Mullawad supporters. Qasim did not openly confront him, instead he quietly retreated to Ardales to resume his job, working as a potter alongside his father.

Now, looking back, it was hard to believe that he and his father had both been deceived by ibn Hafsun but they had not been alone. The man had been charismatic. He had persuaded thousands of men to follow him but who had they been following? A bandit? An opportunist? A political adventurer? Without doubt he was all three. Men saw in him what they wanted to see. Was he a devout Muslim? Unlikely and certainly not a devout Christian. Despite what he had told his followers, ibn Hafsun had only been interested in one thing: furthering his own interests.

Qasim knew he had to distance himself from that man and his losing battle. There was a new Sultan now, Abd al-Rahman III, who was determined to crush the rebellion and everyone connected with it. It was dangerous to be associated with the name ibn Hafsun; the Sultan was waging a bloody war against him and all his followers. Even after ibn Hafsun died it was not over; the Sultan wanted to stamp out any possibility of insurrection. He sent his soldiers to hunt down ibn Hafsun's family and anyone who had supported the rebels. They killed ibn Hafsun's sons and displayed their crucified bodies outside the mosque in Córdoba as a warning against further insurrection.

It was Qasim's father who alerted his son and his new wife to the danger they were facing. The Sultan's men were coming for him, he said; they would surely kill his son too. Qasim and Fatima had fled that very night, not even stopping to look back at the town they both loved. His father had remained. He would face his death in the home he loved, he told them as he kissed them goodbye.

***

The sound of voices could be heard coming from the workshop. Did Omar have some customers? Qasim left al-Mari to get on with the brickwork and went to investigate.

'As-salam alaykum. Can I help you?' he asked.

Two North African merchants were trying, unsuccessfully, to communicate with al-Sagir. There was no sign of Omar.

'Wa alaykum e-salam,' they replied. 'We want to speak to the alfarero.'

'I'm the potter. What can I do for you?'

'We have come from the south and have many things that you might like to see,' one of them said.

'Ivory, inks, dyes, glazes,' the other added.

'Come into my home and have some tea then you can show me what you have brought,' Qasim said, leading them into the house.

He motioned to al-Sagir to follow him.

'Where is my son?' he hissed. 'Where is Omar?'

'He had to go out, sir. He left me in charge.'

'Did he? And what exactly did he leave you in charge of?'

The boy knew instinctively that no answer was expected and scurried back to sweeping the floor, even though it looked as though it had been swept a dozen times already.

'This way gentlemen,' Qasim said. 'Please be seated.'

Fatima appeared in the doorway.

'As-salam alaykum,' she said with a slight bow.

She was wearing her veil; when she saw the visitors, she tugged at it so that its folds covered her face.

'Wa alaykum e-salam, mistress,' the men said.

'Please bring us some tea, wife,' Qasim said.

He turned to his guests.

'So gentlemen, what have you brought that might be of interest to me?'

***

The men had stayed well over an hour, relaying stories of their travels and coaxing him into buying a number of their ready-mixed glazes. Once they had left he returned to his workshop. Omar had returned and al-Sagir was stacking more blocks of clay in the corner.

'Well son, have you finished?' he asked, knowing full well what the answer would be.

'Almost Baba, just a few more to do. I didn't want to rush them. If you work too quickly you make mistakes.'

'So that's your excuse for slipping out to the teahouse?' he asked.

'I was gone no more than a few minutes, Baba.'

'When I leave you in charge, I expect you to stay here, not leave an illiterate boy to deal with whosoever should call by. Do not do it again, Omar,' he said.

'I'm sorry Baba.'

Qasim put three small plates on the table.

'Come and look at these. I got them from the North Africans. What do you think? Pretty, yes? These samples are from Babylon; they were glazed with lead, quartz and something else that they were reluctant to disclose.'

'They are very different. I think they may contain copper,' Omar said, holding one of the plates up to the light.

'You could be right. When we have finished this order I thought I might try out a small batch using the new glazes.'

'How many did you buy?'

'Enough. If they are as good as they look, I wanted to have enough to last until the next time the North Africans come this way.'

Omar rubbed the dry glaze mix between his finger and thumb.

'It's not as good as your lustreware,' he said. 'Why do you need another type of glaze?'

'I know, but the lustreware is expensive and there is a lot of wastage with the firing. This is supposed to give a consistent glaze, time after time. I think we could use both and charge two different prices.'

'Keep the lustreware for the court, you mean?'

'Exactly and sell the rest to the less wealthy. There are plenty of people moving into the town that want to buy well decorated pottery but not at top prices. Also I want to keep my lustreware exclusive. No-one's going to pay highly for something that everyone can buy.'

'Yes, Baba, you're right.'

Qasim picked up his new purchases and put them in the cupboard.

'But for now, let's get this order finished; we have wasted enough time today. Al-Sagir, come here and let me show you how to prepare the clay.'

CHAPTER 13

Yusuf was Omar's closest friend; he spent most of his evenings with him in the bar on the edge of the town, playing chess and drinking mint tea or, when it was available, orange blossom syrup. Neither of them drank wine, Yusuf because he did not like the taste and Omar because his father had forbidden it. Sometimes they wandered through the streets together, chatting to friends or stopping to watch the itinerant conjurers for a while; sometimes, in the summer, they went swimming in the river. They talked about the future and what they dreamed of achieving; they discussed the girls they liked; they shared their doubts and fears and even their secrets. They had grown up together in Córdoba and been friends for so long that Yusuf was regarded as one of Omar's family. Yusuf was more like a brother to him than a friend; he was certainly closer to him than Ibrahim or al-Jundi. Omar's brothers were at school by the time Omar was born and when he too was ready to be educated, they were too old to be bothered with him.

Yusuf was already outside the bar by the time Omar arrived, seated beneath the dark, twisted branches of an old olive tree.

'As-salam alaykum my friend,' Yusuf said.

'Wa alaykum e-salam. Sorry I'm late. My father had a lot of work for me to do. We are trying to get the Royal

Buyer interested in our pottery. Baba thinks we could do well with these new designs.'

'You'll be rich if he decides he likes them. I've seen the quantities he buys. He doesn't just order two or three of something, not even by the dozen; he orders hundreds at a time.'

'Well it's a good job we've got some help now, because otherwise I don't know how we'd cope.'

'Maybe your brother would move down from Córdoba.'

'I doubt it. I think he's got used to being his own boss; he wouldn't want Baba giving him orders again.'

'I can understand that. I wouldn't want to work for my father, either.'

He poured out a cup of the sweet tea for Omar.

'There's a camel race tomorrow evening. Do you think you could get away? It's on the old camping ground by the river,' Yusuf added.

'I'll try. We haven't been to any races for ages.'

In the short time that they had lived in Madinat al-Zahra the amount of land available for such pursuits as camel racing was getting less and less and now the races were held further away from the centre of the city. All the good, flat land was being used for building; the city was creeping ever outwards.

'This place will be as big as Córdoba within a few years,' Omar remarked.

'People always flock to where the money is,' his friend replied. 'As long as the Khalifa lives here, others will want to follow.'

'So, how is your bride-to-be?' Omar asked. 'Is she still in Córdoba?'

He always referred to Zilma as Yusuf's wife-to-be, just to remind him that whilst he, Omar was as free as a bird, Yusuf was about to be married.

'Zilma is fine, thank you. She's coming to stay for a few days so that her mother and mine can discuss the plans for the wedding.'

'Yes, you'll soon be an old married man. No more nights out camel racing,' Omar teased. 'How long is it now? Three months?'

'Two months after the feast of Eid.'

Omar shook his head in mock despair.

'So when does she arrive?'

'This evening. So I can't stay late; I have to go to her uncle's house to meet her. Why don't you come with me? You haven't seen Zilma for ages.'

'Yes, why not. After all I'm going to be a witness at your wedding, so I'd better get used to the idea of you being married.

'It's time you thought about marriage, instead of running after slave girls,' Yusuf said.

'Yes, but what a slave girl. I can't get her out of my mind. She's driving me crazy. If I don't get to see her soon I think I'll go mad. Mad with love.'

'You don't even know her.'

'I've spoken to her. Her voice is like the music of angels. Her smile is divine. She has stolen my heart, Yusuf. I do not think I can go on living if I do not get to speak to her soon.'

'Don't be so ridiculous. You are always the same when you see a pretty girl. What about that Jasmin, last year?

You couldn't live without her, if I remember rightly. Now you never mention her.'

'That was different. She was lovely but nothing compared to Jawhara. She was the moon, cold and aloof; Jawhara is the stars, sparkling and full of promise.'

'You should have been a poet, not a potter,' Yusuf laughed. 'And what about Aisha? What was she?'

'That was a long time ago,' Omar said.

He picked up his tea and drank it hurriedly; he was beginning to get embarrassed.

'I'm just reminding you that this is not the first time and knowing you, as I do, it won't be the last. Don't jeopardise your future for a dream, I beg you.'

'But, I keep telling you, Jawhara is different.'

'Yes, she belongs to the Khalifa. You could have married any one of the other girls if you had wanted to. But not this one. She will never be yours. Face it, Omar. You only want what you cannot have.'

He stared at his friend. Was that true? Was it her inaccessibility that attracted him to her? No, Yusuf was wrong; he had never felt like this before. He was in love; he was sure.

'Rubbish. I am bewitched by her.'

'Maybe, but is that love?'

'Just because you're betrothed, it doesn't make you an expert on love, Yusuf. I cannot dictate to my heart. We have no control over whom we fall in love with.'

He was annoyed with Yusuf; his words made him uncomfortable. His friend knew him very well but this was different; he was certain this was love.

Yusuf put his hand on his shoulder.

'I'm sorry Omar. Don't be angry. I'm only thinking of you; I don't want you to get hurt.'

'I know. You're always looking out for me. Let's say no more about it. Why don't we go and see if that bride-to-be of yours has arrived yet?'

Yusuf's face split into a broad smile. He looked excited at the prospect of seeing Zilma again.

'Yes, her uncle doesn't live far from here. His house is on the Nogales Road.'

'What does he do?'

'He imports silks and wools from Byzantium.'

'A merchant?'

'Yes, and quite a wealthy one at that.'

As they walked back through the medina, Omar remembered the trepan in his pocket. He pulled it out and showed it to Yusuf.

'I must have slipped this into my pocket this morning. Sorry; I hope you didn't need it,' Omar told him.

'No, I have dozens of them. Keep it. Maybe it'll come in handy for something. It's an old one, too blunt for what I need.'

'All right, I will,' he said, adding it to the collection of bric-a-brac in his pockets.

***

Zilma was already waiting at her uncle's house. Her mother and two of her sisters were with her. Omar watched as his friend ran up the path to greet her. He had never seen him so happy before. Yes, Yusuf was certainly in love. And Zilma, he had forgotten what a sweet girl she was. She blushed with pleasure at the sight of her betrothed and could not stop smiling.

'You remember Omar, my love?' Yusuf asked her, pulling Omar forward into the light from the oil lamps.

'Of course. As-salam alaykum, Omar. It is good to see you again.'

'Wa alaykum e-salam, Zilma. I am pleased to see you.'

'Will you come in and have some tea with us?' she asked.

'No, thank you; I have to go. Baba will want me up at the crack of dawn tomorrow.'

'Will I see you at the camel racing?' Yusuf asked.

'Maybe, if I can get away. Insha'Allah.'

He bowed politely to Zilma.

'Ma'a salama, Zilma. I hope you have a pleasant stay.'

What a happy couple they made. As he walked away he felt a momentary twinge of envy. In a few months Yusuf would have everything that he wanted: a beautiful young wife and his own home. But Omar could have that too. After all he was betrothed to Muna. He could have a happy married life just like Yusuf. All he had to do was face up to his responsibilities and stop chasing after rainbows. Yusuf's earlier words returned to him. Was it true that Omar only wanted what he couldn't have? He thought of Jawhara and he knew it was more than that; she was the woman for him; she was the one he wanted to marry.

CHAPTER 14

Isolde thought that after the incident at the market the previous week, she would not be allowed to go again but nothing had been said. Najm was right; the eunuch was not going to tell anyone because he would be punished too. His name was Al-Tayyib, Isolde now knew, and his sole job was to guard her and the others in that part of the harem. His name meant good-natured but he was anything but; his face was always pulled into a sneer as if the women in his charge were a constant irritation to him. Najm said his castration had probably been done badly and now here he was, surrounded by half-naked women and unable to do anything about it. She said that would make any man bad-tempered. Al-Tayyib was an ugly, coffee-coloured man, with no facial hair and a fat, flabby body. Isolde couldn't imagine any woman wanting him even if he wasn't a eunuch.

Today Najm wanted to buy some white muslin to make a new dress, so they had asked for permission from the Royal wife to go to the bazaar again. Since their last visit, Isolde had not spoken about the young man she had met and neither had her friend. Nevertheless his warm smile kept creeping its way back into her thoughts and thinking about him made her feel less lonely. She wondered if she would be fortunate enough to see him again today.

Al-Tayyib was escorting them, as usual and she saw him stop and speak to Najm before they left.

'What is it? What did he say to you?' she asked as they followed him through the narrow passages of the harem and out into the street.

'Nothing. Just the usual stuff about keeping close to him and not speaking to anyone other than the stall holder. I don't know why he always makes such a fuss. It's not as if we were going to run away.'

Najm pulled her veil across her face to protect herself from the sun.

'I think it's because of you,' she added after a moment's thought. 'Yamut is nervous about you. They say that the Khalifa saw you in the garden and asked Yamut who you were.'

'Who told you that? The women in the harem? How do they know?' Isolde asked.

She wondered if Najm had forgotten about the young potter but her next remarks showed that she had remembered the incident.

'There are very few secrets in the harem. You'd be wise to remember that. Everyone always knows who is doing what and with whom.'

She smiled.

'So be careful, little jewel.'

So Najm had heard what the young man said to her. Isolde felt the blood rush to her face and turned her head away so that her friend could not see her blushes.

It was still early and not yet too hot for walking. A slight breeze stirred the leaves in the orange trees as they passed and lifted the hem of her dress, exposing her slender ankles.

She liked the rare occasions when she could leave the harem and walk out in the open, among normal people. True they did not resemble the people she would have seen at home but they were still ordinary people: craftsmen and bakers, gardeners, smiths, women shopping and gossiping just like they would have been doing in her own village. She realised how much she missed her old life and her family. The ache in her heart would just not go away. Maybe it was because of those memories that, as they approached the narrow streets of the souk, she thought she saw her brother. It was just a glimpse but it was enough. A fair-haired young boy, with his back to her, pushed his way through the crowd of shoppers and disappeared. She was certain it was him. Her heart began to pound with excitement. At last she had found him.

'Najm. I've just seen Hans, my little brother. He's here. I've found him at last.'

'What, here, in Madinat al-Zahra?'

'Yes, here in the market. I saw him just now. I know it's him.'

She tugged at her friend's sleeve.

'He went this way. Hurry, I must find him. Please Najm, hurry before we lose him again.'

'Slow down. You don't want to alert Al-Tayyib; if he thinks we're up to something he'll make us go straight home. Just relax. Pretend there is nothing wrong. Remember we are looking for muslin, not missing boys.'

Isolde breathed deeply and tried to quieten her racing heart. She had to find him. She had to find her brother.

'All right, but come this way. I don't want to lose him, not now,' she said.

She linked her arm through Najm's so that she could steer her in the direction of the boy.

'Are you sure it's him?' her friend asked.

Isolde stopped and looked at her. She shook her head, sadly.

'I don't know. Maybe it was a mistake, maybe just someone who looked like him. But I have to know,' she said, tears filling her eyes.

As they turned the corner she saw the boy again. It was unmistakably her brother. He was carrying a pile of plates nearly as big as himself and he looked well. He looked really well. She could hardly believe it; after all this time there he was. The tears coursed down her cheeks and, before she could stop herself, she ran forward, calling out, 'Hans. Hans. It's me, Isolde.'

The boy stopped and turned. He saw her straight away. The plates slid from his hands and crashed onto the floor. Without a backward glance he ran towards her, leaping into her arms, hugging her and bombarding her with endless questions. He was the same unquenchable Hans.

'Isolde. Where have you been? What are you doing here? Why are you dressed like a fine lady? Who's that? Can we go home now? Oh, Isolde, it's so good to see you. I've missed you so much.'

At first she could not speak. She held him to her, feeling his little body against her own. She had found him at last, her own little brother. It was a miracle. She stroked his hair and whispered, 'Hans, we must be careful. I only have a moment. Tell me quickly where you are living.'

The boy understood at once. He turned and pointed to Omar, who was bent over the broken plates in amazement.

So intent was his master on salvaging what he could of the broken pottery that he failed to notice where his slave had gone.

'I live with him. He makes those dishes and things and I work for his family. We live here, in the medina.'

Isolde couldn't believe it. It was the same man who had returned her veil. She would have recognised him anywhere. She felt her heart skip a beat. The potter had bought Hans; her brother belonged to Omar now. How could that be possible? It had to be destiny. The gods had sent Omar to help her; he would be their salvation.

'Isolde, why are you staring at him? Do you know him?'

'No, no, little brother.'

She hugged him again.

'Have you seen Per?' she asked.

He shook his head.

'Look, I have to go but I will try to see you again. If you can, come to the market tomorrow at this time. I will try to be here. And don't tell anyone you have seen me,' she warned.

'All right, Isolde.'

'Look after yourself, Hans,' she said, trying hard not to cry.

The eunuch had not spotted Isolde and Hans; Najm had been quick to create a small diversion by shouting at some innocent bystander and that took all his attention. Her friend had accused the man of pushing her and now al-Tayyib was trying to intervene.

'I'm very sorry, your Highness,' the man she was berating said sarcastically. 'I didn't realise that you needed so much room for yourself and your slave.'

The eunuch was not pleased at the man's attitude and pulled Najm away. Once he had her back under his control he looked around for Isolde.

'Did you see that?' Najm asked, her voice artificially hysterical. 'That man walked straight into me.'

She looked at Isolde and winked.

'So, is it him?' she asked, dropping her voice.

'Yes, it's Hans, one of my brothers. I can't believe he's here in Madinat al-Zahra. It's a miracle. Now I must help him.'

She looked at Najm and said, 'Maybe he could come and live with me in the harem. There are plenty of children living there. I could ask Yamut.'

Najm grabbed her arm and whispered, 'Not so loud.'

'But if I explain that he's my little brother, I'm sure he will let him stay with me; he could work in the kitchens.'

'That won't happen, I can tell you now. Only the children who are born in the harem are allowed to live there and then only if they are the Khalifa's children. The Royal wife would never allow it.'

'But I have to do something for him. I can't just leave him now that I've found him.'

'You don't have a lot of choice. Remember you are a slave now. You might eat good food and wear lovely clothes but you are still a slave. What we have is an illusion of freedom. We only eat and drink because the Khalifa allows it. Even to leave the confines of the harem for a short while requires the permission of the Royal wife. You have to realise that our jailers are watching us all the time. They may not look like prison guards but that's exactly what they are. And our beautiful alcázar is a prison; it is a golden cage. If you want to stay alive, remember this Jawharra, you will never be free to do what you want. Never. Those days are over.'

'I must try to speak to him, at least. I need to find out if he is all right.'

'What did he say to you, just now?'

Isolde smiled.

'Do you remember that man we met last time we came to the market?'

'The handsome one, the one you've been sighing about ever since? Yes, what about him?'

'Hans told me that he works in his house. It was his plates that he dropped.'

'Well that's some coincidence but it doesn't change anything. He's still a slave.'

'I know.'

Isolde felt the hopelessness of it all; she knew she would never be able to help Hans unless she were free.

'Don't cry. You'll make your face blotchy and then you'll get into trouble with Yamut. Just be grateful that you know where one of your brothers is and that he is alive and well.'

Isolde nodded and wiped her eyes with the back of her hand.

'Did he say anything about your other brother, the little one?'

'No. He knows no more than I do.'

'Come on now. Try to look more cheerful. We must finish our shopping and get back. You have your singing lesson soon.'

Isolde hated the singing lessons. She had a reasonable voice but the only songs she had ever sung were folk songs that her mother taught her. Now she was being trained to sing love songs in a language she had yet to master. She also had to learn to play the lute. Luckily her fingers were nimble and she had already managed a few rudimentary chords. To her untuned ears the overall result was discordant but her music teacher seemed quite pleased with her.

When she complained to Najm about it, her friend laughed and said, 'I doubt if the Khalifa will be that interested in your singing. I expect he'll have other things on his mind.'

'That's if he ever sends for me.'

'Once you are ready, he will send for you. First you have to convince Yamut that you're ready to be bedded by the most important man in the land.'

Isolde shuddered at the thought. Najm seemed to think it was good to have the Khalifa take you to his bed but she was sickened at the idea of such an old man making love to her. Somehow she had to get away from the harem.

She was a slave; she belonged to the Khalifa. It was simple. If she wanted to help her brother she had to get free. She tried to remember what it was that Najm had said about getting her freedom; there appeared to be only two possibilities: for the Khalifa to make her a free woman or to run away. The possibility of the Khalifa giving her freedom was remote. As Najm had said, he didn't even know who she was. There had been cases where he had set his slaves free, even his concubines. Not only that, he had arranged for them to marry and given them money and presents to do so. But they had been older women, those he no longer wanted in his harem. As Najm explained it, every so often the Chief Eunuch was given the job of clearing out some space. It was just like clearing out a cupboard in the kitchen. He had to remove some of the women so that others, younger, more nubile and more beautiful, could be brought in. That was no use to her. She was only sixteen; she had only just arrived. Isolde would have to wait many years before she was on the scrap heap and even then she could not guarantee that she would be truly free. She might just end up being the wife or servant of some other man. By then Hans could have disappeared. She wiped her eyes and sighed. So that left her with the second alternative. She would have to run away and take Hans with her. But she couldn't do it on her own; someone would have to help her. She thought immediately of the potter; if only she could speak to Omar she was sure he would come to her aid.

CHAPTER 15

The door to Al-Rahman III's private rooms opened and his son walked in. Al-Hakim was the only one of his children that lived in the private sector of the alcázar.

'Father, may I speak with you?' al-Hakim asked.

'Of course, my son. I want you to tell me what you said to the ambassador. Is he still here?' al-Rahman asked.

'He leaves at the end of the week.'

'I hope he is duly impressed with my court.'

'I am assured that he is very impressed. His advisors could not stop talking about the things that they had seen here.'

'Excellent. So, tell me what agreements have you made with them?'

'They want to buy our textiles, particularly silk. He says that our silk is of a far higher quality than that from the far East. They also like our woollen cloth.'

'Is that all?'

'No. They want mercury.'

'Good. That is something they will find hard to buy elsewhere. So what do we get in return?'

'I talked to him at great length about our libraries, our universities and our schools of music, calligraphy and law. I told him about the hospital in Córdoba with its own baths and running water and how the physicians there are the most knowledgeable in the western world. I have arranged for him to visit it before he returns to Baghdad. I will also make sure he visits our own dispensary here in Madinat al-Zahra before he leaves.'

'So what did he have to say to all that?'

Al-Hakim smiled.

'He expressed some surprise that women were allowed to make copies of the Quran.'

'Did you tell him that here, in al-Andalus, anyone is allowed to make copies if they do it with a pure heart and a steady hand?'

'I did. I said we had many skilled women working in the universities and publishing houses. I told him that we have more than seventy bookshops.'

'So he will spread the word that al-Andalus welcomes men and women of learning?'

'He will indeed. He says he will ask Khalifa al-Muti to send his learned scholars here to exchange ideas with ours.'

'And skilled artisans too.'

'Yes.'

'What about the dyes? Did you speak to him about our need to import good quality dyes?'

'Of course. I explained how our textile industry depended on a ready supply of dyes.'

'I hope you did not make us sound too needy?'

'No, father. I left the minister for trade to discuss the details with him.'

'Good. It is important that we project a powerful image to these people if we are to maintain the peace.'

'There will be a magnificent banquet tonight in his honour. I have spoken to the head of the domestic staff. It is all in order. And tomorrow he will be given a tour of our stud farm. He has expressed a particular interest in seeing your horses.'

'Excellent. But what about entertainment? I hope you have laid on some entertainment for him.'

'Ibn-Ziryab himself will sing for us tonight. The ambassador cannot fail to be impressed by the grandson of the legendary "Blackbird".'

'Indeed. Some say that his talent has far exceeded that of his father and even his grandfather. There is no-one that can play the lute as sweetly as he can.'

Al-Rahman stood up and stretched.

'I am weary, my son. Come and join me in the baths; we can continue our conversation there.'

***

The water relaxed his muscles and made him drowsy. He looked across at his son. How fortunate he was to have such a man to succeed him. It was every great ruler's fear that he would not be followed by someone worthy of him. And when you were dead there was nothing you could do about it if some half-brained idiot undid all your hard work. He was confident that this would not happen with al-Hakim.

'What is it father? You looked worried?' al-Hakim asked.

'I am thinking about the future. I am worried that this beautiful city of ours will never be finished. Last year I spent my whole budget on it and still we have barely begun.'

'It is a big project and one that I will continue for you. Rest assured, my love for this city is as great as yours.'

'It will be a great shining jewel in the heart of al-Andalus,' al-Rahman said. 'People will talk of it for centuries to come.'

It pleased him to think that he was leaving something so precious for posterity.

'Father, I was talking to some of your ministers earlier. They think we have too many dhimmi here. They say that they should all be forced to convert to Islam.'

'That is not our way, my son. There is nothing in the Quran that would support such action. The dhimmi are people of the Book, as are we; they believe in the one God, as we do; they are descendants of Ibrahim, as we are. As long as they do not try to subvert true Muslims to Jewry or Christianity they are entitled to worship their own faith.'

'They say that there are far too many of them. They outnumber the Muslims greatly.'

'Hakim, you have to understand, as you said yourself, we are vastly outnumbered by the Christians. What use would it be to fight them and I'm sure it would come down to that if we tried to force them to convert to Islam. No, it's much better to have them on our side. They don't have a bad life; no dhimmi is a slave. They are free to worship in their own way and they can still hold important jobs. A lot of our tax collectors and secretaries are Christian dhimmis and many of them have already adopted Arab names and customs. Give them time and I'm sure they will eventually convert to Islam, if not to gain greater social mobility then to avoid paying the poll tax.'

'But conversion would give them many benefits: they could rise to prominent positions in the government,' al-Hakim said.

'Yes, that's true, like the Grand Vizier. He was a dhimmi once, an educated Christian. Now he is one of the most powerful men in my kingdom. But nobody forced him to convert; it was his own choice.'

'I never understood why you would promote an ex-Christian to such heights?'

Al-Rahman smiled and tugged at his beard.

'He is a talented man; that is good enough for me. We have need of talented men. Where would I be without our Jewish friend, Hasdai ibn Shaprut? His clever diplomacy has got us out of many a tricky situation over the years. No, leave the dhimmis in peace. Think of the poll tax. They would no longer be required to pay the poll tax if they were Muslims and we need that money to build my city.'

His son stood up, the water running off his oiled body.

'I must go. I will see you later, father,' al-Hakim said, climbing out of the pool.

'At dinner?'

'Yes. Ma'a salama.'

'Alla ysalmak, my son.'

Al-Rahman lay back in the bath and closed his eyes. He had never asked, nor expected to become Sultan of al-Andalus. It had been as much a surprise to him as it was to his brothers and uncles. He knew people thought he must be happy to have so much wealth and power but the truth was that he could count his moments of happiness in days, not in years. One of those moments had been the day when Hakim was born. As soon as he saw him, squalling, wrinkled infant though he was, he knew he was the one

destined to carry on his life's work. So far he had not been
disappointed.

CHAPTER 16

At first Omar was speechless. Then he was angry. He stared at the broken pottery; so many hours of work wasted. What had come over the boy? It was so unlike al-Sagir to behave like that.

'What on earth is the matter with you?' he shouted.

'I'm sorry. Master. I'll pick them up.'

'Pick them up? What use is that? They're smashed to pieces. What good are they now? How can I take them to the Royal Buyer in a thousand pieces?'

'Perhaps we can mend them,' the boy suggested timidly.

'Don't talk rubbish, boy. And get out of the way; let me see if there are any that we can salvage.'

He pulled the boy away and carefully went through the wreckage, rescuing the plates that were still whole; there were about seven or eight that were undamaged. The rest were broken to smithereens.

'Here, sweep up this mess. I'll carry on to the alcázar on my own. And next time don't carry so many at once.'

The boy looked frightened. Something had obviously startled him but he would not tell Omar what it was. He just said that a man had pushed him and he'd lost his balance. Maybe he shouldn't have expected the boy to carry so many plates; after all, he was a bit puny. Well that was what came of buying cheaply. His father should have waited until the next caravan of slaves arrived instead of buying that sorry pair of undernourished specimens.

Omar planned to see the head buyer of the royal household. If he liked the plates, Omar could promise him two dozen more for the next day although he would have to work through most of the night to complete the order. That was, of course, unless al-Sagir decided to break any more.

When he arrived at the alcázar, the guard at the gate waved him through. There were a lot of traders there that morning, all hoping to tempt the Royal Buyer with their wares. It was a strictly controlled procedure and Omar found himself at the end of a long queue. There were local tradesmen and merchants from the East, all lined up in turn with their goods: woollen rugs, fine tapestries, silk sheets, cushions, silver goblets, cutlery, everything that the royal household might require. There were even some other potters waiting but Omar could see that they had brought quite inferior pottery with them, jugs and dishes covered with a simple green and white glaze that allowed the earthenware base to show through in unsightly patches. None of their wares had anything like the iridescent colours of his father's lustreware, nor did they have his meticulous and intricate designs. He examined the plates in his basket, carefully. There could be no flaws, no cracks, no crazing. The buyer would reject them otherwise. He smiled to himself. These were perfect. As good as anything the merchants brought from Baghdad.

'Omar, is that you?'

It was Yusuf. As usual he was covered in white stone dust.

'What are you doing here?'

Omar pointed to the plates.

'Business.   I'm hoping to sell these to the royal household.'

'They're beautiful,' Yusuf said.

He picked one up and held it towards the light.   The colours burned and glowed in the sunlight.

'Is this a new design?' he asked.

'Yes.   I've been working on it for some time now.   But I'm happy with the result.'

'I should think so.   It's magnificent.   It looks as though it's from the East.'

'That's what we were hoping to achieve.   I want to convince the Royal Buyer that he doesn't need to import expensive pottery from Baghdad and Damascus; we can make it here for him in Madinat al-Zahra.'

'I'm impressed.'

'So you think he'll buy them?'

'Without a doubt.'

Yusuf smiled at his friend and added, 'I'm glad to see you do something useful with your time instead of just chasing after girls, especially unattainable ones.'

'Have you found a way to help me yet?' Omar asked, lowering his voice.

'Actually, I have.   I shouldn't be doing this, you know.   It could cost me my job.'

Omar smiled; he knew his friend would not let him down.

'I know, I know, you said.'

'All right.   The thing is, I know one of the ex-maids from the harem.   Last year she was married off to a builder and now lives in the medina. Zilma's cousin has become friends with her. Anyway this woman still has contact with some of her old friends. She has agreed to take a message for you and give it to one of her friends in the harem, who will pass it to your slave girl if she gets the opportunity.'

'Yusuf, that's wonderful. No man had such a good friend as you.'

'Nor such a foolish one, either.'

'I'll never be able to repay you for this,' Omar said.

'Don't get too excited, Omar. There are no promises, remember. The girls will try to get your message to her but they can't guarantee it. It's dangerous for them all. If they were caught and it was found that they were smuggling in a love letter to one of the Khalifa's concubines it would be death for them and her. Consider the risk you are taking, not just for yourself but for others.'

Omar was not listening. He was too excited to consider the consequences.

'I'll bring you the letter tomorrow morning,' he said.

'No. That's too dangerous. I'll see you tonight at the tea shop, as usual. Bring it with you then.'

'Yusuf, I can't thank you enough.'

'It's this once only. I don't want to get involved after that. I'm getting married after Eid al-Adha. I don't want to end up as one of the sacrifices at the feast.'

'No, I promise I won't ask you for anything else. I just want the chance to speak to her.'

'All right. I'll see you tonight then. Give my regards to your father.'

'And Zilma? Is she still here?'

'No, they went back to Córdoba yesterday.'

'So everything is arranged?'

'I believe so. She seemed happy anyway.'

'See you tonight then, ma'a salama, dear friend.'

***

Omar was floating on air. He was one step closer to seeing the woman of his dreams, he told himself. What would happen next he had not decided. Omar liked to take things one at a time. He did not bother his head with long-term plans. That was why he was so dismissive of Muna and any idea of marrying her. Today was what mattered, not the future.

'Well, how did it go?' his father asked as soon as he pulled back the curtain and stepped into the alfarería.

'Great. He loved the plates and wants six dozen by the end of the week.'

'By the end of the week? Allah preserve and keep us. Can we do that? Do we have enough glaze? Do we have enough clay? How many plates are ready for painting? I don't think we can make so many by the end of the week. It's impossible. Why did you agree to such a thing?'

His father was panicking. He turned to the boy.

'Al-Sagir. Drop what you are doing and go straight down to the apothecary and buy me some oxides. Tell him they are for Qasim the alfarero. He will know what I need. And hurry; we have no time to lose. Then you must bring me up some more blocks of clay and prepare it for me.'

Omar put his hand on his father's shoulder.

'We have plenty of time, Baba. You know it's not good to rush the process. We want these to be perfect.'

'Yes, yes. You're quite right, my son. Quite right. But six dozen by the end of the week. I don't know if we can do that,' he said, shaking his head.

He picked up a cone of prepared clay and threw it on his wheel.

'Yes, you're right, my son; we mustn't panic. We have plenty of materials.'

He began to work the wheel with his foot as his hands guided the clay into the shape he wanted.

'How many plates have had their first firing?' he asked, his eyes never leaving his task.

'There are twenty-four in the kiln. I'll get al-Sagir to unload it when he gets back.'

'So he liked them, then?' his father asked, smiling to himself in pleasure.

'He thought they were as good as anything he had seen.'

'This could be the start of a big order, you know. If the Khalifa notices them and likes them he will order many more. We may need to employ someone else to help us.'

'Yes, Baba, but let us concentrate on this order first.'

Omar took a plate that was ready for decoration and began to draw the pattern on it. He was going to be busy but he had to find some time to write to Jawhara; he would not be able to sleep until he had seen her again. To see her, to speak to her, that was all he wanted; his longing for her was beyond reason he knew but he could do nothing to quench it.

CHAPTER 17

Sara had packed a small bag for herself and the children; her husband, Isa was not going with them to her parents' house. He had said from the outset that he wanted to spend Eid in Córdoba, in his own home. He said it was impossible to leave the bakery; people needed their bread. She knew it was because of her, his stupid little wife number two.

She had been furious when he said he was taking a second wife. They did not need another woman in the house; Sara was more than capable of looking after him and their children. They lived with his mother as it was and she ruled the household with a rod of iron; Sara had to tread very carefully with her mother-in-law. The old witch ran to Isa tittle-tattling about Sara at every opportunity. She was sure it was her mother-in-law who encouraged Isa to take another wife; she probably told him that Sara would never give him a son, that he should look elsewhere for his heirs. It was not fair. Sara was a good wife to Isa. It was hardly her fault that the four beautiful children she had borne him were all girls. And now he had brought that skinny little wife into their house; she was no more than a child herself. He said she was fifteen but she looked barely as old as Salma, their eldest daughter. It was unbearable; the girl could hardly look after herself, never mind a husband and a home. No, Sara knew what was going to happen. This chit of a girl would share her husband's bed but Sara would have to continue with all the work of looking after the children, preparing the food, running around after her mother-in-law, cleaning the house and helping in the bakery. She may have the title of first wife but she was nothing more than a skivvy.

That was when she decided; if that was how it was going to be then at least she would make a stand by spending Eid with her mother and father in Madinat al-Zahra. Isa could hardly object. He had another wife now to tend to his needs, she told him. Besides she would be gone no more than four days. Her brother, Ibrahim had agreed to travel with her and had sent his donkey round for them already. The two little ones would ride on the donkey and she and the older girls would walk; it would only take them a couple of hours to get there.

'Run and say goodbye to your father and grandmother,' she told her daughters. 'Then we'll be on our way.'

She parcelled up some of the sweetmeats she had prepared to take with her: almond pastries, biscuits made from cinnamon and honey, sugar snaps, crystallised ginger and lime slices.

'What will we cook for Eid if you are not here?' the new wife asked her.

'How should I know? Ask your mother-in-law. She'll show you what to do.'

She almost felt sorry for the girl. She had been wrenched from her family and given to a man three times her age. She was a docile creature who did not have a clue about how to run a house. Sara wondered what sort of home she had come from where she had not even learned the rudiments of housework. Sara's own daughters had been picking up skills ever since they could walk; they all knew how to sweep the floor and draw water from the pump. They could recognise which herbs to pick from the garden and the older two even helped her to prepare the meals. She did not like to ask them to do too much in the house because she wanted them to go to school and learn as much as possible but she knew that no matter how clever they were at school, at some point in their lives they would have to look after a husband and a family.

'She won't speak to me,' the poor girl wailed. 'I don't know what to do. She frightens me.'

For a brief moment she thought of inviting her to go with them to Madinat al-Zahra but instead she said, 'Then ask your mother. She will help you.'

The girl brightened at that suggestion.

'Girls, are you ready? We must leave now,' Sara called.

She had one last thing to do. She went into the bakery and took four loaves from the latest batch of bread; they were still warm. She added them to her basket of food and went outside. Her husband was standing by the donkey, holding its bridle; the two smallest girls sat astride it, giggling and fidgeting.

'Sit still,' he said 'or you'll fall off.'

He took the bags from Sara and put them in the panniers that hung either side of the animal.

'Where is your brother?' he asked Sara.

'That looks like him now. We'd better be off.'

'Give my respects to your parents,' he said.

'I will. Have a good Eid. We'll be back in four days.'

He kissed each of his daughters in turn and walked back into the house. He was not angry that she was going; he was just disinterested. That made her feel worse. Well let's see how he would manage without her. Maybe, after four days with that child-wife, he would be more interested when she returned.

*****

She was pleased to see the walls of the city ahead of her; her legs were aching and her back hurt. Ibrahim had brought one of his camels with him because he had a load of pots for their father, so the older girls had ridden part of the way on the camel but there was no space for her or Ibrahim.

'Thank goodness we're here,' she said. 'My feet are killing me.'

'You can ride on the camel on the way home,' her brother said, 'unless Baba has anything for me to take back to the city.'

'That would be wonderful.'

'So, sister, how are you getting on with the new wife?' he asked with a grin.

'What do you think? She's a useless creature.'

'I don't know why he wanted another wife. Surely one is bad enough.'

He grinned at her. Ibrahim was still single and happy to be so.

'I don't know. Maybe he did it to spite me. Anyway isn't it time you got married?' she asked, giving him a sideways look.

'Don't you start. You know very well it will be the first thing that Mama will ask when she sees me.'

'Well you are twenty-six. I was sixteen when I married Isa.'

'Yes, but you're a woman. That's all you have to look forward in life, getting married and having children. It's different for men.'

'It's going to be different for my daughters too. They are going to do something other than run around after a husband all day, especially Salma; she's going to go to the university and become a calligrapher. I know she can do it; she's very clever and her handwriting is excellent.'

Ibrahim smiled and nodded in agreement.

'She's certainly very bright but I doubt that Isa will allow her to go to the university? He will want to marry her off as soon as he can.'

'Please don't say that, brother. I pray every day that he will give her the opportunity. It would be such a shame if she doesn't do something with her talent.'

'Then maybe you should try to avoid upsetting him. If he gets annoyed with you, he might decide to take it out on the girls.'

'No, he would never do that. He has tired of me I know but he's not a vindictive man and he loves his daughters. It's just that he doesn't really believe in women working outside the home. You're right; it's my biggest worry that he'll set up a marriage contract for her before she has finished studying.'

'Mama, Mama, there's Seedo,' the littlest girl cried out in delight, as she spotted her grandfather standing outside his house.

She held out her arms to be lifted down from the donkey.

'All right, off you go then,' Sara said as she swung her to the ground.

The child ran straight to her grandfather and jumped into his arms.

'As-salam alaykum, Baba,' Sara said. 'How are you?'

'I'm well daughter. It is good to see you.'

He kissed her on both cheeks and smiled. Then he helped his other granddaughters dismount while Ibrahim led the animals to the house and tied them up. The girls were so excited to see him; they grabbed him by the hands and tried to drag him towards the house.

'Just a minute girls; let me say hello to your uncle and then we'll go and look for Teta.'

'As-salam alaykum, Baba,' Ibrahim said, coming back to kiss his father.

'Wa alaykum e-salam, my son. Have you had a good journey?' Qasim replied.

'Uneventful.'

'Good. Come inside. We have been waiting for you.'

'Where is Mama?' Sara asked.

'She's on the roof, putting the washing out to dry. Go up; she has been so looking forward to seeing you.'

This was the first opportunity Sara had had to visit her parents since they had left Córdoba. She climbed the half-finished staircase until she reached the flat roof. Her mother had finished pegging out her washing and was sitting in the sunshine, looking out across the city.

'Sara,' she cried when she saw her. 'How lovely to see you, my daughter. Come and sit beside me for a moment.'

'Are you well, Mama?'

'Very. And you and the children?'

'We're all fine. And look, here they are. You can judge for yourself.'

Her four daughters burst out onto the rooftop, giggling and chattering, glad to have arrived at their grandmother's house at last.

'Teta, we're here,' they chorused.

'So I see. Come, give your Teta a hug.'

Sara looked about her. Her mother had turned part of the rooftop into a garden and planted herbs, peppers and aubergines in wide earthenware pots; this was where she sat on days like today enjoying the weak sunshine and watching the comings and goings in the streets below. Across the street Sara could see other rooftop gardens and wet clothes flapping lazily in the breeze.

'What a lovely house, Mama,' she said as soon as her mother had finished fussing around her grandchildren. 'You have so much space.'

'Come and look downstairs. I'll show you where you and the girls will be sleeping.'

Their room was light and airy and, like all Moorish houses, opened onto an internal patio; the walls had been painted with a lime wash and it was sparsely furnished with a painted wooden chest to store their clothes, a multi-coloured rug on the floor and five sleeping mats. Ibrahim had dumped their belongings in the corner. She wandered about happily inspecting everything with a keen eye.

'Are these new?' she asked, picking up an embroidered cushion.

Her mother beamed.

'Yes. Aren't they lovely; I picked them up in the market. Qasim keeps telling me how well his business is doing so I thought I'd spend some money on the house.'

'And he doesn't mind?' she asked, thinking how Isa made her account for everything that she spent.

'No. Your father is a very generous man. He has bought us two slaves to help finish the house.'

'It's coming on well,' Ibrahim said, putting his head around the door. 'You've done a lot since I was here last.'

'Yes, it's made such a difference having the slaves to help. I have to admit I thought your father had made a mistake when he bought them but they are both good workers.'

'How long since you got them?'

'About four months. They've done a lot in that time,' she added.

'Is that the goat for the feast?' Sara asked, looking at the animal tied up in the corner of the patio.

'It is, poor thing. I'm sure it knows what's going to happen to it because it never stops bleating.'

'Oh, don't tell the girls that. We'll have nothing but tears from Tara if she finds out.'

'Well she'll find out sooner or later,' her brother said.

Her father came in, a wide smile on his face.

'Well son, I see you have brought me some pots,' Qasim said. 'Excellent. Omar and I have been so busy with making lustreware that I haven't had time to make any simple earthenware. Here I'll help you unload then you can see to the animals.'

'Where shall I stable them?'

'Leave them outside for now. You can bring them into the patio tonight, with the goat.'

'Good. I don't want them stolen.'

'No, Seedo, we don't want to have to walk all the way home,' said Tara, bouncing into the room and hurling herself at him.

'Well we can't have that, little princess, can we.'

'Come here, Tara. Let your grandfather get on with his work,' Sara said to her daughter.

She pulled her towards her and sat down by the fountain in the corner of the patio; the water gushed through a copper spout and ran into a tiny pool, splashing and sparkling in a shaft of spring sunlight. Tara knelt by the pool and let her fingers trail through the water.

'It's lovely, isn't it,' Fatima said, sitting down beside her. 'I asked al-Mari to build it for me. To think I was cross with your father when he brought him home. I thought he was too old and weak to be of any use but I was wrong; he is a good worker.'

'It must be nice to sit here in the summer,' Sara said.

'It is. The sound of running water is so refreshing and at night, when I lie in bed, I can listen to it and it's like music lulling me to sleep.'

She picked up a round white pebble from the bottom of the pool.

'I found these one day when I was walking in the countryside. I thought they'd be perfect for the pool.'

'They're like big pearls,' Tara said. 'All shiny.'

Sara looked up; Salma and Layla were standing in the doorway, holding hands.

'Mama, why can't Salma sleep with me?' Layla asked.

'Yes, Teta, let me sleep in Layla's room, please,' Salma pleaded with her grandmother.

'We'll be very good,' she added.

'Very well, if that's what you want,' Fatima said with a smile. 'But if I hear any noise in the night, you'll both be in trouble.'

Sara looked at her mother's face; she was so happy to have her grandchildren here. They had all missed her since she and Baba had moved to Madinat al-Zahra. Sara vowed that she would make more of an effort to come and visit her parents in future. After all, now that Isa had his new wife to distract him she should be able to get away at least every few months. The children would like that.

CHAPTER 18

It was good to have all her family here, under the same roof; Fatima had missed Sara and the children, so much. When they lived in Córdoba Fatima had seen her eldest daughter every day; the alfarería was in the next street, just two minutes walk from the bakery. Each morning she would take the bread to be baked and spend half an hour, chatting and drinking tea with Sara before going to the bazaar to do her shopping. Sometimes Sara would bring the bread round to her once it was ready and stay for a while and tell her about her day. Layla missed them too. She was the same age as Salma and the two girls had grown up together; they were like sisters. It had been hard to separate them like that. Qasim had said Madinat al-Zahra was only a couple of hours away; he promised they would be able to see the grandchildren whenever they wanted. But it hadn't turned out like that. Neither family had the time to visit the other. Now she hardly ever saw them.

It was because of Sara and the grandchildren that she had been reluctant to move to Madinat al-Zahra but Qasim had convinced her that it was an opportunity not to be missed. He was right, of course. They had a lovely home here in the medina and a thriving business. Besides which they had been able to leave their old house and workshop to Ibrahim. From that point of view it had worked out well; all her sons had a trade. They would be able to marry and support a family when they were ready. She sighed. Not one of her boys had taken a wife yet. Qasim had done his best to find wives for them but so far there had been no weddings. Soon he would lose patience and insist that they marry. Surely they understood how important it was to continue the family line. If it wasn't for Sara they would have no grandchildren and even Sara had only managed to produce girls; there were no boys to take their name forward. She could not understand why her sons hesitated; after all marriage was part of the natural order of things.

Sara and the children had gone off this morning to explore the bazaar and Ibrahim was with his father. At last she had the house to herself. She picked up the bed rolls and stacked them in the corner then she took the broom and swept through the house and out onto the patio. That done, she filled the bucket from the outside pump and watered her plants. She loved her little garden. Qasim had promised her that they would have a proper garden one day but in the meantime she had to make do with a few terracotta pots. Next she took down the oil lamps, cleaned the wicks and refilled them with oil. Her rudimentary housework finished for now, she braided up her hair, placed her favourite green cap on her head and wrapped herself in a thick wool robe.

Qasim liked her to wear a veil when she went out, like she used to do in Ardales but she felt conspicuous in it. None of the other women took the trouble to cover their faces. Sometimes, just to please her husband, she draped a headscarf over her head and held it in place with her cap but she rarely pulled it across her face. Today she would not bother. She was only going to get some extra things for the meal that evening; she would be home long before Qasim returned.

As she stepped outside, the north wind whipped up the dust from the road and made her gasp. She headed for the bazaar; today she needed to buy some more rice and extra saffron for the goat meat then she would return and sit in the shelter of her peaceful patio, away from the biting wind.

She had been all week preparing for Eid al-Adha, the Feast of the Sacrifices. Tomorrow was the first day of the festivities. They would all have to rise early, before sunrise, clean their teeth, wash and put on clean clothes. She had bought some fresh perfume for everyone to use. Then they would eat a small breakfast of sweet dates and recite the Takbir. She went through the words in her head:

Allah is the Greatest, Allah is the Greatest, Allah is the Greatest,

There is no deity but Allah

Allah is the Greatest, Allah is the Greatest

and to Allah goes all praise

Allah is the Greatest, all Praise is due to Him, And Glory to Allah, eventide and in the morning

There is no god, but Allah...

The lines were second nature to her now; she had recited them so many times. Then they would go to the mosque to pray and listen to the sermon. After that came the part that the children liked best, when everyone hugged one another and exchanged presents. She already had the presents chosen for the girls: coral bracelets that she found in the bazaar the other day. For the men in her family she had bought new caps.

After that they would probably visit their neighbours and wish them a happy Eid. Then they would return home and Qasim and Ibrahim would take the goat out and sacrifice it while she and Sara got the rest of the food ready for the feast.

The festivities and prayers lasted for four days and during that time they were obliged to distribute a third of the goat to the poor. That was usually Omar and Qasim's job. The rest of the animal would be shared between their family and any other relatives. She was excited. It was the second most important festival in their religious calendar and she loved the celebrations. Even her oldest son, al-Jundi was joining them tonight although he said that he could not have the full four days off; he had to return to duty.

As she was buying the saffron, she saw Sara approach, with Salma and Layla hand in hand and the other girls skipping along behind. She waved and called across to them.

'Over here.'

The children rushed over and hugged her.

'Are you having a lovely time, girls?' she asked, hugging them each in turn.

'Yes, Teta,' they chorused.

'Where's Omar? I haven't seen him since I arrived,' Sara said.

'He's in the alfarería. He has been working since dawn,' Fatima said. 'There is an important order that must be finished today before sunset.'

'I'll go and say hello,' said Sara.

'I'll join you; I'd like to see what's been keeping him so busy lately.'

She was interested to see what these special plates were like. Her husband had spoken of nothing else all week.

***

Omar was bent over his bench, intent on his work. He was rubbing at the surface of the plate with a soft cloth. As he rubbed she could see the warm colours reveal themselves.

'Hello little brother,' Sara said.

'Sara. How good to see you.'

Brother and sister embraced.

'Have you come alone?' he asked.

'The children are with me. They're playing with Layla.'

'And your husband?'

Fatima saw her daughter screw up her face as she said, 'He decided to stay at home with his new bride.'

'I see.'

'Your brother Ibrahim is here, though,' added Fatima. 'Why not come and say hello.'

'I don't have time. This is the last one then I have to take them to the alcázar.'

'They're exquisite,' Fatima said. 'No wonder your father is so proud of your work.'

'It's not just my work, Mama. It's his too.'

Even as he protested she could see that her son was pleased with the praise. He gave the plate a final polish and stacked it with the others.

'Al-Sagir,' he called. 'I need you to come with me.'

'That's one of our new slaves,' Fatima explained to Sara. 'He was a weedy little thing when we got him but he's fattened out now and he's a good worker.'

She patted the boy's head as he went past.

'Load these into the basket and be very careful with them. Place one of these vine leaves between each plate so that they don't get scratched,' Omar told the slave. 'And don't drop them.'

'Who's the other slave?' Sara asked. 'The old one? Is he al-Sagir's father?'

'No. To be honest we don't know very much about him except that he's from the north. He works hard but he hardly ever speaks. Not even to your father.'

'He doesn't look as though he's from the north. There are lots of northern slaves in Córdoba, all with fair hair and eyes, like the boy. The old man looks more like us.'

'Yes, now you come to mention it, he does. I wonder what he did to become a slave.'

'Ask him.'

'No, I couldn't do that. Maybe your father will ask him one day. Anyway what does it matter. He doesn't cause any trouble and you've seen what a wonderful job he is doing with building the new rooms.'

She turned to Omar.

'Try not to be late for supper tonight. It would be nice for us all to eat together. It's a long time since you've seen your brother and sister.'

'I'll do what I can. Mama.'

As she walked back into her house she passed al-Mari; he was carrying some tiles for the new bedroom. It was true what Sara had said. He looked just like one of them, not a foreigner at all. So why was he a slave? Had he committed some crime and been condemned to slavery? Had he been captured in battle? If that was the case maybe he was one of the rebels. The Khalifa had executed many of the rebels but there were those that had been made slaves; some of them he had put into his own army while others had been sold. She shivered with fear. That could so easily have been their fate if they had been caught fleeing from Ardales.

***

There was nothing more to do until the next day, the first day of Eid. At last she had some time to herself.

'Sara, I'm going to the hamman. Will you come with me?'

Today was one of the two days in the week that women were allowed to use the hamman; the other five days were reserved for the men.

'Of course Mama. What about the girls?'

'Bring them along too. Layla is coming.'

It was a short walk to the bath house which had been built close to the bazaar. Layla and her nieces raced ahead and were sitting on the steps at the entrance by the time Fatima and Sara arrived.

The bath house keeper opened the door for them and they stepped inside.

'Thank you,' Fatima said, handing the woman attendant a couple of small coins and walking down the steps into the cold room.

There they removed their clothes, wound towels around their bodies and put on some wooden sandals.

'Do you want a massage?' the attendant asked.

'Not now, maybe afterwards but I would like to see the hairdresser if she is free.'

'I'll let her know.'

Fatima and Sara followed the children straight into the warm room where they were already pouring water over each other and soaping each other's hair. The hamman was more crowded than usual; everyone had the same idea, to beautify and cleanse themselves before Eid began. She recognised her friend Elvira, happily gossiping with some women and waved across at her.

'It's amazing how children can make a game out of everything,' Fatima said, laughing at the girls as they splashed about in the shallow pool.

'Mama, I've got soap in my eyes,' the smallest of them began to cry.

'Come here, sweetheart, I'll wash it out for you.'

Sara lifted up her daughter and carefully wiped her eyes.

'There, all better now,' she said, kissing the wet face.

Once they had all washed themselves thoroughly, they moved through to the last and hottest room. This was the part that Fatima enjoyed most. The water was deep enough to lie back and soak. It was wonderful for her aches and pains; for a short time they eased, drawn out of her body by the hot, scented water. She leaned back and looked at the steam rising from the pool, floating up to the vaulted arches above them and leaking out through the narrow vents. The flickering oil lamps that stood in the corners of the bath house cast their reflections on the surface of the water, glinting and gleaming like water nymphs. She closed her eyes, remembering when she was young. Qasim used to like to recite poetry. The words of one of his favourites returned to her:

'The river of diaphanous waters
murmuring between its banks

would have you believe
it is a stream of pearls.'

There was more but the rest eluded her. She turned to her daughter.

'Are you still writing your poetry?' she asked.

'No. I never have the time these days. I am always busy running the house and looking after the children.'

'What about when they're in bed? Why don't you write some then?'

Sara had started writing simple poems when she was only a small child; she had a natural gift with words.

'I wish that I could but Isa doesn't approve. He says it's ridiculous for a woman to think that she can write poetry. According to him, only men can do things like that.'

'Don't tell him.'

Her daughter looked at her and her eyes filled with tears.

'What is it, Sara? What's the matter?'

'It's Isa. He never has time for us anymore. I have disappointed him as a wife.'

'How can you say that? You have been a good and faithful wife all these years and you've given him four beautiful daughters.'

'But no son. He desperately wants a son. That's why he has taken a new wife. Now I am supposed to train her, show her how to keep house and tell her how he likes his food. What happens next? Once she gives him a son he will divorce me.'

'Of course he won't. Isa is just like lots of men; he feels it is a slight on his manhood if he has no sons. If this new woman produces an heir, he will be happy again and then he will be kinder to all of you. There is no point railing against him; that won't change anything.'

'But I can't stand her, Mama. She's taken my place. I still have all the work to do in the house but she is the one who shares his bed.'

'I'm sorry, my daughter, but that is the fate of lots of women. Try to think of the positive side; there is an extra pair of hands to share the work. See that woman over there with the henna on her hair? She's my friend, Elvira. Her husband has just taken a second wife and she is perfectly happy about it.'

'But she's old. That's different, Mama.'

'Is it? She's still his wife.'

'But Isa's new wife is a child, not much older than Silma. She is useless. Even Layla has more idea of running a home than she has. How can he do that to me?'

Fatima was not slow to pick up her daughter's jibe against Layla. She knew it was true; neither she nor Qasim expected Layla to do much in the house. They spoiled her. Both wanted more for their youngest child than an early marriage.

'Try to see it from his new wife's point of view. I doubt if it was her choice to marry Isa. Now she is in a strange household, with a wife who resents her and an unpleasant mother-in-law,' she said.

Fatima had met Isa's mother and knew what a sharp tongue she possessed. Isa was her only surviving son and, from the moment he married Sara, she had resented her daughter-in-law. She could not imagine she would feel otherwise about his new wife. She felt sorry for both of the

171

women, having to tread carefully around their mother-in-law.

Sara did not reply; instead she ducked her head under the water and washed away all traces of her tears.

'Did you want me to cut your hair today?' a young woman asked, bending down by the side of the pool and addressing Fatima.

'Yes please. Not too much, mind. Wait a moment and I'll get out.'

Fatima pulled herself out of the hot water, wrapped a towel around her waist and sat on a bench so that the hairdresser could see what she was doing.

'What about you, Sara?'

'No. I'm fine. I'll wait until I get home.'

Fatima watched the locks of grey hair fall about her, casualties of the woman's scissors. Once she had hair the colour of a raven's wing but the passage of time had changed all that. As Sara said, she was old.

'Mama, can I have my hair cut too?' Layla asked, climbing out of the pool and standing before her, the water running off her boyish body.

It wouldn't be long before she was a woman. Already her breasts were starting to swell and her hips were becoming more rounded. Fatima hated the thought that the last of her children would soon be grown up.

'Of course.'

She looked at the hairdresser, who smiled and nodded at the child.

'Yes. I will cut your hair next,' she said, combing Fatima's hair into place.

Sara was lying in the pool, her eyes closed and a look of sadness on her face; her curly dark hair floated about her, like the tendrils of a sunflower. Poor child, what could she do to help her? There was nowhere for a woman to go if she left her husband's home. She would have to stay and make the most of it.

'Where does all this water come from, Mama?' Sara asked, suddenly sitting up. 'Is there an underground stream or a well?'

'There are wells but the medina gets most of its water from the Bejarano River; it flows down from the mountains and into the old Roman aqueduct.'

'So how does it get here?'

'It runs through underground pipes. It takes the water first to the Royal residence and then down to us.'

'You have everything here,' Sara said, admiringly. 'It's as good as living in Córdoba.'

'Naturally. The Khalifa is here. Everything has to be as he would want it and we benefit from that too.'

Maybe Qasim had been right to bring them to Madinat al-Zahra. She was lucky; she had a good husband.

CHAPTER 19

Isolde looked up from her writing practice; her maid was standing before her, her eyes like saucers.

'What is it?' she asked. 'Has something happened?'

'Excuse me Jawhara, this is for you,' the maid whispered. 'Burn it when you've read it and don't let al-Tayyib see it.'

Her hand trembled as she handed Isolde the note then she scurried away. It was from Omar. Isolde knew it was from him before she even opened it. She clutched it to her breast in excitement; this was it. He was going to rescue her.

She looked around her; there was no-one watching. Her maid had chosen the moment well; all the others were busy, walking in the gardens or lounging in the bath house, chatting. Isolde was alone. She opened the message and looked at it. It was written in Arabic. She puzzled over it for a minute or two then decided that she would have to ask Najm for help. She slipped the note into her pocket and went to sit beside her friend. Under the pretext of showing her a page from her school book she laid the message in front of her.

'I'm having trouble translating this, Najm. Please can you help me,' she said with an innocent smile.

'Of course.'

Najm picked up the book and studied the piece of parchment that lay inside it.

'What's this? Where did you get this note?'

She rolled the book shut and looked about her. No-one was paying any attention to the two slave girls sitting by the pool.

'Just tell me what it says, please,' Isolde begged.

'I've told you this is a dangerous game you're playing.'

'Please.'

Najm sighed and took out the letter and read:

'My jewel of the night. I long to meet you. Let me come to you one night and we can walk in the garden beneath the moon and talk. Only send me a message saying that you will allow me to speak to you and I will be transported to heaven with happiness. Your humble servant, Omar.'

'What a silly young man. He's even signed his name. Doesn't he realise what you are?' Najm snorted.

'He sounds romantic.'

'Romantic drivel. The best thing you can do is burn that message and forget all about him.'

She folded the message and handed it back to Isolde.

'But it can't hurt just to talk to him. He might be able to help me speak to Hans.'

'You are playing with fire, Jawhara. How many times do I have to tell you that?'

Najm was cross with her now. Isolde knew she was right. It was dangerous to arrange to meet Omar; it was dangerous to even talk about it. She could be thrown out of the harem; she could even be executed. But she had no other choice. Who else could she ask to help her to speak to her brother? Didn't Najm understand? Besides which she wanted to see this young potter again; she couldn't get his smile out of her mind. Every time she thought of him she felt warm inside.

'You'll get badly burned if you carry on like this. I told you that you cannot keep secrets in the harem. It is only a matter of time before the Royal wife finds out and then nobody will be able to help you,' her friend said. 'Please believe me, Jawhara. I'm only trying to protect you.'

'What shall I do?' Isolde asked her.

'Just concentrate on your studies and forget about your brother and that pathetic potter,' was her reply.

She got up and went inside leaving Isolde sitting by the pool holding the folded message in her hand. But Isolde couldn't forget either of them, neither the potter nor her little brother. It was impossible. She would have to be careful but she would arrange to see him. They would meet in the garden during the Feast of Eid when everyone was enjoying themselves; nobody would notice that she was missing. If anyone asked where she had been she would say she had stepped outside for some air. All she needed was a few minutes, just enough time to tell him about Hans. She was sure he would help her. She had seen it in his eyes.

She waited until she was sure that no-one was about then she took a piece of parchment from her writing materials, wrote him a simple message and handed it to her maid. The poor child looked as though she would drop dead with fright.

'I cannot take this, Jawhara. What if I am caught?' she protested.

'Then don't get caught. Be careful.'

The maid seemed on the point of tears.

'It's just this once, I promise you. Nobody will ever know,' Isolde coaxed.

'Very well.'

The maid took the note and slipped it into the pocket of her robe.

It was done. Isolde would see Omar very soon. She picked up the hand mirror and looked at her reflection. Her heart was beating rapidly and there was a flush to her cheeks. She breathed deeply; it was important to remain calm. No-one must suspect what she was about to do. She took Omar's note from her pocket and dropped it into the flame of the lamp; it spluttered a little then flared and burned. It was gone, no more than a tiny pile of ash.

***

The Chief Eunuch came into the harem. As usual his entrance caused the girls to become flustered; everyone felt that they should be doing something but nobody was quite sure what. The maids flapped around the concubines, re-combing hair that had already been combed, straightening couches and plumping-up cushions. Isolde found herself propelled back to the bath house by her maid.

Isolde began to take off her dress, ready to bathe.

'Where is Jahwara?' Yamut asked. 'Bring her to me immediately and bring me her maid.'

'Jawhara, you must come now,' Najm said.

Her friend looked worried. Was it possible that Najm was right; someone had already told the Royal wife about the potter? She felt her knees trembling. She wrapped her robe around her again, put her silk slippers back on her feet and went back into the main room.

'There you are child. Come here.'

Yamut was sitting on the couch, tapping his cane on the ground; he looked anxious but not particularly angry. She felt her fear subside slightly.

'Jawhara, the Khalifa has shown a strong interest in you; he does not want to wait any longer. You are to dance for him on the last day of Eid al-Adha,' he announced.

She was stunned. So soon. Everyone had said that it would probably be at least a year before he sent for her, if he ever did. Now she was being told that she had four days to prepare herself.

'We have a lot of work to do,' he said to the assembled group.

Everyone looked shocked. This was unusual. The Khalifa had so many women to choose from that there were always virgins ready for when he called. This was different; he was calling for a girl who had been with them barely six months. She was still a pupil, not a graduate of the school. What could she know? No wonder Yamut looked worried. Would she be able to please the Khalifa? What would happen if he were disappointed? They all knew that this was a great opportunity for her; even she realised it. She had been more than noticed; she had been requested, her, an unknown slave girl.

Yamut turned to Isolde.

'I have spoken to your teachers and they tell me that you have a sweet voice. That is good. The Khalifa likes to listen to music. He also likes to watch his concubines dance so I want you to spend as much time as you can practising both dancing and singing during the next four days,' he instructed her. 'Najm will help you.'

He looked directly at Najm.

'Make sure she is ready.'

Isolde thought she could hear a threat in his words. Poor Najm had turned pale.

The Chief Eunuch stood up and left. As soon as the door closed behind him there was a buzz of excitement in the room. The other women liked it when someone from their part of the harem was chosen. It made them all feel special. Najm and Isolde looked at each other.

'You realise what this could mean?' Najm said. 'You could become one of his favourites. Then you would have your own apartment and garden. If he likes you he will shower you with jewels and expensive gifts.'

'He will give you a generous allowance so that you can buy as many clothes as you want,' said one of the concubines.

'Until he tires of you,' said one of the others.

'Yes, but he never takes anything away. You would still live in the apartment and keep the jewels even if he never visits you again.'

'If you become pregnant, it will be even better,' said another concubine.

'And if it's a boy, better still.'

Isolde felt dizzy. This was all going too fast. The women were excited on her behalf but all she could feel was nausea. The Khalifa was an old man. They said his breath smelled.

'Now you must give up all thought of trying to see your brother,' Najm whispered. 'At least for now. It's even more dangerous than before; Yamut will be watching your every move, and mine.'

***

The news of Yamut's message had spread throughout the harem; everyone was talking about it. The teacher from the school had come in person to coach Isolde with her singing and dancing; he did not want to leave it to Najm.

'I thought we would not have to study today as it's the feast of Eid al-Adha,' Isolde said, petulantly.

'That's normally the case, but they're all panicking that you will fail to please the Khalifa,' Najm told her. 'Everyone shares the responsibility for your success. If your dancing is not up to scratch then the school will suffer. If your face and body are not perfect then your maids will be in trouble. Yamut will lose face because he was the one who bought you in the first place and if that happens then he will make sure that we all suffer.'

'Even you?'

'Especially me. So go along and do what your teacher tells you.'

'But we will go to the feast tonight, won't we?'

'Yes, everyone will be there. Why are you so bothered?'

Isolde shrugged and went to join her teacher. She enjoyed the dancing even though it was very different from the dances that they had in her village. This was much more erotic and she danced alone, not with a partner. She wondered what her father would say if he could see her swaying to and fro, moving her head and arms in such a suggestive manner and gyrating her hips. He would be horrified. The teacher liked her to dance barefoot. Her maid tied anklets of silver discs and balls around her ankles and put silver rings on her toes; as she moved they produced a sweet tinkling sound. She wore a filmy gown of blue and gold that was so fine it could pass through one of the rings that glittered on her fingers. Her hair was brushed loose and covered with a long, flimsy veil that she twisted and twirled as she danced.

'Jawhara, the Royal wife has sent for you,' al-Tayyub said.

Isolde stopped dancing and looked at him in surprise.

'For me? Why does she want to see me?' she asked.

'How would I know. Just get along to her rooms as quickly as you can. She does not like to be kept waiting.'

Isolde was scared. She had heard so much about this woman, the Khalifa's wife, but she had never seen her.

'Don't worry, she always like to inspect the Khalifa's concubines. She likes to keep an eye on the competition,' Najm said. 'I'll show you the way.'

Isolde threw a robe over her dance clothes and followed Najm along the corridors and into the sumptuous apartments of the Royal wife. Najm waited by the door and told Isolde to go in. Isolde could feel her stomach churning with nervousness. What if the Royal wife disapproved of her? She approached nervously.

The Royal wife was sitting on a low couch, surrounded by her handmaids. She was old, much older than Isolde had imagined but she was still beautiful. She wore a dress of scarlet, its hem covered in fine embroidery and sewn with tiny pearls; around her shoulders was a chiffon shawl and from her neck hung strings of pearls and chains of gold while her hands glittered with the many rings that she wore.

'As-salam alaykum, your Highness,' she said.

'Wa alaykum e-salam, child. You are Jawhara?'

'Yes, your Highness.

'Come closer so that I can look at you.'

Isolde trembled as she approached her.

'Are you nervous girl? Why are you shaking?'

The Royal wife threw back her head and laughed.

'I won't eat you. I just wanted to see what type of girl my husband has cast his eye on now. Take off your robe.'

Isolde did as she was told and stood there, blushing with embarrassment as the Royal Wife stared at her. When she had seen enough, she smiled and then nodded.

'Yes, you are indeed a beauty. I'm glad to see he has not lost his taste in beautiful women. There was a rumour that he was developing an appetite for young boys.'

She laughed again.

'Lies of course. Young boys. Why would he want young boys when he has hundreds of beautiful women to choose from, I ask you?'

Isolde did not know what to say; she stared at the ground in front of her.

'Here girl, take this. It is a present from the Khalifa. Wear it when he sends for you.'

She handed Isolde a silk veil, embroidered with dedications to the Khalifa and sprinkled with images of birds, flowers and lions. As she looked at it shimmering in her hands she thought that she had never held anything so beautiful. It weighed nothing; a puff of wind could carry it away.

'Thank you, your Highness.'

'Go now, child. Do not disappoint the Khalifa.'

Isolde picked up her robe, bowed to the Royal Wife and left; the woman had already forgotten her and was busy talking to her handmaids.

'What did she say?' Najm asked her as they made their way back to their own quarters.

'Not much. I think she was just curious to see what I looked like. She gave me this.'

She handed Najm the veil.

'It's from the Khalifa.'

'It's gorgeous.'

Najm tossed the veil in the air, catching it as it fell and twirling it around.

'You'll look stunning in it.'

Isolde smiled. It was all moving a bit too fast for her. She found it hard to concentrate on the preparations for her night with the Khalifa when she was due to see Omar that evening. She had to persuade him to bring Hans to her as soon as possible; she had less than four days.

'What is the Khalifa like?' she asked Najm.

'They say he is a gentleman, a kind and tender lover.'

'But he's old, isn't he?'

She thought of the Royal Wife. She was as old as Isolde's mother had been, maybe even older. The thought of her mother made her want to weep. That was her old life. She knew it was not possible to turn the clock back but maybe, just maybe she could recapture some of her previous existence if she had Hans and Per with her again.

'I suppose he must be. He has been the Khalifa for eighteen years and before that he was Sultan for seventeen years. He cannot be very young. But they say he is still very virile.'

'He is probably older than my father,' Isolde said with a grimace.

'There's no point pulling that face. There are hundreds of women here who would swop places with you without a moment's hesitation. I don't understand you, Jawharra. You don't seem to realise how fortunate you are to have been chosen.'

Isolde could see that Najm was envious of her situation. She had been waiting to be noticed for years. As she had admitted once before, it was never going to happen for her now. No wonder she was annoyed with Isolde for complaining. Isolde took her friend's arm and said, 'You're right. I'm sorry for seeming so ungrateful. I'm just scared. I've never been with a man before. I've never even had a boyfriend.'

She started to cry.

'I don't want my first experience to be with a man older than my father,' she sobbed. 'A man I don't love.'

Najm put her arm around her.

'I know it's hard. But that's the way it is here. Love is not for us. We may be taught a hundred and one ways to make love to a man but we cannot fall in love, unless it is with the Khalifa. Even that is not a good idea because your heart will most certainly be broken. I keep telling you, you are no longer free to chose what you can or can't do. You cannot even decide who to love,' she said.

How could that be? Was she never to fall in love? She thought of Omar again and her tears flowed even faster. He was someone she could love; he was young and handsome.

'Come now, wipe your eyes. We have a lot to get through in four days.' Najm said, handing her a handkerchief. 'And I'll tell you something I've heard about the Khalifa, but don't repeat it.'

Isolde nodded glumly at her grinning friend.

'They say the Khalifa is very quick. It will all be over in a matter of minutes and then he will fall asleep. As you said, he is an old man. He doesn't have the stamina of young men.'

She laughed.

Isolde tried to smile but could not. Maybe she should be grateful that she had been chosen by the Khalifa but somehow she could not find it in her heart to accept that her life now belonged to someone else.

CHAPTER 20

The guard was getting used to Omar arriving at the alcázar with his pottery; he waved him through.

'More of those plates?' he asked.

'Yes, this is the last batch for now. Then I can get back to the festivities,' Omar replied.

'It's all right for you. I'm stuck on guard duty all over the holiday. Not even a couple of hours to slip off home and have something to eat,' he moaned.

'Maybe I'll bring you a plate of something, later,' Omar said.

The outline of a plan was forming in his head. He and al-Sagir made their way into the alcázar and were told to wait until the Royal Buyer could see them. The boy put his load on the ground and hunkered down beside it.

'Where are you from Sagir?' Omar asked.

Al-Sagir shrugged.

'I don't know. Our village was called Unterbaum but no-one lives there now. It was a long way away.'

He told Omar how the vikings had raided the village and captured him and his brother and sister; he told him how they had slain his mother, how the men had been away fishing, how they had burned his village to the ground and how they had been brought to al-Andalus and sold as slaves.

'I would like to go back there and find my father,' he said, beginning to snivel a little.

'I don't think that will be possible,' Omar said. 'For a start you don't have any idea where it was and secondly, you belong to my father now.'

'Will I always be a slave?' the boy asked, wiping his tears away with the back of his hand.

'Probably.'

'Is there no way I can get my freedom?'

'Why is it so important to you? Don't we look after you well?'

Omar is surprised at the boy's questions.

'Yes. Your mother is very kind to me and your father treats me well.'

'So why do you want to leave? Where would you go?'

'I don't know but I don't want to be a slave.'

'Maybe when you're older there could be ways of gaining your freedom. You could become a Muslim for instance. All Muslims are free men.'

'What does that mean?'

'It means that you have to believe in the one God and give up the worship of pagan gods.'

'Like the God of War?'

'Exactly.'

'And the God of the Sea, and of Love and of the Woods?'

'Exactly. Muslims don't believe in all those gods. They only have one god and his name is Allah.'

The boy looked worried.

'Maybe I'll just run away,' he said.

'Don't even think about it,' Omar warned. 'If you're caught you'll be beaten. Anyway why so many questions about becoming free?'

The boy looked around to make sure that nobody could hear him then he said, 'I've seen my sister. She's here in the alcázar. I have to help her get away. I can't do that if I'm a slave too.'

'The sister you said was captured with you and your brother?'

'Yes. I saw her in the bazaar the other day and she said she would try to speak to me. She told me to go to the bazaar again the next day and she would come to see me. But she didn't come. She was frightened, I know. I have to help her. Then, when we are both free, we'll go and look for my brother.'

'Well, my little chap, that all sounds very brave but I think it is quite hopeless. I think you and your sister just have to get used to life as slaves. Perhaps one day your sister will meet a Muslim man and marry him then she will be free.'

'I don't think my sister wants to get married.'

'Is she pretty?'

The boy nodded.

'Yes, sort of. She has big ...'

He grinned cheekily and held his hands out in front of him to indicate the size of her breasts.

'Well I'm sure one day she'll meet some man who will want to marry her. Now I want you to stay here with the plates while I go somewhere. I won't be long. Make sure nothing happens to my pottery or all this talk of freedom will be in vain because I will personally kill you.'

The boy looked shocked at this. Omar could see him struggling with the idea that his master's son would be violent towards him. He obviously decided that it was an empty threat because he smiled and said, 'All right, boss.'

That boy was becoming cheekier and cheekier.

***

Yusuf was in his usual place. The panel he had been working on was complete now and he was carving a new one.

'As-salam alaykum, Yusuf.'

'Wa alaykum e-salam.'

Yusuf turned and scowled when he saw it was Omar.

'I told you not to keep coming here. What do you want now?'

'I had to come anyway, to bring the final part of the order for the royal household. I just thought I'd find out if you had a reply for me.'

'As a matter of fact, I have.'

He put down his chisel and searched for a moment in his bag.

'Here it is,' he said, handing a single scrap of parchment to Omar. 'I was going to bring it to the tea shop tonight.'

'What does it say? Will she see me?'

'I don't know and I don't want to know. I haven't read it. The less I know about your harebrained schemes the better.'

'Yusuf, you are a good friend. You are better than a brother to me.'

He hugged his friend close to him.

'I won't forget this.'

'Yes, yes, I know all that. Now go away and let me get on with my work. I'm sorry I can't stop and talk to you. We have a group of artists from Byzantium arriving next week. They are going to train us how to carve the marble capitals for the pillars and how to make the marble window screens. I'm going to be very busy after Eid and I must get this panel finished first.'

He took up his chisel and resumed work.

Omar looked at the piece of parchment in his hand. He was frightened to read it in case she had said she would not meet him. Slowly he opened the fragile leaf. She had written only three words: 'garden, sunset, tomorrow'. So she would see him. Tomorrow. He would be able to talk to her tomorrow. He would tell her to run away with him; he would free her from slavery. They would go north or even over the sea to North Africa.

'Omar, please be careful,' Yusuf said.

His face was serious beneath its coating of white dust.

'It's a dangerous game you are playing; someone could get hurt.'

'I will,' Omar replied but his heart was beating so loudly that he couldn't even hear his own words. 'Don't worry. I just want to talk to her.'

He placed the note inside his robe, tucking it in, close to his heart. Now he had to plan his actions carefully; he could not afford to get caught.

CHAPTER 21

Qasim had been thinking a lot about the past lately, about his life in Ardales. Maybe that was why he thought he had seen him, sitting in the darkest corner of the tea shop. The man's hood was pulled up, partially hiding his face. That in itself was odd. And he was alone, hunched over his mint tea, not speaking to anyone. The tea shop was for socialising, chatting to your friends and neighbours; with its low tables covered in intricate marquetry and the dark wooden ceilings, scattered with patterns of the heavens, it was a welcoming place for locals and strangers alike. Visitors to the town were always certain of a friendly face and hearing the latest news. Yet there he sat, on his own, oblivious to the convivial company around him. It was hard to be sure but there was something familiar about the man. Qasim moved closer so that he could get a better look without alerting him. Yes, he was certain it was him; he was older and his grey hair protruded from beneath his hood, long and unkempt but there was something about his eyes, so cold, like naked steel, that brought the man's name to mind. Qasim had hurriedly made his excuses to his friends and left. He did not want to be recognised, not now, not after all these years. There was too much to lose.

'Baba, do you want me to light the fire?' Ibrahim asked. 'Mama says it's time we started to cook the goat.'

Evening was drawing in and the pale sun was hanging low in the sky. Soon it would sink below the horizon leaving the sky an inky black. They had built a bonfire outside in the street, alongside those of their neighbours. Everyone was turning out now, the women carrying the food in earthenware containers, the men stoking the fires and tending to the meat. Some were roasting whole animals over the charcoal, others had chopped their goat into pieces and were cooking it slowly in the embers of the fire. The air was rich with the smells of cardamon, cinnamon and paprika. Fatima had been all day preparing the goat that he and Ibrahim had slaughtered earlier. It was a good animal, young and tender. He had butchered it into pieces and his wife had marinated it with salt, pepper, dried coriander, cumin, saffron and oil. He had bought the finest saffron specially for the feast. Fatima had put the meat into their largest earthenware pot with layers of aubergine, chopped almonds, meat balls and lavender. Now it would simmer on the fire until it was done and then she would thicken it with whipped eggs and crown it with egg yolks. His mouth watered as he thought about it. It was a recipe Fatima's mother had made every Eid. Now Fatima did it for her family.

'Yes, let's get it lit. It will be dark soon,' he said.

His youngest child rushed up to him, pulling at his robe.

'Baba, I think you're mean. That poor little goat didn't do anyone any harm. I wanted to keep him. He was my friend,' Layla whined, tugging at him in her anguish.

'Don't be silly, princess. We don't have room for a goat.'

'Yes we do. We have lots of rooms now. He could have lived in my room with me. He didn't have to die.'

'Well it's too late now. If you are that upset you don't have to eat any of it.'

At this his daughter burst into tears and ran back into the house.

'Oh, Qasim, leave her be. She's just a child,' Fatima said.

'She'll be a hungry child if she keeps on like that.'

He took the cooking pot from her and lifted the lid. Even uncooked, it smelled delicious. There was a pungent smell of chopped onions and garlic.

'Where's Omar?' he asked her.

She shook her head.

'I don't know what's the matter with that boy these days. He's never here and when he is, his head is in the clouds,' she said.

He could not help but agree with his wife. Omar had been acting strangely for a couple of months now. He couldn't understand what was bothering him. He continued to work well but as soon as he had finished what he was doing he was off out. With Yusuf, he said, when Qasim pressed him.

'I suppose it's his age,' his wife said, poking at the fire. 'You need to damp this down a bit, Ibrahim.'

'All right Mama, don't fuss. Just leave it to us.'

She gave a little snort of laughter.

'If I left it to you and your father we'd never get to eat the Eid feast.'

She turned to go back to the kitchen.

'Wait a minute wife, I need to speak to you.'

Qasim followed her into the house.

'What is it husband? Is something the matter?'

He took her by the arm and led her into their room. Sara was busy with the children and Layla was sulking in her bedroom. Once they were alone he turned to her and said, 'I think I saw ibn Hayyan today, when I was in the tea shop.'

He saw the blank look on his wife's face and added, 'From Ardales. He fought with me against the Sultan.'

'He was your friend. I remember now.'

'Not much of a friend, more a rival. He was a cold, cruel man, a good soldier but that was all.'

She frowned at him. The man in question had asked her father if he could marry her but he was too late; she had already been promised to Qasim.

'Did he recognise you?'

'No, I don't think he saw me. I left straight away.'

'What will you do?'

'Nothing. What can I do? He's probably just passing through. I'm sure he'll be on his way once Eid is over.'

'Are you sure it was him?'

He sat down and put his head in his hands.

'No, I'm not sure. It was dark in the tea shop; it could just have been my imagination.'

'Don't worry. Even if you're right he won't say anything; he has as much to lose as you do.'

'But what if it is him? What if he tells people who I really am? Our lives here will be finished. They will lock me up, maybe even execute me. What will happen to you and Layla then? You'll be thrown out on the streets.'

Fatima put her hand on his shoulder.

'Don't. It won't come to that. Not after all these years. The Khalifa isn't going to be interested in you now, an old man who hasn't held a sword in his hand for thirty years.'

He looked at his wife. She was loyal and true. She had stood by him all these years, sharing his secret. He could not bear to think that her life would be ruined because of him and his past.

'Have you forgotten that the Khalifa crucified my father and all his cousins? Have you forgotten that he had the remains of ibn Hafsun dug up and hung his rotting corpse between them at the main gate to Córdoba? Al-Rahman swore he would wipe out every single rebel that had fought alongside ibn Hafsun. He is a man of his word. I would be arrested without doubt.'

'Well we must make sure this man doesn't tell anyone. Go back to the tea shop and see if he is still there. If he is and it is the man you think it is, bring him here to spend Eid with us.'

'What, are you mad?'

'You don't have to say who you are, just that you are extending the hand of friendship to a stranger.'

'But what if he recognises me?'

'Qasim, you may not realise it, but you have changed quite a lot since you were a young man. He won't recognise your face and he won't recognise your name; you are no longer Muhammed ibn Ahmad. How will he ever know that your father was Omar ibn Hafsun's cousin?'

'I don't know. It seems very risky to me.'

'It's riskier to let him gossip to all and sundry in the tea shop about his days fighting against the Sultan.'

Qasim did not reply. He did not know what to do. Maybe his wife was right, maybe he should confront the man. After all, it might not even be him. Many had been slaughtered after their defeat and those who had escaped would be foolish to return to the Khalifa's court.

'If it's not him, what have you lost? You have just offered hospitality to a lonely man,' she continued. 'Something all devout men do at Eid.'

'Very well, I'll go back there in a minute. But wear your veil tonight, just in case he recognises you.'

'Hello. Anybody home?' a man's voice called.

'Jundi, my little Jundi, is it you?' Fatima answered.

Their strapping son, al-Jundi stood in the patio unbuckling his sword and taking off his helmet.

'I'm so happy you could make it. How many days leave do you have? Your sister is here and her children. And Ibrahim. Have you seen Ibrahim?' she prattled on in her excitement at seeing him.

'Yes Mama. I saw him as I arrived; he was struggling with the fire.'

'Oh no. I knew I couldn't leave it to him. Now the meat will never get cooked,' his mother said, fluttering about like one of the chickens in the hen coop.

Qasim could see that she didn't know whether to rush out and check on the goat or to stay and quiz her son. In the end the goat won and she left her husband and her eldest son to talk alone.

'So son, you managed to find time to come and see us,' Qasim said.

'I did. I have to return to barracks tomorrow but for tonight I am free.'

He looked around him.

'The house is coming on well.'

Qasim nodded. He was pleased to see his first-born son. Al-Jundi was required to work long hours in the Palace Guard and rarely had time to visit them. He had his customary feeling of pride as he regarded this well built young man, his son and heir. He would never admit it to his wife but he had been bitterly disappointed when their first child was a girl but luckily she was followed, in quick succession, by two strapping sons and then, after a few years, Omar had come along. His youngest son was not like his brothers; they were rough and ready lads, always in some fight or other. Omar was more sensitive, more artistic. That was probably why Qasim sometimes found it difficult to understand him. And of course there was his baby, Layla. He smiled as he thought of his little princess. She was not speaking to him now, but he knew she would soon forget about all that silliness with the goat. She was a lovable child and was never angry for long. She was so like her mother. Yes, tonight he would have all his children under his roof. He was not going to let his fears about this man, ibn Hayyan or not, spoil the evening.

'Where's Omar?' al-Jundi asked. 'He wasn't in the alfarería.'

'You know your young brother, he's always wandering off somewhere. He'll be back in time for his meal; you can count on that.'

'I need to speak to him,' al-Jundi said. 'He's been seen loitering around the alcázar and I'm worried he'll end up in trouble.'

'What do you mean, loitering around the alcázar? It's true he has been there recently. He had to take some orders there, new plates that we have sold to the Royal Buyer. I expect that was it. I can't think of any other reason he would be visiting the palace?'

'You're probably right; it's just that some of the guards say he has been up there almost every day on some pretext or other. It's only because he's my brother that they haven't done anything about it.'

'I'm sure it's nothing. You can ask him yourself when he gets back.'

'I hope so.'

The muezzin's voice interrupted them. It was sunset; time to pray. Qasim looked at his son.

'Yes, Baba, I'm going to pray right now. Don't fret.'

***

It took Qasim only a few minutes to get back to the tea shop; the owner was already starting to close up. He had rolled up the blind and was closing the wooden shutters.

'As-salama alaykum, Ali. Closing already?'

'Wa alaykum e-salam, Qasim. Yes, my wife made me promise I would not be late tonight. We have all the family here for Eid.'

Qasim smiled.

'Yes, it's the same with us.'

'Did you want something?'

'Not really. I just wondered what had happened to that man who was here earlier, the one who sat alone in the corner?'

'I know who you mean. He was a strange one. Hardly said a word to anyone.'

'So he's gone then?'

'Only a few minutes ago. If you want to speak to him you'll be able to catch him; he set off towards the river.'

'No, I don't want to speak to him. I was just wondering who he was.'

'He seemed to know you,' the tea shop owner said, slamming the last of the shutters into place.

'What? He said he knew me?'

'Not in so many words but he asked if you were from around here.'

'What did you say?'

'What could I say? I said nobody was really from Madinat al-Zahra; we were all newcomers. I said that I thought you were from Córdoba. That's right, isn't it?'

'Yes, that's right.'

'So, is he a friend of yours then?'

'No. I've never seen him before. It was my wife's idea; she thought it might be a kind gesture to invite him to share our meal tonight. She doesn't like to think of people being on their own at Eid.'

'She's a kind woman, your wife.'

'She is that. Well, I'll say good night, Ali. Enjoy the feast.'

As he walked back towards his house, his mind was racing. Now he was almost certain that it was ibn Hayyan. Why else would he be asking questions about him? He was glad that he had not had the opportunity to see him again and invite him to eat with them. That would have been a grave mistake. No, he wanted that man as far away from him and his family as possible.

***

It was late by the time they had all sat down to eat but nobody was concerned about the hour. Tomorrow the alfarería would be closed. They were on holiday. He looked around the table; all his family were there: his three sons, his daughters, his grandchildren and his beloved wife. He could not ask for more.

'This is good, Mama,' al-Jundi said, mopping up the juices on his plate with a hunk of bread. 'The best meal I've had in a long time.'

'You could come and have some home cooking whenever you wanted, you know that,' she said. 'We always have enough for you.'

'I know Mama, but it's not easy. The Khalifa likes his men to be at the peak of their fitness and he has us training every day. I know some say it's an easy life in the Palace Guard but I can tell you, it's not. We may be at peace now but we have to be ready for whatever might happen. Tomorrow we could be at war. If you don't come up to muster then you're out.'

'I heard that the Khalifa chooses the very best of his soldiers for the Palace Guard,' said Sara, picking a particularly tender morsel from her plate to feed to her youngest child.

The little girl sat curled up on her mother's lap, struggling to keep awake.

'We like to think so,' al-Jundi replied.

'Mama, I think I'll put the children to bed,' Sara said. 'It's been a long day for them.'

'I'll help you,' Fatima said. 'Then you and I can clear up all this mess.'

'So, Ibrahim, how are things in Córdoba?' al-Jundi asked.

'Things are changing. The place is full of foreigners. There are more and more merchants coming from the East with new styles of dress and furnishings. They say that their textiles are the finest to be found.'

He shrugged dismissively.

'Doesn't look as though you have been influenced by them,' his brother said with a laugh.

Ibrahim was not known for his elegance; he always wore the same grey djubba, summer and winter and, more often than not, it bore the marks of his trade around the hem, a dried crust of clay. Fatima had tried suggesting he smarten himself up and try something different but his reply had been one of incredulity.

'What for?' he asked.

When she had mentioned something about a wife, he had laughed and changed the subject.

'They are lots of merchants here too, in Madinat al-Zahra,' Qasim added. 'And textile workers are flocking here from Egypt and Byzantium, starting up their own workshops. People can't get enough of the new fashions. Even the Khalifa has commissioned special bales of silk, inscribed with his name, to give as gifts to visiting dignitaries.'

That was what he was hoping would happen with his pottery. If the Khalifa became interested in your work, your reputation was made. As though reading his mind, his youngest son said, 'It won't be long before the Khalifa is giving his visitors our pottery. The Royal Buyer has twice bought plates from us. Once people know that the Khalifa likes our work they will copy him. They always do.'

'So that's why you've been seen at the alcázar so often?' al-Jundi asked.

Qasim saw his youngest son redden and look down at his plate. Now why was that?

'Of course. First I took him some samples and then, when he placed an order, we had to deliver them.'

'We?'

'I usually take al-Sagir with me.'

'How are the new slaves working out?' Ibrahim asked.

'Excellent. I had my doubts at first but they are hard workers and give us no trouble at all,' Qasim replied.

'Mama seems pleased with them.'

'She does now, but you should have seen her face when I brought them home.'

He laughed at the memory.

'I could do with someone to help in the alfarería in Córdoba,' said Ibrahim.

'A slave?'

'Not necessarily but it's an option. I need an extra pair of hands but someone who is clever enough to learn the trade as well. The only problem is that I'm not making enough at the moment to employ an apprentice.'

Qasim was not really listening to his son; Ibrahim was always going on about needing help. He was thinking about Omar.

'When are you going to the alcázar next?' he asked him.

'Straight after Eid,' Omar replied.

His son did not look up at him when he spoke but continued to stare at his unfinished meal.

'Well be careful. I don't want you seeming too eager. That won't do us any good at all. The Royal Buyer does not like to be pushed. Maybe I should go with you next time, instead of al-Sagir.'

'If you like, Baba.'

'I hear that Yusuf is working there, on the Vizier's new palace,' Qasim said.

'Yusuf?' Fatima asked, coming in to remove the empty plates. 'How is he? He hasn't been to see us for such a long time. Once upon a time he was always under my feet; now we never see him.'

'He's very busy, Mama. Not just with work, he is getting married soon.'

'Of course, to Zilma, the daughter of a shoemaker in Córdoba. I remember. Now what about dessert?'

Qasim thought his wife might make a comment to her sons about it being time they settled down with a wife but instead she turned and went out onto the patio.

'So, he's to be married,' Qasim said, wondering if that was what had been bothering Omar.

He and Yusuf were inseparable; all that would have to change when Yusuf married.

'I have made your favourite sweetmeats. Would anyone like to try them?' Fatima told them, coming back into the room with a large platter of almond and cinnamon pastries.

'Over here, wife.'

Qasim stood up to take the platter from Fatima but by the time he had placed it on the table and sat down again, his youngest son had disappeared.

'Where's Omar?'

'He said he needed some fresh air,' Sara said, as she rejoined them. 'He won't be long.'

CHAPTER 22

Omar just had to get away. He knew if he delayed, his father would involve him in some family task that would make it impossible for him to escape. When everyone's attention was firmly fixed on his mother and her plate of tempting sweetmeats, he slipped out without a word.

It was perfect. Most people were in their homes or sitting around their fires eating their dinner. Nobody was interested in what he was doing or where he was going. It took him no more than ten minutes to reach the entrance to the grounds of the alcázar. The same man was on guard duty. He stood at his post, staring directly ahead of him, his face immobile.

'As-salam alaykum,' Omar said.

'Oh, it's you. What do you want now?'

'I've brought you something to eat. It's goat cooked in spices. My grandmother's recipe.'

He lifted the lid of the pot and showed the food to the guard.

'Hmmn. Looks all right.'

'It's still warm. I told you I wouldn't forget you. It's not fair that everyone else gets to enjoy Eid and you're stuck here.'

The guard took the pot and held it to his nose so that he could enjoy the full aroma.

'Coriander and lavender,' he said. 'Smells all right.'

'It is. Eat it while it's hot. I have to get back before my mother starts complaining that I'm never there.'

'Thanks lad.'

'Good night,' Omar said, turning to walk away.

The guard looked about him. There was no-one around, so he slipped into the guard house to find himself some utensils with which to eat this unexpected meal.

He was only gone a moment but that was enough for Omar; he was through the archway and down the winding passage that led into the palace demesne before the man returned. Now all that he had to do was remain hidden in the shadows. The passageways were lit by oil lamps that spilled golden pools of light onto their cobbled surfaces but left large areas in darkness. He kept close to the walls, edging his way forward cautiously. The passages twisted and turned, sometimes leading to a dead end, sometimes to a crossroads - all designed to confound any intruder. Omar knew that other guards were stationed at various points, all alert and armed, ready for action. It was not going to be easy to reach the gardens of the harem undetected. He couldn't bribe them all with bowls of his mother's stew.

He turned a corner a little too abruptly and almost came face to face with one of them. Just in time he stepped back into the shadows and stood there holding his breath, listening to his heart thumping inside his chest. The guard was tired; he could see that from the way he lounged against the wall, his head dropping forward from time to time. Omar wondered if he could manage to slip past without him realising; it was very risky. Then he noticed that the man was stationed opposite a wooden gate. This was the gateway to the harem gardens; he was sure he recognised it from his earlier reconnaissance. All he had to do was lure the guard away from his post and then he could climb over the gate and into the gardens. He searched on the ground until he found a couple of small pebbles. The guard had not moved. His head was resting on his chest; his breathing was steady. He was half-asleep. Carefully, taking care not to betray his presence, Omar threw one of the pebbles past the guard so that it landed in the shadows beyond him. The man's head jerked up but he did not move. Omar threw a second pebble.

'Who's there?' the guard shouted.

He was wide awake now.

'Who's there, I said. Show yourself or I'll run you through with my sword.'

He unsheathed his sword and brandished it in front of him. Omar could see his face in the lamp light. He was very young, probably not even as old as Omar but he was tall and strong and his muscles gleamed where he had rubbed himself with oil. He was probably not battle hardened, like al-Jundi, but Omar knew that he would not stand much chance if it came to a fight between them. His only chance was to beat him with cunning.

He had one pebble left; it was now or never. He tossed the third pebble, this time further into the shadows.

'I know you're there. Come out, you bastard,' the youth commanded, moving towards the sound.

Omar knew, from what his brother had told him, that the Palace Guards were not supposed to leave their posts under any pretext but this one was inexperienced. It was easy to lure him away. He waited until the guard had moved at least ten metres from the gateway, his attention firmly fixed on finding the source of the noise, then he made his move. As he had expected the gate was locked so he placed his foot on the handle and leapt over it in a single motion. His landing was unexpectedly soft and quiet. He waited, afraid to move, until he heard the guard return.

'Bloody rats,' the soldier muttered. 'Just bloody rats.'

Omar tried to look around him but it was dark; thick clouds covered the moon and made it hard to identify his surroundings. He crouched down and waited for his eyes to adjust to the blackness. He was in a garden; that was certain. And the reason for his soft landing was that he had landed on a bed of sweet smelling thyme; the slightest movement of his feet released the tiny plant's pungent scent. Gradually the garden took form; he began to make out the shadowy shapes of the plants and trees that surrounded him. An avenue of palm trees led from the gate towards the Khalifa's palace, where it sat on a terrace overlooking the grounds, like a glowing jewel in a sea of darkness. A night owl hooted and glided past with barely a flap of its wings. Omar waited a while longer to ensure that the guard remained unaware of his presence behind the gate, no more than a metre away from him. The slightest noise, a cough, a sneeze, would be heard and then it would be all over. But there was no sound from the other side of the wall; he imagined the young soldier leaning against the wall and peacefully dozing once more. As soon as he was certain that he remained undetected, he crept off in the direction of the flickering lights that spilled from the windows of the harem.

She had said sunset. It was well past that now but he hoped she would still be waiting for him. The night was silent save for the sound of a woman singing; the plaintive music floated across the garden from one of the rooms of the palace. A slight movement caught his attention; a pale, filmy figure crossed the path in front of him. He stopped, not daring to breathe.

'Omar?' a gentle voice whispered. 'Is that you?'

'Jawhara?'

She stopped and looked in the direction of his voice. He moved towards her, pulling her gently into the shadows.

'You came?' she said.

'You sent for me, my lady,' he said, smiling. 'How could I stay away?'

'Follow me. It is too dangerous to stay here.'

She led him away from the path, further and further into the garden, past geometric hedges of myrtle, past hibiscus bushes where white flowers gleamed eerily in the dark, past orange trees heavy with bitter fruit, past mimosa trees, whose branches drooped with the weight of their heavily scented blossom until, at last, they came to an ornamental lake.

'We can talk here,' she said. 'No-one will see us. They are all busy with the feast.'

'Won't you be missed?' he asked.

She did not answer. There was a splash as a frog, disturbed by their presence, leapt into the water. The ripples from that tiny splash spread out, wider and wider across the lake. He watched, fascinated, until there was no more to see. Omar suddenly realised what an enormous risk she was taking by agreeing to see him. His actions could have devastating effects on all their lives.

'It's too dangerous,' he said. 'I shouldn't have come. I must leave now.'

'No, do not go. You have to help me,' she cried, pulling at his sleeve. 'You have to help me.'

Instantly he had her in his arms. Her hair smelled of roses and jasmine; he was overcome with longing for her, to hold her, to have her.

'It is my brother,' she whispered, between her tears. 'I have to rescue my brother and you are the only one who can help me.'

The words barely registered with him; he was so overwhelmed by her presence, her touch, her perfume. This was the woman of his dreams and here she was, in his arms, a frail and delicate creature, who rested against his breast, asking for his help. His heart was beating so fast, he could hardly think.

'Can you help me?' she continued. 'You must. Please.'

He trailed his fingers down through her hair until he reached her waist. A thrill of excitement tore through him as his hands encircled her.

'Omar.'

There was an insistence in her voice.

'Omar.'

'Your brother? I don't understand. How can I help you rescue your brother? I don't know who he is.'

He pulled back slightly so that he could look at her but let his hands remain around her tiny waist, his fingertips touching. The clouds parted, allowing the moonlight to fall across her face. She was so beautiful and her sorrow made her even more so; her eyes promised him the world if only he would help her. Whatever she wanted he would do it for her. Anything.

'Come, sit down and tell me what it is you want,' he said, sitting by the lake and pulling her down beside him.

She wore the same scarf he had taken from her that day in the bazaar. Now it slid from her shoulders, exposing skin that glowed like alabaster in the pale light. He desperately wanted to touch her, to press his lips against that shoulder.

'My brother. He was captured at the same time as me. He is a slave. He is your slave,' she said.

She looked at him with sorrowful eyes. Her accent, as she struggled to speak to him in Arabic, was like music; it pulled and teased at his senses making it hard for him to concentrate on her words.

'What? My slave? What do you mean, my slave?'

'He is your slave. I saw him with you, in the market the other day. He told me he works for you.'

'Al-Sagir? Al-Sagir is your brother?'

He was astounded. How could this be? His father had bought the boy in Madinat al-Zahra. This woman was from the north; she belonged to the Khalifa. How had this happened?

'His name is Hans. I have two brothers. I do not know where the other one is but now that I have found Hans, I must help him.'

'He belongs to my father,' Omar said, feebly.

His head was racing. What did she want him to do? How could he help her rescue a boy that was his own slave?

'The vikings came and took us. They killed my mother and they took my brothers and me,' she continued. 'We were separated. I never thought I would see them again.

And now here he is, my little Hans, here in Madinat al-Zahra. I am so happy that I have found him but now I must rescue him. You will help me,' she said, looking at him with those eyes that he could not resist.

This strange exotic creature was asking him for help. How could he refuse her?

'Jawhara, I would do anything for you but how can I help? Even if I could persuade my father to set him free, then what? Where would he go? He is better off with us, at least until he is older. We treat him well and he is learning a trade. One day he may earn his freedom and then he can do as he wishes, but for now he is safer with us.'

She pulled her hand away from his and began to cry.

'At least bring him to me. Let me talk to him. Please.'

It had been hard for him to enter the harem undetected; how much harder it would be with a young boy in tow. But he did not say that. He could not bear to disappoint her.

'I will try.'

'That is not everything,' she sobbed. 'I want to run away. I want to take my brother and leave this awful land.'

'What is it? What has happened?' he asked.

Even with tears running down her face, she was so beautiful. How could he deny her anything?

She swallowed hard and choked back her tears.

'It is the Khalifa. He has noticed me. I am to go to him on the last night of the Eid celebrations. He has specifically asked for me.'

'But that's an honour, isn't it?' Omar asked.

There was a tightness in his stomach as he considered what this meant. He knew he could not bear the thought of anyone else having her, not even the Khalifa.

'He is an old man, Omar. I do not want to give myself to an old man, no matter how rich and powerful he is. I want a man I can love,' she said, touching his cheek as she spoke. 'I have to leave here. I want to get Hans and then we can run away together.'

'But where will you go?'

He liked the idea of taking her and her brother away from here but underneath all his romantic sentiments he was a logical man; he knew how difficult it would be to do what she wanted. Then there was his father, how could he betray his own father?

'I do not know. Back to the north. Back to my people.'

'That won't be easy, Jawhara. The Khalifa doesn't like to lose his concubines. He would rather kill them then allow them to run away. You realise that what you are asking is very dangerous, for you, for al-Sagir and for me. Are you sure this is what you want?'

She nodded.

'I am sure. Bring my brother to me so that I can talk to him. Please.'

'Hush, there's someone in the garden,' Omar said.

There was the sound of footsteps and breaking branches as though someone was stumbling through the undergrowth. Suddenly a voice called out, 'Jawhara, are you there? It's Najm. Hurry. They are looking for you. The Palace Guards are all over the place; they say someone has entered the harem. Yamut is furious.'

'I must go,' Jawhara whispered. 'Come the day after tomorrow at the same time. Bring Hans.'

Before she could go, he pulled her towards him and kissed her lightly on the lips. She tasted of honey.

Jawhara pulled back and looked at him. Her eyes were glowing as she whispered, with her lovely slow smile, 'Tomorrow, my love.'

Then she was gone, slipping through the shadows like a wraith.

'My love', she had called him 'my love'. His heart sang.

***

Allah had looked down on him favourably that night. There was so much confusion amongst the guards that he was able to slip out without being seen. Nobody would have known he had ever been there if he hadn't bumped into al-Jundi.

'What are you doing here, little brother?' he asked.

'Just having a walk. What about you? I thought you were off duty tonight.'

'There's been some trouble. Some idiot was spotted in the gardens of the alcázar.'

'Did they catch him?'

His brother shook his head. He was studying him closely.

'So where exactly were you walking, brother?'

'Here and there.'

Al-Jundi stopped and pulled him into a doorway.

'Now you can stop lying to me. Where have you been?'

'Nowhere, I told you, just walking.'

'Was it you? Tell me it wasn't you,' al-Jundi said. 'It was, wasn't it. How could you be so foolish? Do you know what the penalty is for entering the alcázar of the Khalifa? Do you? Execution. What the fucking hell were you playing at?'

'I didn't say it was me,' Omar protested weakly.

'No, you didn't but we both know it was. What the fuck's going on? Why have you been hanging about the alcázar all the time?'

'I wanted to see someone.'

'Someone? Who on earth do you know in the Khalifa's palace?'

'It's a girl. The most beautiful girl in the world.'

Despite his brother's rage, Omar could not help smiling when he thought of Jawhara. She had called him 'my love'.

'A girl? In the name of Allah and all that's sacred, don't tell me it's someone in the harem?'

Omar did not reply. His brother would not understand how he felt about Jawhara; to him a woman's sole purpose was to produce sons for her husband. Love was not a word he had ever heard al-Jundi use.

'Go home and bloody stay there. Don't speak to anyone about where you've been tonight,' al-Jundi said. 'Tell no-one. I'll be home later. First I must find out if you were seen and if anyone recognised you.'

'Ma'a salama, brother.'

CHAPTER 23

Al-Jundi waited until his young brother had disappeared from sight then he marched into the barracks.

'What the hell's going on here?' he asked, his voice like thunder.

'Some bastard's been snooping around the harem.'

'How did he get in?'

The guards looked at each other sheepishly.

'Well?' al-Jundi thundered.

'We don't know.'

'Someone will pay for this. Don't think that the Khalifa will let it go without someone paying. And it won't be me.'

The Palace Guard was comprised mostly of Slavs; they were slaves, captured in battle, brave men, bold and strong but hardly any of them could speak a word of Arabic. That's why the Khalifa needed a few, like him, to command them. He might not speak their language but he had a way of making them understand him.

'May I have a word, Captain?' one of the local guards asked.

It was the one who had told him about Omar being seen so often in the alcázar.

'What is it?'

The guard looked around him, making sure he would not be overheard, even by his foreign companions.

'It's about your brother, Captain. Do you think it could have been him? He has been here rather a lot lately.'

'He was at home with me, celebrating Eid. You don't need to worry about him. I have spoken to my father about the visits. He has had a lot of work to do for the Royal Buyer recently. No, we must look elsewhere for our culprit. Try to get these Slavic brutes to understand that no-one is allowed to enter the alcázar of the Khalifa without permission. And no-one may enter the harem. No-one.'

'Yes, Captain.'

'Now, tell me exactly what occurred.'

'There was someone walking about in the gardens. One of the eunuchs from the harem saw him.'

'He was sure it was a man?'

'Positive, Captain. He said the intruder was too tall for a woman.'

'Does the Khalifa know?'

'Not yet. Yamut al-Attar wants us to catch the man first before he tells the Khalifa. He doesn't want his wrath to fall directly on him.'

'Well they are supposed to be protecting the women. About all those bloody eunuchs are good for, if you ask me.'

'He's blaming the Palace Guard.'

'Naturally. Well find out who was on duty in that part of the alcázar tonight and punish him.'

'Yes, Captain.'

'Now, I'm going back to my family to enjoy the remainder of my one day of relaxation. I will be here at first light tomorrow.'

'Have you heard the rumours, Captain?'

'What rumours?'

'We are being sent north to quash a rebellion.'

'Where did you hear this idle gossip? There have been no rebellions since Castille fought for independence last year.'

'A messenger arrived tonight from the garrison at Salim. They need our help.'

'Until we are officially told, it is nothing more than rumour. If I catch anyone gossiping about it, I'll have them flogged. Do you understand?'

'Yes, Captain.'

Al-Jundi turned and left. Why was it that the rumours always spread before he was officially given his orders? It was impossible to keep anything secret in the alcázar. He just hoped he could keep Omar's involvement quiet; if anyone discovered that the intruder was his brother, al-Jundi would be the one to suffer. It would be demotion for him at the very least, maybe even arrest. His brother had had a narrow escape. They all had.

***

When he arrived home his mother was still in the kitchen, preparing more food for the next day. His father was sitting on the patio, drinking mint tea; he had removed his cap and his djellaba and looked ready for bed.

'You're back then son,' he said.

'I am.'

'Everything all right?'

'Someone was spotted in the gardens of the alcázar. The Chief Eunuch is blaming the Palace Guard for dereliction of duty.'

'So someone will be punished?'

'Of course.'

'Come, sit down and have some tea.'

Al-Jundi unbuckled his sword, removed his helmet and sat down beside his father. How was he going to tell him about Omar? It wouldn't be easy. Yet he must do it. Omar would be angry with him, feel betrayed. But it was his duty to tell his father about what had happened. His youngest brother only ever saw things from his own viewpoint; he had to realise that his actions could affect the whole family.

'Is Omar home?' he asked.

'Yes, he came in about an hour ago and went straight to bed. Not a word to anyone. I don't know what's the matter with that boy, these days.'

'I have something serious to tell you, Baba.'

His father put down his glass and looked at him.

'About Omar?'

'Yes. I caught him leaving the alcázar this evening. He was the man they saw in the gardens.'

'Allah preserve and save us. Was he recognised?'

'No. I don't know how he managed to be so lucky. There are Palace Guards stationed at every turn.'

'What was he doing?'

'It's something to do with a girl. He just wanted to speak to her, he said.'

'Speak to a girl in the harem? Has he gone completely mad? Doesn't he know the penalty for entering the Khalifa's harem? Have I fathered a complete idiot?' he shouted, leaping to his feet and overturning the table with the tea things.

His father looked as though he would explode; his face had turned quite red. Al-Jundi could not remember ever seeing him so angry.

'What is it? What's the matter?' al-Jundi's mother asked, coming in from the kitchen. 'Has something happened? What's wrong, husband?'

'Nothing's wrong, woman. Get back to what you were doing.'

Al-Jundi saw his mother hesitate then retreat back to the kitchen; his father never shouted at her. She looked hurt and frightened.

'Get him out here. He can tell me to my face why he is putting his whole family in danger like this.'

He turned to where Fatima stood, trembling in the doorway.

'Get your useless son out of bed and bring him here.'

His mother scurried along to Omar's room. He could hear her talking to his brother in low, frightened whispers.

'Sit down, Baba. Don't get so upset.'

'Upset? You think this is upset. That boy will learn what "upset" is by the time I'm through with him. Get me my stick.'

He looked at his father in amazement. He could not remember even one occasion when Baba had beaten any of them. Yes, there had been plenty of cuffs and clips around the ear for being cheeky but never a beating. Was something else worrying his father? After all Omar had not been caught. Al-Jundi just wanted his father to impress the seriousness of his actions on his young brother, not beat him.

Omar appeared in the doorway, bedraggled and half-asleep. Fatima stood behind him, her face stained with tears.

'Come here boy.'

'What is it Baba?'

'You know perfectly well what it is. Why, in the name of Allah, have you been putting our family's name at risk? The harem. Are you mad? Why were you trying to get into the harem?'

His father was still angry but more composed now; he was not about to beat Omar. Seeing his son standing there in front of him had calmed him down.

'I wasn't trying to get into the harem. I was meeting someone in the gardens,' Omar replied.

He shot a furious look at al-Jundi.

'Who?'

'A girl I met in the bazaar.'

'A slave?'

He nodded.

'Belonging to the Khalifa?'

Again he nodded.

'Have you lost your mind? Why do you think there are Palace Guards? To keep out idiots like you. The Khalifa's harem is a sacred place. No-one may enter, no-one, yet my stupid son thinks he can just walk in there and talk to one of the Khalifa's women.'

He brought his stick down on the ground with such force that it splintered in two. Even al-Jundi felt himself jump at the ferocity of his father's action.

'Think yourself lucky that it's not your head,' he said. 'Now, my lad, under no circumstances are you to go back there. Never. You hear me? Never.'

Omar nodded his head.

'You are fortunate that your brother has covered up for you. This time you've been lucky. Allah has protected you but he will not be so forgiving next time. Now go to bed.'

His father sat down again, staring at the broken tea glasses on the floor.

'Fatima, bring me some more tea,' he said, but his voice was softer, his rage had died away.

He looked a tired old man, exhausted by his outburst. Al-Jundi sat next to him.

'What is it Baba? Is there something else? Why were you so angry? I told you that Omar had not been discovered. No harm has been done.'

His father sighed.

'Yes, I know. You are right, my son; something else is troubling me. Something I should have told you about a long time ago.'

He hesitated and continued to stare at the floor.

'What is it Baba?'

He had never seen his father like this before; he was normally a man who looked you straight in the eye and said what had to be said. Now he would not look at him. At last Qasim spoke.

'I've been keeping a secret from you, al-Jundi, from all of you. I am an old man now; I think it's time I told you about my past. I know you are a member of the Palace Guard but you are my son and heir; you deserve to know the truth.'

What did he mean? What truth did he need to know? What had his father been keeping from him all these years?

His mother came in with some fresh tea and more glasses. They waited while she swept up the broken shards and mopped up the spilt tea. Then, once she had returned to the kitchen, his father said, 'You have heard of the rebel Omar ibn Hafsun?'

'Yes. He and his men were defeated by the Khalifa many years ago. It was the last big rebellion.'

'He was your grandfather's cousin.'

'What? How could that be? You told me grandfather was a potter.'

He could not believe that he was only learning this now. He was related to a rebel. In the Khalifa's eyes that made him a traitor.

'He was but before that he fought alongside his cousin, Omar ibn Hafsun.'

'So what happened?'

'We were related to ibn Hafsun through marriage; his mother was the sister of my grandfather, who had been a soldier in the early campaigns. Omar ibn Hafsun's father, on the other hand, was a descendent of a Visigoth nobleman called Alfonso; he was rich and owned much of the land near the town of Iznate. But that was not enough for ibn Hafsun; he wanted more. He was in and out of trouble for years then he raised an army and rebelled against the Sultan. My father supported his cousin at first but Omar ibn Hafsun was an opportunist and thought nothing of changing sides whenever it suited him. It didn't take long for my father to see through him. He returned to his trade as a potter and would have no more to do with ibn Hafsun or the rebellion.'

'But legend says he was a hero to his followers.'

'He was a bandit, a murderer and a thief. Worse than that he abandoned his religion. When it suited him he renounced Islam and converted to Christianity.'

'So that's why you don't want the Palace Guard looking too closely at Omar's escapades,' al-Jundi said.

'There's more.'

His father poured some tea into his glass and stared at the swirling green liquid for a moment.

'I too fought in the rebellion.'

'You were a soldier like your father?'

'Yes, but unlike my father, I fought against Abd al-Rahman. I was a young man, a Mullawad and I believed I was fighting for the rights of all Mullawads. That was what ibn Hafsun told us. But then, when he thought he could get more support from the Mozarab Christians he joined them and abandoned us. It was never about the Mullawads; it was only about power for Omar ibn Hafsun.'

'Does anyone know this? Does anyone know that you were a rebel?'

Al-Jundi's position was growing worse by the minute. His own father was a traitor and had been in hiding for years. As a captain in the Palace Guard he knew it was his duty to report it.

'Only your mother. We ran away to Córdoba. That was before Sara was born. We wanted to build a new life. I changed my name and took on a new identity. We were lucky; we made our escape just in time. The soldiers came and wiped out the rest of ibn Hafsun's supporters. Your grandfather was killed along with the rest of our family. We are the only survivors.'

'Why didn't you tell me about this before?'

'It wasn't safe. It still isn't safe. If the Khalifa knew that I was still alive and that my son was a member of his Palace Guard, I fear it would be over for all of us.'

'So I am not Makoud ibn Qasim, Makoud the son of Qasim?'

'Yes you are. It no longer matters that my name used to be Muhammed. Now I am Qasim and you are my son.'

'But.'

'No buts. That's how it is. What is important is that no-one finds out our secrets.'

'He thought he saw an old soldier, yesterday, someone from the army,' Fatima said.

She had been standing by the door, listening to them.

'Did you?'

'Maybe. I could have been mistaken,' his father said.

His mother was crying.

'What if he talks? What if he tells people who you really are? I cannot bear the thought of moving again,' she said. 'I am too old to start a new life in another city. If we are discovered, I will just stay here and take my chances.'

'Don't be silly, wife. Nothing will happen as long as your stupid son keeps away from the alcázar.'

His father drank the last of his tea and got up.

'I'm tired. I'm going to bed,' he said.

He turned to al-Jundi and asked, 'Will I see you in the morning?'

'Maybe. I have to leave early before it's light.'

'Allah be with you, my son. Tisbah ala-kheir.'

'Tisbah ala-kheir, Baba.'

'I have made a bed for you in Omar's room, with Ibrahim,' his mother said.

Al-Jundi followed her into the new bedroom.

'Tisbah ala-kheir, son. Sleep well,' she said.

He laid his sword and helmet beside his bed and lay down. His brothers were both asleep but for him sleep was unlikely. His mind was racing with the news that his father had just revealed. Where did it leave him? He was a captain in the Palace Guard whose father had been the right-hand man of Omar ibn Hafsun. Not only was ibn Hafsun a rebel but he had been the man whom the Khalifa hated more than any other. What could he do? The answer was clear; he could do nothing. This had been a secret for thirty years; it would have to remain a secret for another thirty. If it came to a choice between his family and the Khalifa, he had to stand beside his family, no matter what the consequences.

He looked across at the sleeping figure of Omar.

'You're playing with fire, little brother,' he murmured. 'Don't get burnt and don't pull your family into the flames with you.'

CHAPTER 24

The shouting had woken al-Mari but he did not move; he lay there in the dark and listened. Qasim was angry about something, something that his son had done. Well that was what happened when you had children; they never behaved as you wanted them to. He had never been blessed with a family but he could see that it was not all light and joy. He heard his master send for Omar and warn him about something, his voice raised and angry once more and then it went quiet. Al-Mari rolled over onto his side and was about to go back to sleep when he realised that Qasim was talking again; this time the tone was different, quiet but urgent and he was speaking to the oldest one, the soldier. There was something about his voice that alerted al-Mari; it was almost apologetic as if he wanted his son to forgive him. He got up and moved to the doorway so that he could hear better. It was as he suspected; Qasim was telling the soldier about his past. So no-one knew about it, not even his family. That was strange; Qasim had kept the secret to himself all these years. That was probably best; in his experience you couldn't trust anyone these days. He crept back to his bed and lay down again.

So he had been right. He knew he recognised that pock-marked face despite the years that had passed. He had spotted him in the tea shop asking questions about Qasim, so he had hung about and waited to see what he would do. First the man set off towards the Dar al-Sina'a where all the tradesmen worked and then he stopped and asked directions to the alfarería. So the crafty devil was looking for his master. Now what did he have in mind? Was he after money? Was he planning to blackmail Qasim? Or was he planning to slit his throat? Whatever it was, it wasn't good news. So it seemed that Qasim had spotted him as well. He would be worried. Al-Mari wondered if he should speak to his master and confess who he really was, see if he remembered him. But what would be Qasim's reaction to someone else from his past? He might throw him out. Al-Mari didn't want that to happen; he was comfortable here. There were worse places to spend his last years. Then there was the boy, al-Sagir; he had grown very fond of him. He reminded him of his own brother when he was young; he had been a cheeky little thing, always getting into mischief, always following him around. Then his brother had got the fever and died. Many died that year, coughing their lungs up until they had no strength to go on. The fever had raged through their village taking most of the children and many of the women, including his own mother; he and his father were the only ones to survive.

So many years ago and here he still was. He had never thought he would live into his sixties, never thought he would survive the battles, the galleys. He had been born a free man but that man was dead now, reborn as a slave. His thoughts drifted back to those days, to memories that he usually kept shut away in a black hole of forgetfulness. Tonight they wanted to resurface; tonight they would not be repressed.

He had been a young soldier then. They had fought bravely but in the end their defeat had been bloody and total. Those that survived al-Rahman's slaughter were rounded up and marched back to Córdoba; al-Mari was among them. They were stripped of their armour and weapons and those that were uninjured were given the choice of changing sides, joining al-Rahman's army or becoming slaves. He had served ibn-Hafsun well but he was first and foremost a soldier; he would serve al-Rahman equally well. Then that weasel, ibn Hayyan interfered. Only Allah knows how he managed to convince the commander that al-Mari could not be trusted but he did. Instead of letting him serve as a soldier they sent him to work as a galley-slave. His hand automatically reached down to his ankle where the scars of the leg-irons had never healed; on cold nights his ankles ached as though he were still shackled in the ship. For twenty years that was his life; he, who had been a proud, loyal soldier was less than nothing, a slave that was treated worse than a dog, who sat in the bowels of the ship and rowed to the ends of the earth. At first many died, dropping from exhaustion where they sat, their backs bloody from the lash of the whip. There were three of them to an oar, thirty in total. He was on the inboard seat; his job to get to his feet to push the oar forward and to sit again to pull it back. The other two just sat, pulling at the oar in unison. When one died he was thrown overboard and another replaced him. That was his life for what seemed like an eternity. Then one day they decided that he was too old. They dumped him in the port of Almeria. He felt no rancour; that was what happened. If you were a slave, life threw shit at you.

Now here he was, back where it all began. But nobody recognised him; certainly not the general. He was a slave and as such he was invisible.

CHAPTER 25

His father was still angry with him, Omar could tell. If only he could explain to him how impossible it was for him to abandon her. Jawhara was all he could think about. Her perfume, her soft skin, her silken hair, he could think of nothing else. She had filled his dreams with an unbearable longing and, even now, the image of her would not leave him. Despite the warnings from his brother and his father he would take al-Sagir to meet her, just as he had promised.

All day he had struggled with the temptation to tell his slave about Jawhara but he knew the boy would not be able to keep the news to himself. He longed to ask him about her, what she had been like as a sister, as a daughter; he longed to ask if she had had any suitors. Had she been betrothed as a child? All these questions and many more ran around in his head; he wanted to know all about her.

Tonight, as soon as they had had dinner, they would slip away and head for the alcázar. He knew it was risky to try to trick the guards again but he had to keep his promise to her. What happened after that would be down to Allah.

He was impatient. The day had dragged by so slowly and now that they were all seated, ready to eat, everything seemed to be moving in slow motion. It took an interminable length of time for his mother to serve the food then there were delays because one of the children felt sick and Baba would not let them start until Sara had seen to her; Ibrahim would not stop talking about his plans for the business, how he was going to supply the pedlars that visited all the small villages outside Córdoba, how he needed to get extra help for the shop. His mother wanted to know when he would take a wife. Omar listened distractedly to all that was said but his mind was racing ahead to the cool, leafy garden where she would be waiting for them. He had no appetite for food. His stomach churned with the fear that they would arrive too late, that she would not wait for them.

'Eat up, Omar. You've hardly touched your food,' his mother scolded him gently.

'I'm not very hungry, Mama.'

'Well I never thought I'd hear those words pass your lips, little brother,' Sara said, with a laugh. 'You are either ill or in love.'

He did not reply but stared down at his plate. He could feel his father's eyes on him. This was not going to be easy.

At last the meal was over. He wiped his mouth and put down his fork.

'Thank you Mama. That was good.'

'A sparrow could have eaten more than that.'

'I'll take some of the leftovers to al-Sagir, if you like. He always has room for more.'

'Very well, although they have both eaten already.'

She put some of the chicken on a plate and handed it to him.

'You're not going out tonight, I hope,' his father said.

'No, Baba. I thought I'd work on one of my new designs before I go to bed. I'll be in the alfarería.'

'Don't work too late. It's still a holiday, you know,' his mother said.

The slaves sat outside in the porch of the alfarería. The dog was curled up beside them.

'There's some more chicken if you'd like it,' Omar said, putting the plate down beside them.

The dog raised its head and looked at the food.

'Not for you, old boy. You'll get yours later.'

The dog lay down again. Al-Mari looked at Omar with those knowing eyes of his and said nothing; he just nodded and took a chicken leg to chew then passed the plate to the boy.

'It's good. Your mother is a wonderful cook,' al-Sagir said, popping a chunk of chicken in his mouth and licking the juice from his fingers.

'Al-Sagir, I want you to come with me. We have a job to do.'

'Now? Tonight?' the boy asked, helping himself to another piece of the chicken.

'Yes, it won't take long. Finish that and come along with me.'

Once they were out of sight of the alfarería, Omar turned to the boy and said, 'I've found your sister. We are going to see her now.'

'Isolde? You've found Isolde?'

'She's no longer called Isolde; her name is Jawhara. She is one of the Khalifa's concubines.'

He could see that the boy did not understand. Well there was no point trying to explain it to him.

'She is a slave like you,' he added. 'But she belongs to the Khalifa.'

'Will we be able to free her? Are we going to rescue her?'

'Perhaps. She wants to speak to you but it's very dangerous. We have to be very careful not to get caught. There will be guards all over the place. Do you think you can do that?'

Al-Sagir nodded, his face grave like an old man.

'I will be as quiet as a mouse. I will be as swift as a bird. I will be invisible.'

'Good. You will need to be all three. Now keep close behind me and do everything I say.'

He knew it would not be easy. After the fuss last night the guards would be more alert than usual. He and the boy stood in the shadows, opposite the entrance to the grounds of the alcázar, watching and waiting. The same guard was on duty as the previous night but he was not going to be so easily fooled a second time. Omar would just have to wait for the right moment to slip past him. The man had left his post the night before; it was quite likely he would do so again.

As they waited, the sound of raised voices came from inside the guard house; it sounded like a wrestling match. The guard on duty hesitated and then went inside to see what was happening. Instantly Omar grabbed al-Sagir by the arm and ran through the entrance and down the passage. This time he knew exactly where he was going and what he would do.

'Stay close to me,' he whispered to the boy.

They crept along the passage until they had almost reached the gateway to the garden. As expected a guard was positioned there, his feet planted firmly in front of the entrance. Omar motioned for the boy to stop. It was vital that they didn't alert the guard to their presence. Could he rely on al-Sagir to keep quiet?

'What will we do?' whispered al-Sagir.

'Shush. Don't make a sound. We're going over the wall.'

The boy's eyes widened with fear. The wall was over two metres high.

'Don't worry; I'll help you. Come back here, where we can't be seen. Now take this rope and don't let go of the end. Once you're over, look for a branch and tie the rope to it.'

The boy nodded, his eyes still like saucers. Omar felt a twinge of guilt at having brought him here into such danger but there was nothing he could do about it now. They had to go on.

'Now put your foot here, in my hands and scramble up. I'll follow you over.'

He cupped his hands into a stirrup and half-lifted, half-pushed al-Sagir over the wall. He heard a muffled gasp as the boy landed and then there was a pause while al-Sagir scrabbled about; Omar feared that the guard would hear them and come to investigate but he continued to doze at his post. After what felt like an eternity, Omar felt a gentle tug on the rope. He pulled at it, testing it for his weight. It would hold. Quickly he scaled the wall and dropped down into the garden then he pulled the rope up behind him.

'Do you want me to untie it?' the boy asked, his voice quavering.

Poor little chap, he was scared and who could blame him. If they were caught it would be the end for all of them.

'No. We'll need it to get out. Now follow me. Be careful where you tread and don't make a sound.'

This time he knew the way. He followed the paved path through the garden and around the pond, leaving the lights of the alcázar behind them.

'Is that where she lives?' al-Sagir whispered. 'Is that the palace?'

He had stopped and was looking back at the lamplight playing on the fountains. A flight of steps led down from the palace into the garden; waterfalls cascaded into the pond below, every splash a glittering jewel. Al-Sagir seemed more relaxed now, interested in everything around him.

'Yes, now come on. We haven't much time.'

'It's like fairyland,' the boy said. 'The Khalifa must be very rich.'

'He is. Very rich and very powerful, so we don't want to get caught. Now come on.'

She was waiting by the lake, sitting there in the moonlight like an alabaster statue. It took his breath away to look at her.

'Hans, is that you?' she whispered.

'Isolde.'

Instantly brother and sister were in each other's arms, crying and whispering in joy. Omar watched, trying to quash the feelings of jealously that rose in his throat. If only she loved him half as much.

'I never thought I would find you again,' she said, her tears soaking the boy's hair as she hugged and kissed him.

'I was here all along,' he said. 'The gods took care of us, just like you said, Issy.'

'Yes, my darling, they did. Now that we are together again, I'm never going to let you go.'

'Are we going to run away together?' al-Sagir asked.

She pulled away from her brother and turned to Omar.

'Thank you so much for bringing him to me. I am forever in your debt.'

Her smile wiped away all Omar's doubts and fears He was her slave; he would do anything for her.

'Issy, are we running away?' al-Sagir repeated, wiping the tears from his face with the back of his hand.

For the first time Omar saw him as he really was, a frightened child with a tear-streaked face, defenceless, expecting his sister to make all this go way, expecting her to turn back the clock and make things better.

She looked at Omar.

'Are we?' she asked.

Yes, of course they were. He had been thinking of what to do all day. He could not abandon them now. His plan was sketchy but he believed it would work. Once they had got out of the palace grounds they would get some horses and ride north. Nobody would know they had gone until the morning and by then they would be miles away. He was sure that the Khalifa would not bother to send his soldiers after one slave girl. They said he had hundreds of women in his harem; one less would mean nothing to him.

'Yes, but we must move quickly.'

'And quietly,' added al-Sagir.

She grabbed Omar's hands and looked up at him with her luminous eyes.

'Thank you so much, Omar.'

He felt his heart skip a beat. They would leave here and she would become his wife. She would be his forever.

He took her hand and they headed back towards the wall. This time, instead of keeping to the paved path, which he thought might expose them to prying eyes from the alcázar, he led them through the undergrowth, stumbling through bushes and overgrown trees until, at last, they arrived at the gate in the wall.

'Be very quiet,' Omar whispered. 'The guard is just the other side of that gate.'

Hardly daring to breathe, they crept past it and began to search for the tree where al-Sagir had tied the rope.

'It's just here, somewhere,' the boy whispered. 'I know it is.'

He sounded frightened.

'Is this it?' Jawhara asked, grabbing at something.

In the gloom Omar could see the rope exactly where he had left it. Now all they had to do was scale the wall and get out of there. Suddenly there was a movement to the left of them.

'Who's there?' a high pitched voice cried. 'Stop or I'll call the guards.'

'Oh no. It's al-Tayyib,' Jawhara wailed. 'Hurry before he catches us.'

The stout figure of the eunuch was waddling up the path towards them. His robe flapped behind him and Omar could hear the harsh gasping of his laboured breath.

'I know you're there. Stop in the name of the Khalifa,' the eunuch shouted.

They were in the darkest part of the garden; it was unlikely that he could see them. Omar gave Jawhara a gentle shove and said, 'Hide behind this bush and don't make a sound. I'll see to him.'

Next he grabbed al-Sagir and pushed him up and over the wall.

'Get out as quickly as you can. Just run. Don't stop for anyone. Go home and hide,' he said. 'We'll be along as soon as we can.'

Al-Sagir tumbled out of sight just in time.

'I see you. Guards, guards. I have him. Here by the gate,' the eunuch called.

His voice was rising in his excitement as he closed in on them. Omar froze. There was no way he could get Jawhara over the wall without al-Tayyib seeing them. He turned. He would have to do something to silence him before the guards heard and came to his aid.

'Stay here. I'll try to lead him away. As soon as we've gone, go back to the harem as though nothing has happened.'

'But.'

'Do as I say. If they catch you they will kill you. You are as nothing to them. You are less than nothing. Do as I say.'

'May the gods keep you safe,' she whispered.

He turned and ran, heedless of the noise he was making. The eunuch followed.

'I have you now,' he shouted. 'I see him. Guards, here he is.'

Omar was sure that he could outrun this portly slave. He would lead him away from Jawhara then make his own escape. Then he stumbled over a tree root and fell. It was only a moment before he was up on his feet again but that was enough for the eunuch to be on him. For such a fat, flabby man, he was surprisingly nimble.

'You can't escape now,' he squeaked, his breath coming in short sharp gasps. 'I have you.'

Omar struggled to free himself but the eunuch had him tight by the arm, his fingers gripping his flesh like pincers. He thrashed out at him but he would not let go. He punched him with his free hand but it made no difference. His fist sank into the man's unresisting soft white flesh but still he held on.

'Let go of me, you ridiculous little man,' he cried in anger.

'I have you now,' the eunuch repeated. 'I have you.'

Why had he come unarmed? It was a stupid mistake. If only he had something to defend himself, something to prise this limpet from him. He thrashed about with his free arm but couldn't locate anything to defend himself. He felt in his pocket. Something sharp pricked his finger; it was the trepan that Yusuf had given him. That would do; it wasn't much of a weapon but it might be enough to make the eunuch let go of him. He pulled it out and thrust it at his attacker.

'Arghh.'

The eunuch let out a long, low cry. His hand dropped to his side and he fell to the ground with a thud. Omar was loose at last. But for how long? The guards were searching the gardens. He could hear their heavy footsteps crashing through the bushes. He looked down at the eunuch; he was lying on his back, not moving. Had he hit his head when he fell? Why was he so still? Something didn't seem right but there was no time to worry about it. Omar could hear the guards getting closer; he turned and ran back to where the rope still hung, waiting for him. He swung himself over the wall and he was free.

'Got you.'

His heart seemed to stop. A heavy hand held him by the collar.

'By all that's holy I never thought you would do it again. You must have crap for brains.'

It was al-Jundi.

'Quick, put this on and follow me. And try to look like a soldier. Hold yourself upright and stop that bloody panting.'

He handed Omar his red cloak. Together they walked slowly out of the alcazaba and into the medina. Omar's heart was beating so loudly he was sure that everyone they passed could hear it. He tried to look like a soldier, walking with his head erect and his eyes forward, hoping all the time that nobody would recognise him. One of the guards saluted his brother as they went by but nobody questioned them. Nobody dared to question al-Jundi.

'Have you seen al-Sagir?' Omar whispered, once they were away from the alcazaba. 'Did the guards catch him?'

He was trembling now. What had happened? It had all been so fast. That fat eunuch had appeared from nowhere and ruined everything. The events raced through his head, tumbling over and over, making him giddy.

'Yes. I caught the little bastard. He's at home, shaking like a leaf. Why you involved him in your escapades I'll never know. Do you want everyone to go down with you?' al-Jundi replied.

His brother was very angry; that was clear. But he had saved him. He could have dragged him into the guard house and told them Omar was the intruder but he hadn't. What would he do? Would he tell Baba? And what of Jawhara? His heart sank when he thought of her; she would be so worried about her little brother. But was she safe? Had she done what he told her to? Had she made it back to the harem without being discovered? And the eunuch, when he recovered what would he say? Had he seen enough of Omar's face to identify him? Had he seen Jawhara? Omar groaned aloud as he thought of what could have been. It was over. He knew that now; even if they were not identified it would be very difficult to get Jawhara out of the harem now. He had breached the Khalifa's private quarters; no-one would be allowed to do that again.

CHAPTER 26

Once Omar had led the eunuch away from Isolde's hiding place and it was quiet again, she crept carefully back to the alcázar. There were loud voices and the sound of shouting in the distance. The guards had been alerted and were looking for the intruder; she could hear them crashing through the bushes. She was careful to keep away from the pools of light cast by the many oil lamps and moved like a cat amongst the shadows. The women in the harem had come to the jalousie windows of the harem and were gazing out; she could see them moving behind the wooden slats, the flickering candles elongating their bodies into strange, ghostly forms. She must be careful. No-one must suspect her. She had been in the harem only a few months but she was already aware of the jealousies and rivalries that existed between the women. If they knew that she had tried to escape, there would be no hesitation in giving her up. Najm was her only friend; she was the only one she could trust. But would Najm stand by her if she were caught? She doubted it. What good would it do either of them? No. She was on her own.

She crept round to the side door and opened it quietly. There was no-one about. Everyone was too busy staring into the garden, wondering what was happening. She could hear their voices, high and shrill, like so many starlings. But she could not join them; they would know at once. Not only was her dress torn and muddy, her yellow hair pulled loose from its braids, she was shaking all over. Her body was trembling, out of control. She had to wash and change before anyone saw her. Luckily her room was close by. She pulled aside the curtain and went inside. Her maid was curled up on a mat, asleep.

'Wake,' she said, gently pushing the girl with her foot. 'Wake up.'

The child, because she was no more than that, ten years old at the most, sat up, rubbing her eyes.

'Bring me hot water. I need to bathe,' she told her.

'Are you all right?' the maid asked. 'You are trembling. And what happened to your dress?'

'I fell in the garden,' Isolde replied. 'It was so silly of me to go out in the dark and now I fear I have caught cold.'

'Shall I bring you something?' the maid asked.

'No, I will be all right soon. Just bring the hot water for my bath.'

While the maid went for the water she took off her ripped dress and hid it in the cupboard then unbraided her hair and lay down on her bed. She was safe she told herself. She was safe. Nobody would ever know that she had been in the garden. She was safe now. But she could not stop her heart racing nor her hands from trembling.

'Jawhara, you're missing all the excitement,' said Najm, coming into the room. 'There has been another intruder.'

She stopped and looked at her friend.

'What's the matter? You are as white as a sheet. And why are you trembling? Are you unwell?'

She sat on the bed, next to her.

'Has something happened?'

244

Isolde could not reply. She shook her head and began to cry, hot salty tears that ran down her cheeks, soaking her pillow.

'Is it about the Khalifa?'

Najm took her hand and stroked it gently.

'I told you, it will be over very quickly. Don't let it upset you. And don't start crying when you are with him, whatever you do. He will not like that. You must smile and be happy. Remember this is a big chance for you. All the women here would give anything to change places with you tomorrow, me included.'

'I know. I'm sorry,' Isolde whispered.

Better to let Najm think she was scared of the Khalifa than to tell her the truth. It would only put her friend in danger too.

'What is happening outside?' she asked, at last. 'Have they caught him?'

'No, he has escaped.'

'So no-one knows who he is?'

She looked away as she said it; it seemed that Najm was looking at her a bit too closely.

'No they don't. Do you?'

'Me? Of course not. Why would I know anything about an intruder? I have been here all evening.'

'Well whoever he is, he's in plenty of trouble. He has killed al-Tayyib. Stabbed him in the throat. The man bled to death where he lay.'

'Al-Tayyib is dead?'

'Yes, as dead as mutton. So we will be getting a new guard to accompany us on our shopping trips.'

'But that's awful. Dead?'

She could not keep the horror out of her voice.

'Yes it is awful; al-Tayyib wasn't a very nice man but he didn't deserve to die.'

This was dreadful news. What had happened after she left? Who had stabbed him? Did Omar kill him? She groaned in despair. It could only have been Omar. The guards knew al-Tayyib; they would not have mistaken him for an intruder. She felt as though the bottom had dropped out of her world. What would happen to Omar now? Would she ever see him again? Once more she felt the soft touch of his lips on hers as he kissed her. Was she never to feel those lips on hers again? Would he abandon her now? Or would he risk coming back for her? And Hans? Would Hans be implicated in this murder? Her head began to spin.

'Excuse me, Najm. I'm going to be sick,' she said.

CHAPTER 27

Qasim had just dropped off to sleep when he was awoken by a loud banging on the door. At first he lay there thinking he was back in Ardales, his heart racing with fear. Soldiers. He would have to flee. A movement from his wife, tossing restlessly by his side, brought him back to the present. Who could it be? Who was making such a terrible racket at this time of night. He got up and pulled his robe around him.

'Who's that?' Fatima asked, her voice thick with sleep.

They both feared the worst. A knock on the door in the middle of the night was never good news.

He heard al-Mari open the door and let someone in. His servant sounded surprised.

'Who is it?' Qasim called.

'It is al-Sagir.'

For a moment Qasim was bewildered. He thought al-Sagir was asleep on the patio with al-Mari. Why was he trying to get into the house? When had he gone out? He sighed. There was no alternative; he would have to see for himself.

He shuffled slowly out onto the patio, feeling the chill of the night air creep into his bones.

'What's this?' he asked. 'Where has the boy been at this hour? And why so much banging on my door in the middle of the night?'

'I don't know, master. He refuses to say.'

Qasim hated his sleep to be disturbed, whatever the reason. He stared at his young slave; he was crouched in the corner of the patio, shaking. Something had given him a fright; that was clear. Well, there was no point shouting at him; he'd tell them nothing then.

'Come now boy, I'm not going to hurt you. Where have you been? Why are you shaking so?'

Al-Sagir still said nothing; he sat watching the door, terrified.

'Ask him why he is so frightened,' he told al-Mari.

But even the old slave could not get the boy to respond.

'Something has scared him.'

'Something or someone,' said Qasim. 'What is it lad? You can tell us. We'll help you.'

But the boy just stared at the door, unblinking.

Now Fatima came in to see what was happening; she was followed by a sleepy-eyed Layla and one of the grandchildren.

'Get him something to eat,' he told his wife. 'And send those children back to bed.'

She brought a bowl of the leftover aubergines, covered with a sprinkling of sesame seeds and offered it to al-Sagir. He did not seem to even notice her.

'Well whatever it was, it has scared him good and proper,' Qasim said. 'I've never seen him like this before.'

Suddenly the boy jumped further back into the shadows. Someone was coming. Heavy footsteps could be heard approaching the house. The door opened and Omar and al-Jundi came in.

'Praise be to Allah,' Qasim said. 'Now maybe we'll get some sense out of the lad. Where have you been Omar? This boy has been sitting here like one of the half-dead for the last ten minutes. We haven't been able to get a word out of him. Maybe you can tell us what has been going on.'

'As-salam alaykum, Baba,' Omar said, looking down as he spoke.

'We need to speak to you, Baba,' said al-Jundi, shutting the door behind them. 'In private.'

Qasim motioned to al-Mari and the others to leave. He saw Fatima cast a worried glance at Omar then she too, went to her room.

The three men stood looking at each other. Qasim was frightened to ask what had happened. If al-Jundi was here again, it was not good news. What had Omar been up to this time?

'I think you should sit down, Baba.'

'No. I'm quite all right. Just tell me what he's done.'

He saw Omar give him an injured look. He turned to him and said, 'You've been back to the alcázar, haven't you? How many times do you have to be told? Are you completely stupid, boy?'

He struggled to keep his voice calm. It did no good to get angry. First he had to hear all the details.

'Yes, Baba. He was back in the alcázar and this time he took al-Sagir with him,' al-Jundi confirmed.

'What?' Qasim thundered; he could no longer keep his voice down.

'But Baba, wait until you hear it all. Then you'll understand,' Omar protested.

'I understand well enough. You have lost your wits to some slave girl. Instead of thinking with the good brain that Allah gave you, you're letting your loins do the thinking for you.'

'But Baba I was trying to help her. I love her.'

'Love?' he exploded. 'Do you think you are the first man to think he is in love with some slip of a girl? You know nothing of love. It's the demon lust that has turned your mind.'

Omar sat down on the floor and put his head in his hands.

'And why did you take the slave with you? What was that all about?' his father continued.

'I've been trying to tell you, Baba. He is her brother. She just wanted to speak to her brother, that was all.'

Qasim looked at the boy in the corner. He was crying now. Poor child, what misfortune had Omar got him involved in?

'Go to bed, boy,' he said.

The slave scurried to his corner of the patio and curled up on his bed; he was glad to get away from Qasim's anger.

'Let me explain, Baba,' said al-Jundi. 'I'm afraid it's much more serious than that. They managed to get into the gardens of the harem and meet the girl, though only Allah knows how, with so many guards on duty. She belongs to the Khalifa; she is a member of his harem.'

'Allah save us from stupid sons,' Qasim groaned.

How could his son do this to him, to the family? If he had been caught it would have been the end for all of them. He struggled to keep his temper.

'They were discovered by the eunuch al-Tayyib. The woman escaped, unseen and, as far as I know, unidentified. Omar and the boy ran away with the eunuch in pursuit,' al-Jundi continued.

His son spoke in a cool, impersonal way, as if he were recounting the details of some military skirmish.

'We had doubled the guard after last night's farrago, so everyone was on alert.'

'That's what I don't understand, Omar. You knew it would be even more dangerous to go back there. Did you want to get caught? Did you want to bring disgrace to your family?' Qasim asked.

'No Baba.'

'I was waiting outside the gates when the boy climbed over. I sent him straight back here,' al-Jundi continued.

'Thanks be to Allah that it was you, al-Jundi and not someone else.'

'The worst is still to come, Baba.'

'Come inside, my son and tell me the worst.'

Qasim went into the main room and sat down on the couch, waiting to hear what al-Jundi had to say. He knew this was going to be serious. His eldest son was not given to exaggeration.

'Omar says he was caught by the eunuch. There was a scuffle and the eunuch was stabbed.'

He looked at Omar. His son sat motionless, his head still in his hands. Qasim could not believe it; Omar was not a violent man. He never got into fights like many of the other boys and he certainly never carried a weapon. How had this happened?

Omar's shoulders began to shake as he wept.

'It was an accident, Baba. I swear it was an accident. I never meant to hurt him. I was just trying to get away,' he sobbed. 'I couldn't get free of him; he was hanging on to me like a limpet. I just wanted him to let go.'

'You stabbed him?'

'I didn't mean to harm him,' Omar cried. 'I just wanted to hurt him so that he would let go.'

'Is he all right?' Qasim asked, looking at al-Jundi.

'I don't know,' al-Jundi said. 'I hope so, for Omar's sake.'

'Will he be able to identify Omar?'

They both looked at Omar.

'It was dark,' he said. 'I don't think he would recognise me again. I've only seen him once before.'

'He's seen you before?'

Qasim could not believe his ears.

'When? Where did he see you?'

'It was in the market, the first time I saw Jawhara, but I don't think he noticed me. He was more interested in the other girl.'

'What other girl? How many people know that you were involved with this slave girl?' al-Jundi asked.

'She was with a friend, another slave-girl. They were buying things in the market. That's all. I just spoke to her once.'

'Did you tell her your name?'

Omar looked down at his feet and mumbled something.

'What's that? What did you say?'

'Yes.'

'Allah preserve us from fools and madmen,' Qasim said. 'This is getting worse by the minute. So if the eunuch survives and remembers the young man stupid enough to approach one of the Khalifa's concubines in the market, what do you think he will do?'

Omar said nothing.

'He will ask the women who you were.'

He turned to al-Jundi.

'What can we do? What will happen to him?'

'First I must find out if the man is alive or not. Then we will decide. Whatever happens we will have to move quickly. There's a rumour that we may be going up north, to deal with a rebellion. If that's true, I won't be here to protect Omar anymore,' he said. 'I'll go back to the barracks now and try to find out what has happened then I'll come straight back. In the meantime stay here and do not go out.'

This last remark was directed at Omar.

'Thank you, brother,' he said.

Qasim locked the door behind his son and turned to Omar. His son looked exhausted; he was not a bad man, just a foolish one.

'Go and rest,' he told him. 'Who knows what will happen tonight.'

Qasim went into his room and lay down beside his wife.

'Is everything all right, husband?' she asked.

'Go back to sleep, wife. I will tell you all about it in the morning.'

***

He must have dozed because the next thing he heard was a tapping at the door.

'It's me, Baba, let me in.'

It was al-Jundi. He pushed past Qasim and stormed into the house.

'Bolt the door,' he said. 'It's bad news; the eunuch is dead.'

There was a gasp from Omar who had heard his brother arrive and stood there, white-faced, listening to every word.

Qasim felt his knees turn to water. This was worse than anything he could have imagined. His son had murdered a member of the Khalifa's personal household. The punishment for that was death. All this time he had been worried about his own safety and now it was his son and family who were in danger. Qasim looked at Omar, with tears in his eyes. He was no longer angry with him. This went beyond anger. He believed his son when he told him that it was an accident. He had never known Omar to be violent; he rarely lost his temper Even this woman could not have changed his son that much. He would never have meant to kill anyone, he was sure. He sighed. It was too late now; the deed could not be undone. All that remained was for him to find a way to save his son and to save the family's honour.

'Go back to your room. I need time to think about what we will do,' he said.

'I must get back to the barracks, Baba, before I am missed. I will let know if I hear anything else,' al-Jundi said.

'Very well son. Thank you for what you have done tonight. Alla ysalmak. May Allah protect you from all harm.'

And from the stupidity of your brother, he wanted to add.

***

Long before dawn Qasim was up and dressed. He knew exactly what had to be done. He had prayed all night for Allah to give him guidance. There was clearly only one solution: his son had to disappear.

'Fatima, tell Sara and Ibrahim that they must leave today. Go and help them get ready. I want them on the road before daybreak.'

'But there is still one day left of Eid al-Adha.'

'Just do as I say; I will explain it all to you later.'

'Yes, husband.'

He went to where al-Mari was still sleeping and shook him by the shoulder. The man was awake in an instant. Qasim had the sensation that he too had not slept much that night.

'The boy must leave. I am sending him to Córdoba to work with my son. Make sure he is ready by the time Ibrahim leaves.'

Al-Sagir was awake already. He sat up and, when he heard Qasim's words he started to cry again. He cried like a very young child, with his mouth open and snot and tears running down his face.

'What about my sister?' he asked. 'Will I never get to see my sister again?'

'Listen child. You have been badly advised by my son. If you stay here and they discover that you went into the

255

harem to see one of the Khalifa's concubines, whether she is your sister or not, you will be executed. Not only that, your sister will be killed too. Do you want that?'

The boy shook his head sadly. Poor child, he had been separated from his sister once and then, against all odds, he had found her again; now he was being told that they could never be together. It was hard for an innocent boy to understand. But understand it he must because there was no other way.

'You will be well treated in Córdoba. My son will look after you. Now get your things together and hurry.'

Fatima had the grandchildren up and was feeding them bread and honey. He could see from the expression on her face that she was unhappy that they were leaving so soon. It was for the best for all of them; it was not safe for them to stay in Madinat al-Zahra now. Who could tell when the soldiers would come knocking at their door?

'Is Omar awake?' he asked her.

'Yes. He's talking to Ibrahim.'

Qasim found his two sons sitting on their beds, in the dark. No-one had bothered to light an oil lamp. No-one wanted to shed a light on the shame that had befallen them.

'Have you decided, Baba?' Omar asked.

His voice was no more than a whisper. For a moment Qasim was reminded of him as a child when he and his brothers had got into mischief. Omar was rarely to blame. Ibrahim and al-Jundi were always the naughty ones; Omar was gentler, kinder, an altogether more pleasant child but he still got pulled into their pranks.

'I have. Get your things together at once. You are leaving here today. Right this moment. You are going on a pilgrimage to Mecca to beg Allah for his forgiveness.'

His son's face was ashen. Whatever he had expected his father to say, it was not this.

'And al-Sagir?'

'He is going to Córdoba with Ibrahim.'

He looked across at his middle son and said, 'You said you needed some extra help. Well now you have it. Do not question the boy about what has happened. It is better that you and your sister know nothing of the details. It is sufficient to know that Omar's actions could have serious repercussions on all of us. Now hurry. Not a moment's delay.'

While Ibrahim gathered up his clothes and his bag and went out to look for his sister, Qasim turned to Omar.

'Go to the outskirts of the town. There you will find the camel train that arrived a few days ago. I know that they plan to leave for North Africa today. Go with them. When you get to North Africa you can pick up a ship to Alexandria. From there you can make your way down to Arabia and to the Holy City of Mecca.'

'But Baba, how long must I be away?'

Omar's eyes were filled with tears. Soon they would both be crying. There was a pain in his heart as Qasim realised that he would probably never see his son again.

'Do not come back Omar. It will never be safe for you to return to Madinat al-Zahra, not while the Khalifa is alive. You must make a new life now. That is the consequence of your actions. Do not fear; Allah will guide you. It has been my life's ambition to make a pilgrimage to

257

Mecca. Now you will do it for me. Make this pilgrimage for me, your father, who has never had the opportunity to do it, make it for your family's honour and above all make it for your own salvation.'

'Yes, Baba.'

'Here take this money. It is not much but it is all I have. It is enough to pay for your journey and to get you to your destination. After that Allah will take care of you.'

He hesitated, tears already running down his cheeks.

'And this is for you. It was always for you, my son. Maybe it will help you to make your way in the world. Guard it carefully and may it bring you prosperity.'

He handed his son a folded piece of parchment; it was the secret recipe for his glazes.

Omar threw his arms around him and sobbed. Qasim could feel his son's lean body through his robe and hear the beating of his heart mingled with his own. Would he ever hold him in his arms again? The memory of Omar as a baby came flooding back to him. Another son. How proud he had been.

'Allah be with you my son,' he said. 'Now go, quickly before it is light.'

CHAPTER 28

They had kept Isolde busy all day with extra singing lessons, dancing and extra language classes. They said her Arabic was poor; she must practice harder. The Khalifa was a cultured man they said; he liked beauty in all things even in the way the women of his harem spoke. It was not enough to be beautiful she had to be accomplished too. They brought in a new tutor, a young woman who taught at the university. She was a Jewish girl who read and spoke perfect Arabic; she showed Isolde how to form the letters and curl her tongue around the strange sounds.

'Try to hear the music in the language,' she told her. 'Once you have the rhythm then it will flow more easily.'

She made her repeat the sounds after her, half saying, half singing them. At last Isolde began to feel that she could understand this foreign tongue. She recited the phrases back to her. It was like reciting the nursery rhymes her mother used to teach her.

'That is much better, much softer,' the woman told her. 'Good. I will come back again tomorrow and we will work on it some more.'

'Thank you,' Isolde said. 'Ma'a salama.'

The tutor smiled at her and added, 'Good luck, tonight.'

They all wanted her to please the Khalifa. Everyone, the maids, the dancing teacher, the tutor, the singing instructor, the eunuchs, the other concubines, Najm and even poor al-Tayyib had contributed to her preparation. No-one wanted any blame for her shortcomings to fall on them. She felt weighed down with the responsibility of it all.

Najm pulled back the curtain and came into her room.

'It's time to get ready,' she said.

Isolde felt herself go cold; it was as if a blast of icy wind had entered the room. There was no going back. She could not escape her destiny now. Whatever might happen in the future, tonight was inevitable. The Khalifa wanted her and she was powerless to refuse him.

Najm was smiling at her.

'Come along now. You look as though I have just announced your death sentence. It really won't be that bad. I keep telling you, the messy part will be over very quickly. Just make sure you please him with your dancing. Remember your job is to make him happy, to give him pleasure. So try practising that lovely smile of yours. Come on. Think of something that makes you happy. Think of the wonderful life you will have if he falls in love with you.'

'I don't think the Khalifa would ever fall in love with me,' Isolde said, trying to imagine what it would be like to have such a powerful man enamoured of her.

'They say he was besotted with al-Zahra; he couldn't get enough of her. But now she is old, at least twenty-two and he is looking for someone new. It could so easily be you he chooses.'

At this Isolde let out a laugh.

'There, that's better. Keep that thought and it will help you to smile.'

'You are very kind to me, Najm,' she said. 'I don't deserve your friendship.'

She was tempted to tell her friend what had happened the night before in the garden but as she struggled with the idea, her maid came in.

'You have to come into the baths with us now. We need to prepare you,' she said.

'Prepare me? What do you mean.'

'Come with us please, Jawhara.'

She looked at Najm.

'It's all right. They just want to get your body ready for this night of love. Don't worry. And remember keep smiling.'

As she spoke, Isolde could see that she was envious of her. Nothing like this had ever happened to her and was not likely to now.

She followed the maids into the baths and stood there while they removed her clothes. The water was warm and perfumed. First they bathed her in scented soap then they shaved all the superfluous hair from her body until she was as smooth as a baby. Next they dressed her in a flowing robe of white muslin that was embroidered with rosebuds and tiny bluebirds then they placed perfume made from water lilies behind her ears and on her ankles and wrists. They sat her on the couch and slipped her feet into white silky slippers embroidered with gold thread and wound fine chains of pure gold around her ankles. She felt like a lamb being prepared for the slaughter, a pure white virgin held by golden chains but a captive nonetheless. If only all this preparation was for her to see Omar; if only her first night of love was to be with him.

'Now for your make-up,' her maid said with an envious smile.

She drew lines around Isolde's eyes with kohl to make them seem larger and rubbed walnut shell on her lips to redden them; she rubbed henna into her finger nails. They brushed her hair until her scalp tingled and caught it up loosely into a white satin cap. They hung emerald earrings from her ears and encircled her throat with diamonds; then, when she was ready, they stood back and looked at their handiwork with unconcealed pleasure. She was their creation, their princess, their perfect virgin.

Now the others gathered round; all eager to comment on her good fortune. She was to be blessed with a child, a son no less; she was to make the Khalifa fall in love with her; she was to become rich and famous, her beauty more renowned that al-Zahra herself.

Isolde felt faint. Would she be able to please him? Thoughts of Omar and her brother kept running through her head. It was all her fault. It was she who had insisted he bring Hans to see her. Had she caused her little brother's capture or even death? Najm told her to smile but how would she be able to keep from weeping when she did not know what had happened to them.

Najm came close to her and whispered in her ear, 'I have just heard some news. They have identified al-Tayyib's killer. It's a stone mason called Yusuf. He works here in the alcázar.'

'So what was he doing in the gardens?' she asked, incredulous.

'Nobody knows. They have arrested him and thrown him into the dungeon.'

'Was he alone?'

'They didn't catch anyone else if that is what you're asking.'

She stared at Isolde for a moment then moved away. Had she guessed what Isolde really wanted to ask?

So it was not Omar. She closed her eyes and whispered her grateful thanks to Frig, the goddess of love; she had kept them safe. Someone else was to blame for al-Tayyib's death not Omar. Now maybe she would be able to smile for the Khalifa.

All the women in the harem had gathered around her. They were to accompany her to the Khalifa's bedroom. Najm took her arm and gently led her forward; the rest of the women whirled about her, singing and dancing as they went. Najm's eyes were shining with happiness. Isolde looked at them; it all felt surreal. Everyone was so happy. This was what they all wanted so why did she feel numb? Their happiness and the general air of celebration clashed with the emptiness in the pit of her stomach.

They led her through the palace to the door of the Khalifa's most private rooms. Two Palace Guards stood, one on either side, their feet apart, their javelins at their sides. The women stopped; only Isolde, her maid, two musicians and Yamut were allowed to enter.

The Khalifa lay on a couch that was covered in purple velvet and strewn with cushions. He regarded her in silence. She looked about her; the walls of the room were lined with silk tapestries, each one woven with gold and silver thread in the images of peacocks. Even in the subdued light from the candles that flickered in each and every corner, their red, blue and green colours were bright and vibrant. She almost expected to hear the birds' mewling cry or see them flap their wings and fly towards her.

'I have brought you the new concubine, Jawhara,' Yamut said at last.

The Khalifa nodded gravely and at once the musicians began to play.

'Now you must dance,' Yamut hissed at her.

She stretched out her arms, letting the folds of her robe hang free and began to turn slowly. The delicate muslin floated about her like a cloud. Her feet caught the rhythm of the music and soon she was lost in the movements she had practised so assiduously, giving herself up to the sensuous pleasure of the dance. The heady perfume of the burning incense that filled the air was intoxicating. She swayed and turned, gyrating her hips as she moved; she whirled and twirled and shook her body at him. She was a snake, sashaying sinuously around the room, never taking her eyes from the man seated before her. She was dancing for the Khalifa, the most powerful man in all of al-Andalus. The musicians played faster and faster until she fell to the ground in a final swirl of her skirts and knelt there looking up at the Khalifa. She knew it was perfect. She had done exactly as she had been taught.

The Khalifa was smiling now.

'You have done well, Yamut,' he said. 'Leave us now.'

Everyone knew what they had to do. The musicians bowed and backed out of the room; the maid approached Isolde nervously to disrobe her. She removed her outer dress, leaving Isolde wearing only the finest of cotton robes then she pulled at the cap that pinned her hair in place, letting it cascade down her back.

'You can go now,' Yamut told the maid.

Once she had gone he too bowed and left. Isolde was alone with the Khalifa. His bodyguards had retreated to the other side of the heavy oak door and closed it tight. Nobody could help her now.

'Come child. Sit beside me,' the Khalifa said.

His voice was gentle and for a moment she relaxed. She approached the couch and sat at his feet. He was old, even older than she had expected. His eyes were keen and blue, like hers but the flesh below them was soft and baggy. He had probably been a handsome man once, but now, apart from the proud hooked nose that spoke of his Arabian ancestors, his face gave witness to the ravages of his years. He was not a man she could fall in love with and she saw once again the face of the young potter in her imagination.

'Jawhara,' the Khalifa murmured. 'You have been well named.'

Isolde looked up at him. She knew that whatever happened that night she would never be the same woman again; her life was about to change whether she wanted it to or not.

CHAPTER 29

He hardly knew what he was doing; Omar's mind was in turmoil. All he wanted to do was run away and hide. Instead, he did as his father had told him and headed out through the south gate of the medina, searching for the caravan. He walked as briskly as he could without actually breaking into a run; the last thing he wanted to do was draw attention to himself. There were Palace Guards everywhere. He recalled his father's instructions as best he could; he had to find the North Africans and persuade them to take him with them. But where were they camped? It was dark; what moon there was had slipped behind the clouds and it was hard to see exactly where he was. He stumbled over a sleeping body and was rewarded with a series of obscene oaths.

'Sorry,' he muttered and veered away to the right, wishing he had thought to bring a torch with him.

He had seen their camp earlier when he had been to watch the camel racing and he knew it was somewhere to the south-west of the city walls, so he kept heading in that direction and hoped he would eventually come to it. There was no-one about to ask; most people were asleep, their lights extinguished and their doors closed tight. The embers of one or two campfires still glowed dully and stray dogs scavenged about looking for food. One of them sprang out at him, snarling angrily. He leapt back, his heart racing.

'All right, boy. It's all right,' he whispered, trying to calm the animal.

The dog growled menacingly then fell silent. Then Omar realised he must be close to their camp; he could hear the grunting, snuffly sounds of the camels and the pungent smell of camel dung was unmistakeable. He edged his way towards the dying fire.

'Who's there?' a gruff voice called. 'What do you want?'

'As-salam alaykum,' Omar said. 'I am the son of Qasim the potter; I'm looking for the North Africans.'

'What do you want with them at this hour of the night?'

'I want to speak to them.'

'Come closer.'

As Omar moved nearer to the fire he saw the hunched figure of one of the Africans squatting beside it. The man lit a torch from the embers and stood up to examine his visitor.

'Wa alaykum e-salam,' he said. 'I recognise you; your father is a most hospitable man. Does he need more glazes for his pots?'

'No, thank you. My father did send me but not to buy glazes.'

'Well, what is it that you want?'

'I heard that you were leaving for North Africa and I want to come with you.'

The man did not reply; instead he motioned for Omar to sit beside him. He lifted a pot from the fire and poured out a small cup of sweet-smelling tea.

'Thank you,' Omar said, accepting the ritual drink from his host.

He sipped it in silence. Now he would have to wait until the North African spoke to him. He looked at the flickering flames. Some said you could see your future in the dying flames of a fire but all he could see were blue and silver glimmers amongst the ashes. The man poked the fire with a stick and then the flames danced gold and red in the darkness, flaring up as if to welcome him. For a moment he thought he saw Jawhara's face but, just as quickly, it was gone.

The man stroked his beard thoughtfully and regarded Omar in silence. At last he spoke.

'So you want to come with us?'

'Yes. I'm going on a pilgrimage to Mecca.'

'Mecca is a long way,' the man said.

'I know. I have money,' Omar said.

'Oh, you have money, do you?'

The man's teeth gleamed white in the firelight.

'Yes, I can pay you. All I want is to accompany you until we reach the Maghreb and then I will take a ship to Alexandria.'

The man nodded, all the while continuing to stroke his beard. Omar began to feel nervous. He had heard tales of these nomads; without warning the smallest altercation could blow up into a fight to the death. They were fiercely independent men whose sole loyalty was to their families; a slight on their honour could only be expiated by the blood of their enemy. He wondered if he could trust them. Omar was a stranger to them. Did that also make him an enemy?

'Very well, for one hundred silver dirhams I will take you to North Africa. You must pay now.'

It was a lot of money, almost half of what his father had given him; but Omar had no choice. His father would not have sent him to these men if there had been an alternative. If he stayed in Madinat al-Zahra and he was arrested it would not only be him to suffer, his whole family would be dishonoured. He counted out the money and handed it to the man but it pained him to do so. His father had saved this money bit by bit over the years; Omar knew it was his Mecca fund, as they all called it. The whole family were aware how much Qasim had wanted to make the pilgrimage. Now he would never do it; he had given his savings to Omar.

'There is no time to sleep,' the nomad said. 'We are leaving before the sun rises.'

He went into the nearest tent and roused his companions.

'Can you ride a camel?' he asked Omar.

'Of course.'

'Good. Come with me.'

The camp was suddenly alive with men and animals. Within a short time the tents were dismantled, the camels were laden, the fires extinguished and everyone was ready to leave. Omar climbed onto his camel. He pulled up the hood of his long djellaba.

'That will be no good when you get to the desert,' the nomad said. 'You need a maghrebi; here, wind this around your head.'

He handed him a long strip of green and yellow material and showed him how to wind it into a simple turban. Omar did as instructed. Not only would it shield him from the dry winds of the desert it would hide his face from prying eyes.

The man kicked his camel into action and loped to the front of the caravan, leaving Omar sandwiched between a couple of mules, some women on foot and a very fat man on a dromedary. With a lurch, his camel moved forward; his exile had begun. He was about to leave behind everyone that he loved: his mother, his father, his brothers and sisters, Yusuf and his beloved Jawhara. Feelings of sorrow and guilt overwhelmed him. Would he ever see any of them again?

***

He expected the journey to the coast to take five or six days but he had not allowed for the fact that his hosts still had business to transact. They stopped in all the sizeable towns on the way, exchanging their wares for sacks of olives and almonds, buying cloth and silverware and distributing the news. On the second day, he was disturbed to hear them tell some of the market stall holders in Medina Antaquira about the murder of the Khalifa's eunuch.

'It happened in the alcázar itself,' one of the Africans said. 'An enormous man strode in and hacked at the eunuch with his sword. He would have killed more of them but the guards came and he ran away.'

'Did they catch him?' asked an old man, with baskets full of oranges.

'I don't think so. They say he disappeared without a trace.'

'It's only a matter of time before they catch him,' one of his companions added. 'All the Palace Guard are looking for him.'

'But surely it's impossible to enter the alcázar without being seen?' said a woman with jars of honey for sale.

'Some say he was a djinn. He could only have escaped by the use of magic,' said another of the nomads. 'The place was surrounded by guards and yet nobody saw him enter or leave.'

'There are no such things as djinns,' said the old man.

'We have seen one,' said the African. 'Once, many years ago, in the desert. He appeared in the guise of an old woman, promising to lead us to a well of fresh water. Then, when we arrived at the well, it was dry. We turned to berate the old crone but she changed into a black crow and flew off.'

'But why would a djinn want to kill one of the Khalifa's servants?' asked an important-looking man in a white robe. 'It doesn't make sense.'

'Maybe it was an omen. The Khalifa is about to go to war again. Maybe the djinn was warning him,' said one man.

'Just some idiot trying to get into the Khalifa's harem, more likely,' said another. 'Got his eye on a juicy slave girl.'

Omar listened carefully. Everyone liked to have an opinion on such an exciting piece of news and people vied with each other to state their views. As usual the rumours were a mixture of fantasy and truth but he was pleased that so far it seemed that no suspicion had fallen on him.

'And who are you, young man?' asked the woman with the honey. 'You're not one of these nomads, I can tell that, even though you wear their turban and you arrived on one of their camels.'

'I'm just a traveller. I'm making a pilgrimage to Mecca.'

The men stopped chattering for a moment and looked at him with new respect.

'A hajj? That is very noble. I have always wanted to make the hajj but somehow there was never the time and now I'm too old,' said the old man. 'Good luck to you, my son. May Allah go with you and protect you.'

The old man and his companions collected their purchases together and left, walking back towards the fortified town from which they had come and leaving the nomads to continue on their way. The caravan moved south until they came to an empty field on the outskirts of the town, next to some ancient stone monoliths.

'We will rest here,' said the leader. 'There's a stream for water for the animals and some trees to give us shelter.'

Some of the women were unhappy at this; they muttered about being so close to the standing stones.

'It's not good,' one said. 'This is a place of witchcraft. It will bring us bad luck.'

'The only bad luck that will fall on you is if you don't get our food ready soon,' her husband said.

'She's right. It's unlucky to camp here. This is where they sacrificed people to the old gods,' said another of the women.

'Don't be stupid, wife, and see to the animals.'

'May Allah protect us,' the women muttered as they led the animals to the stream, to drink.

The men may have dismissed their wives' fears as groundless but nevertheless they didn't complain when their wives placed the cooking tents as far away from the evil spirits as possible. The women started to organise the camp, feeding the animals and preparing the food; at last the smell of cooking began to drift through the air. Omar felt himself relax as the men continued to gossip. He lay back in the shade of an olive tree and listened to them; some were drinking mint tea but others drank fermented camels' milk and, as they became more intoxicated, the stories grew.

From where they were camped they could see for miles across the golden plain of Medina Antaquera, its wide expanse broken only by the occasional outcrop of rock. There was no corn now; it had been harvested some months ago but patches of stubble remained where the plough had passed them by.

'See that hill there?' one of the Africans said, taking a deep draught from the jug of camels' milk. 'The one that looks a sleeping man? Some say that, long ago, a djinn terrorised this town and, when he was caught, they imprisoned him inside the hill. He has lain there ever since.'

'Well I heard that two lovers, one a Muslim merchant and the other a Christian girl, threw themselves to their deaths from the top of the rock and now their bones lie beneath it,' said another.

'Why would a good Muslim fall in love with a Christian woman? Weren't there enough pretty Muslim girls for him?'

'Why didn't he just marry her and make her become a Muslim like him?'

'It's probably just a legend. Who knows what's true and what's false by the time the story has been told and retold hundreds of times,' Omar said.

The African nodded in agreement.

'That's true, my friend. Maybe she was the Muslim and he was the Christian.'

'Of course. Now that would be different.'

The men were intrigued by this sudden twist in the tale.

'Her father would not have allowed her to marry a Christian,' said one.

'He would have killed her first,' said another.

While they continued with their speculations, Omar stretched out his aching limbs. He was unused to riding a camel and every muscle in his body hurt. The sun was almost overhead; it was time for the midday prayers.

He had made himself a vow that he would pray five times a day, no matter what else he was doing. He would become a good Muslim and make this pilgrimage for his father.

The realisation that he had killed another person, someone he did not even know, upset him deeply. He had not meant to harm anyone; it had been self-defence he told himself over and over again. Nevertheless an innocent man had died because of him. He could not escape that fact. Would Allah ever forgive him? And what of Jawhara? If all went well and, some time in the future, his father allowed him to return, he would look for Jawhara; he had to explain to her that the eunuch's death had been an accident. Surely she realised that he would never intentionally kill another person, that he was not a murderer. Surely she did not believe that he had abandoned her to save his own skin. He had only been trying to prevent her from being caught, he told himself and now he could not bear the thought that she might hate and despise him. He groaned. If only he could get some word to her. If only he could explain what had happened.

Even as he thought it, he knew that this was an impossibility. It would never happen; any foolish act on his part would endanger his whole family and Jawhara herself. No, he had brought enough suffering on them already. His guilt was eating away at him but he knew this was to be his punishment; he would never see her again and he could never tell anyone what had happened. He would just have to suffer the knowledge that he had sinned and pray that Allah would forgive him. Omar unrolled his prayer mat and, making a guess at the direction of Mecca, knelt down to pray.

***

On the tenth day they arrived at Jebel Tariq, the northern pillar of Hercules, a gigantic outcrop of rock overlooking the narrow straits that separated al-Andalus from the Maghreb. Across that tranquil, blue water lay the home of their ancestors, a land of sandy wastes and mauve-tinged mountains, of huge sand dunes and isolated villages, a land of fierce independent nomads. Tomorrow he would be over there looking back at his homeland. He felt an emptiness inside him at the thought of his future exile. Was he never to return to al-Andalus? Would he ever see his family again? His mother? Little Layla? Would he ever see Jawhara again? He felt his throat tighten and his eyes fill with tears. There was no going back now.

They made their camp on the beach at the base of the rock and waited while the leader of the caravan went to negotiate a crossing for them. Once again the women turned their attention to the camels. He had never spent much time with camels and now here he was, eating and sleeping beside them. They were strong patient animals who seemed able to journey for days without eating or drinking. He realised that the nomads depended on them for many things: milk to drink, dung to burn on the campfires and he had even seen the women weaving garments from the animals' coarse hair.

He was beginning to enjoy the company of these people. They were a tight-knit tribal group, united against their enemies but open-hearted and generous to their guests. The fact that he was going on a hajj accorded him great respect in their eyes.

'Hey, potter, come and sit here with us,' one of them called.

He handed him a platter of stewed goat. It smelt very strong, rank even, nothing like his mother made but he took it nonetheless; he was hungry and to refuse their food would be an insult.

'Tell us a tale, potter. We need entertaining.'

The men were all seated around the fire, eating their evening meal. The women and children sat with the animals.

'I'm not very good at storytelling,' Omar said. 'But I'll try.'

All eyes were on him. He tried to remember a story that he had told his sister, about dragons and castles and rescuing a princess on a magic carpet but the details eluded him. Instead he began:

'Once, a long time ago, a poor young man met a beautiful slave girl. She was the loveliest girl he had ever seen and he fell instantly in love with her. But the slave girl belonged to a rich man who lived in an enormous castle with hundreds of servants. He was known to be a cruel and ruthless master. They said he beat his slaves for the slightest thing and at night he tethered them in the animals' quarters with the goats. The slave girl was very unhappy; she missed her family and she wanted to go home to them. She cried and pleaded with the young man to save her. Although he knew that if he was caught it would mean certain death, he promised to help her escape from the castle. At the dead of night he crept into the gardens of the rich man's house to meet her. He waited but there was no sign of the girl. He searched the gardens and all the outbuildings but could not find her. He waited until dawn but still she did not appear. Each night he returned to the gardens to look for her but he never saw her again.'

He stopped and looked at his audience; they were hanging on his every word.

'Is that it?' one of them asked.

'Yes,' said Omar.

'So what happened to her?' asked another of the men.

'The rich man caught her and killed her,' suggested one of them.

'She had been turned into a dove by a djinn and flew away,' said another.

'She met someone else, handsomer and stronger,' said a third man.

'The young man went to the wrong castle,' said the first, with a hearty laugh.

'He never found out what happened to her,' Omar said. 'She just disappeared. But the young man continued to look for her, night after night.'

'Stick to making your pots, potter. That's the worst story I've ever heard.'

The others laughed and someone started to beat a rhythm on a small tambourine.

'Afra,' he called. 'Come and dance for us.'

A young girl came out from inside the tent and the men moved back to give her room. She was about six years old and her skin was the colour of nutmeg. Something about her cheeky smile reminded Omar of his sister, Layla. One of the men began to play a lively tune on a reed flute and the girl twirled her skirts and clapped her hands and weaved her body back and forth until the music stopped.

'Well done, child,' said the leader. 'Now it's your turn, Harun.'

The girl skipped back to sit with her mother and sisters and one of the men stood up and pulled some wooden clubs from under his cushion. His talent was juggling and Omar sat mesmerised, watching the tumbling clubs in the firelight.

As the last club fell into the man's outstretched hand, their leader returned. He strode up to the fire and waited for them to fall silent.

'It's all organised,' he said. 'We cross at dawn.'

He sat down beside them and took off his cloak. One of the women brought him some wine and someone else handed him a plate of the goat stew.

'So, Hajj?' he said looking at Omar. 'What have you learnt today?'

'He's a bloody awful story-teller, that's what he's learnt,' said one of the men, with a laugh.

'I have a riddle for you. What is as light as a feather and has nothing in it, but a strong man cannot hold it for more than a minute?' Harun asked.

'That's easy, the wind,' said one man.

'No, clod-head. How can a man hold the wind?'

'A breath,' said Omar.

'Ah, so the Hajj has learnt something today. Yes, his breath. Your turn now.'

'What is it that you can keep after giving it to someone else?' asked Omar.

'How can you keep something if you have given it away?'

'I know. You steal it back while he is sleeping,' suggested one of the young boys.

'No. That's not the answer.'

'You can keep your word,' said their leader. 'After you have given it to someone.'

'Correct,' said Omar with a smile.

'As I will keep my word to get you safely to North Africa.'

'That's a good one. I must remember that one,' said Harun.

They continued like that, late into the night, each trying to outdo the other with some trick or riddle. They passed the wine round for all to share and, at last, too drunk and too weary to dream, Omar staggered to his bed and fell into a deep sleep.

***

The next morning was bright and sunny; the straits lay before them, a narrow stretch of glistening, gleaming sea. It was the ancient gateway to the Mediterranean world, the crossing point to Africa, the meeting of two seas. As Omar waited with the others on the beach he could see two ships approach, their oars breaking the shining surface and leaving ripples of white water in their wake. Their sails hung limp, waiting for a breeze to help them along. But today there was no wind, no cloud, not a wave; it was a perfect day for crossing the straits.

'Get the animals ready to board,' the leader of the Africans shouted.

They all dismounted and prepared to lead them up the ramp and onto the ships. The nomads had promised to take him along the coast to the port of Orán where he could get a ship to Alexandria and from there he would cross the Sinai peninsula and make his way to Mecca. He had a long journey ahead of him but he was not worried; not the thought of jackals nor lions bothered him, not the threat of sandstorms, not thirst nor hunger, not pirates, nor shipwreck. This was his life now; he was a nomad, a wanderer. He would follow the stars and, one day, he would return to the land of his birth, to al-Andalus.

CHAPTER 30

Abd al-Rahman III sat at the council table, in the Dar al Wuzara, the House of the Viziers, surrounded by his ministers. Although he had every confidence in his Grand Vizier he liked to be kept informed of everything that was going on.

'My lord, I have some disturbing news for you,' the Grand Vizier said.

'Well what is it?' al-Rahman asked.

'A messenger, from our garrison in the north, arrived late last night. He says he must speak to you urgently. There have been rumours of an attack by the Christian princes. They are in need of reinforcements.'

'Send him in. I want to hear exactly what he has to say.'

'Very well, my Lord.'

He raised his hand to signal for his servant to bring in the messenger. At once, the doors swung open and two of the Palace Guards escorted the man into the council chamber. The guards stopped by the door and allowed the messenger to approach the council table, alone.

'What is your name, messenger?' al-Rahman asked.

'O merciful ruler, my name is Idra al-Jazuli. I am a soldier from the garrison town of Salim.'

'And why have you come here to my court?'

'The governor has sent word that there have been sightings of an army massing near the frontier. He respectfully asks if you could send him reinforcements in case there is an attack.'

'Indeed. And does the governor know whose army this could be?'

'It is believed to be the army of one of the Christian princes from the kingdom of León, my lord.'

At this, al-Rahman stood up; he was angry at the news. Was the peace that he had struggled to gain for his country to be broken now by these troublesome princes? Were all his efforts to be undone by some power-hungry princeling?

'Once again? Allah give me patience. When will these infidels understand that I will never let them take my land? I thought that we had reached an agreement over a decade ago; I would not interfere with them and they would stay behind the frontier.'

'It is probably just posturing on the part of one of them,' ibn Shaprut, the minister of foreign affairs said. 'They can never hope to take that garrison. It is well fortified.'

'I expect you are right but this posturing cannot be tolerated. It must be met with a show of force.'

He turned back to the messenger.

'Go and rest now. I will give you my answer in one hour.'

'Very well, my Lord.'

He turned to his servants and said, 'Make sure this man is given food and get a fresh horse ready for him. He must leave before nightfall.'

The messenger bowed and backed out of the room.

Once he had left, the Khalifa said, 'Tell Prince al-Hakim I want to speak to him, right away.'

'Yes, my Lord,' replied his servant.

'So, Hasdai, what do you think of this? Is it just posturing, as you suggest or could it be something more?' he asked ibn Shaprut.

He trusted the advice of his minister and friend; he could be relied upon to state his opinions freely.

'It is difficult to say, my Lord. King Ramiro has not threatened your kingdom for many years. This could just be someone who is trying to make a name for himself.'

'An upstart, you think? One of the princes of León, the messenger said.'

'There are a number of these princes and they are always quarrelling amongst themselves. They resent the power and wealth of King Ramiro. It could be nothing,' added the Grand Vizier.

'How can it be nothing if an army is gathering at the frontier?'

'That is true, my Lord but we do not want to break the peace that you have fought so long to obtain.'

'I know. That is what makes me so angry. If this is just some young renegade, why isn't Ramiro making him toe the line?'

'It is possible that King Ramiro is watching to see what you do. Even though he may have nothing to do with this threatened attack, I am sure he will take advantage of any weakness that he may see in your response. You need to send a signal to them that the Khalifa will not stand for any insurrection, not from anyone,' ibn Shaprut advised him.

'How do I do that? I am too old to go to war now.'

'Send Prince Hakim. He is your heir and his presence there will make it plain to King Ramiro that any attack on their part will not go unchallenged.'

'Mmn. You could be right. It would be good for Hakim to go to the frontier and see the rest of my kingdom. He spends far too much time with his nose in a book. The heir to the Khalifa must be a warrior as well as a scholar.'

The doors to the council chamber opened once more and al-Hakim strode in.

'Father, you wanted to see me?' he asked.

'Ah, Hakim, my son. Have you heard the news? The governor of Salim has asked for our help. I have discussed it with my ministers and have decided that we must go to his aid. I want you to take an army to help him defend the garrison.'

'Very well, father, I can have the troops ready to leave by noon.'

'Excellent. We will send ten thousand mercenaries and two thousand horsemen from the Palace Guard. I want some trusted men there, people I can rely on to monitor the situation and report back to me.'

'And arms?'

Al-Rahman turned to the commander of his army.

'Load one thousand mules with extra bows and javelins and enough equipment for three months. If they do decide to attack, who knows how long the siege could last.'

'Yes, my Lord.'

'I want to review the troops before they leave. Have them on the parade ground by noon.

'Yes, my Lord.'

'And send for my official historian. I want to speak to him. But not in here. I will see him in the garden.'

As one of the servants went in search of the historian, al-Rahman turned his attention back to his council of ministers.

'Unless anyone has any more unpleasant surprises for me this morning, I think I will close our meeting now. The rest of the business can wait until tomorrow. Al-Hakim, accompany me please.'

He rose and walked out into the garden, followed by his son.

'So. What do you think of this business in the north? Do you think there is any truth in the rumours or is the governor just angling to get more troops out of us?' he asked.

'We cannot tell, my Lord. We only have the word of the messenger,' al-Hakim replied.

'True. But if I ignore his request and the rumours are true then the garrison will fall. Worse still, it will send a signal to the Christian princes that we are weak or even disinterested. No, I cannot ignore it. He will get his reinforcements but I need you to go as well, Hakim. What better signal can I send to the Christians that the Khalifa means business, than to send my own son and heir?'

'Of course, father, I understand.'

'Ah, here is my historian. Good morning to you, al-Gafur.'

'Good morning, my Lord.'

'Walk with me in the garden and tell me how you are progressing with the history of this, my greatest project?' he said, waving his arm to encompass his alcázar and gardens.

'Excuse me father, I must leave to prepare for my journey,' al-Hakim interrupted.

He bowed to al-Rahman and then to the historian.

'I will see you before you leave, my son. Goodbye for now.'

As they strolled along the paved stone paths of the garden, al-Rahman listened as the historian told him about the detailed record he was making of the building of Madinat al-Zahra.

'Forgive for saying, but you are not a young man, al-Gafur. Who will continue your work when you die?'

'I do not work alone, as you know, my Lord. There is one of my assistants who is more than capable of taking over my work when I am gone. He is a young man and most meticulous in his recording. His hand is excellent.'

'Good. Now do you have anyone I can send on an expedition to the northern provinces? I want someone to make an accurate record of what is going on in these frontier towns but I don't want to take anyone away from the work here.'

'Yes, I have a man who could do that.'

'Excellent. Make sure he is ready to leave with the soldiers at noon. It will be his job to report back to me all the details of the battle, if there is to be one.'

'I will see to it, right away, my Lord.'

Al-Rahman knew that al-Gafur was a competent man who would make accurate and detailed accounts of his buildings, but his books would never have the impact of the elergy 'Urjuza' written by Ibn Abd Rabbihi. What a court poet he had been. That talented man had written about al-Rahman's previous war exploits with grace and eloquence.

Anybody reading Abd Rabbihi's work could not fail to acknowledge that al-Rahman III was a just and powerful ruler, a generous man, a wise and cultured man, a great Khalifa who had united his country and carried the Omeyyad dynasty forward. Sadly ibn abd Rabbihi had died a few years previously, an old and respected man; he was not here to record al-Rahman's greatest achievement, the building of Madinat al-Zahra. Al-Rahman had other court poets now, but none with Rabbihi's poetic gift nor his skill as a panegyrist.

'Is there anything else, my Lord?' al-Gafur asked.

'No, that is all. Make sure that your man is ready to leave by noon,' he repeated.

He looked at the sun; it was already quite high in the sky. He would return to his rooms and pray for a successful outcome to this campaign.

CHAPTER 31

Qasim sat on the patio, listening to the water trickling into the pool. The sound was soothing but it did nothing to ease his aching heart. In the next room he could hear his wife weeping; she had not stopped all morning. Nothing could comfort her.

'Baba, I have some news for you.'

It was his son, al-Jundi; he stood in the doorway dressed in his full uniform. A shaft of sunlight glinted on his helmet.

'What is it, son?'

'I am leaving today. We are going north to sort out a disturbance on the border,' he replied.

'War again?'

'No, Baba, nothing like that. It's not even an uprising, just some Christian princes who think they're strong enough to threaten us. The Khalifa just wants to make a show of strength. As I say, it's nothing really. I doubt if they'll even be any fighting.'

'So the Khalifa is leading you?'

'No, not this time. He's sending Prince al-Hakim instead.'

'Is that good? I thought he was more of a scholar than a soldier.'

'Of course it's good. The prince is a fine soldier; the men all respect him. He is brave in battle and just in peace.'

His son was very loyal to the Khalifa and his family. It had come as a shock to him to learn of his father's past, Qasim knew that. And for Omar to violate the sacred grounds of the alcázar, not once but on two occasions, well, it was hard for al-Jundi to accept such disrespect. He had been forced to put his family before his duty and Qasim was grateful to him for that sacrifice.

'How long will you be away?' he asked him.

It was a foolish question; al-Jundi would not know and if he did he would not tell him.

'A few months, maybe more. It all depends. Once the border is secure then we will come home again. Don't worry, Baba; it will soon be over.'

Qasim sighed. He could still hear his wife weeping and now he would have to tell her that her eldest son was going off to war. She was in danger of losing two of her sons, not just one.

'I'll be back in no time, you see,' al-Jundi reassured him. 'Just be careful while I'm gone.'

Qasim gripped his son by the hand. At least he had that to look forward to; al-Jundi, all being well, would come home. It was Omar he would never see again.

'I'll call your mother; she will want to say goodbye to you,' he said, blinking the tears from his eyes.

'No, not yet. I have something to tell you before I leave, Baba,' his son said. 'It's bad news.'

'More bad news? I can't believe it. What now?'

'They've identified the weapon that killed al-Tayyib. It wasn't a knife as originally suspected; it was a trepan.'

'A stone mason's tool? What on earth was Omar doing with that? We never use such things.'

For a brief moment his heart leapt; it had been a mistake. Omar hadn't killed the man after all; he had become confused during the struggle, thinking he had stabbed the eunuch when he hadn't. Someone else had killed him. Qasim would send word for him to return. He would tell him he was innocent. Their lives could continue as before.

'So it was all a mistake?' he said.

'No. Listen to me, Baba. The trepan belonged to Yusuf, Omar's friend. He has been working in the alcázar for many months,' al-Jundi explained.

'I don't understand. Why was Yusuf in the gardens? Omar never mentioned him.'

'He wasn't.'

The words hung in the air for a moment while al-Jundi struggled to control his anger.

'He wasn't there. Omar used to visit him regularly, using him as a pretext to enter the alcázar. If you remember, my sergeant told me about Omar wandering about the place. I should have done something about it then but I thought a warning would be enough,' al-Jundi continued. 'I blame myself for letting things go so far.'

'You were not to know that this would happen.'

'I could have threatened him with arrest. If it had been anyone else that is exactly what I would have done, instead I trusted him to heed my advice.'

'Omar was always a bit headstrong,' Qasim said.

'He is my brother. He relied on me to help him out and now look where it has led.'

'So are you saying that Omar stabbed the eunuch with Yusuf's trepan?'

'It seems so.'

'But why? Did he take it as some sort of weapon? Was this a planned attack? Are you telling me that it wasn't an accident after all, that your brother intended to kill this man?'

The news seemed to be getting worse by the minute. Qasim put his head in his hands. He could not believe that his son was a cold-blooded murderer.

'No, Baba, I'm sure it was as Omar said, a dreadful accident. I believe him. You know what he's like; he's always picking up things that aren't his and then forgetting to return them. The trepan was probably in his pocket. I imagine that he looked for something to defend himself and it was the first thing that came to hand.'

His son was pacing up and down like a caged lion; Qasim had never seen him so agitated before.

'What will happen now?' he asked 'What will we tell your mother?'

The sound of Fatima's sorrow reached out and enveloped them; her tears had turned to a wailing despair. His oldest son looked at him and punched the wall in frustration.

'I don't know Baba. There is nothing that we can do. They have arrested Yusuf. He will be executed tomorrow at dawn.'

'But...'

Qasim was shocked. The enormity of Omar's crime suddenly hit him; he did not know what to say. Yusuf, who was like another son to him, who had spent so much of his youth running in and out of their house, who had been inseparable from Omar, who had grown from a tousle-headed boy into a serious young man on the verge of being married, was innocent. He had killed nobody but now he had to die because of Omar's mistakes. What should they do? How could they help him?

'He's innocent, you say?' he asked al-Jundi.

'He says he is and I believe him.'

'So we must tell them that. We must tell them that he is innocent.'

'And then what? If we told the commandant that Yusuf was innocent it would not make any difference. They would still execute him and punish you and the rest of our family as well for helping Omar to escape. As for me, there would be no mercy. I would be stripped of my rank and executed like a common criminal. No, we cannot tell anyone.'

'But how did they find out that the trepan belonged to Yusuf?' Qasim asked, his voice cracking as he spoke.

'His name was carved on the handle. He never denied that it was his tool. He just said he must have dropped it somewhere.'

'But he must have protested his innocence more strongly than that?'

'Of course but he was not believed. He admitted that he worked in the alcázar but he said that he had never been in the gardens. Then to make it worse, one of the workmen said that he saw him slipping a note to a palace maidservant earlier in the week.'

'Did they identify her?'

'No. The man is a foreigner; he has not been here long. He said that the girls all look alike to him.'

'So there is no way to link Yusuf to Omar?'

Despite his despair at the news, Qasim's mind was already racing ahead to see whether his son would be implicated.

'No. Although I'm sure people know that they are friends.'

'Did he mention Omar's name?'

'I don't think so. Why would he?'

'Surely he has guessed who the culprit is? He is Omar's oldest friend. They have known each other since they were toddlers. Omar must have confided in him about the woman. Maybe it was him who set up the initial contact between Omar and the concubine. Maybe that was what the note was about.'

'You could be right. Possibly that was why Omar was always hanging about the alcázar but I don't think Yusuf has any idea that Omar was there that night. If he does, he is not saying.'

'I must go to see him to explain what happened. I need to talk to him, to ask for his forgiveness.'

He picked up his cloak. He would go straight to the alcazaba and ask to see Yusuf. Al-Jundi put his hand on his arm and stopped him.

'No Baba. You can't do that. It's pointless. It won't help him and it won't help us. I tell you, no good will come of it, only more suffering and heartbreak. The best thing is for you to keep well away from the alcazaba. Promise me you won't go there.'

'But ...'

'Promise me. I'm telling you, it will do no good.'

'There has to be some way to help Yusuf,' he insisted.

'There isn't. Believe me. I know how this works. Yusuf's fate is sealed. Now promise me that you will stay away from the alcazaba and don't mention this to anyone.'

Qasim felt defeated; he was caught in a web of lies and intrigue that was not of his making and he had no way to escape. He had no alternative but to let an innocent man take the blame for his son's crime; that was something which would weigh on his conscience for evermore.

'I promise.'

His son hesitated and then asked, 'Have you seen any more of that man?'

'You mean ibn Hayyan? Yes, I saw him lurking near the market, yesterday.'

'So, he's still around? Well keep an eye on him. If he's still here when I get back I'll see what I can do to scare him off. Now, I must go; we leave at noon.'

'Say goodbye to your mother first. She will never forgive me if I let you leave without seeing her.'

He waited, listening to his son's heavy footsteps and then his murmured farewells to his mother. He half expected to hear Fatima's cries of anguish as another of her sons left her but there was only silence. Her crying had stopped. His heart ached for her; he knew her grief was beyond tears now.

'Ma'a salama, Baba.'

'Alla ysalmak, my son. May Allah protect and keep you safe.'

'Remember what I said. Speak to no-one.'

Al-Jundi pulled his red cloak around his shoulders and was gone. The house felt empty without his bulky presence. He knew his son was right; there was nothing that Qasim could do to help Yusuf. The damage that Omar had unwittingly caused could not be undone. It was Allah's will. Qasim had given al-Jundi his promise and now he sat there, a broken man, unable to help his son and unable to help an innocent man. Allah would never forgive him.

The sound of the muezzin rang out across the city. Today he would go to the mosque to pray. He grabbed his cap and, throwing his djellaba around his shoulders, he hurried out.

***

He joined the queue of people heading for the mosque; there was a greater number than usual at this hour, probably because the news was spreading about the soldiers leaving. The busiest time was normally at evening prayers which he sometimes attended although he usually only went on Fridays. The mosque gardens were crowded with people cleansing themselves before entering the mosque. He waited until there was a space at the fountains then washed himself down in the cold water, removed his shoes and went inside. He found a space near the front, facing the mihrab and knelt down on one of the straw mats that covered the dirt floor.

The mosque had been the first building to be completed in the city; it lay outside the alcázar but adjacent to its walls so that everyone, the local people who lived in the medina and the residents of the alcázar, could use it. It was a beautiful building, its craftsmanship the equal of the mosque in Córdoba.

Qasim had barely closed his eyes and touched his forehead to the ground when there was a slight disturbance which caused him to look up from his meditation. It was the Khalifa. He had entered through a covered passageway which led from the gardens of the alcázar straight into the mosque and now he took up his usual place in the maqsura. He was a devout man who took his role as Defender of God's Faith seriously. His son al-Hakim was also present today, praying for the success of his troops. Qasim had read the notice plastered on the wall of the mosque informing all the citizens that their borders were under threat. Today they would include in their prayers an exhortation to Allah to bring them victory.

No sooner had the Khalifa taken his position than the imam began to lead the congregation in prayer:

'In the name of Allah, the Merciful, the Compassionate...'

The prayer room was dark, its oil lamps unlit, the only light creeping through the openings in the ceiling high above. Yet from somewhere a light infused the horseshoe arch of the mihrab with a warm glow. The holy words of the Quran had been inscribed on this beautiful facade. Men had created a masterpiece of coloured mosaics on a background of pure gold. Looking at it Qasim was reminded that he too was a craftsman, that all that he made with his hands was for the glory of Allah not for man, not for wealth and riches, not for fame, not for power. How could he have forgotten that? He, who loved Allah so. He had sent his son into temptation, telling him to sell their pottery to the Khalifa. Why had he not been content with the life he had in Córdoba? Why had he strived for more? Why had he coveted a new house and fancy possessions? What use were they to him now that he had lost his most treasured possession, his son?

The imam continued with his sermon and Qasim listened, hanging on every word but his mind refused to be quiet; it returned again and again to his son. Had Qasim failed him? Was there anything else that he could have done for Omar? And Yusuf, what could he do to help him? The congregation began to pray and Qasim repeated the words that by now were engraved on his heart. Gradually the power of the prayers calmed his spirit and he felt a peace descend on him. He knew that there was nothing he could do. What was done was done. As Qasim chanted the ritual prayers he knew that Allah would forgive him. The Quran promised all true believers salvation, no matter what their sins. Omar had gone on his pilgrimage not just to be saved from eternal damnation but to intercede for them all.

As he left the mosque and headed for home, he caught a glimpse of a dark figure watching him from the shadows. He stopped and would have spoken to the man but before he could do anything, the man pulled his djellaba over his head and hurried away. Was it ibn Hayyan? And if it was, what did he want? It wasn't just Omar's actions that threatened the family, Qasim's past was about to resurface too. May Allah protect them all.

CHAPTER 32

Al-Rahman made his way back to his private rooms. The mosque had been full this morning; that was good. They had prayed for victory and he was sure that Allah would give it to them. Not that he was one of those religious dolts that believed you would receive everything you prayed for; no, he believed that Allah helped those who helped themselves. They would win this campaign because his troops were the best; they were well-armed and well-trained. The fact that Allah was on their side just gave them an extra advantage.

Gassan was waiting when he entered the bedroom.

'Is there anything you need, my lord?' his servant asked.

'No, thank you, Gassan. Leave me for now.'

'Very well, my lord.'

Al-Rahman fancied some time alone so that he could think back to the previous night. He had been very surprised, not just by the girl herself but by his reaction to her. The problem with being able to have any woman you wanted was that after a while there was no-one that really stirred you. Until last night. Maybe the potion that Hasdai had prescribed for him had helped; something had certainly got his blood racing. She was a beautiful young girl and just the type he liked, tall and blonde, not unlike his mother when she was young, but it was more than that. There was something about her that was bewitching him.

He had many beautiful women in his harem; he tried to sleep with a different one each night and still there were those he had not tasted. This one was different. She was haughty, as though she was indeed a princess and not the peasant girl that he was certain she was. But her aristocratic way of looking at him, meeting his eye as an equal, did not anger him, instead it stirred his loins in a way that had not happened since he had first met al-Zahra. He had wondered of late whether he was losing his virility which was why he had approached Hasdai about a remedy. He had even started to consider other ways of exciting his flagging libido; Yamut had brought him a delightful boy a few weeks ago but even that had not satisfied him. Jawhara on the other hand had given him great satisfaction. He had kept her with him until dawn, unable to quench his thirst for her. When she left he had lain there, looking at the painted stars on the ceiling above him, feeling like a young buck. He no longer thought of his aching back and the pain in his thigh; he was seventeen again. She had restored his youth to him. He would send for her again, tonight. That was unprecedented and he knew what gossip it would set in motion amongst the women of his harem. Al-Zahra would be furious; he never sent for a concubine two nights in a row. He would probably even have his Royal wife interrogating him about it. Well let them gossip. He had not felt so happy for a long time. He would have her again tonight and this time he would dispense with Hasdai's potion; he would discover what spell it was she had cast over him.

'*My eye frees what the page imprisons: the white the white and the black the black,*' he quoted aloud and taking up a book of poetry, he sat by the open door to read. The book he had chosen was by his favourite court poet, Ibn Abd Rabbihi; he turned to the poem that reminded him so much of his new concubine. It was called 'White Skin'.

'I have never seen
nor heard of such a thing
her modesty turns
pearl into carnelian.
Her face is so clear
that when you gaze
on its perfections you see your own face
reflected.'

He had read the poem many times before but now when he read it, he could see her face, smiling up at him.

'Excuse me, my lord,' Gassan said, bowing as he entered. 'May I speak with you?'

'Of course, Gassan. What is it?'

'The troops are ready, my lord. His Royal Highness, the prince, wants to know if you would like to do the inspection yourself?'

'Tell him that I will be right there.'

It was gone noon already; it was time to send his troops to war. He walked out onto his private terrace and looked down at them. They were lined up on the parade ground, row upon row of immaculate foot soldiers, their shields glinting in the sun, spears and javelins by their sides. Magnificent fighting men, they would put fear into the hearts of those cowardly Christian princes. Behind them stood the archers and the slingers. To the right were the jinetes, the light cavalry, the pride of his army; their horses were the best in the land, bred of Arabian stock. His son, al-Hakim was at the head of his troops, astride his favourite horse, a chestnut beauty that fidgeted with impatience. Although not one of them moved a muscle as they waited for the Khalifa's command, he knew that the men were as impatient as the animals to be off. Even from this elevated position he could feel the tension, the excitement, maybe even the fear of what lay ahead; no man nor beast was immune from it. He raised his hand and watched as a ripple of reflected sunshine ran along the line of troops, glinting on their helmets. They awaited his signal. The sun was directly overhead; it was time for them to leave. He dropped his hand. Immediately al-Hakim wheeled his horse round to the right and led his army out and down the ramp. With heads held high and completely in step, they marched past al-Rahman, first the Palace Guard in their bright red cloaks then the mercenaries, mostly regulars but some conscripted from North Africa, next Berbers and with them tall negroes from the interior. Now came the horsemen, some carrying javelins and their heads shrouded in red and green turbans, others with short bows and round shields. At the rear came the mule train laden with all their provisions: tents, food, water barrels, spare bows and replacement arrows.

Al-Rahman watched until the dust had settled and the last of his army had left. From his vantage point, here on the palace terrace, he could look across the plain below the medina and see his troops disappearing into the distance. It would take them at least two weeks to reach the garrison town of Salim. He had no doubt that, if it came to a battle, his troops would win. They were disciplined, loyal, armed with the finest equipment and, more importantly, his son, al-Hakim was leading them.

CHAPTER 33

Her mother had helped Sara pack all their things together and get ready to leave. She did not explain why they had been woken in the middle of the night to flee from the house; she just said it was for their own safety. What was she expecting to happen? It seemed to have something to do with Omar. He had been up to some mischief again, no doubt.

Sara sat the two eldest girls on the camel but put the younger ones on the mule so that she could walk beside them. Mariam had her arms around Tara's waist and Tara clung to the animal's mane; the children nodded sleepily from time to time. It was a mild night and the sky was a carpet of stars above them; before long the sun would rise and chase them away. That was what her mother used to tell her when she was a little girl.

'Why are there so many stars, Mama?' asked a sleepy Tara.

'I don't know, sweetheart.'

'Where do they go when the sun comes up?'

'They don't go anywhere; they are still there; it's just that you can't see them because the sun is so bright,' she explained.

Although the explanation her mother had given her was very sweet, it was not true. She wanted her daughters to develop enquiring minds, not have them filled with stories.

The elder girls, Salma and Maysa were wide awake now and excited at leaving while it was still dark. They giggled and chattered and bombarded their mother with nonstop questions from their perch on top of the camel.

'Why do we have to leave so early, Mama?'

'Has something bad happened?'

'Are we running away?'

This was accompanied by the onset of more giggling. Then Salma asked, 'Where is Layla? Why can't she come with us?'

'Why was Teta crying?' her sister asked.

'Has someone died?'

'Why is that boy with us?'

'Is he a slave boy?'

'Will he be our slave now?'

Sara had no answers for them; she had no answers for herself.

'Do you know what has happened?' she asked her brother.

'I'm no wiser than you, sister. But whatever it is, it's serious. I've never seen Baba so upset before and Omar could not even bear to speak to me. Something has happened that's for sure.'

'And the boy? You've got the slave-boy with you.'

'Yes. He's to work for me from now on. That's good; I have lots for him to do. I've told Baba hundreds of times that I needed help.'

'So Baba just gave him to you?' she asked, looking at al-Sagir, who walked behind them in silence, his face streaked with tears. 'I thought he was pleased with the boy?'

'Yes, so did I. I'm just as mystified as you are, sister, but I'm not going to complain.'

'What about Omar? Is it something he did? Do you know what will happen to him?' she asked.

Nobody was telling her anything. She resented the way she was being treated like a child; after all she was the eldest in the family but because she was a woman that counted for nothing. It was always the boys, her brothers, who mattered.

'All I know is that he's going on a hajj.'

'A hajj? Just like that? No warning? No planning? I don't understand; nobody spoke of it during Eid. Nobody said a word.'

She looked at her brother but he didn't reply.

'Don't you think that's strange? I mean nobody just gets up and says they're going on a hajj, just like that. You need money to travel to Mecca. It's something that everyone would be talking about for months beforehand, like a wedding. No. Something's not right. I know it.'

Ibrahim stopped the camel to adjust its load.

'You girls all right up there?' he asked.

'Yes, uncle,' came their replies, followed by more giggles.

'I don't see why Baba and Mama can't tell us what's going on. Why are they being so secretive?' Sara continued.

'I expect they have their reasons.'

Either her brother knew more than he was telling her or he was not really interested; she didn't know which it was.

'Yes but what are they? What reason could there be to throw us out in the middle of the night?'

'Look Sara, I know as little as you. All I can tell you is what Omar told me and that wasn't much. He said that he had done a bad thing and didn't know what to do about it. That's when Baba came in and said he was to go on a hajj.'

'Just like that?'

'Yes, exactly like that.'

'No explanation?'

'I don't think one was needed. Omar seemed to understand why it was happening.'

'You don't seem very upset about it?' she said.

'Why should I be? It's not me that's going.'

'But Omar is your brother.'

'Yes he is but maybe now Baba will pay more attention to me and my work and less to Omar. I have been slaving away in the alfarería for years and yet it is always Omar who gets the interesting, more prestigious jobs to do. It's always Omar's designs that are praised, never mine. Without Omar around, Baba will have to rely on me for once.'

She suddenly realised that Ibrahim had been jealous of Omar all this time but had kept it hidden. She wasn't the only one who had been unhappy when their father decided to take his wife and his youngest two children to Madinat al-Zahra. Ibrahim had felt abandoned when they had moved to the exciting new city and left him behind. She remembered how Baba had not even made a pretence of it; he had said outright that someone had to stay behind and do the rudimentary work and that Ibrahim was best suited to it. No wonder he resented his brother.

'This is an opportunity for me to show Baba what I'm capable of,' he continued.

'You will have to learn to do what Omar was doing,' she reminded him. 'You don't have much experience in decorating pottery, do you?'

'It can't be that difficult. I have already made some designs of my own but when I suggested showing them to Baba, he said I should stick to what I was good at. Well now he might be more interested.'

'Mama, are we nearly home yet?' asked Mariam, her youngest daughter. 'My bottom's sore.'

'Not much longer, sweetheart. Would you like Mama to carry you for a little while?'

She lifted the child down from the mule and settled her on her hip.

'My, you're getting a big girl, Mari; I won't be able to carry you for long,' she said.

'Just until my bottom's better?'

'All right then.'

'Here, give her to me. Come on my little princess, climb onto my shoulders,' Ibrahim said.

Sara smiled at her brother. He was always so good with her children, far more affectionate to them than their own father who could never conceal his disappointment that one of them was not a boy.

'It's time you had children of your own, brother,' she said.

'One day, sister. One day.'

***

It was almost as if Isa had known they were on their way; as if he had been waiting for her. When they arrived her husband was standing at the door of their house, tapping his foot on the stone threshold. He did not look very pleased. Sara felt nervous. What had happened in her absence? Was she to be made to pay for it?

'As-salam alaykum, wife. Did you have a good time at the home of your mother?' Isa asked, coolly but politely.

He rarely showed her much affection these days and never took her to bed anymore.

'Wa alaykum e-salam, husband. Yes, thank you.'

'As-salam alaykum, brother-in-law,' said Ibrahim, depositing Mariam at her father's feet.

He unloaded his sister's possessions and carried them into the house.

'You have returned early,' Isa said. 'I didn't expect you until tomorrow.'

'The children wanted to come home,' Sara replied. 'They missed their friends.'

She wasn't going to discuss her family's problems with her husband and, as it was, she was unable to do so, as she didn't know what they were.

'Come in, wife, come in. I must speak to you.'

Her husband seemed agitated about something and, as soon as she was over the threshold and her brother had left, he started to berate her.

'It was wrong of me to let you spend Eid with your parents. It was a stupid idea. I have been far too generous to you and because of that I have suffered. I have had a terrible time. Look at me; I am half-starved.'

Sara bit back a smile; her husband looked anything but half-starved. Like many bakers, he was a round, well padded man with a rosy face and a liking for his own bread.

'That girl has no idea how to feed a man. Why was she not better instructed before you left? If I had known that you had left me with a half-wit that couldn't even make a bowl of almori and whose meat balls would be better used for juggling, I would have forbidden it.'

So it was the new wife who had upset him. She wanted to laugh but instead she said, trying to keep the amusement from her voice, 'But you didn't, husband. You thought that your new wife would be able to satisfy all your needs. You said that you could manage without me. But I am sorry that you had a miserable Eid. I will cook you some lamb pasties for your lunch today, with fried aubergines and some wild asparagus that we picked on the way home.'

That brought a smile to his face.

'Excellent, but I want you to show my new wife how to cook as well as you do. Make sure she is in the kitchen with you all the time. Everything you do, I want her to do. She must learn and learn quickly.'

So now she had to instruct this child how to cook. What else must she do? The situation was no longer so amusing. He had brought a new wife into their home and made her Sara's responsibility. Didn't he realise how hurtful that was? She had been married to him for eleven years and now he treated her like a housekeeper, or worse. He hadn't even missed her when she was away; all he had missed was her cooking. Sara turned away from her husband before she answered, 'Yes husband, I will do that for you.'

'I must go back to work now,' he said. 'Remember what I said.'

'Of course.'

The new wife was waiting for her in the kitchen; as usual she seemed to be in a dream.

'Good morning Ghayda,' Sara said as pleasantly as she could, even though she was seething inside at her husband's attitude.

'Good morning, Sara.'

'Our husband wants me to teach you how to cook so we will prepare the meal together today. First I want you to go to the butcher and buy some lamb. Tell him to cut it into small pieces and to leave all the fat on it. In the meantime I must rest for a while. I am tired; it was a long walk from Madinat al-Zahra. Call me when you return.'

'Yes, Sara.'

The girl seemed pleased to have been given some directions. She smiled at Sara and said, 'I'm so pleased that you're home. I think Isa is angry with me because I burnt his supper.'

'Well, don't worry. We'll cook him a hearty meal today.'

She went to her room and lay on her bed. Her feet ached from so much walking but that was nothing compared to the pain in her head; it was as if there was an iron band around it. Her conversation with Ibrahim had done nothing to ease her worries about her family. Something awful had befallen her brother and now her father was worried that they would all get involved; that was why he had sent them home early. It was obvious. Her mother had implied that it was no longer safe for them in Madinat al-Zahra. If that was the case then were they also in danger in Córdoba? It was only two Arab miles distance, not enough to protect them from harm. And what could she do to keep her daughters safe? For now, Isa would protect them but if his new wife gave him a son then he might throw her and her daughters out. It was a simple thing for him to divorce her. It had happened to her friend. Her husband had pronounced the talaq three times and that was it; they were no longer man and wife. If that happened to her, who would protect them then?

'Mama, it's the lady who cuts your hair,' Salma called. 'She says do you want her today?'

'Yes, tell her to wait; I'll be right down.'

It was Halawa. She would help her. Halawa was not just a hairdresser, she also acted as a midwife, a masseuse and a clairvoyant. Sara had known her for many years; she had helped to deliver all four of Sara's children. However it was her skill as a clairvoyant that interested Sara at that moment.

'As-salam alaykum,' Halawa said.

'Wa alaykum e-salam,' Sara replied. 'I am so pleased to see you.'

She sat down and waited while the woman rummaged in her capacious carpet bag and pulled out a comb and some scissors. Her daughters gathered round to watch. They loved Halawa; they loved to see her flamboyant clothes, her robes of bright reds and oranges, the beads and silver coins that she sewed along the seams to bring her luck, her henna coloured hair, the bangles that jangled around her wrists and ankles.

Halawa ran her comb through Sara's hair.

'Are you sure you want me to cut your hair today?' she asked. 'Or is there something else on your mind?'

She rested the palm of her hand on Sara's head.

'Something is troubling you.'

'Salma, take your sisters out to play; I want to speak to Halawa alone.'

The women waited until the girls had gone into the yard and they could hear the young voices arguing about which game to play then Sara said, 'Yes, something is bothering me but I don't know what it is. I have just returned from Madinat al-Zahra where I spent Eid with my family. There is something wrong and I am worried that whatever is causing problems for my father will cause problems for us too.'

'Give me your hand.'

She took Sara's right hand and turned it over so that she could read her palm. For a while she said nothing, just stared at the open palm and stroked it with her forefinger.

'Something very bad has happened. A death perhaps. It is to do with a close member of your family. I cannot see clearly what it is but it could affect all your lives.'

She paused.

'There is something else; something that happened long ago. This is going to return to bring trouble to your family.'

She stopped and looked at Sara.

'Do not go to Madinat al-Zahra again. It is not safe for you or your daughters. You must stay here in Córdoba.'

Sara felt a chill in the room. So it was true; her daughters were in danger. She had been right.

'Is there anything I can do to protect them?'

Halawa rummaged in her bag again. This time she pulled out four small pieces of polished stone and handed them to Sara.

'Take these amulets and sew one in each of your daughters' clothes. They must wear them all the time, even when they sleep. They will protect them from evil. But do not tell anyone that you have done it and do not tell them that I gave them to you.'

Sara looked at the stones; they burned with a dull amber glow. She closed her hand over them and immediately felt that she could sense their power.

'Thank you.'

She handed the woman a couple of silver coins. What she was doing was against the law. Witchcraft was a sin but many of the women went to Halawa when they were in trouble. She helped them with the birth of their babies and she helped them to conceive sons; she could even make wayward husbands return to their wives. She had potions and herbs for every ailment from broken hearts to broken legs. Sara wondered if she should talk to her about Ghayda but at that moment the new wife returned.

'I have bought the lamb, sister,' she said.

Sara gritted her teeth. Why did the silly girl keep calling her sister? She was not her sister; she was her rival.

'Good.'

'Are you having your hair cut?' Ghayda asked.

'Yes, I am just about to start,' said Halawa. 'Would you like me to do yours afterwards?'

The new wife smiled and clapped her hands like a small child.

'Oh yes please.'

'Well go and put the lamb in a pot with some garlic and dried coriander, first. Then pour a little vinegar over it. Not too much mind,' Sara instructed her. 'I will see to it after that. Then Halawa will be free to see to you.'

Sara watched the black curls drop to the floor one by one as Halawa began to cut her hair.

'I will come again next week,' Halawa whispered 'to see if you are all right.'

'Thank you.'

Sara decided that she would write to her mother that night and tell her what the clairvoyant had said. In the meantime she would endeavour to be the wife that Isa wanted her to be. For the sake of her children she would befriend the new wife and help her to please their husband. She would put aside her own ambitions and her pride; she would bow to the commands of her husband. If she did all this then Allah would reward her by protecting her daughters.

CHAPTER 34

They left Isolde alone. Even Najm did not interrogate her although she was sure that the questions would flow soon enough. Isolde lay down and closed her eyes. She needed to sleep. Maybe later she would be able to unravel the knot of emotions that clutched at her heart but at the moment it was impossible. She felt that she was outside of herself, looking down at someone else lying on her bed, dressed in her clothes, wearing her face. It was not her. Isolde was back in Saxony with her parents and her brothers. She wore homespun clothes not silk and satin; she milked the cow and fed the pigs instead of playing the lute and reciting poetry; she helped her mother cook the porridge and ladle it into wooden bowls rather than eat chicken breast from silver plates.

Her maid tiptoed into the room and stood by her bed, uncertain whether to disturb her. Her young face was white and pinched with crying.

'What is it?' Isolde asked.

'May I speak to you, Jawhara?'

'What is it? Speak.'

'You have heard that they have arrested someone for the murder of al-Tayyib?'

'Yes, a stonemason.'

The girl began to cry.

'It is the man who gave the message to my friend,' she whispered. 'She says it is the same man. His name is Yusuf.'

Isolde sat up. She had not known how Omar had managed to get the message to her; in fact she had never given it a thought. Now she could understand why the girl was so upset; if they discovered that a man was trying to contact someone in the harem they might trace a connection to her and to Isolde.

'Come here,' she said. 'Sit down and wipe your eyes. No-one will know what you did as long as you don't tell anyone. You haven't told anyone have you?'

The girl shook her head.

'Good. In that case you have nothing to fear. Just make sure that your friend keeps quiet and we won't speak of it again. It will be forgotten.'

'But what of the man? They say he is to be executed today.'

'He won't be able to say anything if he is dead, will he?'

The words came out before she could stop them; they sounded cruel and unfeeling.

'No, Jawhara,' the maid whispered. 'But he says he is innocent. He says he was never in the gardens; that he knew nothing about it.'

'Who said this?'

'One of the eunuchs told us.'

'It's just tittle-tattle. If they have caught him then he must have been the one in the gardens. So no more crying or someone will become suspicious and start asking you questions.'

'Yes, Jawhara.'

'I think I'll have my bath now. Prepare it for me please.'

So the man was to be executed. Then it would be over; the matter would be closed. Omar would hear about it and, once everything had quietened down, he would contact her again. At the moment the harem was still buzzing with excitement. Admittedly some of the elation was generated by Isolde's visit to the Khalifa but the news of the man's arrest had also set tongues in motion. Why had he entered the gardens when everyone knew it was punishable by death? Who was he looking for? What did he want? At the moment no-one had any answers but that did not stop them speculating.

'You're awake then,' Najm said, coming into Isolde's bedroom. 'So?'

Isolde looked at her friend's happy face. Najm wanted her to tell her all about last night.

'So what?'

'You know. How did it go with you and the Khalifa? All over in a flash, I bet.'

'It happened.'

'Is that all you have to tell me? The others won't let you get away with just that. We want something more. What was he like? Did he seem pleased with you?'

'I don't know. I don't know what he is like when he is pleased. He is a very serious man.'

'Of course you do. Come on Jawhara, don't be mean.'

Isolde sighed. There was no way to avoid it.

'All right. He seemed to be pleased with my dancing. He made Yamut smile, anyway.'

'That's a good sign. And later?'

'He was just as you said, a gentle man.'

'There, what did I tell you. I bet he was finished almost as soon as he started.'

'Najm, I don't know how long these things are supposed to go on but it wasn't over quickly. He did not let me leave until dawn. Is that what you mean by "over in a flash"?'

'Dawn? He kept you with him until dawn? I don't believe it. No wonder you couldn't wake up this morning.'

'Look I must go and have my bath. Rebecca is coming later to give me my lesson in Arabic.'

'Did you enjoy it? Did he hurt you? Tell me how you felt,' Najm pleaded.

Isolde realised that last night had changed things between them. Najm was still a virgin and would remain so until the Khalifa sent for her or gave her to someone in marriage. Isolde was no longer a virgin; she was now one of the Khalifa's concubines and would always have that status even if he never sent for her again.

'I could never love him,' was all she said.

How could she tell Najm how frightened she had been? How could she explain that her fear had disappeared as his hands caressed her body, that she had been able to relax and give herself up to a pleasure that she never knew existed? True she had cried out when he entered her but this only seemed to please the Khalifa more. Her emotions had been in turmoil. He was an old man. He was a stranger. He was not Omar. She did not love him but still her body had betrayed her; it had melted under his touch.

Her maid came scurrying in.

'Jawhara, your bath is ready. But first Yamut wants to speak to you.'

Isolde pulled her robe around her and went out onto the terrace. The round, black face of the Khalifa's chief eunuch was shining with delight; his big white teeth gleamed at her.

'Jawhara, my dear. What a prize you are indeed. The Khalifa is very pleased with you. He says that you have given him great pleasure. It is not often that I hear those words on his lips.'

He chuckled and rubbed his hands together as though he was contemplating a delicious meal. She had never heard him speak so ingratiatingly before. Did this mean that things were about to change for her?

'Thank you, Yamut. I only did as I was instructed.'

'You must have done a lot more than that, my dear girl. He wants you to go to him again tonight.'

'Again?'

She could not keep the horror from her voice. Najm had convinced her that it would happen only once and that it would be over quickly. Already she had been proved wrong. Last night the Khalifa had been insatiable. They had made love many times. Now he wanted to have her again. She struggled to keep back the tears.

'What is it, child?'

The smile had disappeared from the eunuch's face.

'Nothing Yamut.'

'You should be happy, my girl. This is unprecedented. The Khalifa obviously thinks very highly of you. It is an honour. The highest of honours,' he said.

'Yes, Yamut.'

'Make sure you are ready at the same time tonight. I will come for you.'

'Yes, Yamut.'

She held back the tears until he had gone then let them flow freely.

'Jawhara, whatever is the matter? Is Yamut angry with you? Is it about last night? What has happened?' Najm asked, fussing around her friend like a startled hen.

'I am to go again tonight,' Isolde sobbed.

'Where?'

'To the Khalifa.'

'Praise the gods. That's wonderful. Oh, Jawhara, you don't know how marvellous that is. He has indicated that you are someone special, a favourite. Yamut must be so pleased.'

'It's not Yamut's happiness that concerns me,' Isolde snapped. 'What about mine?'

She was tired of being treated as a chattel. Why did no-one consider her feelings? Why did no-one ask her what she wanted? Was she to be used night after night like a woman of the streets? Was she never to have someone she could love, someone like Omar? And what of the handsome potter, would he still love her after what the Khalifa had done to her?

Najm stared at her, the smile fading from her face.

'Look Jawhara, you have to get used to the idea that you are no longer free. You are a slave. You have no rights. Nobody cares about your feelings or your happiness. All you can hope to get from life is someone who will take care of you and not beat you. You are lucky; because of your beauty you have done much better than that.'

Najm was angry with her; she turned and walked back into the harem. Already the news was spreading that the

Khalifa was about to honour Jawhara with a second night. The air of excitement and jealousy was bubbling more than ever.

***

After their mid-day meal Isolde went for a walk alone in the gardens. Her mind was in a state of confusion. How could she get in touch with Omar again? She could not ask her maid to act as a go-between; the girl was so terrified that she would surely get caught. There had to be some other way.

'Jawhara, come quickly. Yamut wants you,' her maid called from the terrace.

What did he want now? Had news of her tears reached him? It was very possible; she felt she was under constant scrutiny from all the other women. Someone must have told Yamut how ungrateful she was.

'Yes, Yamut? You wanted me?' she asked.

'The Khalifa has sent instructions to move you to a new apartment, where you can be alone. Your status has changed and you are to have four maidservants instead of one. I have it all organised. Just tell your maid to collect your things and to follow me.'

'But I like it here,' she protested.

The Chief Eunuch glared at her.

'Follow me.'

'Can Najm come with me?' she asked, softening her voice into a plea.

'Oh, very well. Tell Najm she is to accompany you.'

Najm was sitting with the other women, drinking tea. She looked up when Isolde approached her but did not smile; she was still angry with her.

'Najm, I have some news. I am going to have my own apartment and you are to come with me,' she said.

At once the women began with the questions. What had Yamut said? Did this mean that she was to become one of the Khalifa's favourites? Which apartment would she have? Was one of the other favourites being usurped? Isolde felt her head would burst with so many questions.

'I don't know,' she answered. 'I don't know anything more than I've told you. Please Najm, come with me. I don't want to be alone.'

Najm was already up; she hugged Isolde tightly and whispered, 'Everything will be all right now, you'll see. You'll be treated with more respect. Even the Royal wife will not be able to harm you.'

Together they followed Yamut through the palace until they came to the inner part of the harem, the zenana. Here he took them to a splendid room with its own courtyard and steps leading down to a secluded part of the garden. Isolde's maid trailed behind them carrying a few of her mistress's possessions.

'This is where you will live from now on,' Yamut told them. 'I will send someone to talk to you about anything you need. Do not forget that I will come for you tonight at the same time.'

'Yes, Yamut. Thank you.'

Once the Chief Eunuch had left, Najm hugged her again and danced her around the room.

'Isn't this wonderful.'

She pulled Isolde down onto the couch beside her and said, laughingly, 'Everyone is talking about you and they say that al-Zahra is furious with you.'

'Why would she be furious with me?'

'You have taken her place as his favourite, of course.'

Isolde stood up and walked around the room; it was so big and airy.

'What does Yamut mean, he will send someone to talk to me?' she asked Najm.

'He means that you can have anything you want. You may choose the tapestries and curtains, change the couches and beds, whatever you want to do to make it more comfortable.'

Isolde looked at the room with its gleaming marble floor and the delicately carved wall panels; its jalousie windows opened wide onto the garden, letting in the heavy scent of the last of the winter jasmine. It was perfect as it was.

'I don't think I could make it any more comfortable,' she said.

'Well, wait until you talk to the Royal Buyer; he will show you things that you won't be able to refuse.'

'It's all so overwhelming,' Isolde said.

She thought she might start crying; only the thought of her friend's certain irritation if she saw her shed more tears, stopped her. She took a deep breath; here, in the zenana, it would be even more difficult for Omar to reach her.

'The Khalifa likes to visit his favourites in their own rooms occasionally. That is why you must make sure it is furnished fit for a king; it is not solely for your pleasure,' Najm informed her.

There was so much to learn. She thanked the gods that she had Najm to guide her through this labyrinth of customs and procedures.

'It is certainly a beautiful room,' she said, tracing the design of the wall carvings with her finger.

The man who was arrested was a stone mason; had he carved this? Who was he? His name was Yusuf but that was all she knew. She longed to know more about him. He must be a friend of Omar, someone that he could confide in. What would Omar do when he heard about his arrest? Would he go and confess? Would he tell them about her part in it all? No, she was certain he would not betray her. Poor Omar, it must be hard for him to decide.

'Do you think that man carved these panels?' she asked Najm.

'What man?'

'The one who was arrested.'

'The murderer? Possibly. What a strange question. I sometimes wonder what goes on in your pretty head, Jawhara. You shouldn't be wasting your time thinking about a murderer; you are about to be one of the Khalifa's favourites. You should be thinking about how to continue to please him.'

'But what if he didn't do it? They said he insisted that he was innocent.'

'Look, by this time tomorrow he will be dead and buried. Don't think of it anymore.'

Isolde shuddered at these words. Her friend was looking at her strangely.

'Is there something that you know about al-Tayyib's death that you're not telling me?' Najm asked. 'You seem very interested in the man they have caught.'

Isolde looked away; she could not bear to face her friend. Now was the time to confess, to explain why she was so unhappy but she hesitated. What was the point? If she told Najm about Omar it would put them all in danger. Slowly she was beginning to realise that the game of life was played differently here. Yes, she was a slave; yes, her life was not her own but, if she was careful, she could regain at least some of her independence. All she needed was the backing of the Khalifa. He could be her champion.

CHAPTER 35

Fatima knew she had to stop crying but it was impossible. The house was empty without Omar and now the soldiers were leaving and al-Jundi was going with them. Two of her sons going into danger. Al-Jundi was a soldier; he would be able to protect himself but Omar had never even used a sword. She had heard of the perils that pilgrims faced on their journey to Mecca; there were pirates that sailed along the Barbary coast, thieves and murderers that would slit a man's throat for a purse of silver coins. She knew it had always been Qasim's wish to do a hajj, but Omar had never mentioned it; she was sure that it had not been her son's idea to go. When she questioned him, her husband would say very little but she had a feeling in her bones that something bad had happened. Qasim would never have sent Omar on a hajj if it had been some small misdemeanour. No, something dreadful had befallen her son. She tried to piece together the bits of information that she had picked up from her brief conversation with her husband. There was a woman involved somewhere, she was sure; she had seen the signs before. Was she married? Yes, that was it; her son had been making love to a married woman. Stupid boy. For that he was banished from the home? But why had al-Jundi been involved and the slave boy? No, it must be something more. She sighed. She would have to wait until the right moment and then ask her husband for all the facts. She deserved to know. She knew Qasim too well to ask him now, so soon after the event; she would wait until his mind had calmed and his temper cooled.

A knock at the door startled her. She wiped her eyes and straightened her hair. Who could it be? Maybe it was Elvira, hoping for a chat and a glass of mint tea. That would be nice; she could do with the company, anything to take her mind off her worries. She opened the door and stared in surprise. It wasn't Elvira; it was a young woman.

'As-salam alaykum. Can I help you?' she asked.

'Are you the mother of Omar ibn Qasim?' the young woman asked.

'I am. And you are?'

'I am Zilma bint Zakariya, the betrothed of Yusuf ibn Yusuf.'

'You are Yusuf's wife-to-be? How nice of you to call and see me. I am delighted to meet you. Please come in. How are you? And how is Yusuf?'

'I want to speak to Omar,' the woman said, ignoring Fatima's questions. 'Is he here?'

Her face was pale and streaked with tears. What had happened? Had Yusuf jilted her? Is that why she wanted to talk to Omar, to ask him to speak to Yusuf on her behalf?

'I'm sorry but my son is not here,' Fatima explained. 'He has decided to go on a hajj. I do not know when he will return. But tell me, how is your betrothed?'

'Yusuf is dead,' the girl said.

She spoke plainly, her voice dry and hard and, as she spoke, her eyes filled with tears.

'Dead? How is that possible?' Fatima asked.

She wondered if she had heard correctly.

'Yes.'

What had happened to him? Fatima thought of the last time she had seen Yusuf, just a week ago when he and Omar had come back from the camel racing, laughing and joking, as they always did. He had eaten some of her almond tart, making her promise to give the recipe to his betrothed.

'He was executed this morning for something he did not do,' Zilma continued.

Fatima felt faint. Little Yusuf executed? How could that be? What had he become mixed up in?

'What happened?' she asked, her voice trembling.

'I don't know. That's why I need to speak to Omar. I want to know what Yusuf said to him the last time they met.'

'Oh my dear, I'm so truly sorry to hear about Yusuf but Omar cannot help you. He isn't here.'

'When did he leave?'

'A few days ago,' Fatima lied.

Something told her to be careful. Was it possible that her son's disappearance and Yusuf's death were somehow linked? She had to know more before she confided in her.

'So, it was planned for some time?' Zilma asked.

'Yes, of course. You can't do a hajj without lots of planning beforehand.'

'It's strange that Yusuf never told me that his best friend was going on a pilgrimage to Mecca. We thought he would be coming to our wedding.'

'I'm sorry; I don't know what he had arranged with Yusuf. As you say they were best friends. I'm sure he wanted to go to your wedding but his duty to Allah was obviously stronger.'

She could see that the girl did not believe her. Omar had never demonstrated a strong religious fervour and he had talked incessantly about Yusuf's forthcoming marriage.

'Is there anything I can do to help you?' she asked.

'No-one can help me now. They might as well have chopped off my head at the same time. What future have I got with Yusuf dead? No-one will marry me now, the betrothed woman of a convicted murderer. Innocent or not I will carry that shame to my grave.'

'I'm sure that's not true. You are a very comely girl. Someone will want you for a wife.'

'Maybe, but not Yusuf. Some old man, who fancies taking a second or third wife, might take me in. So I will pass my years in drudgery. Yusuf loved me. I loved him. We were going to be so happy together. Omar knew that. Omar understood how we felt.'

She cried silently for a while, mopping her tears with a white linen cloth. Fatima wanted to hug her but something held her back. Yusuf had been a lovely young man, well educated and clever. He had moved to Madinat al-Zahra at the same time as her family. She remembered her husband talking to Yusuf's father and explaining what great opportunities there were in this new city for a talented sculptor like his son. Yusuf's father had agreed and convinced him to apply to the alcázar for work. Yusuf had been working there ever since, saving money for his wedding. Unlike her sons, he was eager to marry and settle down; he had been betrothed to Zilma since they were children.

'Do you still live in Córdoba?' asked Fatima.

'Yes, I just arrived here this morning but too late to see Yusuf. It was all over. My beloved was dead.'

The woman swallowed hard, trying to control herself then continued, 'So I came straight here. I was sure that Omar would know what had happened. Didn't he say anything to you before he left for the hajj? Didn't he speak of Yusuf at all?'

'No, he never mentioned Yusuf once, not to me. I am so sorry.'

The girl started to cry again.

'I was so sure Omar would tell me what was happening. When I came here to sort out the arrangements for our wedding, I saw them together; they had been to the tea shop. Later Yusuf told me that he was worried about Omar; he said that he thought Omar was heading for trouble if he wasn't careful.'

'Did he say why?' Fatima asked.

'No. He was too loyal to Omar to even confide in me, his future wife.'

Fatima thought she detected some bitterness in her tone as she said it.

'Let me make you some tea,' Fatima suggested.

'No, thank you. I must go back to his mother; she is distraught with grief.'

Fatima had an image of Yusuf's mother, a frail woman, years older than her, breaking her heart at the death of her only son. In the name of Allah, she prayed, please don't let this have anything to do with Omar. Please do not let him be responsible for this young man's death. Please let there be no blood on his hands.

After Zilma had left, Fatima put on her outer robe and wound a scarf around her head, so that her face was partially covered. She could not stay in the house; she had to find Qasim and she did not want to antagonise him by appearing in the tea shop without a veil. She need not have worried; no sooner had she left the house and turned the key in the lock when he came round the corner. He did not see her at first and she watched him unobserved. He looked so old and tired; his shoulders were slumped forward and, as he walked, his right leg, where he had been wounded many years before, dragged. He did not look like her active, energetic husband; he had become an old man overnight. Whatever had happened with Omar had affected him badly.

'Fatima? Where are you going at this hour?' he asked, looking up and realising it was her.

'I was going to the tea shop to look for you, husband.'

'Well you wouldn't have found me there. I have been to the mosque to pray for our family.'

Fatima took the key from her pocket and unlocked the door again. She stood to one side to allow her husband to enter first.

'What is so important that it couldn't wait until I got home.' he asked. 'Not more bad news, I hope.'

He sounded more weary than irritated, not angry with her, just empty of emotion. Something terrible was bothering him. She had to know what it was. She waited until he was seated on the patio in his usual place by the fountain.

'I had a visitor today,' she began but her husband did not look up. 'It was Yusuf's betrothed. She came to tell Omar that Yusuf was executed this morning.'

She expected some reaction from her husband but he still did not look at her.

'She said he was innocent but nobody would believe him. She wanted to talk to Omar, to see if he knew anything about what had happened.'

'You told her he had gone on a hajj?' Qasim asked, continuing to stare at the tumbling water in the fountain.

'I did.'

'Good.'

'Husband, you must tell me the truth. Why did Omar leave so suddenly? He never even said goodbye to me or his sister. That is so unlike him.'

'He had to hurry because the caravan was leaving,' Qasim said.

Fatima knelt by her husband's side and took his hands in hers.

'Husband, we have lived together for many years. I have always respected you and obeyed you because I believed that you were a truthful, honest man. Please tell me why Omar left so suddenly. Does it have anything to do with Yusuf's death?'

Then he raised his head and looked at her. She meant what she had said; he was an honest man. He would have to tell her now.

'I did not want to tell you, wife, because I wanted to protect you. The least you know about this sorry affair the better but, as you have pressed me, then I will tell you. When you hear what I have to say you will understand that no-one must know this, not Sara, not Ibrahim and definitely not Layla.'

'What about al-Jundi? Does he know?'

'Yes, my oldest son knows. He was the first to know. Now sit here beside me and I will tell you everything.'

She listened in silence while he explained all that had happened, how Omar had sworn that it was an accident, that he had not meant to kill anyone. He had gone there to help the woman, only that. He was reuniting brother and sister, nothing more. He was in love.

'So Omar doesn't know about Yusuf?' she asked.

'No. He had left for the hajj before they arrested his friend.'

'But you knew? You knew that they had arrested Yusuf?'

'Al-Jundi told me.'

'Why didn't you tell them that he was innocent?'

He groaned and put his head in his hands.

'How could I, wife? That would have meant putting all my family in danger. I couldn't take the risk.'

She stared at him, trying to understand what was going through his mind. An innocent man had been executed and Qasim had done nothing to prevent it.

'Do not think that I made the decision lightly. I have prayed to Allah the Merciful for guidance. I have lain awake searching my conscience. There was nothing I could do. Believe me, I did this for our family, for all of them, for Omar, al-Jundi, Ibrahim, Sara, for you and Layla,' he said, looking straight at her. 'It was not to save my own skin.'

'So now Yusuf is dead and our son is a wanted man, exiled from his homeland,' she said.

Her voice was flat, emotionless.

'But he is alive. That is what is important. Omar is innocent of all this. He does not know what happened to his friend. One day he will marry and have a family of his own; our line will continue.'

'But who will he marry? Some girl we know nothing about? A foreigner? And what of Muna, his betrothed?'

'I know, wife. It is troubling me also. I will speak to Ibrahim; if he is agreed I will tell the father of Muna that he will marry her.'

'Do you think Ibrahim will agree?'

'Why not? He has to get married some time. She is a comely girl and the family are well positioned. I think Ibrahim will be happy to marry her, even if it is only to stop you nagging him.'

'But what will you tell her family?'

'I will say that it is better for her to marry Ibrahim than to wait for Omar to return from the hajj. Everyone knows that a pilgrimage can take many years; it depends on the pilgrim.'

'And what of Yusuf's family? His wife-to-be? His mother and father? They have no more sons to continue their line.'

'Enough, wife. I have told you what you wanted to know. I did not say that you would like it. Now leave me in peace.'

Fatima got up. Why had she pressed so hard for the truth? Now that she had it, it upset her more deeply than ever. In her heart she knew that her husband had had no choice; he had to put his family first but it pained her to think of that innocent young man, dying for a crime he did not commit.

'Oh and there is something else. I have found a husband for Layla,' he said.

'What?'

She cannot believe her ears. They had agreed when Layla was born that she would have an education; she would not be given in marriage to the first man that came along. Now Qasim had arranged a marriage contract for her. She felt betrayed.

'I know. I remember perfectly well what we planned for Layla but things have changed. I do not know how long I will be here to protect her; I must make sure that she has a husband to look after her if anything happens to me,' he continued.

'She will not like it,' Fatima said.

'Since when do I have to ask my daughter if she likes something before I can do it?' he snapped.

For a moment there was a spark of the old Qasim.

'Who is it?' she asked.

'A respected family. It is the son of the apothecary. I spoke to him today; he is very happy to marry his son to our daughter. In fact it was he who first suggested it, two or three years ago.'

'But he does not know of your past, nor of Omar's deeds.'

'He would refuse if he knew either of those things. That is why it must be done as soon as possible.'

'She is still very young, husband. Can we not wait until she is older, until she has finished her education?'

'No. I want her out of harm's way. She will never be safe in this family any more. Our secrets are secure for now but one careless word could put us all in danger. I do not care for myself but I will not endanger my little Layla. They are a good family; they will take care of her.'

'But she is still so young. She is not yet a woman. How can you marry her off so soon?'

'I have spoken of that to the apothecary. He says his son will respect her until she reaches womanhood.'

'When will you tell her?'

'You will tell her, wife, right away. I have told them that we will start making arrangements for the wedding as soon as possible. I would like it to happen immediately but if I seem in too much of a hurry they may think something is wrong.'

Fatima could no longer hold back her tears. She was losing all her children. It was more than she could bear.

'There is no use crying. Tears will not mend what has been done. Now go and make me some tea,' her husband said. 'And when you say your prayers ask Allah to forgive your son for what he has brought down upon our heads.'

He was not angry with her; his voice was soft and gentle. She knew that it pained him to part with Layla as much as it did her.

She poured some water from the jug and put it to heat on the stove. This stupid infatuation of her son's had disrupted all their lives. She knew that Layla would be unhappy at the news. She would feel that her mother had betrayed her. Fatima had promised her daughter a different life, the sort of life she had wanted for herself.

Now someone else would be in control of her daughter's future.

Fatima remembered how excited she had been when she had arrived in Córdoba all those years ago. She had never been to a city before and although she had been overawed by it she was not frightened. In fact she had enjoyed the hustle and bustle of the crowded streets and bazaars. What had amazed her then, someone who was used to seeing women living very restricted lives, raising children and caring for the animals and the home, was the freedom that the women of Córdoba possessed. That was what she had wanted for Layla. Now it would never happen.

CHAPTER 36

Layla was scared. Something was wrong. She had woken up that morning and the house was empty except for her mother. She remembered that there had been some kind of disturbance in the night; al-Sagir had come home in tears and Baba was shouting at Omar but then she had been sent back to bed and didn't know any more until she had woken to a house weighed down by its silence. Everyone had disappeared: Sara, her cousins, her brother Ibrahim; they had all gone home her mother told her. They had left without saying goodbye. She couldn't believe it. Sara wouldn't do that to her. And Salma, she thought that Salma was her friend; how could she just go home without a word? Something terrible must have happened. She would go to the alfarería and ask Omar; he would know. She pulled her dress over her head and slipped on a pair of cork-soled sandals. Her mother was in the kitchen but there was no smell of cooking; she just squatted by the stove, watching the water boil.

Layla slipped out the front door and went into the alfarería. It was empty. There was no sign of Omar, nor her father. No heat radiated from the kiln; it was cold to her touch. She opened the door and saw that it was still fully laden with pots. Nobody had been in to empty it. Where was everybody? Where was al-Sagir?

She went back to the kitchen, her anxiety growing all the while. Her mother remained squatting in the same position.

'Mama, what's wrong? Where's Baba and Omar? I can't find them. Nobody's been into the alfarería this morning.'

Her mother stood up and looked at her; her face was streaked with tears. Layla could not remember seeing her mother cry before; it frightened her.

'Omar has gone on a hajj,' she said. 'He will be away a long time.'

At this news Layla burst into tears. It was as if everybody she loved had abandoned her.

'But why Mama? What's wrong? What's happened?' she sobbed.

'Don't cry, little one.'

'Tell me Mama. Tell me what has happened. Why has Omar gone on a hajj?'

'It is something that he has always wanted to do and Baba said that he could go.'

'But Mama, I don't understand. Why did he leave so suddenly? Has he done something wrong?'

'Yes, child, your brother has done something very foolish and for that he must go away for a while but you don't need to worry. Nothing can harm you. We will always look after you.'

Her mother's words did little to comfort her because as she spoke them she burst into fierce sobs and hugged Layla to her bosom. So her mother felt it too; something was very wrong.

The door opened and her father came in. Layla pulled herself away from her mother's grasp and ran to him.

'Baba, you'll tell me, won't you. What has Omar done that is so bad? Why has he gone away and where is everyone else?'

'So many questions, my little princess. You mustn't worry your pretty head with all these things. Your brother has gone on a hajj. That is all you need to know. Now run along and get yourself properly dressed. Fatima do her hair for her. She is coming out with me this morning.'

Layla stared at him and then at her mother, who had turned very pale.

'Don't look at me like that wife. You know it's for the best.'

'What is? What's for the best, Baba?' Layla asked.

'Haven't you told her yet?' he asked, looking straight at her mother.

'No. I couldn't bring myself to do it.'

He sighed and sat down on the couch, pulling Layla beside him.

'I have something to tell you, Layla. It is very good news.'

He smiled at her and stroked her hair.

'I have found you a husband, my child.'

Layla looked at him in amazement; she could not believe what he was saying. She pinched her arm to see if she was still sleeping. So many strange things were happening this morning; surely she was dreaming. A husband? Why would she want a husband?

'Well, what do you have to say to that? Don't you want to know who the lucky man is?'

Her father was smiling but only with his lips; his eyes were sad.

'But, Baba, why do I need a husband?'

'Every girl must find a husband; that's how things are in the world, princess.'

'But I don't want to get married; I want to stay here with you and Mama.'

'I know it's all a bit sudden, my child but you will be happy when you know what I have arranged for my princess. Come, can you guess who it is?'

She had no idea what to say. The only boys she knew were friends of Omar, boys like Yusuf, with whom she had grown up and the two sons of the baker.

'No, Baba,' she whispered.

'His name is Muhammed al-Hasam; he is the son of the apothecary.'

'Muhammed "The handsome",' she said. 'Is he? Do you think he is handsome?'

'I don't know. What do you say, wife? Is he handsome? Will he be a good match for our beautiful daughter?'

'Yes, husband. He is a good looking young man, tall and with a fine head of hair and a full beard although he is only nineteen.'

She wiped her eyes and looked down at Layla.

'He will make you a good husband, my daughter. They are a fine family.'

'I know the apothecary,' Layla said. 'And I think I know his son. He works in the shop sometimes.'

She knew exactly who they were talking about; she had seen him in the shop when she had gone on errands for her father. Muhammed was a thin, pimply-faced youth whose beard did little to hide the ravages of his acne; he wasn't handsome at all.

'But what about school, Mama? I am supposed to go back to school tomorrow.'

'Don't worry about that. Just go and get ready,' her father said, rather sharply.

At that moment she wished with all her heart that Omar was there; he would have known what to say to her father. He would have spoken up on her behalf. But her brother was goodness knows where, half-way to Africa by now she guessed. He couldn't help her. She looked at her mother for support but her mother turned away; she could not look her daughter in the eye. No, Mama could do nothing to help her either. Layla was on her own.

'But I have to go to school,' she insisted. 'We are having a test today. I cannot miss it or the teacher will be angry with me.'

'Don't worry about the teacher; I will explain to her later. She will understand,' her father said.

'Come child, let me braid your hair,' her mother said.

She brushed Layla's long dark hair until it shone then parted it down the middle and braided each side into equal plaits. These she looped up so that they covered her ears and finally pinned the ends neatly to her head. It was a traditional hairstyle that she only wore on special days and now she had to wear her best clothes too, because today her father was taking her to meet her future husband.

'Shouldn't she have a veil?' Baba asked.

'No. She's still a child; she doesn't need a veil,' her mother replied. 'Let them see what a lovely girl she is.'

***

She knew the pharmacy well. Her father often sent her there to collect supplies for him. The apothecary was an old man who had three wives and many children. He was a jolly man who often gave her a piece of sugar cane to chew or a sugared almond. This son was said to be his favourite, born to his third wife and the only one still unmarried and living at home. Her mother told her that she would have to live with her in-laws after the wedding because Muhammed was expected to take over his father's business when he retired. This would be her new home.

When they reached the pharmacy her father stopped and turned to her.

'Are you all right, Layla?' he asked. 'Do you want to ask me anything before we go in?'

'Do I have to do this?'

'Why do you ask, child? Can you think of a better match for you?'

'No Baba, but it's just so sudden. I don't understand what is happening.'

'Don't worry Layla. You must have known that you would have to marry one day?'

She nodded sadly. It was what was expected of every young girl but she had wanted to do something more with her life. Many of her friends did nothing but talk about boys and who they would like to marry. She was clever; she had her sights set on going to the university. Her mother had talked to her about it ever since she could remember. Her teacher had encouraged her. Even Baba had been happy with the idea. Now everything had changed.

'Is he a good man, Baba?' she asked.

'Yes, child. You know I would never give you to someone who would be cruel to you. I believe he will be a good husband and, more importantly, the family will take care of you.'

'Who decides when the marriage will take place?'

She felt very grown-up talking about such things.

'It has been decided already. You will be married early next month.'

She looked at him in horror. How could that be? She had assumed he was talking about a marriage that was to take place sometime in the future, when she was older, when she had left school. How could she become a bride so soon? She was still a child.

'No Baba, I'm not ready,' she croaked. 'I'm too young.'

She swallowed hard; even her voice was failing her. The thought of meeting her future husband made her feel faint; she wanted to turn and run home. She knew nothing of being a wife. She had watched her mother preparing the food but never actually done it herself; her mother did all the cooking. Layla helped her by bringing in the water, feeding the donkey and doing a bit of sweeping but most of the time she was left to play or study. Her mother made few demands on her. She had often told her how important it was to learn as much as she could while she was at school and so that was how Layla passed her days.

Her father took her hand and squeezed it gently.

'Don't worry, princess, it will be all right. You will be well looked after in their household. Trust me.'

She could not move; her feet felt rooted to the spot. Her heart was pounding. No, she couldn't do this.

'I can't Baba. Don't make me do this, please. Let me go home.'

'Come along now. I'll be right beside you,' her father said.

He was patient and kind but she could see the anguish in his eyes. There was some other reason that had prompted him to make this hasty step towards her marriage, something he wasn't telling her.

She looked up at him and said, 'All right Baba, but don't leave me there. Please don't leave me on my own, not today.'

'No, of course not, princess.'

The apothecary was serving a customer when they entered the shop, a podgy lady with enormous rings on her fingers. The counter was littered with dozens of small pots and the woman was taking her time examining the contents of each one. She poked a plump finger in them, one by one and rubbed a little of the contents on the back of her hand. The apothecary looked up and smiled at them.

'As-salam alaykum, Qasim. Welcome to my home.'

'Wa alaykum e-salam, I have brought my daughter Layla to meet you and your family.'

'As-salam alaykum, Layla. How are you?' he said and gave her a wink. 'You have not come on your father's business today, I take it.'

'Wa alaykum e-salam. No,' she said shyly.

She had no idea what to say to the man who would soon be her father-in-law. The woman he was serving had finally made up her mind and chosen a rose coloured pot of cream. The apothecary wrapped up the customer's purchase and gave it to her. The pharmacy had always fascinated Layla with its high, marble counter that she could barely reach even now and the strange smells, some sweet and pleasant, others so pungent they brought tears to her eyes. She tried to identify them; there were aniseed and camphor and today, because he had been making up some cosmetics, there was also the heavy scent of musk in the air. Whenever she went in there, the apothecary and his son were always busy, mixing syrups for coughs and colds, creams for skin ailments, lotions for the hair or salves to place on wounds. Rich and poor came to their pharmacy; they prepared deodorants, face powders and perfumes for the rich women who lived in the medina and they dispensed free medicine to the less fortunate.

'Did you make those jars, Baba?' she asked her father, pointing to the tall green and black majolica containers that the apothecary used to store his ointments and dried herbs.

'No, princess. We don't make anything as large as that. He probably bought them in Córdoba.'

'From a peddler, actually,' the apothecary said, closing the door behind his departing customer and pulling down the blind. 'He comes from Italy and brings me two or three every year. Come, let me take you to meet my wife and son. Follow me.'

The apothecary's wife and the man who was to be Layla's husband were sitting in a room above the shop, waiting for them. Muhammed was not wearing the usual grey djubba stained with chemicals that he wore in the shop; instead he wore a brown one and had a red cap on his head. His beard was neatly trimmed and his hair was short, in the latest fashion; there was no sign of his acne.

She had to admit that he did look rather handsome. He stood up as they came in; he was tall, taller than Baba.

'Come in child and join us,' the wife said to her.

She was much younger than the apothecary and had a pretty, round face that creased into dimples when she smiled. Muhammed did not look at Layla but greeted her father, warmly.

'Wa alaykum e-salam,' her father replied.

He seemed as nervous as she was.

The family were very kind to her, offering her tea and treating her like a lady. Most of the conversation was about general things: the price of wheat, the number of people that were moving into the city and of course, the news of the rebellion in the north. Nobody spoke to her directly, except to offer her more tea or cakes but Muhammed stole glances at her from time to time and she felt herself blushing. Then, to her relief, the men went into a separate room and she heard them discussing the arrangements for her bride price and the wedding party.

None of it made sense to her. It was too soon; she was not ready. Of course, she knew that one day she would have to marry; that was the way for all women. But now, next month? It was such a surprise; nobody had mentioned anything about marriage before. She thought she would continue at school for another four years at least. Why had her father changed his mind? He was not happy about it; she could see that in his eyes. Despite his comforting words and smiling face she knew he was as unhappy as she was. So why the hurry? Perhaps this was to do with Omar's disappearance.

'So, Layla what do you enjoy doing?' the apothecary's wife asked her when they were alone. 'Do you like to sew?'

Layla hung her head in shame; she knew how to sew but she was not very good at it.

'Not much,' she said. 'I can never keep the stitches straight.'

The woman laughed.

'I used to be like that. It's just a question of practice. You are very young yet. What about cooking?'

'My mother does the cooking.'

'Oh. So what do you do to help your mother?'

'I feed the donkey.'

'My goodness, is that all?'

'I study a lot. My mother wanted me to be a doctor.'

At the thought of her lost opportunities she burst into tears.

'Now, now, there is no need to cry. I'm not going to treat you like a slave. I just want to know that you will be able to look after my son when you are older. A woman has to know how to sew and cook and keep a well-run house.'

She smiled kindly at her.

'But you are young; you will soon learn how to do all those things. If you are interested in medicine then maybe you can also help my husband in the shop. I will speak to him.'

She leant across and patted Layla's hand.

'Do not worry. I'm sure you will make my son an excellent wife.'

'I can play the lute,' Layla said, feeling that she ought to contribute something positive to this catalogue of her non-achievements. 'And sing. And draw.'

'That's wonderful. You can sing for us next time you are here. Now I think your father is ready to leave. Ma'a salama, my child and shed no more tears. This is a happy time for both our families.'

'Alla ysalmak, auntie.'

She followed her father out of the shop but not before stealing another glance at her prospective husband. After greeting her formally when she arrived he had not spoken to her but he was gazing at her now from the doorway and when he saw her look back at him, he smiled.

***

Her mother was waiting anxiously at the door when they returned. She hugged Layla as though she had been away for weeks.

'How was it, husband?' she asked as Layla wriggled out of her embrace.

'Fine. The wedding will take place in six weeks time but the groom has agreed not to consummate the marriage until Layla is ready.'

'And the bride price?'

'Yes, it has been agreed, a substantial amount.'

'Good. He is getting a beautiful, healthy young wife who will bear him many children.'

'I have decided that it will be paid directly to Layla,' he added. 'She will have control of it after the marriage.'

'Why can't I wait until I'm old enough to marry?' Layla asked. 'Why do I have to live with them?'

'Because, in six weeks time you will be his wife. It would not be proper for you to live here with us.'

Her father sat down and pulled her onto his knee; he looked sad.

'Listen, princess, we do not want to lose you but this is the way of the world. I have done all that I can for you; I have found you a young husband from a well-respected family. I have negotiated a good bride price so that you will have some security if anything happens to your husband and you will continue to live here in the same town so that you can visit your mother and me whenever you want. I can do no more. Please give me a smile. It breaks my heart to see you so unhappy.'

She laid her head on his shoulder and whispered, 'Very well Baba. I do not understand why this is happening but I will do as you say. I know you only want my happiness.'

She did not feel like smiling but she managed to find a smile for her father and hugged and kissed him. But later, in her room, lying on her mat, she thought of her lost opportunities and the man who was soon to be her husband and wept.

CHAPTER 37

Someone was banging on the door. Fatima felt her heart begin to race; ever since Zilma had visited her she had been frightened that someone was going to come round asking about Omar.

'Who is it?' she called.

'I am looking for the wife of Qasim the potter,' a male voice replied.

'Who wants her?'

'I have a letter for her from her daughter.'

Fatima opened the door and looked at the youth standing outside. He held a folded piece of parchment in his hand.

'Are you the wife of Qasim the potter?' he asked.

'I am.'

'This is for you,' he said and thrust the letter into her hand.

'Wait. Take this for your trouble,' she said, giving him a small coin.

A letter from Sara, how strange. The only letters that Fatima ever received were from her parents and then not often. Sometimes, if there was someone passing through Ardales who was going to Córdoba, then her mother would ask them to take her a parcel of herbs and a brief note telling her how the family was but that only happened perhaps every two or three years. She opened the parchment and sat down to read it.

'Dear Mama, I had to write to you because I am so worried. When I arrived home Halawa came to the house to cut my hair - you remember me talking about her, she can tell fortunes and see into the future. I know you don't like me doing it but I was so worried about what Baba had said that I let her read my palm. What she told me has frightened me, Mama. That is why I am writing to you. She said there's been a death that threatens all the family. Do you know what she means? Is this to do with why Omar had to go away? She also said that something bad happened in our family, a long time ago. She said that both these things mean that we are all in danger and that I mustn't take my daughters to Madinat al-Zahra again until it is resolved. What happened? Do you know what this bad thing was? And who has died?

I haven't said anything to Isa. He hates Halawa and he is already annoyed that I left him alone with his child-wife for Eid so there is no point talking to him.

Please write to me or, better still come and see me.

Your loving daughter, Sara

Fatima rolled up the letter and placed it in her pocket. Poor Sara, she had been sent home with no explanation; no wonder she was worried.

Who was this woman? How could she know about their past and what death was she referring to, the eunuch or Yusuf?

Fatima did not believe in soothsayers and fortune tellers. She knew that people like Halawa had a great deal of influence over the women that they met, lonely women, women looking for answers to their problems, but she had never listened to them; she wasn't going to start now. In her opinion it was usually guesswork on their part. They were clever; there was no doubt about that, picking up on things that people said and piecing together a likely story. But that wasn't the same as seeing the future. It would have been easy to suggest to Sara that the family's problems stemmed from something in their past; Sara would neither be able to confirm nor deny it. After all everyone had skeletons in their cupboards. And the mysterious death, that could be anyone. Surely the news of the eunuch's murder had not reached Córdoba yet. Yes, she was sure Halawa was just up to her usual tricks; no wonder these women were condemned as witches.

She sighed. What should she do? She couldn't leave Layla now, what with the wedding to organise but Sara needed her. She would talk to Qasim and see what he suggested.

***

Qasim was in the alfarería, emptying the kiln; al-Mari was helping him.

'What is it, wife? You look upset.'

'I have had a message from Sara; she is worried.'

'We all have our worries,' he replied, stacking the last of the pots by Omar's bench.

She looked at them; who was going to decorate them now? Qasim couldn't do it. What would he do without Omar?

'You are busy. I will speak to you later, husband.'

Her husband had turned to al-Mari.

'Go and bring me in some blocks of clay,' he said. 'Then I'll teach you how to prepare them for the wheel.'

'So al-Mari is to work in the alfarería, now?' she asked. 'What about the house?'

'The house will have to wait. What do we need so many rooms for anyway? In a few weeks time there will just be you and me. This is what my pride has brought us to,' he added bitterly.

'Do not say that, husband. It is not your fault that these things have happened. You have always done the best for our family.'

'So, what is it that is worrying Sara?' he asked, heaving some clay onto the wheel and starting to work it with his hands.

'She has been talking to a soothsayer,' Fatima said.

'A soothsayer? You mean one of those old hags who spins a good tale for gullible housewives?'

'She has warned her that we are all in danger. She says that something from our past is putting us in danger. Is it possible that she means ibn Hayyan?'

Al-Mari came back in with the clay and set it on the ground.

'How many blocks do you want?' he asked Qasim.

'Two will do, for now.'

They waited until al-Mari had left then Qasim said, 'It's a coincidence, that's all it is. Tell Sara to pay no heed to the woman.'

'But it's true. Sara and the children would be in danger if it were known about your past.'

'Do you think I don't know that, woman? That's why I want them to stay in Córdoba. They will be safe there. What else can I do? I can't wipe it out, much as I would like to. What is done, is done.'

Her husband was angry with her but Fatima's concern for her daughter made her continue, 'She wants me to go to see her. Maybe I should tell her the truth then she would know exactly what she had to do.'

'No, don't say anything. It is best that Sara knows nothing. Then she can't tell that gabby husband of hers, who would probably divorce her and then delight in telling all his customers about the shame of his ex-wife and her family. No, the least said, the better.'

'I have to tell her something. The woman also mentioned a death that would affect us all.'

'Just guesswork. Tell Sara to pay her no heed and to spend her money on more worthwhile things. Go and see her, if you wish. Al-Mari can go with you. But one day only; I can't do without him for longer.'

'What about Layla?'

'Take her with you. It might be the last chance she has to see her sister before the wedding.'

'Are you sure you can manage without us?'

'Of course, wife. Just hurry back.'

***

Sara was delighted to see them. They had left before dawn and were knocking on her door soon after sunrise.

'You came, Mama,' she said, hugging her mother as though she hadn't seen her for months.

'Yes, but we must leave today, before it is dark. I can't desert your father for too long; he has a lot of work and no-one to help him, except al-Mari.'

She nodded at the slave as she spoke. Sara smiled at him and said, 'Come in and have some breakfast with us. I'll run over to the bakery and get some fresh bread.'

'Where are the children?' Fatima asked.

'I'll wake them; they're still sleeping.'

'No. Let me. I'll get them,' said Layla, running off towards her nieces' room.

Fatima sat down; her feet ached from walking so far. She was no longer as fit as she used to be. Once she could have walked to Córdoba and beyond with no complaints but now just two Arab miles and the pain in her hip was excruciating. Still it would pass once she had rested and at least she was here, with her daughter and her grandchildren. The pleasure on Sara's face when she greeted them had been worth the long walk. Squeals and shrieks of delight came from her granddaughters' bedroom; they were awake and obviously pleased to see Layla. Poor child, it was difficult to imagine that she would be married soon.

'They're up, I hear,' said Sara.

The smell of the newly baked bread was delicious; Fatima could feel her stomach rumble. As she watched her daughter put some fruit and oil on the table, she realised just how hungry she was.

'Isa sends his regards. He will come in later, when he has finished,' her daughter said, cutting the bread into thick slices. 'Girls, come and eat your breakfast.'

She passed some bread to al-Mari and then sat down beside Fatima.

'When the girls have gone out, we must talk, Mama.'

Fatima took her daughter's hand and stroked it gently.

'Try not to worry so, Sara. You must learn to trust in Allah; he will keep and protect you.'

'Mama, Mama, Layla is getting married,' Salma cried.

The girls tumbled into the room and rushed towards Fatima.

'Teta, why does Layla have to get married? Does that mean we can't play with her anymore?' Maysa asked.

'Will Salma have to get married too?' asked Tara.

'I want to get married,' squeaked Mariam, excitedly.

The children could not contain themselves; they bounced around the room in excitement. Only Salma and Layla looked serious

'Hello my lovelies. Here, give your Teta a big hug.'

'Is that right, Mama?' Sara asked.

She looked shocked. It was no wonder. She was not expecting to hear this news for another few years at least.

'Yes. Isn't it wonderful. Baba has found her an excellent husband. They are to be married next month.'

'So soon?'

She thought for a moment that Sara would burst into tears. This must seem to her like confirmation that her fears had been correct, that something was wrong. Fatima managed as broad a smile as she could for the sake of the children and nodded. She could not trust herself to speak.

'I don't understand, Mama. Why did nobody mention it over Eid, when we were all together? Does Ibrahim know? And al-Jundi?' Sara asked.

'It has only just been arranged.'

'What do you think, little sister?' Sara asked, pulling Layla towards her. 'Are you ready to become a bride?'

Layla looked at her mother.

'He is a good man,' she said, quietly.

'So you know him?'

'He is the son of the apothecary,' Fatima said. 'I expect you know the family as well; they used to be in Córdoba. They lived near the Jewish quarter.'

Sara shook her head.

'No, I don't remember them.'

She kissed Layla on the cheek and said, 'Run outside and play with the girls. Be a child while you can.'

After they had left she looked at Fatima and asked, 'Why?'

'Your father thought it was for the best. They are a good family and they will look after her. It had to happen one day.'

'But she was happy. You always said Layla would have the opportunities that we missed. What has happened to change that?'

'Sara, I cannot explain it all to you. There are things that have happened in our family that are best not discussed. Your father says it is safer if you do not know the details. Please trust him. Everything that he has done has been for the good of our family. His only wish is to keep you all from harm.'

'Is it to do with Omar?'

'Do not press me, child. I cannot tell you any more than I have already done.'

'I'm frightened, Mama. Halawa says we are all in danger. How can she know that? And how can she know about our past? Who can have told her?'

'Tell me exactly what she said.'

'There were two things. One was about a death that could affect all our lives and the other was something that had happened long ago. She said we shouldn't return to Madinat al-Zahra; that it was unsafe for us.'

'Is that all she said?'

'Yes.'

'Sara, I think you are reading too much into her words. You were probably tired after your journey and upset at having to leave so suddenly. I think this woman took advantage of your vulnerable state. Please put her words out of your mind and stop worrying.'

Despite everything she had said to her daughter, Fatima was worried. How did the woman know about their past? And what was the death she spoke of? Either the woman was genuine or someone had been talking to her. She feared it was the latter.

'But I agree with Halawa on one thing; you and the children should stay in Córdoba.'

'What about Layla's wedding? Should we go to her wedding? The girls will be so disappointed if we don't go.'

Fatima hesitated. Qasim didn't want them to go anywhere near Madinat al-Zahra at the moment but it was he who had insisted that Layla should marry. What could they do? If Layla's closest relatives did not attend the wedding, people would think it very strange. Weddings were occasions for all the family to get together. People might think they were trying to hide something if Sara did not attend. It didn't take much for rumours to start.

'You should certainly be there and Isa. Your father is sure to ask Isa to be one of the witnesses.'

'What about Ibrahim?'

'Yes, Ibrahim too. They are the only two male relatives we have at the moment with Omar and al-Jundi away.'

'Mama, I want to go to Layla's wedding,' Salma said.

She had been standing in the doorway listening to them. Fatima wondered how much she had overheard.

'Layla says she wants me to be there. She says I'm her best friend. Please Mama.'

Sara looked at her mother.

'Of course you can go, sweetheart. We are all going. Now run along and play,' Sara said.

The girl clapped her hands in delight and ran outside; they could hear her calling out to Layla with the good news.

'Do you think that is wise?' Fatima asked.

'If Isa and I are going then they must go as well.'

'You could leave them here.'

'What with his mother, you mean, or with his new wife? No. We will go as a family and pray to Allah that nothing happens to spoil the day.'

'Very well, but I don't know what your father will say.'

'There's not much he can say, is there. That would mean explaining to Isa that our family has secrets that he does not know about.'

Her daughter was right. They must all behave naturally if they did not want anyone to suspect that something was wrong.

'Very well. I will tell him what we have decided. And now, aren't you going to introduce me to Isa's new wife?'

'If you insist, Mama. Although she is probably still in bed.'

But Ghayda was not in bed; she was sitting in her room, sewing. She looked up when they entered but did not speak. Fatima thought she looked very apprehensive. She hoped that Sara was not bullying her.

'Ghayda. This is my mother,' Sara said.

'As-salam alaykum, auntie,' the girl said, putting down her sewing and standing up.

'Wa alaykum e-salam, my dear,' Fatima said. 'Don't interrupt your work, please.'

She picked up the garment. It was a tunic made from blue cotton and the girl had been sewing some beads along the hem.

'This is very nice. Do you like sewing?' she asked.

The girl nodded shyly then said, 'It's for Salma.'

Fatima noticed the surprise on Sara's face.

'For Salma?'

'Yes, I thought she would like it.'

'I'm sure she will,' said Fatima. 'It is very pretty. You have a neat hand.'

The stitches were small and even. She might not be able to cook but she could certainly sew.

'We are going to have some tea, would you like to join us?' Fatima said.

The girl nodded again and smiled. She was a pretty little thing, not very old; in fact she seemed a mere child. Fatima could not help but think she would have been better off playing outside with the rest of the girls than sitting in her room, sewing. Once more she thought of Layla and what this marriage would mean to her; her childhood would be over before it had hardly begun. She sighed. That's what it was to be a woman.

***

Fatima helped her daughter prepare the lunch and, when it was ready, went in search of al-Mari. He was standing outside the bakery talking to an old man.

'Al-Mari. Where have you been? Come and have something to eat. I would like to leave straight after lunch.'

'I've been to see your son, Ibrahim,' he answered. 'I wanted to see if al-Sagir was well.'

'Oh,' she said, surprised at the slave's actions. 'And is he well?'

'Yes, mistress. Your son says he is working hard and has a talent for drawing. He is helping him with his new designs.'

'That's good news indeed. I expect he learned from Omar,' she added.

'He is a very bright child,' al-Mari replied. 'I am pleased that he has settled in.'

'Come and eat, before the food goes cold,' she said, setting a plate of food on the patio for the slave.

She went inside and joined the others at the table in the kitchen. Her youngest daughter was happier than she had been in days; Layla and the girls had not stopped talking and laughing since she had arrived. It was so good to see them together. Again, as she looked at Layla's laughing face, she wondered if Qasim really knew what he was doing, marrying off his little princess so soon.

'So, I hear that our little Layla is to be married,' Isa said, as he helped himself to a hunk of fresh bread and dunked it into his stew of lentils and squash.

'Yes, Baba, and we're all going to the wedding,' Miriam squealed with delight.

They were so excited by the news. Typical little girls, they could talk of nothing else but what they would wear.

'Maybe it's time I started to think about finding a husband for Salma,' he said, wiping the gravy from his beard. 'What do you think about that, my lovely?'

Fatima looked at her granddaughter. The colour had drained from her face. She was sitting next to Ghayda; there was little difference in size between them. If anything, Salma was plumper and Fatima noticed for the first time that her breasts were already taking form; she too would soon be of marriageable age.

'Well, speak up, child. Would you like Baba to find you a rich husband?' he asked.

'Leave her alone, Isa. There is time enough to talk about that. First we have Layla's marriage to think about. Baba wants you to be the chief witness at the wedding. Would you do that for him?' Sara said.

Fatima noticed how she kept her voice soft and non-challenging. Her daughter was learning that Isa was not a man to be confronted head-on; she could get her way better through cajolery.

'Yes,' Fatima said. 'May I tell Qasim that you will be able to come and officiate as a witness?'

'Well, of course I would like to but you know the bakery keeps me very busy. People can't do without their bread.'

'I realise that but surely someone would look after things for you for one day so that you could celebrate your sister-in-law's wedding? I don't know what Qasim will do if you can't come. My son Ibrahim will be there; he will be the other witness but, as you know, we need a minimum of two.

It would impress the groom's family if both witnesses were men with their own successful businesses,' she added.

She was making it up as she went along. Qasim would simply ask one of his friends from the tea shop if Isa did not come. But she wanted her son-in-law to feel that his presence was important to them. He was a man who liked to be at the centre of things and there was nothing better than a family wedding for that.

'Well I wouldn't want to let my father-in-law down,' he said, puffing out his chest and beaming at her. 'You will have to help me, Sara. We will bake extra bread the night before and Ghayda can look after the shop while I'm gone.'

'That's wonderful, Isa. Qasim will be so pleased,' Fatima said, giving him a winning smile.

'Of course we won't be able to stay overnight. We'll set off early and leave at sunset.'

'But, Baba ...' Salma began.

'No buts, daughter. That is my final word on it.'

'It sounds an excellent compromise, husband,' Sara said. If she was disappointed, she did not show it.

'Well we must be on our way now,' Fatima said. 'Thank you for a lovely meal, Sara. We will see you all at the wedding then. Come, Layla, kiss your sister and your nieces goodbye. It is time to go.'

She could see Layla was holding back the tears now that it was time to leave, so she hurried her out of the door before she began to cry; if Layla started weeping then the girls would join in and Isa would be annoyed.

'We're ready to go now, al-Mari,' she said.

The slave mopped up the juice on his plate with the freshly baked bread and stood up.

'Here, Mama, take some bread back with you,' Sara said, handing her a couple of loaves still warm from the oven.

'Thank you, my dear.'

She hugged her daughter to her.

'Now, don't worry. Everything will be all right, you see,' she whispered in her ear.

***

As they walked back to Madinat al-Zahra, Fatima could not stop thinking about her eldest daughter. She had told her not to worry but the truth was that Sara's life was less secure than before. Now that Isa had taken another wife she would have to be careful not to upset her husband. But Sara was a clever girl; Fatima was sure she would do what was best for her and her daughters. She was reminded how quick Sara had been to point out that her husband would have asked some awkward questions if all their family had not been invited to the wedding. Her daughter was right; they must try to carry on as if nothing had happened.

Sara seemed to think that her husband had lost interest in her family since he had a new wife but Fatima could see that this was not true. When they told him about the wedding and asked him to officiate as a witness, he had blustered a bit about being a very busy man but in the end Fatima saw that he was delighted to have been asked. He had always liked and admired Qasim and now even more so since he had heard how his business was prospering.

Luckily he did not suggest that his new wife should come along; Sara would not have been happy with that. Fatima could see that the two women did not get on well together. It was understandable; they were very different and Sara had felt hurt and betrayed when Isa had brought the girl home. But she was a sweet child and, before she left, Fatima had tried to explain to Sara that it was important for the harmony of the home that the women became friends. Sara had nodded in agreement but Fatima could see that it was too soon; her daughter was still very bitter about it. She promised she would try to get on with the girl and help her as much as she could but Fatima knew that it would not be easy for her. Her daughter had a strong character; she would have made a good soldier, Fatima thought with a smile, but she was not much of a diplomat.

CHAPTER 38

Sara's daughters could do nothing but talk about the wedding. They wanted Layla to come and visit them again but Sara explained that Layla had to stay at home now, until the day of her marriage. Forty days was the customary period. She wondered how her lively little sister would cope having to stay in the house all that time.

Once the children had accepted that they wouldn't see their aunt until the day of the wedding, they turned to the next thing on their minds. What would they wear? They badgered her day and night about it.

'Mama, we have nothing to wear for the wedding,' Salma said. 'Why won't Baba buy us some new dresses?'

'I have spoken to your father about it and he says that I can go and look for some material today, while you are at school.'

'White?'

'Yes, white.'

'With embroidered flowers?'

'Yes. Now run along or you'll be late and take Mariam with you.'

Salma ran back to her sisters to give them the news. Isa had not been keen to spend money on four new dresses for his daughters but when Sara had pointed out to him that it would be a slight on the honour of the family if his children were not properly dressed for their aunt's wedding, he relented. So today she was going to look for the material and find a tailor to make them up for her. Normally she would have made the dresses herself but there was no time. That was the problem with having a rushed wedding; there was insufficient time to get everything prepared.

'Sara, may I speak to you?'

It was Ghayda.

'I'm just about to go out to buy the material for the girls' dresses. Can it wait until I get back?'

'I wanted to tell you that I will make the dresses for you. I know you won't have the time but I can do it.'

'You will sew them, all four of them?'

'Yes. My mother was a tailoress. I know how to sew. I will make you four beautiful dresses. I promise. Look, I made this for my own wedding.'

She held up the dress she had been married in, for Sara to inspect. It was lovely, beautifully stitched and a simple but flattering design.

'Well, I'm not sure.'

'Please Sara, I would love to do this for you.'

'But will you be able to do them all in five weeks? It's a lot of work for one person.'

Ghayda smiled.

'Of course. I'll even have time to embroider the hems with flowers, like Salma wants.'

'Well you'd better come with us to buy the material, then.'

The girl's face lit up with pleasure. Maybe Sara had been too hard on her; after all she was not much more than a child herself.

She waited until her two older daughters had left for school then she, Ghayda and the two little ones set off. She knew the shop she was looking for; it was in the Jewish quarter. She walked along the river bank, past the flour mill where Isa bought his flour, past the royal stables, until she came to the mosque.

'Are we going to the mosque today?' asked Miriam.

'No, sweetheart. We're going to buy the material to make your dresses for the wedding. Surely you haven't forgotten?'

The little girl smiled up at her.

'No, Mama.'

They waited for a man and his donkey to pass then they crossed the road and went round the north side of the mosque and down one of the roads that led to the synagogue. The Jewish quarter was a maze of narrow streets and alleyways, packed with small houses and workshops. Here you could find almost anything you wanted: silver jewellery, shoes, silks and satins, precious stones. There were moneylenders and men who dealt in gold; there were copyists and scribes, physicians and teachers. Today, as usual, it was crowded with merchants doing business and shoppers, many like herself, looking for a bargain.

'Keep tight hold of your sister's hand,' she told Tara. 'We don't want to lose her.'

'No, Mama, because then she won't be able to go to the wedding.'

'I won't get lost, Mama. I won't,' Mariam cried.

She squeezed her sister's hand so tightly that Tara cried out.

'I'll look after her,' Ghayda said, taking Mariam by the hand.

'Well, just behave, both of you. We are almost there,' Sara told her daughters.

The first street they came to was where all the goldsmiths and silversmiths lived. There was nothing displayed on the pavement; in order to see their beautifully crafted jewellery you had to step inside their shops. She peered into one of the dark interiors but was met only with the suspicious eyes of the jeweller. She was not the sort of rich customer that would entice him out into the open. Halfway down the street they turned left and found themselves in the street of the tanners; here skins and hides were hung in the doorways for everyone to inspect. There were many things to look at: slippers, leather vests, saddles, purses and leather tablecloths. The air was heavy with the rank smell of the animal pelts and she was glad when they reached the street of the tailors.

The shop she was looking for was just in front of them. A swarthy Jewess, with her black hair oiled and plaited and coiled round her head, sat behind a table laden with bales of cloth. Most of it was of wool but at the end Sara noticed some pure white cotton.

'As-salama alaykum,' she said to the woman. 'I'm looking for something to make dresses for my daughters.'

'Wa alaykum e-salam. You have come to the right place. What is it that you have in mind? Maybe something in this nice soft wool for the winter? What about this lovely red one? It is warm and hard-wearing.'

'No, we're looking for something to wear to a wedding.'

'My aunt is getting married,' Tara informed her.

'Well that's very nice.'

'I think something lighter, maybe cotton or muslin and in white. They want it to be white.'

'Of course. All girls want to wear white to a wedding. I have just the thing for you.'

She rummaged under the table and pulled out a small bale of white cotton and handed it to Sara to inspect. It was a heavy weave, with a diamond pattern woven into it.

'They won't want anything too lightweight. The weather is very unsettled at the moment' Ghayda said.

'That's true. What about this one?' Sara asked her.

'That would be fine. The cotton has been washed and bleached in the sun; it will look lovely when it is made up,' said Ghayda.

'Yes, it looks perfect. But I need enough for all my daughters; I have four of them. Those two are the smallest,' Sara told the shopkeeper, pointing to Tara and Miriam who had lost interest in the shopping and were busy watching a juggler in the street outside.

'Well, let me see.'

The shopkeeper unwound the bale and spread the material out. There was plenty and maybe there would even be some left over. Ghayda took the fabric between her fingers.

'It's just right. The weave is close and the colour even.'

'Good. I'll take it all,' Sara said.

She hoped it was not too expensive or Isa would moan at her. Carefully she counted out the money Isa had given her while the woman folded the cloth and placed it in Sara's basket.

'Do you need a seamstress?' she asked. 'I can recommend someone very good and not expensive.'

'No, thank you. I am going to make them,' Ghayda interrupted.

'Very well. I hope you enjoy the wedding.'

'We will. Ma'a salama.'

'Alla ysalmak,' the woman replied.

Sara took her basket and stepped into the street. The girls had moved on and were watching two acrobats somersaulting in the square.

'Mama, Mama, have you seen those men? They are so funny. Look, that one is so strong that he can hold the other one on his shoulders,' Tara said.

Sara felt a tap on her back; she turned around to see Halawa standing behind her.

'As-salama alaykum, Sara. I don't often see you here in the Jewish quarter,' she said.

As usual Halawa was dressed in one of her multi-coloured robes and today she seemed to be wearing even more bells, bangles and rings than ever. There was a constant murmur of tinkling bells and jangling bracelets every time she moved.

'Hello, Halawa. We're getting new dresses for the wedding,' Mariam said.

'Are you my dear? Now whose wedding would that be? Not yours, is it?'

Mariam laughed delightedly at that idea.

'No, I'm too young. It's my aunt's wedding.'

'Yes and they're going to be white,' added Tara.

Halawa looked quizzically at Sara and then at Ghayda.

'That's right; we are going to my sister's wedding at the end of the month. I'm pleased to see you here, because I'd like you to do my feet before we go.'

Halawa was an expert at drawing the traditional henna designs. Everybody went to her to have their feet decorated.

'I'll come round one day next week. Will that be all right?' Halawa asked.

'Yes, that would be fine.'

Halawa looked at the girls; they were still busy watching the acrobats. One man was bent over backwards and was holding his ankles while the other was trying to lift him as though he were a basket of shopping.

'I hope you have taken my advice,' she whispered to Sara.

'Yes, I have sewn the amulets in their clothing.'

'Good. Well, take care my dear.'

She turned and with a swirl of her musical skirts, she was gone.

'Come along, girls. We must get home so that Ghayda can get started or you will not have any new dresses for the wedding.'

Reluctantly the girls pulled themselves away from the acrobats and followed their mother.

'Ghayda take the girls home for me; I'm going to call at my brother's house on the way back.'

'Very well, Sara. I can measure them for their dresses. You'd like that, wouldn't you, girls?'

The girls clapped their hands with pleasure. They were so excited about the wedding.

'I won't be long. And don't worry about preparing the meal for Isa; I'll do it when I get home,' Sara added.

She wanted the new wife to start as soon as possible. She was still a bit doubtful whether the girl could do as she promised; she hoped she hadn't made a mistake by agreeing to let her do it. Her daughters would be bitterly disappointed if their dresses were not ready on time.

***

As usual her brother was working in the alfarería and he was covered in clay. How was he ever going to get a wife if he didn't smarten himself up a bit, she thought.

'Sara, this is a surprise. How nice to see you.'

He kissed her on the cheek, leaving a smear of clay on her face as he did so. She wiped it carefully away.

'How are you brother?'

'Fine. Busy as usual.'

'Where's your new slave? I thought he was meant to help you in the alfarería?'

'He does. He's gone out to buy me some supplies.'

'Is he any good?' she asked.

'He is, surprisingly. He's going to be a real help to me. He'd picked up quite a bit from working with Omar, you know and he knows all about how to prepare the clay and load and unload the kiln. He's also quite a good draftsman, so I've got him copying out some designs for me. I think Baba will be very surprised when he sees my next batch of plates.'

'Have you heard about Layla?'

'Getting married, you mean?'

'Yes. What do you think about it?'

He looked at her.

'What do I think about it? Nothing really. It's a bit inconvenient, to be honest. I will have to close the alfarería for a couple of days and that will cost me money. Why?'

'Don't you think our sister is a bit young to be married?'

'Well it had to happen one day.'

Her brother continued to remove the fired pottery from the open kiln. He wasn't really interested. She sighed. Why had she expected anything different? Like all men he expected his sisters to find husbands at some time in their lives; the fact that Layla was still a child barely registered with him.

'Ibrahim, I'm worried. Isa is talking about finding a husband for Salma,' she said. 'I'm not happy about it. She is too clever to give up her schooling. She deserves the chance of something better.'

'If he finds her a good husband, what could be better than that?'

'But you know what a good memory she has. She is only ten and already she almost has the Great Recitation off by heart. In another year she would be able to quote you anything from the Quran.'

'I didn't know that. That's impressive,' her brother said.

'I don't think he's really concerned for Salma's happiness; he is only interested in the dowry. The younger she is, the more he can ask.'

'Isn't that normal?'

'Baba is giving Layla's dowry to her, so that she will always have some money if anything happens to her husband,' she told him. 'That's the normal practice.'

'Well there's no point worrying about it yet. It might not happen for a long time.'

He turned back to the kiln and his pots. She watched him for a while then said, 'I'm going now. I promised to teach the new wife how to make churros, today.'

'You can bring me some, next time you come round,' he said. 'I'm fond of churros.'

He turned to look at her.

'How is the new wife? Have you two come to terms yet?'

'She isn't so bad after all. She has offered to sew the dresses for the girls to go to the wedding.'

'That's nice of her. I knew you'd win her round eventually, with your smiles and kind words,' he said, laughing.

Sara picked up a piece of clay and threw it at him. It stuck to his cheek, making them both laugh.

'What do you know of wives, brother? You haven't even got one yet, never mind two.'

And before he could retaliate she ducked under the curtain and out into the street. Seeing Ibrahim always cheered her up, even though he didn't really understand how she felt.

***

Ghayda had already made a start on the sewing by the time Sara returned; she had cut some of the material, enough to make the smallest of the dresses and was busy measuring it against Mariam.

'It's beautiful cotton,' she said to Sara, with a smile on her face. 'It will be so easy to sew.'

The girl seemed delighted to be doing something that she was good at. Maybe Sara should make an effort to be nicer to her; after all it wasn't her fault that Isa had taken her as his bride.

'Ghayda, there is one thing I want you to do for me but you mustn't mention it to our husband.'

'Of course, Sara. What is it?'

'Promise you'll say nothing to Isa.'

'I promise.'

'In the hem of each of the girl's dresses I have sewn some amulets; they are supposed to protect them from harm. On the day of the wedding I want you to sew them into their new dresses, without them knowing. Can you do that?'

'Of course, Sara. Did you get them from Halawa? My mother used to buy things from her.'

'Yes, but Isa does not like me speaking to Halawa about these things. He thinks she's a witch. He will be very cross with us both if he finds out.'

'I won't say anything, Sara. I promise. It will be our secret.'

'Good. Now would you like me to teach you how to make churros the way our husband likes it?'

The girl smiled with pleasure and carefully folded up the cotton and put it to one side. Maybe Sara's mother was right; maybe they could work together.

CHAPTER 39

Al-Jundi rode his horse with an easy gait; the horse's head was held high, the bit tight and his chin tucked in. He was a beautiful animal; originally a light grey colour he was now pure white with a long thick mane and tail which switched excitedly to and fro. His back was short but he was sturdy with strong hindquarters. Al-Jundi would not have changed him for any other in the Khalifa's stable. He was a good steed, agile but steady in battle and quick to respond to his rider's commands. He had been with al-Jundi for years and was part of the reason that he had survived so many campaigns.

They advanced at a steady speed; there was no need for a faster pace. The prince wanted his men to be fresh when they arrived, not exhausted from a forced march. It would take them ten days to reach Toledo and then another ten days to get to the frontier south of Léon. The soldiers marched four abreast, in perfect unison. The standard bearer, in his mail coat and pointed blue and gold helmet led the way; the Khalifa's son rode behind him. As they passed through the villages and towns that lined their way, the local people came out from their houses to watch them go past. Who could blame them; they were a splendid spectacle, ten thousand of the Khalifa's best men and two thousand jinetes, the infantrymen in their soft cotton armour, with their crossbows and leather shields, the jinetes splendid astride their horses with the afternoon sun glinting on their chainmail hauberks and rounded helmets. Just seeing them march into the garrison town would strike fear into the insurgents and then it might not be necessary to do battle. He smiled to himself; he did not really believe that. There would be a battle, no matter what. The men would be ready for it. They were all true fighting men. Some fought for the Khalifa, some for the love of Allah, some for the blood-lust that ran through their veins, others for money. Al-Jundi, he was a career soldier; he fought because it was his job and he was good at it.

Already he could feel the adrenalin coursing through his blood. It was always the same when they left for a campaign; he craved the excitement, the adventure. He loved being a soldier; it was what he was born for. His father had wanted him to join him in the alfarería when he finished school and his mother wanted him to marry but al-Jundi would not hear of either. He had wanted to be a soldier since the day he stood by the Roman bridge, a skinny five-year old, and watched the Khalifa's army march into Córdoba.

He enlisted at sixteen and became one of the Khalifa's foot soldiers; his father could do nothing to dissuade him. They sent him north to one of the garrison towns on the frontier and there he learnt his bloody trade fighting against the Christians, turning from a raw recruit into a seasoned soldier. After a few years duty on the northern frontier he had returned to Córdoba, battle-hardened and already promoted to the rank of captain at the age of twenty-five. When the Khalifa moved his court to Medinat al-Zahra, al-Jundi had been picked to accompany him as a captain in the Palace Guard. It had been an honour to have been chosen and for that he would serve the Khalifa until his dying breath.

He had never imagined that the Khalifa's court could be so magnificent. Like everyone else, he had heard tales of gold ceilings and marble fountains, of peacocks and exotic animals but he had never thought that the alcázar would be so richly endowed. As one of the Khalifa's trusted men, he was free to move around the grounds of the alcázar and still, after all this time, he could not get used to the splendour of the place. All this would be lost to him if they found out about his father. He thought over what his father had told him. This man from his father's past was planning to make trouble. He could not allow that. When he returned from this campaign, he would seek him out and find out exactly what he wanted with Qasim.

Ahead of him he saw Prince Hakim wheel his horse around and ride back towards him.

'Captain, this looks like a good place to halt and rest the men. There is water and shade from those trees,' he said, pointing to the nearby river. 'What do you think?'

Al-Jundi looked up at the sky. The sun was low but there were still a few hours of daylight left.

'No, my lord. I think we should keep going until sunset. We can follow the river for a while then make camp when it is dark. The men will be fine for another couple of hours.'

'Very well, Captain. If that is your advice, we will continue.'

The preparations for the journey had been thorough; he had overseen them himself. There were two dozen mules laden with supplies for both men and horses, camels to carry their tents and barrels of water; there were crates of arrows, fresh javelins and hand axes. They had enough basic food to last two months and anything fresh they planned to purchase on the way. The local people liked to sell their produce to the army. The Khalifa insisted that his army pay a fair price for it, so instead of hiding their animals from the soldiers, the farmers came out eager to display what they had. The Khalifa was a fair man when it came to things like that. He knew that if the people felt oppressed or unfairly treated by their ruler then they would one day rebel against him. The greatest army in the world would not keep him safe forever; the rule of law was important too. That was why al-Jundi knew that his brother could expect no mercy if he were caught. He had committed a crime and he would have to pay for it. The law made no exceptions. Not that the soldiers were beyond helping themselves to the odd chicken or pillaging the occasional farmhouse but if they were caught by one of the officers they were punished. Of course none of that applied when they were in enemy territory; then they were encouraged to help themselves to whatever was at hand, be it food, money or women. Nothing was safe from the victorious soldiers. It was the spoils of war. It was what motivated many of them.

His thoughts returned once more to the danger that threatened his family. His brother had been exiled so that should be the end of the matter. As far as the Khalifa was concerned they had caught the guilty man and even though al-Jundi knew of his innocence, Yusuf had been arrested and punished. No-one would be looking for Omar now. No, it was his father that he worried about. It could be the end of al-Jundi's career if it was discovered that his father was a traitor. More than anything else he needed to distinguish himself in battle this time, to prove to the Khalifa that he, al-Jundi, was a loyal subject, no matter what was said about his father.

CHAPTER 40

It had been almost a month and still Isolde had heard nothing from Omar. The almond blossom had come and gone, the rosemary bushes in her garden were thick with new growth and the trees that shaded her patio were filled with quarrelsome birds looking for places to nest. It was spring and the cold winds of winter were behind her yet still there was no word of him or Hans. Every night she prayed to the old gods for help but they did not seem to be listening to her. So she lived a double life. Alone in her garden, she sat, sad and thinking of her past, her sorrow gnawing inside her like an evil spirit waiting for the right moment to emerge. But, in the presence of the Khalifa she smiled and danced and did all she could to please her master. He was to be her salvation; she would do nothing to disappoint him.

It was fortunate for her that the Khalifa's passion for her had not diminished. If anything it had grown. She felt sure that she would become pregnant soon and then she would ask him to help her find her brother. He would not refuse her, not if she were carrying his child.

'Jawhara, the Royal wife has sent for you,' her personal maid said, coming down the steps into the garden. 'She says she will see you in her private gardens.'

'You had better help me get ready then. I can't see the Royal wife looking like this. Get out my blue robe and help me dress my hair.'

***

The Royal wife was sitting in her garden, surrounded by her maids when Isolde arrived. Her younger son and two of her daughters were with her. They all looked at Isolde with unconcealed curiosity.

'Jawhara, come and sit by my side, my dear,' she said with her most charming smile.

Despite her newly acquired confidence as one of the Khalifa's favourites, Isolde could not help but feel nervous in this woman's presence. She was smiling at Isolde as a cat might smile before pouncing on its prey. Najm's words came back to her, 'Be careful, the Royal wife has the power of life and death over you.'

'As-salam alaykum, my lady,' she said. 'You wanted to see me?'

'Yes, my child. I have heard glowing reports of you. It seems that my husband, the Khalifa, is bewitched by you. I wanted to reassure myself that you were not a sorcerer,' she said with a little laugh.

She might have been smiling but Isolde could see that her eyes were hard and cold. She was not pleased that her husband was paying quite so much attention to his new concubine.

'I am happy to please my lord,' Isolde replied, bowing her head.

She did not want to antagonise this woman, the most powerful woman in the harem.

'What do you think, ladies? Can you understand what your father sees in this creature?' she asked her daughters.

'No, Mama.'

'And you, my son? Would you like her for your own when your father has finished with her?'

Her son, a callow youth not much older than Isolde, smirked and leered at her.

Isolde did not move; she was sure that whatever she said or did would bring the Royal wife's wrath down upon her. The thin veil of politeness that had been covering their conversation was already cracking.

'Well then child, do you practice witchcraft?' the Royal wife asked. 'Is that what keeps you in the Khalifa's bed night after night?'

'No, my lady.'

Now Isolde was scared. Witchcraft was against the law.

'But you northerners believe in magic, don't you?'

'No, my lady. My mother forbade me to have anything to do with the soothsayers and spell-makers. She said that the gods would punish me.'

It was a lie. Her mother had put a great deal of trust in the sayings of the wise old women that came to their village and she used their potions and spells for everything from removing warts from the back of her hand to making sure their cow gave the sweetest milk.

'I am pleased to hear it. Our beloved prophet forbids all forms of sorcery.'

Isolde did not reply.

'Are you pregnant yet, child?' she asked suddenly, causing Isolde to look up and blush.

'No my lady, I don't think so.'

'So maybe your magic is not working after all,' she said with a cruel laugh.

She stood up and signalled for her maids to follow her. Isolde had been dismissed. She waited until the Royal wife had left then went back to her apartments. Najm was waiting for her.

'What did she want?'

'Just to check up if I was pregnant yet and to make sure I understood how powerful she was. She even accused me of bewitching the Khalifa.'

'Well others have been saying the same thing. He does seem to be under your spell.'

'Maybe he loves me,' Isolde said.

Najm threw her hands into the air.

'Do not think that, Jawhara. You always dream for the impossible. Understand this: Khalifas do not fall in love. It may look like love but it is infatuation and it will pass when he is tired of you, just as it has with all the other women he has made love to over the years. Look at al-Zahra; he never visits her anymore and she is heartbroken. She was his favourite for many years; they say he even named this city after her. If he can abandon her, he can abandon you. If you start to think of love, your heart will be broken.'

'Then I had better become pregnant soon, before he tires of me.'

Najm smiled.

'I am so glad that you are settling into the life of the harem and have given up all that talk of running away. You see, it's not such a bad life for someone as lovely as you. Already you have all this luxury.'

Najm waved her arm to indicate the splendid rooms that they occupied. The walls of Isolde's new apartment had been hung with tapestries, rivers of silk depicting birds and forests. Isolde's favourite, which she had hung above her bed, showed two peacocks of iridescent blue facing each other, their glorious tail feathers spread wide. Beneath her feet were finely woven Indian rugs of many colours, by her bed, lamps made from gold and boxes of carved ivory. Isolde had been given the best that the Royal Buyer could find to furnish her rooms.

'If you have his child, he will shower you with more gifts than you can imagine,' Najm continued.

'I am going to ask the Khalifa if I can send for Hans and have him here in the palace, with me,' she said.

'Really?'

'Yes, I'm sure he will agree. He promises me anything I want. He tells me, when his passion is spent, that he will give me anything; all I have to do is ask.'

'And do you? Do you ask for emeralds and rubies?' Najm said, her eyes gleaming.

'No. I never ask him for anything.'

'What nothing at all? Not silver nor gold?

'Nothing. That's why I know that when I ask to have Hans here with me, he will agree.'

Najm looked away.

'What is it?' Isolde asked.

'I'm sure you're right, Jawhara. I'm sure he will let Hans live here in the harem if you ask him but are you certain that is what you want?'

'Of course. It is what I want more than anything.'

'Have you really thought about what you are asking?'

'What do you mean? It couldn't be more simple; I want my brother to live here with me. In these very apartments. I want us to be together again.'

'Ah, Jawhara, you will never understand the ways of the harem. The Khalifa is besotted with you, that is obvious. I am sure he will give you whatever you ask for but he will not break the rules of the harem. He will send his men to find Hans and bring him here.'

'That's all I want, to be with my brother again.'

'Then they will castrate him. Then and only then will he be allowed to enter the harem. You know that. Only eunuchs may enter the harem and only sandali, those that have had all their male parts removed. That is the law. Do you want that to happen to your brother? Do you think he will thank you for that? It is a horrible thing to happen to a young boy; they slice away everything. He could bleed to death from the wound or even die from blood poisoning. If he survives he is condemned to the life of a eunuch, never to have a wife of his own, never to have children, to carry forever the knowledge that he is no longer a man and it was his sister who did this to him. Is that what you want?'

Isolde felt her blood run cold. Najm's words horrified her. Why did she say such things? Surely the Khlaifa would not do that to her brother.

'But the Royal wife has her youngest son here with her,' she protested. 'I saw him today.'

'True, but he is the son of the Khalifa. If you have a son, he too will be brought up in the harem. But not your brother. His only entrance to the harem is as a sandali.'

Isolde began to weep at the thought of her brother being mutilated; it had never occurred to her that anything so horrible could happen to him. She wanted to protect him not destroy him.

'I didn't know,' Isolde sobbed.

What could she do now? Was there no other way she could reunite her family?

Najm put her arms around her.

'Jawhara, you must give up all these ideas about your brother. You are the Khalifa's favourite. You have a wonderful life ahead of you. Accept your destiny.'

Destiny. What was it she had read in her classes of Arabic? *'Destiny was as changeable as the coat of a chameleon.'* Maybe she could change her destiny.

CHAPTER 41

Layla could still not believe this was happening to her. In a few days she would be married. The wedding was to be a simple affair; both her parents and Muhammed's parents wanted it that way, they said. To her it did not seem simple; the preparations had been going on for weeks and she had been virtually a prisoner in her own home. It was traditional that she stayed inside for the forty days leading up to the marriage ceremony. She had asked if she could continue to go to school but Mama had said she must forget about school now; she had to learn how to be a good wife. So she had spent her time learning how to cook. Surprisingly Layla found that she actually enjoyed cooking. Mama had let her cook a whole meal the previous day, her special lamb tagine and Baba had wiped his plate clean and insisted that it was the best he had ever tasted.

The door opened and her mother came into the room, followed by the bridegroom's mother and two sisters. They looked excited.

'We are going to have a henna party, the Laylat al Henna,' she said with a smile. 'So that we will all look beautiful for your wedding.'

Layla felt a thrill of excitement; she had seen women with henna-painted hands and feet and longed to have her own done but Baba would never allow it. He said she was too young. Now here she was at her own henna party, about to become a bride.

'Sit down here and relax because this will take a while. I don't want you fidgeting about as you usually do,' her mother instructed her.

'Will Salma have henna on her feet as well?' she asked.

'I don't know, sweetheart. I don't know if Salma's father will allow it.'

'But she is my best friend and my niece,' she added to give weight to her argument. 'She has to look her best.'

'We'll talk about it later. Now put your feet on this stool.'

It was Muhammed's mother who was going to decorate her feet. She placed a pot of henna paste on the ground beside her and pulled a cloth over her lap.

'Have you ever seen this done before?' she asked, smiling at Layla.

Layla shook her head; she still felt shy of the woman who was soon to be her mother-in-law. She let her take her left foot in her hand and begin to draw on it with the paste. It tickled and she wanted to laugh.

'Keep still, child. I don't want to make a mistake.'

'Will it wash off?' she asked.

'Eventually. It should last at least two weeks, more than enough time for the wedding. Look, I did my feet a week ago and they are still perfect.'

She lifted the hem of her dress to show Layla her feet; they were covered in a network of fine, interwoven patterns that had been drawn with the red henna paste. They reminded Layla of the designs Omar drew on his plates.

'They are very pretty. My brother can make patterns like that,' she said.

Her mother frowned at her; they never spoke of Omar these days.

'Well your feet will be even prettier.'

'What about you, Mama? Are you having patterns on your feet, too?'

'I am. We all are. It's the tradition. It will bring you good luck.'

Layla had never been to a wedding before; her sister, Sara had married before she was born. Despite her fears she couldn't help being excited by all the attention. They had even been giving her special food to eat so that she looked plump and healthy; everything to make her more attractive to her new husband was being done.

Her mother sat down beside her and let one of Muhammed's sisters paint her feet. It was a pretty pattern but not as elaborate as Layla's.

'How long will it take?' Layla asked.

'A couple of hours. And then I have my daughters to do,' Muhammed's mother said. 'You must be patient and keep very still.'

'Do all brides have henna on their feet?' Layla asked.

It was hard to remain shy of her future mother-in-law when she was holding her foot in her hand.

'Yes. The Laylat al Henna is an important ceremony. It isn't just to beautify the bride, it is to ensure she has health and good fortune.'

Layla could feel her bottom going numb. She tried a little wriggle but an exasperated look from Muhammed's mother made her sit still again.

'Mama, my leg aches,' she said, looking across at her mother.

'Just keep still, Layla. You don't want auntie to make a mistake now, do you.'

'Will your other children be coming to the wedding?' Muhammed's mother asked.

'Of course,' her mother said. 'One of my son's has gone on a pilgrimage and another is away on a campaign in the north but my children in Córdoba will come; both my son and my son-in-law are busy men but they will be there.'

'Oh, good. It will be a lovely day. It is an opportunity for our families to meet; after all a wedding is about two families being joined together. We must all get to know each other.'

She looked up at Layla.

'So, Layla, are you excited about getting married?'

'Yes, auntie.'

'And what about those plans of yours to become a doctor?'

Layla blushed. She did not know what to say.

'I've spoken to my husband. I told him that you were interested in medicine. He has agreed that you can help him in the pharmacy, at least until you are old enough to become a real wife to my son. If you are good at it then maybe you can study and become an apothecary too. It is a family business, after all.'

Layla beamed. She liked the idea of mixing the medicines and serving in the shop. Perhaps life in this family would not be so bad after all.

'Thank you, auntie.'

'But you will still have to help me in the kitchen. Your mother tells me that you have learned to cook now.'

'Yes, auntie. I can make lamb tagine and ziriabì beans.'

'Well that's a good start. My son loves beans.'

Layla saw her exchange a smile with her mother.

'Has your mother explained to you what will happen during the ceremony?' she asked.

Layla nodded.

'Muhammed's eldest brother will be one of the witnesses,' she told her.

'And my son, Ibrahim and my daughter's husband will be the others,' Layla's mother added.

'And your dress? Is it ready?' she asked Layla.

'Yes. It was finished yesterday.'

She liked her wedding dress; it was white, plain and long with a short veil to cover her face. She thought it made her look very grown-up.

'She looks beautiful in it,' her mother added.

Muhammed's mother sat back and looked at her handiwork.

'That's one of them finished. It will be dry in a few minutes then I'll spray it with lemon and sugar to make sure the dye soaks into your skin. In the meantime you can get up and move around a bit; I can see you've found it hard to keep still. Then we'll do the other one.'

Layla stood up, careful not to smudge her hennaed foot. It was so lovely. She couldn't stop looking at it. She was never going to wash it off; she wanted it to stay like that forever.

'Thank you auntie; it's beautiful.'

'Well as I said, we still have the other one to do. It will only bring you half the luck if we leave it like that.'

She laughed, standing up and stretching her back.

'Would you like some tea?' Fatima asked.

'That's an excellent idea. Let me help you,' Muhammed's mother said.

The two women went into the kitchen together and Layla could hear them laughing about something. The coming wedding had put everyone in a good mood.

***

The day of the wedding arrived sooner than Layla expected. She woke up with a terrible feeling of dread in her stomach. What if he was a bad husband? What if he hit her? She had overheard one of Mama's friends telling her mother about a husband who beat his wife. What if Muhammed didn't like her? Maybe he had had no more to do with choosing her than she had had with choosing him. Maybe he loved someone else. Her head was swimming with doubts and unanswered questions but there was no-one she could turn to. Her mother would just say it was last minute nerves; her father would tell her that he would never have chosen anyone who would treat her badly and her sister was miles away in Córdoba. She couldn't even talk to her friends about it; she hadn't seen them for weeks. If only Omar was here; he would know what to tell her. He wouldn't let anyone beat her, even if he was her husband.

'Layla, my child, are you awake? We have come to prepare you for your wedding,' her mother said, coming into her room and pulling back the bedcovers. 'We must make you beautiful.'

'Oh Mama, I'm tired. I don't want to get up yet.'

'I know, sweetheart but we have to wash and anoint you. There is a lot to do. You must be perfect for the wedding ceremony. Come with us.'

Reluctantly Layla crawled out of bed. Muhammed's sisters were there too; they were going to help to get her ready.

'Just stand there; we will do the rest. Today you'll be treated like a princess,' her mother said.

The women bathed her then washed her hair with jasmine and ambergris; they rubbed her body all over with sweet smelling oil and combed a perfumed cream through her hair. Then they sat her down and painted her eyes with kohl.

'Shall we do her lips?' one of the women asked.

'Just a little. She is too young to have much make-up,' her mother said, taking the walnut shell and rubbing a little on Layla's lips.

'Now for the dress,' said her mother.

They carefully dressed her in her white gown, then braided her hair in the traditional fashion and placed flowers in it.

'My mother gave me this necklace on my wedding day,' she said, placing a coral and amber necklace around Layla's neck. 'I want you to have it.'

'It's lovely, Mama. Thank you.'

She slipped some silver bracelets onto Layla's arms, adding, 'These bracelets are a gift from your mother-in-law. Be sure to thank her later.'

'Yes, Mama.'

Everyone was being so kind to her. She raised her hands above her head and let the bracelets slip down her arms; they made a lovely jangling sound. She shook her arms and did it again.

'You look so beautiful, my little Layla,' her mother said and hugged her.

'Be careful,' said Ulla, Muhammed's older sister, 'you'll crush the flowers.'

Mama was crying now. Was she sad that Layla was getting married? Did she think that Muhammed would beat her?

'What's the matter, Mama?' she asked. 'Why are you crying?'

'It's because you look so lovely, my little princess and I'm sad that I'm going to lose you. Today you will become a married woman; you will be independent. You will not need your Mama any longer.'

'I will always need you, Mama,' she cried, hugging her mother tightly.

Her eyes filled with tears.

'No, don't cry. You'll smudge your eyes,' cried Ulla. 'Then we'll have to do them again. And look at those flowers; I told you you'd crush them.'

Layla took a deep breath.

'I'm not crying,' she said. 'Anyway, what does it matter? I have my veil.'

She pulled the veil over her face.

'Are you ready yet?' her father called. 'It's time we left for the mosque.'

'Just coming. A minute more.'

'Well, my child, is there anything you want to ask me before we leave?' her mother said.

There were a hundred things Layla wanted to ask and the first of them was 'why today?' but instead she smiled and shook her head.

'No, Mama. I'm ready.'

The time for questions was over. This was something she had to do. If she was lucky, if Baba had chosen wisely for her, then everything would turn out well. If not, there was nothing she could do about it now. To rebel against her father's wishes would mean expulsion from the family. Her future had been chosen for her; now she must follow its path.

***

The wedding ceremony was long and tedious; the imam talked for more than an hour. He read from the Quran and he blessed the bride and groom, then he read some more. Layla wanted it to be over. Wearing the veil was good; she could look at her new husband without him seeing her. It was the first time she had seen him since that day at the apothecary's home. Today he was dressed very simply in white, with a garland of flowers around his neck. His beard seemed fuller than she remembered it and there was no sign of the acne. In fact he looked very handsome. She remembered how he had smiled at her that day at his house and she felt a flutter of excitement in her stomach. She was marrying this man. He would be her husband and they would live together forever.

At last the ceremony was over; they were man and wife. The witnesses signed the documents that the imam had prepared and then they filed out of the mosque. Everyone was waiting for them, all their friends and family, cheering and clapping and throwing money over her. The coins glinted in the sunlight, falling in front of her like a shower of silver rain. Still she wore her veil; still the groom kept his distance. Her mother had explained that it wasn't until after the wedding feast that he would speak to her and that she wasn't to worry because that was the custom. Even so, she might have been concerned if it wasn't for the fact that she had seen him look across at her repeatedly during the ceremony. He had looked nervous but happy.

Both her mother and her mother-in-law had gone through all the stages of the wedding ceremony with her; there was so much to remember that her head had been spinning. The night before she had lain in her bed worrying that she might make a mistake or do something foolish in front of so many people but now her worries had dissipated; she was married and now there was the party to enjoy.

The wedding procession wound its way down the road to the enormous tent that Muhammed's family had put up for the feast. They were all in a happy mood; she could see that Muhammed was smiling and joking with his friends. Baba was laughing with the apothecary and Mama and Sara walked together, arm-in-arm. Everyone carried presents for the bride and groom and the air was sweet with the scent of jasmine flowers. Today was her wedding day and she was happy.

Once in the tent the women sat themselves along one side and the men, the other. She sat with the women, next to her mother and Sara and her husband sat at a separate table with his male relatives; they seemed to be joking and teasing him about being a married man. Despite his beard she could see him blushing.

'Stop staring at your husband, child. It is not polite,' her mother warned her. 'Here, try some of this delicious cold soup.'

Layla pulled back her veil and began to eat. Her mother was looking at her and crying.

'What is it, Mama? What's wrong?'

'Nothing, my dear. It's just that you look so lovely. I shall miss you.'

'Don't cry Mama; I'll come and see you every day. I promise.'

Her mother wiped her tears and tried to smile.

'Of course, my child. Remember we will always be there for you. Now, take no notice of your silly mother; today is a day to be happy, to rejoice that you have such a fine husband.'

Layla could not resist looking across at Muhammed again; this time he caught her eye and smiled quickly before turning back to his raucous companions. Her mother was right; he was a fine husband. She was very lucky.

At the end of the room was a table spread with all the wedding gifts; she had never seen so many beautiful things.

'Mama,' she whispered, 'are those for us?'

'Yes, my dear, they are for your new home, to start your married life.'

'But it's too much. Why do we need so many things?'

'Your father-in-law is very highly respected; people like to show their appreciation by giving generously to his son and his new bride.'

She turned to look behind her, saying, 'And look who's here, my little Salma.'

'Salma, come and sit beside me,' Layla said, pulling her niece down beside her.

'Layla, you look so beautiful and so grown-up,' Salma said.

'Yes, she's married now,' Sara said, smoothing her daughter's dress. 'But you look beautiful too, sweetheart. Your new dress is very pretty.'

'Will I be getting married now?' Salma asked. 'Will I marry someone as handsome as Muhammed?'

'One day. One day,' Sara replied, hugging her daughter tightly.

How strange it was, Layla thought; one minute her mother and Sara were happy and the next they were sad. They didn't want Salma or her to get married but they couldn't do anything about it; that's what was making them sad. A solitary cloud passed across her face; maybe she should have resisted Baba's plans, maybe she should have insisted that she was not ready to be wed yet. But what could she have done? She was a child and she had to obey her father. She thought of his words, 'I would never do anything to hurt you, my princess.' Once more she looked across at the table where her new husband was sitting; her father had chosen well for her.

She was not very hungry and only picked at the food she was given; course after course was served until nobody could eat any more. The feasting seemed to go on forever, only interrupted by the guests standing up and saying nice things about both families or someone singing. At one point her father stood up and read out a poem that Sara had written; it was lovely, all about new beginnings and hope and springtime. When he had finished reading it, her mother leaned across and whispered, 'I am so pleased that Sara has started to write again. She is a very talented poet.'

Layla agreed; she wished she could string words together as beautifully as her sister did.

At last the feast was over, the speeches ended and her mother said, 'Now it's time for you to sit with your husband, Layla.'

She and Muhammed's mother led Layla to the table where her husband was sitting. Immediately his companions stood up and moved away, leaving a space for his new bride. There they were, her and Muhammed, sitting side by side at last. His mother covered their heads with a dupatta; the ritual scarf was made of reddish silk, embroidered with flowers and birds and edged with pearls. It was enormous and covered both her and Muhammed easily but it was so fine that she could look through it and see the wedding guests. They sat together under its voluminous folds, hidden from the eyes of the guests, while more prayers were read. They did not speak but this time he looked at her openly and smiled and she reached out and touched his hand.

After the prayers the couple set off for the apothecary's house, followed by their families. The ritual of Rukhsat was the next ceremony to be performed: Baba would offer Layla's hand to her new husband and ask him to take care of her and Muhammed's mother would hold a copy of the Quran over Layla's head as she entered her new home for the first time. Then she would be truly married.

CHAPTER 42

The house was empty without Omar and Layla and echoed with silence. It was his punishment, Qasim knew, to no longer hear her voice. His lovely little daughter now belonged to someone else.

The wedding party had been lavish but discrete; Qasim had insisted on that. He wanted her to have a wedding she would remember, a happy occasion to look back on in years to come but he was still worried about drawing too much attention to themselves. Her husband's family had been happy with the arrangements and now it was done. She was married. She was safe. He sighed. How he missed her voice. She was like a little nightingale, humming and singing from the moment she awoke until she tumbled into bed at night, the happiest child they had ever had.

'I'll need you to help me in the alfarería, later,' he said to al-Mari, who was laying the bricks for the upstairs floor. 'We may have to leave this room for now.'

There was no need now for extra rooms. Suddenly the house seemed far too large for him and Fatima. They rattled around in it like beans in a jar.

'Yes, sayyad.'

For some reason al-Mari had started calling him 'sayyad'. He didn't know whether it was a sign of respect or if it was sarcasm; he preferred to think it was the former.

'Finish what you are doing then go to the apothecary and collect my usual order of manganese and cobalt,' he said. 'Then I'll show you what you have to do.'

The old slave laid the final two bricks and went to do his master's bidding while Qasim returned to the alfarería. He did not know how he was going to complete the order for the Royal Buyer without Omar there to help him. He had studied Omar's designs and was sure he could replicate them but it would take time and he was already late with the order. He would have to send a message to Ibrahim; maybe he could help him. He needed to see him anyway, to discuss Muna and whether his son would be prepared to marry her. Qasim knew he did not have to ask for Ibrahim's agreement; he was the one who decided whom his sons should wed but he wanted to hear his opinion. Nevertheless he felt sure he would agree; his son would do the right thing to save the family's honour.

Qasim mixed up a new batch of glaze and began to paint it on the plates; it wasn't anything like Omar's uniform style, more freehand and loose but it would have to do for now. He suddenly realised that he had almost no white tin glaze left; he would have to go to the apothecary himself, after all. He could not continue without the all-important white background; white was the colour used to represent the Omayyad dynasty. No Royal Buyer would purchase plates without it.

He placed his cap on his head and hurried out; with any luck he would catch al-Mari before he got too far and then he wouldn't need to go all the way to the pharmacy himself. As he rounded the corner he saw his slave standing outside the inn, arguing with someone; it was ibn Hayyan, the man he had seen that day in the tea shop, the one he thought was looking for him, the one he thought he had seen outside the mosque. He stopped and watched them for a moment; there was certainly some disagreement between them. Something was not right; al-Mari was a quiet man who barely spoke and yet there he was, a slave, arguing and gesticulating in the street with a complete stranger. A few passers-by stared at the men but no-one intervened. At last the man turned and headed for the centre of the medina and al-Mari continued on his way. Qasim hesitated for a moment then decided he would go back to the alfarería; he would question al-Mari as soon as he returned.

He busied himself loading the kiln with plates while he waited and all the time his head spun with questions about what he had just witnessed. He had no doubt that al-Mari knew this man; it had been obvious from the way he spoke to him, threatening him even. What was it about? Was it just a coincidence that he was also someone al-Mari knew from his past or were they both connected to ibn Hayyan in some way?

The curtain in the doorway was pulled aside and his slave came into the alfarería carrying the supplies.

'Good, you're back.'

'I have what you asked for, sayyad. Your daughter was there, in the pharmacy; she sends her respects to you and her mother,' he said, unpacking the packages and stacking them on the shelf.

'Leave that, al-Mari. I must speak to you.'

'Yes, sayyad.'

There was no point wasting time; he would ask him straight out.

'Who was that man you were talking to outside the inn? You told me that you didn't know anyone here in the medina.'

'I don't, sayyad.'

'So who was he?'

Al-Mari dropped his eyes and did not answer.

'Come now, I know that you know that man. Just tell me who he is and how you came to meet him.'

'You do not remember me, sayyad, do you?' he asked.

'What do you mean, remember you? Should I know you?'

Qasim stared at his slave. The man had been living in his house for almost a year and yet he had hardly looked at him. If asked, he would not have been able to describe his face, nor told anything about him except the name which he, himself had given him. A feeling of shame washed over him. Had he been too busy to even get to know a member of his own household?

'My name is Abram ibn al-Attar; I served under you, my general,' he said, lifting his head proudly and staring straight at Qasim.

Of course, he remembered the name instantly; al-Attar had been one of his most loyal and brave soldiers. How could he have failed to recognise him? His feeling of shame deepened. True the man's appearance had changed greatly in thirty years; before he had been clean-shaven, now he had a grey beard but, nevertheless, Qasim should have recognised something about him.

'Come, we will go inside and talk more of this,' Qasim said.

He had not thought of al-Attar in many long years.

'Fatima,' he called. 'Bring us two cups of tea.'

His wife looked at him in surprise; he could see her wondering why he had asked for two cups.

'Tell me what happened to you?' he asked when he and the slave were both seated on the patio. 'How did you become a slave?'

'You remember how it was then? The rebel army was put to rout, virtually wiped out. It was chaos. Those that weren't killed, fled for their lives or were taken prisoner.'

'I remember. What happened to you?'

'I was captured and marched back to Córdoba in chains with the others. That's when we were given the chance to renounce the rebels and fight for the Sultan. We all had a choice, change sides or go into exile. Now I was a soldier through and through; if our cause was lost then I was willing to fight for a new one.'

'So you joined the Sultan's army?'

'I wanted to.'

'So what happened?'

'That pig of a man happened, ibn Hayyan; may the curse of Allah fall upon him. Somehow he wheedled his way into the confidence of the commander; he said he would help him identify those that would not be loyal to the Sultan, those who would always secretly support the rebels. Then he pointed his finger at me.'

'So you were sold into slavery?'

'Yes. Sent to the galleys. Better than execution, some would say.'

'Al-Mari, I mean Abram.'

'No, do not call me that. Abram ibn al-Attar is dead; I am al-Mari, the slave.'

'Why is ibn Hayyan here? What does he want?'

'He wants money. It was by chance that he came to Madinat al-Zahra; he didn't know that you were here. Like many others he thought that there would be easy pickings in a new city. He wanted to make some money and move on. But then he recognised you. Or he thinks he has; he is not sure, that is why he hasn't approached you yet.'

'So he wants me to give him money or he will reveal my identity?'

The slave nodded.

'What about you?'

'He cannot hurt me. I have been punished. I spent twenty years in the galleys. How I survived, Allah alone knows. I certainly prayed to him enough to release me, to let me be swept overboard and drown.'

'Why did you never tell me who you were?' Qasim asked.

'I told you, as far as I am concerned, Abram ibn al-Attar is dead. There is nothing to be gained from resurrecting him now.'

'So what should I do?' he asked his slave.

'Nothing. As I said he does not know for certain that you are not who you say you are. He will not make a move until he is sure.'

'But nobody here knows my real identity, only my wife and one of my sons.'

'So you are safe. He will get tired and move away, looking for someone else to make him rich.'

'I hope you are right.'

The slave drank the last drop of his tea, smacked his lips with enjoyment and said, 'So what is it that you want to teach me?'

Qasim was confused for a moment until he realised that his slave was talking about the alfarería.

'Follow me. We have a lot of work to do.'

CHAPTER 43

Al-Mari could hear Qasim moving around on the patio; he had been like that for hours, pacing up and down, unable to sleep. Al-Mari was finding it hard to sleep as well, despite the hard work he had done all day. His mind was in turmoil.

He was glad it was out in the open now. Once Qasim had recognised him he had welcomed him with open arms; now he wondered why he had doubted that it would be otherwise. Qasim gave him his freedom immediately but said that he could stay and work for him if that was what he wanted. Al-Mari had no plans to move. He was happy here and the work was not arduous so he agreed to continue as before.

'You are a free man now al-Mari; I will sign a document to that effect. However I think it might be best if we keep it between ourselves; we don't want people asking unnecessary questions,' Qasim had said.

That was all right by him. He too didn't want people looking too closely into his past. Some things were best left hidden.

He stretched his legs to relieve the cramp that sometimes crept up on him. No longer was he expected to sleep on the patio with the dog, he had one of the new rooms to himself. Not that he had objected to the dog's company; it was far preferable than some of the strange bed fellows he had had over the years. But to have a room to himself was a luxury he had never expected to have.

'You might as well sleep there,' Qasim had said. 'There are only three of us now.'

He liked the room; it was the best place he had slept in many a year. Not that he was usually bothered about where he bunked down; soldiers were used to a rough life. But he was old now and his bones ached; it was good to be able to sleep out of the cold wind. The high plains were a bitterly cold place in the winter and Madinat al-Zahra was as bad, despite being in the lee of the mountains.

He rolled onto his side. He wondered what the boy was doing. He had liked the lad; he was bright and willing. Funny that, how you could miss someone you hardly knew. Still the boy would be all right. They were a good family; they would treat him well.

It was strange, the way they had sent him off like that, in the middle of the night, with no warning. Something had happened, that was obvious, something to do with that young son of Qasim's. Gone on a pilgrimage? He had never seemed to al-Mari like someone who wanted to go on a pilgrimage, not according to the way his father was always urging him to say his prayers. No, he was more interested in his friends and chasing after the girls, a normal young man, in fact.

Al-Mari was not a good Muslim, he knew that. He had been once but life had changed him; it had eroded his beliefs until they no longer had any meaning for him. He knew that if he changed and went to the mosque regularly he could redeem himself but he wasn't bothered now. It was too late. A few more years and he would be no more, just dust that blew across the plain. The idea of death did not frighten him; he had faced death many times and survived. One day he would die, that much was sure. He had never expected that he would die in bed.

He turned over again. It was too soon to be thinking such morbid thoughts; he had unfinished business to attend to first. His conversation with ibn Hayyan came back to him. He had only intended to follow him, not tackle him, to keep in the shadows and see what he was up to. In the end the temptation was too great; he had to confront the bastard. When he stood there, face to face with the man who had ruined his life, who had condemned him to a life of slavery, the old anger welled up inside him and he wanted to knock him down and strangle him there and then. But common sense prevailed. There were better ways to take his revenge on this man; an incident like that would start people asking questions and it would be damaging for the General.

Ibn Hayyan had recognised al-Mari straight away. He thought he could make an ally of him, confiding his plans to him. He had heard that the General was still alive and he was looking for him. Fortunately he didn't know that Qasim was the man he sought, not yet. But it wouldn't take him long to discover the General's new identity; al-Mari was sure of it. Ibn Hayyan was the sort of man who would never give up until he had what he wanted; he was like a dog with a bone, worrying away until he had all the information he needed. It wasn't blackmail that ibn Hayyan had in mind; no, it was worse. He planned to find the General and then betray him to the Khalifa. He reckoned he would be paid handsomely for the information.

'If you find out anything, let me know,' he said. 'I will reward you well.'

That was when al-Mari lost his temper.

'You treacherous viper, don't you remember what your lies did to me? You ruined my life. I spent twenty years in the galleys, thanks to you. Now you want me to help you? I should knock you down and strip you of all your money right now.'

'You can't turn the clock back, Attar. I'm giving you a chance to make some money then you can buy your freedom.'

'May Allah take you and your money and throw you into hell.'

'Do as you wish. I don't need the help of a broken-down old slave, anyway. Someone will talk; there is always somebody who will sell their soul for a bag of silver dirhams,' he said, turning away from al-Mari. 'Anyway, if you change your mind you can find me at the inn next to the shoemaker's.'

If al-Mari had had a sword in his hand he would have run him through there and then. Instead he made himself a vow; he would have vengeance on this man, one way or the other.

Now that vow came back to him and, as he lay there admiring his handiwork on the ceiling above his head, he began to plan how he would stop ibn Hayyan from betraying the General's identity.

***

The next morning he waited until Qasim had gone to the mosque and he slipped out. He knew the inn where ibn Hayyan was staying and within ten minutes he was there. The man was sleeping in the room at the back.

'Hey, wake up,' he said, pushing the sleeping figure with his foot.

'What in the name of Allah's going on?' ibn Hayyan said, pulling back his cloak and sitting up.

'I want to talk to you.'

'At this hour? Go away and let me sleep.'

'It's Attar.'

'I know who you are. What do you want now?' ibn Hayyan asked. 'I thought you'd condemned me to burn in hell.'

Slowly he got to his feet and pulled his cloak around him. He grinned at al-Mari, revealing a mouth of broken and blackened teeth; he smelled as though he had been drinking something stronger than mint tea.

'So?'

'I've been thinking about what you said. Maybe I was too hasty. The truth is I could do with the money. I'm old now. I don't want to die a slave. How much will you pay me if I find out where the General is hiding?'

'Fifty dirhams.'

'Is that all? Make it a hundred and we've a deal.'

Ibn Hayyan had stopped smiling; he stared at the slave, his eyes steely. Al-Mari could see he was not sure whether to believe him.

'You've changed your tune, haven't you. I thought you didn't want to do business with me?'

'I need the money,' al-Mari said. 'I can't get my freedom if I have no money.'

That seemed to be good enough for ibn Hayyan. He leered at al-Mari and said, 'You're no better than I am. It's always the money that counts when it comes down to it. All right. I'll pay you one hundred dirhams.'

'In silver.'

The man nodded.

'Meet me tonight at midnight, outside the city walls, near the south gate. I'll have some news for you by then,' al-Mari said.

'Right,' the man grunted. 'Now let me get back to sleep.'

Al-Mari hurried back to the alfarería; he would be back before Qasim knew that he had gone.

***

He waited until the house was quiet; only the rumbling snores of Qasim broke the silence. It was time to go. As he got dressed, the dog, always alert, lifted his head but did not move. He watched al-Mari for a moment then closed his eyes and went back to sleep. Al-Mari moved quickly, unbolting the door and slipping out into the black night. There was no moon and the stars were hidden by thick clouds; it was perfect for what he had in mind. He looked around him; there was no-one about. He pulled up the hood of his djellaba and set off towards the south gate. He wanted the deed done.

As he approached the meeting place there was no sign of ibn Hayyan. It was just as he planned; he was the first to arrive. He knew where to hide so that he wouldn't be seen;

he had checked the area beforehand. Now all he had to do was wait.

It did not take long. His enemy had obviously been drinking again but he was eager for information; he staggered towards al-Mari's hiding place but seeing no-one in the darkness, stopped and turned round. He had a purse in his hand; al-Mari could hear the jingle of the coins as he fidgeted with it.

'Where's that bloody turncoat? I thought he said midnight,' he muttered.

He pulled a flask from his pocket and took a long drink from it.

'Come on, you old bastard; I've got your money for you,' he called. 'Where are you?'

He tossed the bag of coins in the air. Al-Mari waited. He could see that ibn Hayyan was getting impatient. Soon he would give up and leave.

'I knew you didn't have any information. You don't know where the General is, any more than I do. Why did I listen to you? I knew you wouldn't come,' he said, wiping his lips and putting the flask back in his pocket. 'You're a stupid bastard Hayyan; you should have known that old slave would have nothing for you.'

'Well that's where you're wrong,' al-Mari said as he stepped from the shadows.

Before ibn Hayyan knew what was happening al-Mari had drawn his dagger and slashed it across the man's throat. With barely a grunt, ibn Hayyan slumped to the ground, the blood gushing from his wound. Al-Mari bent down to pick up the purse of coins and then walked quickly away; there was no need to check if ibn Hayyan was dead or not. Al-Mari knew his work.

CHAPTER 44

Fatima burst into the alfarería. Her hair had come loose and straggled free from her cap.

'What is it, wife? What has happened?' Qasim asked.

His wife began to wail and wring her hands in anguish.

'They've found a body, at the place where they hold the camel races. Oh, Qasim, do you think it is Omar? Isn't that near where the North Africans were camped? Do you think it could be him?'

Qasim put his arms around his wife and tried to calm her.

'Hush now. Why would it be Omar? I am sure he is far away by now. But I will go there straight away and see who it is, so that you will stop worrying. Go into the house and wait for me.'

He grabbed his cap and djellaba and hurried out. He had tried to appear calm for his wife's sake but his heart was racing. Was it Omar's body? Had the guards executed him and thrown his body out for the crows? May it please Allah, let it be someone else, he found himself praying. Please Allah, don't let Omar be dead.

As he left the medina, he could see a crowd of people in the distance and others flocking to join them. There was nothing people liked more than a grisly death. As he approached he caught snatches of conversation.

'Who is he?'

'No idea.'

'Do you know him?'

'Nearly took his head off.'

'I've seen him around; I'd know him anywhere.'

'Never seen him before.'

'I've never seen anything like it. Must have died in a flash.'

'Slaughtered like a goat at the feast.'

He pushed his way through to the front. He was just in time, two of the Palace Guards had come to remove the body.

'Who is it?' he asked a man standing next to him.

'No idea. A stranger, I think; I've never seen him before.'

He had to know. He stepped up to the guards and said, 'Can I help?'

'Unless you're a bloody miracle worker, I shouldn't think so,' one of them said, lifting the body onto a sheet.

The man's head rolled to one side and Qasim found himself looking into the vacant eyes of his enemy, ibn Hayyan. He leapt back in horror.

'Never seen a dead man before, hajj?' one of the guards asked with a laugh. 'This one's had his throat cut from ear to ear.'

'Looks like a professional job, if you ask me,' said the other.

The soldiers rolled the man in the sheet and hauled him away while Qasim stood open-mouthed. He did not know what to think. It seemed strange that the man who was planning to blackmail him should suddenly be found with his throat slit. Could it just be a coincidence? He found that hard to believe. Had he made other enemies in Madinat al-Zahra or had al-Mari done this to protect him?

'You seem very upset, hajj. Did you know the unfortunate man?' asked one of the bystanders.

Qasim shook his head.

'No, I've never seen him before,' he lied. 'But it is a terrible way to die, like a slaughtered animal.'

'Indeed. May his soul rest in peace.'

He stared at the pool of blood that had soaked into the bare earth. What should he do? If he questioned al-Mari he would deny it; he would have nothing to gain by admitting it and everything to lose. Qasim had no way of proving that his slave had committed this atrocious act but neither could he believe that it was just a coincidence. There was nothing he could do; the man was dead. Then he remembered Fatima; she would be waiting for news. He had to get home.

***

His wife was sitting on the patio, staring at the water cascading into the pool. She looked up when he came in but did not speak. He knew she was too frightened to ask him about the dead man.

'It's all right wife, the man is a stranger. Some poor traveller that was robbed and murdered last night. No need to fret any more about Omar.'

She buried her face in her hands and sobbed with relief.

'Allah will punish me for being so happy,' she said. 'It's not right to rejoice in another's misfortunes but I can't help it.'

He understood what she meant. Now that the shock of seeing ibn Hayyan's blood-covered face had worn off, he was beginning to realise what the man's death meant. There was no-one who could reveal his identity now; only al-Mari knew about his past and Qasim was certain that he would never betray him.

His slave was already in the alfarería, preparing a batch of clay for him. He looked up as Qasim came in.

'Have you heard the news?' Qasim asked. 'Ibn Hayyan is dead. Someone robbed and murdered him.'

Al-Mari's face was impassive.

'So you don't need to worry about him any more then,' he said and returned to his work.

'No, I don't.'

Should he have expected more of a reaction from al-Mari? It was as if he already knew that the man was dead. Maybe his fears were justified after all. Had al-Mari murdered his enemy? It made sense. He had plenty of motive: revenge for what ibn Hayyan had done to him and protection for Qasim and his family. On the other hand, within a few days he would be a free man, just as soon as the documents had been legally ratified. Why would he jeopardise his future by committing murder? He looked at al-Mari. The slave was softening the clay block with his feet; he did not look at Qasim.

'The guards don't seem to have any idea who did it,' Qasim continued. 'But they think it was someone who knew how to handle himself.'

'Probably got into a fight with a man younger and stronger than himself,' al-Mari said.

'Yes, I expect that's what happened. Strange coincidence though, isn't it.'

'They say life is stranger than fiction,' al-Mari replied. 'Now where do you want this clay?'

'Just put it straight onto the wheel. I'll use it now.'

He sat down at the wheel and began to shape the clay. So was this something else he would always have on his conscience? Qasim had let an innocent man be executed in place of his own son and now he was going to remain silent about the murder of ibn Hayyan. He had no choice. He was responsible for the actions of his slave; people could say that he had forced al-Mari to kill the man in order to protect his family. He could not prove otherwise. No, better that he questioned al-Mari no further and let the matter rest. He sighed. Allah would have a lot to forgive him for when he died.

CHAPTER 45

They arrived at garrison of Salim on the evening of the twenty-fifth day. Al-Jundi could see the fortress long before they reached it; it stood proud on a steep bluff, a winding path leading up to its gates. The evening sun was setting behind it, casting a golden glow over the rough-hewn stone walls and its square tower.

'So that's Salim,' the prince said. 'It looks impenetrable.'

'Shall I send word to the governor?' al-Jundi asked.

'Yes. Let him know that we are here.'

He watched as the rider raced across the plain and up the hill to the fortress. Along the open parapet he could see soldiers watching their progress; their arrival would be no surprise to the governor. His garrison was well positioned to see all who approached. It was a well fortified building; al-Jundi estimated that it was at least half an Arab mile round its perimeter. It would resist an attack by the rebels without any problem. So why had the governor sent for them in such a panic?

He turned and looked at his men; they were in good spirits and ready for whatever might happen.

'Tell the troops that we will stop here tonight,' al-Hakim said. 'While they are setting up the camp I want you to bring some horsemen and follow me.'

Al-Jundi was confident that this uprising would be easily quelled and they would soon return home. Now as they neared the garrison gates he could see the armed guard, waiting for them. He signalled for his men to stop and waited while the Prince surveyed the scene before him. The cobbled path had led them up to the main entrance, a narrow archway that would allow no more than a single horseman to enter at a time. Beyond the archway, armed guards stood either side of the studded wooden gates. It had the look of a place already under siege; he had forgotten what it was like to live in a frontier town, constantly on guard against attack.

'Captain, bring half-a-dozen men and come with me,' al-Hakim said. 'I want to be sure that this is not a trap.'

'Yes, your Highness.'

He signalled to six of his best horsemen and they filed behind him and the prince.

'The rest of you wait here until we return,' al-Jundi instructed the remainder of his men.

'Let's see what this is all about,' al-Hakim said, urging his horse forward with his heel.

As they approached the gates, the governor's men stepped forward, barring their way.

'Halt,' one of them said.

'Tell the governor that we have come to bring him help. Tell him that the Khalifa's son, al-Hakim is here in person. And be quick about it; my men are tired and need somewhere to rest,' al-Jundi said.

Immediately the men stood to one side and the gates swung open. The prince rode straight in, followed by al-Jundi and the six horsemen. No sooner were they inside the garrison then the gates closed behind them. Al-Jundi's hand went straight to his sword. Was this indeed a trap? There had been times before when governors of remote garrisons forgot their loyalty to the Khalifa and thought to become autonomous.

'Where is the governor?' al-Hakim asked.

'The governor respectfully asks if you would follow me, your Highness,' one of the guards said.

A groom stepped forward and took the reins from al-Hakim.

'Give my horse some water and rub him down,' the prince said.

'Yes, your Highness.'

'Captain Ibn Qasim. Follow me.'

'Yes, your Highness.'

Al-Jundi motioned for the men to dismount and follow him. He had no intention of leaving his prince unprotected.

They followed the guard into the garrison building, through a labyrinth of narrow, winding corridors until they came to a large reception room. Al-Jundi marked carefully in his mind each twist and turn of the route, counting the arches they passed beneath, noting the guards positioned along the way; if they needed to make a hasty exit he would be ready. At last they arrived in a large, well-furnished room; the governor sat on a low couch at the far end of it. He rose to greet them.

'Welcome your Highness, welcome. Thanks be to Allah that you have arrived. The rebels are massing more and more troops every day. I would not be able to hold them off without your help.'

'As-salam alaykum, governor al-Madanish. My father, Abd al-Rahman ibn Muhammad ibn Abd Allah al-Nasir li-Din Allah, Defender of God's Faith and supreme ruler of Al-Andalus, has sent me to find out what is happening here,' al-Hakim said.

'And you are most welcome, esteemed Prince. Please be seated and I will send for some refreshment.'

Al-Hakim sat on the low couch and the governor sat down opposite him. Al-Jundi and his men stood to one side, close enough to protect their prince.

'I trust you had a good journey?' the governor asked, as they waited for a servant to place a silver pot of mint tea and a plate of almond sweetmeats on the table between them.

'It was uneventful.'

'May I pour you some tea?' the governor asked.

'No, thank you. Let us get down to business.'

'Very well, your Highness.'

He waited until the servant had left then asked, 'You have brought me some reinforcements? Fighting men?'

'I have my army, that is true and we have marched for more than three weeks to reach you. But tell me, governor al-Madanish, where exactly are the rebels of whom you speak so fearfully? You say they are massing more men every day but I do not see them. Where are they?' al-Hakim asked.

'I have it on very good authority that no more than two Arab miles from here there is an encampment of Christian rebels. My scouts came across them more than a month ago and have been watching them every since. They are led by a young cousin of Ramiro II.'

'Is King Ramiro supporting them?'

'I don't think so; he is busy with internal affairs of state. He is not interested in challenging the authority of the Khalifa. It looks as though this young upstart has decided to raise his own army and challenge not only the Khalifa but his cousin as well.'

'He must be either very foolish or very rich. How has he managed to raise an army strong enough to challenge the Khalifa's men?'

'I don't know, your Highness. I do not think he is rich but he is certainly foolish. He promises his followers that he will throw out the infidel and restore the land to the true rulers, the Christian princes. He says God and Saint James are on his side.'

'What nonsense. He is a fool indeed. That Saint James is nothing but a character in a fairytale. No ghost is going to come and help him fight against the Khalifa,' al-Hakim said.

Al-Jundi had heard the rumours of how the people of the north believed that this Christian saint had led them to victory before, against Abd al-Rahman II in the year 844. Saint James had appeared before King Ramiro I's army, dressed as a soldier and riding a white horse. They said that the apparition had fought alongside them and slew many of their enemies. The Christians had been lucky that day and somehow managed to beat the Moorish army even though it outnumbered them greatly. That's how the myth had started, but al-Jundi didn't believe that the Christian's victory was down to saintly intervention. He didn't believe in such folk tales; it was more likely, as with all battles, a matter of luck and good judgement on the part of Ramiro

I and mistakes on the part of Abd al-Rahman II. It would not happen again, not with al-Hakim leading them. The Khalifa's army was the best in the land. It would not be beaten by a young upstart hiding behind the legend of a saint.

'I agree, your Highness, but the people believe him. They are flocking to join him from all over the north. They say that Saint James has returned to help free them from the Moorish infidel,' the governor said.

'Then we will stop him before his army gets any bigger. Send your generals to me and we will prepare to attack as soon as possible.'

He turned to al-Jundi.

'Send some scouts and find out where this army is camped and how many men there are.'

'Yes, your Highness.'

'So, tell me Governor, how many men do you have stationed here?' al-Hakim asked. 'How many can I rely on?'

'Armed and able-bodied, some three thousand,' the governor replied.

'That is substantial. And you did not think to attack this prince as soon as you knew of his plans, before his followers had grown in number?'

'I did not know how many men he had, your Highness. I thought it best to keep my men here, to protect the garrison from attack. I did not want it to fall into enemy hands.'

'I see.'

Al-Jundi could tell that the prince was not pleased with this reply. Part of a governor's duties was to squash any uprisings along the frontier before they got out of control. That was why he was equipped with a heavily armed garrison of well-trained fighting men. Instead of dealing with the insurgents himself, al-Madanish had simply called for help.

'It would be a great honour for me, your Highness, if you would stay the night, here in the castle,' the governor said, obsequiously. 'I will arrange a banquet and entertainment for you and your men.'

'No, thank you for your hospitality but I prefer to rejoin my men. I will sleep in the camp tonight. Send your generals to my tent.'

'Very well, your Highness.'

The prince stood up.

'My men need fresh water and meat,' he said.

'I will arrange for provisions to be taken out to them at once.'

'Good. Now I must leave you. There is much to do.'

The governor bowed as low as his corpulent frame would allow. Al-Jundi signalled for his men to lead the way and he followed behind the prince. There was something he did not like about the governor. He was too fat and too complacent. His black beard was oiled and curled and his robes were a little too fancy for the governor of a provincial garrison; he did not have the air of a frontier soldier, rather the sycophantic manner of a wily courtier. Why had he not dealt with this uprising himself as soon as he had become aware of it? Why had he wasted time waiting for the Khalifa to send him more men? He had admitted already that with every day that passed the Christian prince gained more recruits. It was necessary to act quickly; even the biggest simpleton could see that. Al-Jundi had met men like him before, men who had grown fat and lazy during peacetime and were not prepared to defend their territories. Well it was not his business. He was here to fight for the Khalifa and to protect his son, al-Hakim.

***

The scouts returned at midnight. They had found the rebels' camp and they estimated that there were no more than five thousand men.

'Five thousand men?' al-Hakim exclaimed. 'Is that all? That dolt al-Madanish has sent for reinforcements when he has only five thousand men to face.'

'What do we do, your Highness?' al-Jundi asked.

He knew what they would do. They would send in the skirmishers with slings and javelins to attack them first. Then the jinetes would ride in and finish off any resistance. If they were lucky they would capture or even kill Ramiro's cousin. It would be over very quickly.

'We attack at first light. Tell your men to rest and to be prepared to leave just before dawn.'

Al-Jundi knew there would be little rest for anyone that night. The men would be too excited about the prospect of battle. He walked through the camp, checking that all was in order. Some of the men sat by the camp fires, chatting and playing chess, others lay in their tents trying to sleep; some tended their horses, grooming them and talking to them like close friends, others cleaned and oiled their weapons, checked bindings and sharpened the points of their javelins or waxed the flax strings of their bows. They had eaten well. The governor had been as good as his word and sent whole sheep to be roasted and fresh vegetables from the surrounding farms. Now each man wanted to be sure that he was ready for the battle. They all wanted it over and done with.

'Want a game, Captain?' someone called out to him.

'Not now, soldier. I'll play you after the battle, when we're on our way home.'

'I'll keep you to that, Captain.'

Al-Jundi had a good relationship with his men. He stood no nonsense, no insubordination but he liked to talk to them man-to-man. If there were any grievances he listened to them and, if he thought they were just, he tried to help them. At first some of the men had thought he was a soft touch but they had soon learned otherwise; a few of them had felt the lash for their misdemeanours and he had not hesitated to deal with the man who was caught stealing from a fellow soldier. He received the punishment of all thieves even though it meant the end of his career as a soldier; there was no room in the Khalifa's army for a man with an amputated hand.

His tour of inspection completed, he went into his tent to try to get some sleep. He took off his armour and his helmet and lay down on the straw palliasse. He did not want to sleep; he wanted to be riding into battle. He closed his eyes but his mind was racing; he could feel a pulse banging away in his temple. It was always like this; he was impatient for the battle to begin even though he knew how important it was to conserve his energy. He needed to be fresh and clear-headed tomorrow. Soldiering was a dangerous occupation - nobody denied that - but preparation, both physical and mental improved the odds in your favour. His body was firm and hard, his muscles finely tuned and there was not an ounce of fat on him. More importantly than that, his mind was clear and his reflexes were sharp. Tomorrow he would do what he was best at, fight for his sovereign.

***

He was up and ready before the sun rose and moved quietly among the men, rousing those that had managed to sleep and encouraging the rest. The dew lay thick upon the ground and his boots left a trail of footprints as he walked through the camp. He rubbed his hands to warm them; the air was chill and his breath hung white in front of his face as he gave out the orders. A streak of silver light began to creep along the horizon and, by the time the sun had started to stain the night sky pink, they were already in formation and ready to move out. Prince al-Hakim rode to the front to face them.

'Today we are going into battle. Some of you may die but you will die fighting for your country, your Khalifa and for Allah. Let us pray to Allah to bring us victory,' al-Hakim said.

He lowered his head and began to pray, the soldiers echoing his words as they would in the mosque.

'Allah will bring us victory today and help us to defeat these infidels,' he said. 'Praise be to Allah.'

'Praise be to Allah,' the soldiers chanted.

'We will approach from the east,' al-Hakim told his generals, 'with the sun at our backs. Send in the skirmishers first.'

He turned to al-Jundi.

'And hold your horsemen ready for my signal.'

'Yes, my Prince.'

***

The rebels were taken by surprise. Al-Hakim's troops were trained to move quietly and quickly; they were into the camp before the enemy was aware of them. The sleeping soldiers were wrested from their dreams to find themselves in a maelstrom of fear and killing as their attackers fell upon them, cracking open skulls, thrusting and stabbing at close range. From where they waited in a grove of oak trees above the rebels' camp, Al-Jundi and his jinetes could watch the carnage. Tents were set alight and soon the camp was in flames, black smoke billowing into the pale morning sky. It seemed too easy at first but the rebels were by no means defeated; they fought valiantly, hand to hand, until many of their attackers lay dead. Al-Jundi waited for the prince's signal; he was desperate to join the battle but experience told him to hold back. It would soon be over; the Christian rebels would not be able to hold off the attack for long.

Suddenly one of the scouts came running towards them.

'Your Highness, there are more soldiers coming from the north. Five hundred of them at least, maybe more, foot-soldiers and horsemen,' he gasped. 'They must have been camped in the forest.'

Al-Hakim wheeled his horse round to face al-Jundi and the jinetes.

'Take your men and try to cut them off. We will finish off here.'

'Yes, your Highness.'

He lifted his arm and signalled for the men to follow him. If they could keep the two armies apart it would be easier to defeat them. There was no need for subterfuge now; silence was no longer necessary. He spurred his horse on and, shouting to his men to raise their javelins, they rode as fast as they could to face their foe. His horse ran like the wind, his tail held high and his nostrils flaring; he sensed the excitement too.

Al-Jundi's blood was up. The moment had come to do battle and that was all that was in his mind - to kill and not be killed. The men were the same. They rode like madmen straight for the enemy, hoarse inhuman cries coming from their throats as they whipped themselves up into a battle frenzy.

As al-Jundi and his men burst into a clearing on the edge of the forest, the two sides met head on. There had to be a thousand of them but they were a motley collection of soldiers, conscripts rather than regulars, who made up for their lack of experience with religious fervour. Some were on horseback, some on foot, some carried pitchforks, others lances and swords; all were ready to fight to the death. The clash of steel on steel rang through the cold morning air; the screams and groans as weapons sliced through human flesh, the frantic neighing of the horses as they pranced and swerved trying to avoid the slashes and cuts of the short swords, all were just music to his ears. Al-Jundi threw his javelin at an enemy soldier, watched as it pierced him in the neck and he fell to the ground. He pulled his sword from its scabbard and slashed at the Christians, splitting open heads and cutting men down, their blood spurting up and covering him in gore.

The battle raged for an hour or more and then the enemy turned and fled. His men were all for chasing them and killing off the stragglers but he called them back.

'Leave them. We must go back and support our brothers-in-arms,' he said. 'The Prince may need us.'

They galloped back to the enemy camp where the battle was still raging. It had not been as easy as he had first thought. The camp was littered with the dead and dying, as many of their own men as the enemy. But where was the prince? Where was the standard of al-Hakim? Then he saw him. He was no longer on horseback; he stood with his back to a tree, fighting hand to hand with two Christian knights. Blood was running down his face from a jagged cut in his head. His helmet, with its distinctive jewelled crown, lay on the ground beside him. His standard bearer was dead, pinned to a tree with an axe. Al-Jundi did not hesitate. He grabbed a javelin from the body of a dead soldier and threw it straight at one of the knights, burying it deep in his back. The man slumped to the ground without a sound. Then al-Jundi rode up to the other knight, slashed him across the throat with his sword and, leaning down, swung the prince up onto his horse.

'My crown,' the prince said.

Al-Jundi leaned down again and scooped up the crown with his sword.

'Here, your Highness,' he said, handing it to al-Hakim. 'No infidel is going to wear the crown of an Omayyad prince.'

The prince placed his crown back on his head; it was caked in mud and streaked with blood but it was a royal crown and a symbol of his power.

Al-Jundi rode up onto high ground so that they could survey the scene. The battle continued but it was obvious

that the Christians were outnumbered. They fought
fiercely and bravely but soon they would all die.

'Where is their leader?' asked al-Hakim. 'I'm sure that I
saw him go down.'

'Maybe he's dead.'

'Send some of your horsemen down there to search for
him. I want him, alive or dead but I want him.'

'Yes, your Highness.'

He climbed down from his horse, leaving the prince
clinging to its back.

'You are injured my Prince. Are you able to ride?'

'Yes, thanks to you. Get me a horse.'

'You can have my horse, your Highness. He is as gentle
as he is brave.'

'Very well.'

'I must go back to my men,' al-Jundi said.

He could not abandon his men to fight alone; he set off
back down the hill into the camp. Behind him, he could
hear his horse neighing and pawing the ground; he wanted
to be with him.

The battle was soon over and the Christian rebels
defeated; they were all dead or had run away, back across
the frontier from which they had come. The soldiers
indulged in their usual orgy of stripping the dead bodies of
anything of value and, as instructed by al-Jundi, searched
for the leader of the rebels. They found his standard and
his standard bearer but the man himself seemed to have
vanished. Nobody could find him or his body. A few
stragglers who were too slow or injured to escape were
caught. They would be taken back to the garrison to

become slaves but in the meantime al-Jundi set them to work digging graves for the dead.

'How about that game of chess now, Captain?' one of the men asked.

His tunic was covered in blood and his left arm hung lifeless by his side but he was alive and smiling. He carried a heavy lance in his good hand and wore a rebel's helmet on his head, spoils from the battlefield.

'You fought well today, soldier. All the men fought well. The Khalifa would be proud of you.'

'That's why we won, Captain. We don't rely on some Christian saint to fight our battles for us.'

The man staggered away, following his companions back to the camp.

'Don't forget about that game of chess, Captain,' he called.

'I won't, soldier.'

CHAPTER 46

A year had passed since Abd al-Rahman's army had left Madinat al-Zahra to quell the rebellion in the north. News of their victory had already reached the Khalifa; his son had written to him of the battle. Now word had arrived that they would be here, in Madinat al-Zahra, any day. Abd al-Rahman III was eager to see his son and learn all the details.

'Will that be all, my Lord?' Gassam asked.

'Yes. You can leave me for now. No, wait. Send in the Royal Buyer. I want him to get me something special.'

'Yes, your Highness.'

She deserved something very special, a jewel for his jewel, his Jawhara. That very morning she had given birth to a son. Now her place was secure in his heart. He would shower her with gifts to show her how grateful even a Khalifa could be to be given a son.

'You wanted to speak to me, my Lord?'

The Royal Buyer stood near the door.

'Yes, come closer. I want you to find me an ivory casket. I want it carved with the words of the Prophet and set with amber. Then I want you to fill it with necklaces of fresh water pearls, a gold ring set with emeralds and earrings made from amethysts and rubies. Bring it to me as soon as you can.'

'I have just the casket for you, my Lord. It is exquisitely carved and comes from Damascus. I have never seen finer.'

'Excellent. And the jewels.'

'They will be no problem. There are such items already in the Royal treasury. I will see to it.'

'Good.'

He waited until the Royal Buyer had left then he picked up his book of poetry. Tonight he would read something to Jawhara in celebration of their child. His eyes lighted on a verse:

And although it was still night,
when you came, a rainbow
gleamed on the horizon,
showing as many colours
as a peacock's tail,' he read aloud.

'Yes that will do well. Her eyes are the colour of a peacock's tail,' he murmured to himself.

The court musician was waiting in the next room. Al-Rahman clapped his hands and the man entered and bowed.

'Play me something, but nothing sad. Today is a day for rejoicing.'

The man bowed again and, after adjusting the strings on his lute began to play. He had a soft touch and the gentle music reached out and touched the Khalifa's heart. Yes, today was a day for rejoicing: his first-born was returning to him and a new son had been born. What man could ask for more.

***

They were waiting for him in the throne room, all his generals, officers, the commander of his army and Prince al-Hakim. He had already had a private audience with his son, who had gone through the details of their campaign at length; now it was time to address his men.

He took his place in front of his throne and, standing proudly before them, said, 'Welcome home. You have achieved a great victory over the Christians and you have taught them that they cannot threaten the caliphate of al-Andalus without reprisals. Thank you men. I hear from Prince al-Hakim that you have fought bravely for your country and your sovereign. You will be well paid for your efforts and today we will say special prayers to Allah to thank him for your safe return and for our glorious victory.'

He waited while his commander led the officers out. At the bidding of his son, one of them stayed behind; he was a captain by the look of his uniform. Al-Rahman looked at him quizzically.

'Father, this is the soldier that saved my life,' al-Hakim said.

The man knelt before him, his head bowed. So this was the man to whom he owed his son's life. He felt a surge of gratitude to this unknown soldier.

'Stand up, Captain and let me see your face,' he said.

Slowly the man stood up.

'What is your name?'

'Captain Makoud ibn Qasim, my lord.'

'You did well, Captain ibn Qasim. It seems you saved the heir to the throne of al-Andalus, Crown Prince al-Hakim, from certain death.'

'I did what any true soldier would have done, your Majesty,' the captain replied.

The Khalifa was content; his army had fought well and returned home to a tumultuous reception from the cheering citizens of Madinat al-Zahra. As was normal in battle, many soldiers had died but the losses were not severe; they would soon find replacements. His son, al-Hakim, had acquitted himself bravely; he was wounded but he would live. For that al-Rahman thanked Allah and now he had to thank the soldier standing before him.

'No doubt, but for that action you must be rewarded. My son tells me that the governor of the garrison at Salim is lax and slothful, that he should be replaced. I will make you governor in his place.'

'Thank you, your Majesty.'

'You don't look very pleased at the prospect. What is it, man? Do you not fancy yourself as governor of one of my garrisons?'

'The truth is, your Majesty, that I am happy here, serving in your army. I would prefer to remain a soldier than become governor of a garrison.'

The Khalifa looked at his son.

'Well what do you say to that?'

'I will have him as my personal bodyguard,' al-Hakim replied. 'He is a loyal, trustworthy soldier and I need someone like that by my side.'

'Very well. What about that, soldier? Would that suit you?'

'I would be honoured, my Lord.'

'Right. It shall be so. But that is not enough. You have saved the life of Prince al-Hakim, my son and heir; I must reward you in some other way as well. What is your desire? Money? Women? Land? Speak and you shall have it.'

Al-Jundi remained standing in front of the Khalifa, his head bowed.

'Come on man, speak up.'

'There is only one thing that I would request from your Majesty,' al-Jundi replied.

'Yes, well what is it?'

'That all the members of my family should have your protection.'

The Khalifa frowned.

'That is an odd sort of request. All my subjects have my protection. Why would your family in particular need my protection? Are you from a tribe of cut-throats and thieves?'

'No, my liege. My father is a potter and so are my brothers; I am the only soldier in the family.'

'As long as I live, your family will have my protection,' said al-Hakim. 'That I can promise you.'

The Khalifa nodded.

'Very well. My son is right. You shall have the protection of the Khalifa and his son for you and your family, as long as we shall live.'

'Thank you, your Majesty.'

'Now you may leave us. I wish to spend some time with my son. I have some news for him.'

'Yes, my Lord.'

The soldier bowed and backed away, in the customary manner. Before he had time to leave the room, al-Rahman had turned to his first-born with a broad smile and said, 'You have a new brother, Hakim. Jawhara gave birth this morning'.

CHAPTER 47

Isolde lay back on the cushions, the child in her arms. Najm sat by her side, chattering happily away; her maids darted in and out, desperate to do things for her, bring her a glass of peach juice, rub her swollen ankles, brush her hair. Everyone was delighted that she had given birth to a boy. Not only was her future secured but so were theirs; the Khalifa's generosity would extend to them all.

She was tired; it had been a long and difficult confinement. Isolde was no stranger to the mysteries of giving birth; she had been present at the arrival of both her brothers and she had helped to deliver their cow of a healthy calf. She knew that things could go very wrong if the gods were not looking over you. She had prayed to Ostara, the goddess of spring to protect her and her child and her prayers had been answered. She had not told Najm about this; her friend had said that she must stop praying to the old gods and pray to Allah now. Her son would be brought up as a Muslim. One day he could be an important man, maybe even a ruler.

She looked at his pink, wrinkled face; he was like a little old man with a fuzz of blond hair on his head.

'He's so beautiful,' Najm said. 'Even the physician said he was handsome.'

'Do you think so? I think he looks too much like his father. He's going to have a big nose.'

'That's good. Now the Khalifa will know for certain that it is his child.'

Isolde was surprised at Najm's remark. How could it be anybody else's? She was a captive here; the only real man she ever saw was al-Rahman. If only it were Omar's child. She had tried to push thoughts of him out of her mind but they kept returning. Yet she knew there was no point in thinking of him; that was a dream that could never come true. She was the Khalifa's now. Her fate was sealed.

'You have a son now. This will change your life. You'll be elevated to an even higher status,' Najm continued. 'The Khalifa may even marry you one day. Anything could happen.'

Everyone was so happy that there was another royal baby to fuss over. She held him closer to her; he was like a doll, so perfectly formed, with such tiny hands and feet. For now he slept; his lashes lay like a miracle on his cheeks. She wondered at his perfection.

'Are you happy, Jawhara?' her friend asked.

'Of course I'm happy. Why wouldn't I be?'

Sometimes she thought that Najm could read her mind; she was certainly very sensitive to Isolde's mood changes. Did she know that she was still in love with Omar?

There had been no word from him since that fateful day in the gardens. She had persuaded her maid to make some discrete enquiries about his whereabouts in the market but all she could find out was that he had left Madinat al-Zahra. Of her brother there seemed to be no trace. She had often wondered if it had been her insistence on seeing him that had led to this. What had happened to Omar? Had he been caught and imprisoned? Or had he taken

Hans and left the city for somewhere safer? She felt she would never know and sometimes, at night, she lay in her bed and wept that she had lost the two people she loved because of her own impatience.

The baby began to cry so she sat up and let him fasten onto her teat. As he sucked away happily, she stroked his head. He was so tiny, so helpless; he depended on her totally. She was overwhelmed with love for this child, her child. Yes, her life was going to change but not for the reasons that Najm and the others said; it was going to change because now she was a mother and the most important person in her life was no longer Omar, nor her brother, nor the Khalifa; it was her son. She would never leave this child, not for Omar, not for Hans, for nobody; if it meant she would live her life in the zenana, then so be it. That was what the gods had ordained.

CHAPTER 48

So the concubine had had a son. Well that at least should persuade Omar that it was a lost cause pursuing her; she wouldn't be interested in a mere potter now. Her life was secure; she would be rich beyond belief. The Khalifa was well known for his generosity when it came to his wives and concubines.

Al-Jundi was glad to be back in Madinat al-Zahra; they had been away much longer than he anticipated. That was due to that incompetent wretch who called himself governor of Salim. Al-Hakim had said that they could not leave until he was sure that the garrison was secure; he believed that the Christian princes would attack again as soon as they were gone and the governor would do little about it. Then all their efforts would have been for nothing.

So al-Jundi had led some sorties across the frontier, routing out any Christian soldiers that were still in hiding. They had cleared the area of the insurgents but their main worry was the disappearance of Ramiro's cousin. As long as he was alive there was the danger of him raising a new army and making another attack on the garrison or even on other towns along the frontier. It had taken several months but eventually they found him, licking his wounds in a cave in the mountains. He had a small band of followers with him but they were easily dealt with. They bound him in chains and dragged him back to Salim.

Al-Hakim had not even hesitated; he ordered the immediate execution of Ramiro's cousin and then had his head stuck on a pole outside the garrison walls. The message would soon get out to his followers. The rebellion was over.

Al-Hakim was right. There were no further signs of resistance and so, finally, they were given the orders to return to Madinat al-Zahra.

So here he was at last and promoted too; personal bodyguard to the Royal Prince was an honour he had not expected. He was very happy with the appointment; he would receive more pay, be treated with greater respect and live in the alcázar. Besides which, he liked al-Hakim; they had become friends during the campaign. The prince was a cultured man, a scholar but a good soldier as well. He fought with his head as well as his sword. Yes, al-Jundi respected him.

He didn't need to report for duty until the next day so he decided to visit his parents and let them know that he was alive and well. He went to the alfarería first.

'As-salam alaykum. Where is my father?' he asked al-Mari.

The slave was kneading a block of clay with his feet; his feet and legs were covered in it. So Baba had got him working in the alfarería now. Not surprising now that Omar had left.

'Wa alaykum e-salam. Your father has gone to get some supplies from the apothecary.'

'And my mother?'

'I don't know. In the house maybe?'

He went straight through to the inner part of the house. It was very quiet. Only the dog came forward to greet him, wagging his tail cautiously as if he was unsure of who he was.

'Hello boy. You haven't forgotten me, have you?'

'Who's there?'

'Mama, it's only me, al-Jundi.'

'You're back. Thanks be to Allah.'

She rushed towards him and enveloped him in her arms.

'I thought I'd never see you again,' she sobbed.

'What's all this, Mama? I've been away before and I've always come back, haven't I?'

His mother was holding him at arms' length now, inspecting him. He could see her eyes checking every part of his body.

'And you're not hurt? You're all right?'

'Yes, Mama. I'm fine. Don't fuss so. This is not like you. What's the matter with you?'

'Nothing, my son. I'm being silly, I know. It's just with you on a campaign, Omar away and Layla gone the house has been so empty.'

'What do you mean, Layla gone? What's happened to my little sister?'

'Your father gave her hand in marriage to the apothecary's son. She lives there now.'

'Oh, is that all? I thought something dreadful had happened. Well, they're a good family,' he added. 'Although I must say that I'm surprised you didn't wait until I got back.'

His mother wiped her tears and beamed at him.

'But you're here now. Would you like some tea? Or maybe something to eat?'

'Tea would be good. Al-Mari said that Baba was at the apothecary's collecting some supplies.'

'He's always there. He won't send al-Mari anymore; he wants to go himself so he can see that Layla is all right. I told him it's not necessary but every week he has to go. They let her help in the shop, you know. Her father-in-law is teaching her how to mix creams and potions for his customers.'

'Is she happy?'

'She wasn't at first but now she seems a lot better.'

'Well it's a bit of a surprise, little Layla getting married. I can't say I expected it.'

'But you understand, don't you?' his mother said. 'Your father was trying to distance her from us, so that if anything happened she would be safe.'

'Baba made the right decision.'

He sighed. He had forgotten about it; he still had to find this man who was threatening his family and silence him. Now he was home he would see what he could find out.

'Is that you son? Back from the wars, eh? And how are you?'

His father stood in the doorway, a wide grin on his face.

'Wa alaykum e-salam, my father. I am well.'

'Praise be to Allah. Come, tell me all about the battle. Not wounded, I hope?'

'Just a scratch or two, nothing really. Yes, it was a complete success. The rebellion has been crushed and the perpetrators punished.'

He told his father all that had happened and when he got to the part about saving al-Hakim's life, his father jumped to his feet and hugged him.

'You will be well rewarded for that, my son,' he said.

'I have been already. I am now the prince's personal bodyguard.'

'Fatima, do you hear that? Your son has been promoted. He works in the inner sanctum of the alcázar now. Allah has been good to us.'

'That's wonderful news,' she said, placing the teapot and glasses on the table in front of them.

'But that's not all. I have the Khalifa's promise that you and all our family will have his protection and that of al-Hakim as long as they live. You don't need to worry about your past any longer.'

His father stared at him.

'I can't believe that you have done this for us? Allah be praised. What a son I have; you have saved us all.'

'Not really, Baba, but if anything is ever said about what happened when you were young, we have the Khalifa's word that he will protect you.'

'I have something to tell you, my son. The man I told you about is dead. He was murdered a few months ago.'

'The one who you thought had recognised you?'

His father nodded.

'That's strange. Did they catch the murderer?'

'No. It remains a mystery.'

'Well that is even better news.'

Now he wouldn't have to find out about the man; there was no more need to worry. He was dead and al-Jundi wasn't going to waste time worrying about the death of an old man. Whoever had killed him had done them a favour.

'Excuse me, sayyad. There is someone to see you,' al-Mari said. 'He is waiting in the alfarería.'

He stood in the doorway, his feet and legs covered in dry clay.

'I wonder who it is,' his father said.

'A new customer, perhaps,' Fatima said.

'Maybe. I won't be long. You're not in a hurry, are you my son?'

'No, Baba. I have plenty of time.'

'Let me pour you some more tea,' his mother said.

He leaned back, stretching his long legs in front of him. He could understand his mother's unhappiness; one minute she had a house full of people and the next they had been scattered to the wind. She would miss Layla especially.

'So, when do you get to see Layla?' he asked.

'She and her husband come to eat lunch with us at the beginning of each month but she also comes in to see me if she's passing. She is very busy, working in the apothecary's shop and helping in the house. Her mother-in-law is a nice woman; she is teaching Layla how to cook and sew.'

'I never thought our Layla liked that sort of thing.'

'She's young but even she realises that all women have to learn certain tasks. In fact she is a nice little cook; sometimes she brings me things to try: pastries and tiny biscuits. They are very good. Her sewing is dreadful though; I think she spends more time unpicking her work than she does sewing.'

She smiled sadly at him.

'I think I might look for a wife now,' he said. 'My new position is more secure. I could take a wife. I will talk to Baba about it.'

He smiled to himself when he saw the look of pleasure on his mother's face. All she ever wanted was for her sons to marry and give her grandchildren. Before she had time to say anything however his father came bursting into the room.

'Look at this. Look at this,' he cried, holding a plate up for them to see.

'What is it husband? What's the matter?'

'A traveller just brought me this. He said a man he met in Alexandria asked him to bring it here to Madinat al-Zahra. He was paid to deliver it personally to Qasim the potter.'

'But what is it?'

'It's a plate. Look at the glaze. It's my glaze, the lustre glaze. And look at the pattern; it's Omar's. I'd recognise it anywhere. He's alive.'

'It's signed,' al-Jundi said. 'Look here; it says ibn Qasim and then there's an O.'

'Allah be praised; Omar has sent us a message to say that he is well. That's his signature; I told him to always sign his work. He thought I didn't know about the extra O but I did. I didn't mind. If he was proud of his work then so was I.'

'Do you think he has made the pilgrimage to Mecca, already?' Fatima asked.

'I think he has, wife. Look at this writing around the edge of the design, where it speaks of the blessings of

Allah. You can just make out the word "hajj". He is telling us that he has completed the hajj.'

'So he'll come home now?' she asked.

Al-Jundi looked at his father. He was no longer smiling.

'No, wife. I don't think he will; remember he doesn't know that Yusuf took the blame for the killing. He will still think his life and those of our family are in danger. It could be a long time before he ventures back to Madinat al-Zahra but at least we know he is safe. We can sleep easier in our beds at night, knowing that Omar has completed his pilgrimage and that Allah has forgiven him.'

He took the plate from his wife's hands and placed it on the table. The colours glowed in the morning light, amber, greens and reds that burned with their own fire. There was no mistaking it; it was the product of father and son, of the family of Qasim. Al-Jundi had a feeling that life was going to be more tranquil for his parents from now on.

EPILOGUE
Córdoba
987 AD

Omar stood on the bridge, watching the swallows swooping past, soaring and turning then diving to snap at the insects that swarmed around the reedy beds of the river Guadalquivir. It was forty years since that fateful day when Omar had been exiled from his home and family, yet it seemed like yesterday. The memories came flooding back to him. Omar had travelled far and wide after he completing his pilgrimage. For a few years he stayed in a small town, north of Mecca and worked at what he knew best, making beautifully glazed plates, but he had been unable to settle. He made his way up to Damascus and, for a while, he studied with the best artisans in the country then, still restless, he had headed west to Mesopotamia, just for the pleasure of seeing the glorious city of Baghdad. He had been disappointed and saddened; it reminded him too much of his beloved Córdoba and filled him with longing for his homeland. He yearned to see his family once more, so he continued west and travelled through Byzantium and along the north coast of the Mediterranean Sea.

It was while he was in the ancient city of Rome that he received the news of Yusuf's execution. He had met a merchant who knew Córdoba well. Like many merchants, this man carried messages for people he might meet along the trade routes. As soon as he realised that Omar was the son of the potter, Qasim, famous now for his magnificent earthenware, he had given him a letter from Omar's mother. The news it contained had torn at his heart. He knew instantly that Yusuf's death had been his fault and he could not forgive himself. Yusuf had warned him to be careful; he had said that someone could get hurt. If only Omar had realised that it was going to be his friend, who instead of marrying his sweetheart had been arrested and executed for something that Omar had done. There and then he had vowed he would never marry. Instead Omar had led a solitary, sometimes lonely life. It was a self-inflicted punishment.

How different things could have been, he told himself as he looked into the fast-flowing river below his feet. If he had heeded Yusuf's warnings he need not have spent his life as a lonely bachelor; he could have married Muna, his betrothed, and had sons of his own.

The bridge was old but still sturdy; it had been built in Roman times and would last many centuries more. He was half-way across and he stopped to gaze back at the city, the memories crowding into his head. Córdoba was once again the centre of power for al-Andalus; it was bustling and vibrant and he wouldn't have wanted to live anywhere else. Now, with the hindsight of old-age he could see how selfish he had been as a young man. His love for Jawhara had clouded everything else; his duty, his family, his friends were as nothing in the passion that had consumed him. He had destroyed his friend's life and put his family in danger, all for a pretty face. Despite all that had happened, that face had never left him; it had stayed with him through the long days and nights he spent travelling with the nomads; it had been with him in the storm-tossed ship that took him to Alexandria; it appeared to him in the sandstorms of the Sinai desert and as he journeyed down the Red Sea. It was with him as he approached the holy city of Mecca and after, as he journeyed to Damascus. When he realised that he was no longer a wanted man, that his dear friend had been executed in his place, he had returned to al-Andalus filled with remorse but still with the irrational idea that Jawhara would be waiting for him. How blind he had been. Ten years had passed. He had not been the only one in love with Jawhara; the Khalifa too had been captivated by her. The slave, for whom Omar had sacrificed everything, was now a rich woman, mother of two of the Khalifa's sons and her future assured. And his best friend, Yusuf, lay dead in the ground because of his foolishness.

The thought of Jawhara still stirred his soul but the memories now were bitter-sweet. Just as his beloved Madinat al-Zahra was crumbling to dust so was his heart. He had tried to live a good life and now all he could hope for was that Allah, in his compassion, would forgive him. He picked up his walking stick and headed slowly back to the city.

GLOSSARY

Al-Andalus the Islamic name given to Moorish Spain

Alcázar palace, fort or castle

Alcazaba walled fortification

Alfarería pottery

Alfarero a potter

Alla ysalmak response to goodbye

Almori a Moorish pastry

As-salama alaykum Hello

Arab mile is between 1.8 and 2 kilometres

Baba father

Churros a sweet fried batter

Dar al-Sina'a the House of trades

dirhams units of currency

Djubbah a simple tunic

Djellaba a hooded cloak

Djinn a mythical being from the spirit world

Dupatta large headscarf

Eid al-Adha the Feast of the Sacrifices

Ghifara a crocheted cap

Hajj a pilgrimage to Mecca, sometimes used as a polite term for an old man

Hadith reports of the deeds and sayings of Mohammed

Hamman baths

Imam holy man

insha'Allah God willing

Jarrah jug

Jinete horseman

Laylat al henna

Ma'a salama goodbye

Maghreb the region of North West Africa bordering the Mediterranean Sea

Maghrebi a turban used by the North African tribes

Maqsura the area in the mosque where the sovereign prays

Medina a town

Mihrab niche in the wall of the mosque

Quran the central religious holy book of Islam

Quibla the wall that faces Mecca

Rukhsat   part of the marriage ritual

Sandali a eunuch who has had all his genitalia removed

Sayyad master or sir

Seedo nickname for Grandfather

Tagine North African stew of spiced meat and vegetables

Talaq divorce procedure

Teta nickname for grandmother

Tisbah ala-kheir Good night

Wa alaykum e-salam Peace be upon you

Zenana   the innermost apartments where the women live

Ziriabì broad beans

LIST OF CHARACTERS

Qasim a potter
Fatima, his wife
Makoud ibn Qasim, eldest son (al-Jundi)
Ibrahim ibn Qasim, middle son
Omar ibn Qasim, youngest son

Sara the eldest daughter of Qasim
Isa her husband
Ghayda Isa's second wife
Mariam
Salma
Maysa
Tara

Layla youngest daughter of Qasim
Muhammed al-Hasam - her husband
Ulla his sister

Muna, Omar's betrothed
Elvira a friend of Fatima

Al-Mari - Abram ibn al-Attar a slave and former soldier
Al-Sagir   - Hans, the brother of Isolde

Yusuf ibn Yusuf - Omar's friend

Zilma bint Zakariya - Yusuf's wife-to-be

Ibn Hayyan from Ardales
Halawa clairvoyant

Abd al-Rahman ibn Muhammad ibn Abd Allah al-Nasir li-Din Allah, Defender of God's Faith and supreme ruler of Al-Andalus, (Abd al-Rahman III, Khalifa)
al-Hakim, son of al-Rahman
Gassan, a slave
Al-Gafur, historian
Grand Vizier
Hasdai ibn Shaprut, royal physician, minister and close friend of al-Rahman

The Royal Wife
Al-Zahra, concubine
Al-Tayyib, eunuch
Yamut al-Attar , the Chief Black Eunuch - in charge of the Khalifa's harem
Jawhara/Isolde, concubine in love with Omar
Najm, her friend
Governor al-Madanish, the governor of Medina Salim
Omar ibn Hafsun, rebel leader

THE AL-ANDALUS SERIES
BOOK 2

THE EYE OF THE FALCON

CHAPTER 1

It was barely light when she came to his room. The night sky was turning to milky white on the horizon but the songbirds were still asleep; even the cock had not yet begun to crow. She stood by his bed, looking down at him. Her nightdress shone and glittered in the flickering light of the night lamps; it reminded him of the kingfishers that stole in to the palace gardens to steal fish from the lakes. Gently her hand stroked his hair.

'Hisham, my son, are you awake?' she asked.

'Yes mother. What's happened? Is something the matter?'

He was well aware of the commotion in the women's quarters; the wailing and crying, the sound of heavy footsteps as the guards marched through the palace, the slamming of doors and loud voices all spoke of some catastrophe. It had broken into his sleep and woken him before his mother arrived at his bedside. Now she knelt by his side and said, 'You must get up, Hisham. The Khalifa is dead.'

Dead? Baba was dead? He felt a chill pass over him and hot tears sprang into his eyes. He looked at his mother; her face was impassive, not a tear marred her beautiful face. She pulled the covers off him and took his hand in hers.

'Do not cry, Hisham; there is no need for tears. You are the Khalifa now, my son. You will be a great and glorious ruler,' she continued, her eyes gleaming, 'like the Omeyyads before you. Al-Andalus will thrive and prosper with you as Khalifa and with me by your side.'

She bowed low so that her face touched the carpet next to his bed, her long blonde hair cascading over the elaborately woven silks, and would have kissed his hand but he snatched it away. Baba was dead. Who was this woman who did not weep for her dead husband? He had seen her shed more tears when her pet peacock died.

He turned his face away from her. Was she telling him the truth? Was Baba really dead? His father had been unwell for some time, confined to his rooms, only able to walk a few steps at a time, but Hisham had never really expected him to die. He was sure he would get better. He believed the doctors who came each day and gave him potions made from *habba souda* and warm milk, said by the Prophet to cure everything but death, who made him infusions of anise and applied myrrh to his lips to sweeten his breath, who massaged his legs and prescribed salt water baths. He believed them when they said that with time he would recover, that he would return to his books and be as he was before. But they had been wrong. Baba had not recovered from the affliction that had twisted his face and stolen the strength from his limbs. He had lain in his room surrounded by his ministers, listening silently while they told him what was happening in his kingdom. Then, tired from his inability to do anything, he had sent for Hisham and asked him to read to him.

What would Hisham do now? He had loved his father. Al-Hakim had been more than a father; he had been Hisham's friend and his teacher. Each day, when his father had finished with the business of the court, he went into the harem to look for his son and together they walked in the palace gardens while he recited the great Persian poetry of times past. He recounted the exploits of his father, Hisham's grandfather, the mighty al-Rahman III, who had died before the boy was born, of how he had subdued all the rebellious tribes and united al-Andalus into the most powerful kingdom in Europe, of how he had defeated the Christian princes yet allowed Christians, Jews and Moslems to live in peace, side by side. Hisham had listened to his stories and was proud to be part of such a powerful family. On other occasions he accompanied his father to the great library, al-Hakim's pride and joy, and there he learnt the secrets that were held within his countless books, sharing his father's excitement when a new manuscript arrived from some distant land or a copyist presented him with something fresh to read and explore. Hisham loved to trace his finger over the beautiful illuminated characters and follow the words across the page or watch as books in Latin or Greek were carefully translated into Arabic. His father had taught him many things it was true, but Hisham was not sure that he had taught him how to be Khalifa of Muslim Spain.

'Hisham, you must get up, the ministers are waiting to see their new Khalifa. Come child, I know you are upset at the news but you have responsibilities now,' his mother whispered so that his attendants could not hear her.

He looked at her and wished he could just pull the covers over his head and stay there until she went away but he knew he could not. Queen Subh umm Walad was not someone to be easily ignored; she was as fearsome as she was beautiful.

His mother stood up and clapped her hands. She looked annoyed with him. At that signal Hisham's personal slaves hurried across to him and, reluctantly, he rolled out of bed so that they could begin to prepare him for the day. Khalifa? How could he be Khalifa? It was only a few months since he had celebrated his eleventh birthday.